For those who have given us pride, and for those who suffer at the hands of prejudice

Chapter 1: Graduation

My mum has always been a fan of Bringing People Together. It's why we have so many stressful family gatherings. She'll invite loads of people round for a ridiculous reason, then panic about it and spend the whole time fanning herself in another room, leaving Dad happily commandeering the kitchen and the four of us trying to make sure everything happens as it should. More often than not, she'll find a way to introduce at least one of her children to an unsuspecting single guest with good prospects. She's always been more interested in the size of her future in-laws' bank accounts than their gender. I suppose she's rather progressive that way.

Of course, my graduation was not an occasion to be brushed over quietly – we had to have an enormous party, or at least as big as our small sitting room would allow. The whole family was there, as well as family friends, neighbours, any of my university friends that Mum had somehow managed to add on Facebook, and, it seemed, someone else's cat.

While the party itself was fairly awful, it was nice to spend some time with my best friend, Charlotte, and my sister Jane, who had just arrived back from Thailand. Jane was on her fifth gap year now; Charlotte and I have a bet going on to see if she can make it to a gap-decade without actually having to get a job. She's always gone for the typical gap year approach of finding a charity project overseas where you build a school or a water pump or help feed endangered animals or something, and then applied for countless grants and donations to help her pay for the trip. The thing about Jane, though, is that there aren't enough charity projects under the sun for her, so she keeps going on new ones. So far, she's helped build three schools, two hospitals, five water pumps, helped homeless children in three different South American cities, helped run a tiger rehabilitation project and taught maths to children in six different villages in Ethiopia. You would think that the number of people willing to give her money to do these things would dwindle, but it doesn't. Her sheer determination to go and help all these causes, combined with that trademark-Jane-smile and kind words, makes her completely irresistible to both the unsuspecting bake sale victim and the millionaires that give away cheques to 'plucky young people who want to change the world'. Even when she's at home she's helping at a hospice, volunteering at a homeless shelter or standing on the street with just a collection pot and that winning smile.

Jane's seemingly only goal in life was to be helpful, on whatever scale. She was kind to the point that it was almost a flaw. Now, though, she had clearly decided that the most helpful thing she could do was to take over as hostess, a job which suited her well; she was happily mingling with the assorted guests, smiling and taking a genuine interest in what they were saying, before handing them a glass of wine or a cupcake and moving on. Having her there made up for my less-than-stellar party attitude; I was perfectly content chatting to Charlotte, making small talk with whoever came my way, then moving on.

Mum's attitude wasn't exactly helping the party spirit either; she was on her usual 'overcompensating' train, pointing out (loudly) which guests were out on Facebook, and asking (again, loudly) if I'd dated any of them, which, thankfully, I hadn't. I was happily running on auto-pilot, making the usual "No, Mum", "Yes, Mum", "Shh, Mum" noises, until she said something that shook me out of whatever dreamland I was in.

"I invited the new neighbours," she said, looking far too proud of herself. "I thought it would be a good way to let them get to know the people in the area – help them settle in!"

Inviting neighbours to any and all events was standard Mum-behaviour, but something about the look in her eye told me that this time, things were different.

"Really? What are they like?" I asked, trying to come across as nonchalantly as I could, not catching Charlotte's eye as I sensed that she would burst out laughing if I did.

At this my mum seemed to grow at least three inches taller, beaming with pride at the knowledge that she held over us.

"I'm surprised you haven't heard! It was all we could talk about at the book club." I have yet to hear about them actually discussing a book at book club. Ever. "A young lady and gentleman, about Jane's age – they've just moved into one of the houses on Netherfield Court, you know, those swish new buildings? With the pools in the gardens and the solar panels on top? I saw how much one of those cost and, well, let's just say that it's more money than I have ever seen in my life!"

I rolled my eyes at Charlotte, who's face had now relaxed into its usual your-mum's-crazy position, before interjecting.

"Mum, those houses are ridiculous – we live in England, having a solar panel and pool are pointless. Besides, you've always said money isn't important, which is why you refused Gran's when she offered."

I got the haughty, 'that was a completely different situation and you know that,' look as she grabbed Jane, insisting that she also ought to hear this. She had a slightly mad glint in her eye and continued as though I hadn't said anything, lowering her voice to a stage-whisper.

"Anyway, Gladys – you know Gladys, she goes to book club – paid her son to find them on the Twitter, and the man's called Charlie Bingley, and apparently he's a professional musician! Not one of these pop people, he plays the piano! Properly! He's very good, he's also on the YoobToob thing that Mark spends all his time on. And Janet – you know, Janet who is in book club and also brings cake – she actually saw them from her sitting room window when they were moving the last of their things in. Don't give me that look, Lizzy Bennet, you know she keeps binoculars by the window for bird-watching – and apparently, they were both in designer clothes and *very* attractive!"

At this she leant back and looked across our silent faces, clearly expecting praise and excitement. When it was obvious that we weren't going to respond, she pushed some more.

"Well, girls? Aren't you excited? Don't you want to know more?"

I huffed, exasperated, before responding, knowing that no matter what I said, the outcome would be the same.

"Why should we care so much about this rich young couple moving in down the road, Mum? I'm moving out soon anyway, it's not like there's much point in getting to know new people."

I should have said something ridiculous, like 'but do they have a flying pet cat? You know I can only be friends with people with flying pets,' because it would have had the exact same reaction. A gasp, a taken aback look, and a hand flying to her mouth in shock.

"Why should you care? I'll have you know why you should care!" And we were back to conspiracy, big-secret-sharing mode. "They're not a couple. They're just friends. They're both single, and that Charlie Bingley seems *perfect* for Jane!"

This is the first thing that shocks me. Mum? Setting someone up with Jane? Mum has been known to say that Jane is 'too good for this world, let alone any mortal man', in complete sincerity, and I'm not going to lie, I sort of agree. Of course I want Jane to be happy, but I have yet to meet any man who could match up to being the sort of man she deserves. This Charlie guy must be really nice, really good-looking, really rich, or a combination of all three, for Mum to think he's a possible match for Jane.

As soon as she dropped this bombshell, Mum ran off to go and gossip with her book club friends, presumably about these new neighbours. Whenever Mum spoke at length about anything, I always left feeling a bit like a miniature whirlwind has just happened right in front of us, leaving a pile of confusion and mild annoyance.

I turned around, hoping that just looking at other people would help me recover, when I realised that I had some serious damage control to do. Gran was talking to some friends from uni – more specifically, the LGBTQ society – and was fishing for information.

"I'm very supportive, you know, as Lizzy's grandmother, but I *am* a bit intrigued about what, exactly, lesbians do," was the line I heard drifting over to me as I approached them, ready to do some Gran-watch. I interrupted the stunned silence by dragging the nearest person I could over to them with me.

"Hey guys!" Loud, cheerful voice, fake smile. The perfect way to save your friends from your Gran who, whilst less homophobic than she was (a *lot* less, thanks Dad!) was still lacking in any basic understanding. "Have you met…" I turned around to see which unsuspecting victim I'd dragged with me. "My brother! This is Sander." I pushed him forward before realising that he was not, by any stretch of the imagination, sober. He took a second to orientate himself before giving these poor girls the creepiest expression that I'd ever seen.

"Heyyyyy, giirlsh," he waved and nearly fell over. "Hey, do you like my shmoul – my smuuulllll – smoulder? That's the worrrrd, right? Smooooooouuuulder – hey, thatsh a – thatsh a cool word! Smooouuuuuldeeeeeerrrrrrrrrrr I like it I like it a lot!" He stopped his monologue for long enough for me to drag him away, and say a quick apology to the two girls, who now looked pretty glad to be stuck talking to Gran.

"Are they yourrr lesbo friendsss, Lizshy?" Sander asked, now kicking his own foot determinedly. I made a mental note to set some really loud, awful music ready for his hangover tomorrow – all in the name of justice, of course.

"It is seven o'clock," I hissed, not really caring that none of this was going in. "What the hell are you doing?! You're completely hammered, we didn't even put that much booze out, and you're embarrassing yourself and all of us! For God's sake, you only turned eighteen last month!"

If looks could kill, then this would be one of those times when a drunk took a swing at you. Completely missed the mark, but you still got the intention behind it.

"Look at you, all high and might, Lizshy Bennetbennetbennet, she has a degreeeeee now so she's allowed to boss us all around! Huh! Isn't that right! Mark, ishn't that rigghhtttt!"

He looked to his side for his twin brother, but of course Mark wasn't there and hadn't been for the course of the afternoon. Although identical, no one had ever had any problems telling them apart. Two genetically identical people had never been so different.

I sighed and grabbed his arm, determined to drag him out of the sitting room before he could make a mediocre party turn bad, but was stopped in my tracks by Jane.

"Lizzy," she said, calmly and in those hushed tones that we all knew meant that she was trying to intervene and calm you down, "is everything okay?"

I tried to be angry. I really, really tried. But when Jane is looking at you, with those big eyes that you never want to see lose their innocent sparkle, it's really difficult. But I was damn well going to try.

"It's still light outside and he's completely off his face," I hissed, determined not to draw attention to myself. "He's running round – or attempting to, anyway – and making an absolute fool of himself. How did he manage to drink this much in such a short space of time?!"

Even in his drunken, disoriented state, Sander looked sheepish at the look of disappointment on Jane's face.

"You are coming upstairs and we're going to talk about this, away from Lizzy's big day. You really should know better than this, Sander," she said, indicating for him to follow her upstairs. I'm sure it would end in him crying because he'd let her down and then being tucked up in bed with two paracetamol left for him, ready for the next morning. Jane really is an angel.

As I watched Jane lead Sander upstairs, I let out a deep, relaxing sigh. Maybe this party was going to be alright, and maybe I should take the opportunity to celebrate my achievement and look forward to the next stage of my life! I'd just got a first class degree from a top university, and the world was my oyster – shouldn't I be allowed to have a great time at a party that had been thrown for me? And so I made my way back to Charlotte, so wrapped up in my little bubble of self-congratulation that I didn't hear the doorbell ring.

Chapter 2: Guests from Netherfield

Just as I had firmly resolved to enjoy this party, to have fun with Charlotte and my friends, my mum tapped me on the shoulder. I turned around, a bit shocked (she has a way of creeping up on people), only to see that dreaded 'I'm plotting something' grin on her face, and two people I didn't recognise standing just behind her.

"Lizzy," she said, still grinning manically as she indicated towards the two strangers, "this is Charlie Bingley and Darcy Williams. They've just moved in at Netherfield Court." She gave me a look that probably meant that I was supposed to act like this was brand new information and that they hadn't been gossip fodder for the last week and a half.

As my mother left us to it, I turned to look at our new guests who both looked like they'd walked straight out of a magazine. Charlie Bingley was at least six feet tall and quite muscly, but his dark brown eyes, short black curls and skin that was only a shade lighter, combined with his soft expression, made him look about as threatening as a teddy bear, even as he loomed over my five-foot-tall mother. His friend was a good half a head taller than me, with long dark hair and pale brown skin. Her eyes, though also brown, were piercing, like she was trying to assess everything about you in the few seconds of looking that she was allowed. She was much slimmer than me, and though these things don't usually bother me, I was suddenly very conscious of my stockier build. She had a way, just by being there, of making me feel inferior.

I decided there and then that I would never let that happen.

"Hi, I'm Charlie!" A beaming face was sent my way, followed by the offer of a handshake.

"I'm Lizzy, it's nice to meet you!" I smiled back, shaking his hand. I was reminded instantly of Jane; even if I hadn't wanted to shake his hand, I wouldn't dare refuse it because I wouldn't have been able to bear seeing the look of disappointment on his face.

"Hi," I smiled again, turning with my hand out to The Friend.

"Darcy," she said curtly. Not even a hint of a smile. I saw her reach into her pocket for her phone, but her hand was stopped by Charlie.

"Come on, Darcy, we're at a party! Have fun, get to know people! Don't just stand there texting!"

I had never seen such a withering look in my life.

"Unlike you, Charlie, I have an actual job that requires work, and that involves doing things like replying to emails. *Even* in company." She turned to me, "If you'll excuse me," then turned on her heel and walked back into the hallway, rapidly typing on her phone.

"Sorry about her," Charlie said, obviously genuinely apologising for his friend's behaviour. "She gets like this around large crowds of people, I'm sure it's nothing personal."

"Don't worry about it," I said. "What brings the two of you to Longbourn?"

"Oh, it's just me. Well, obviously Darcy's here too! And she's certainly making herself at home, so I'm sure she'll be staying a lot, but she's mostly just helping me move in. And this was all her idea – buy a house for the financial security and everything! I live in London usually, so I just wanted something a little bit away from the city to escape to. But enough about me, tell me about you! You've just graduated, right?"

I nodded, glad that Charlie didn't seem too bothered by the awkwardness of before. "Yes, I studied English Literature. What about you, what are--"

But I couldn't get any further before he interrupted. "Wow, that sounds amazing! What are you hoping to do with it? I bet there's so many options for you!"

I'm sure I must have looked at him suspiciously. No one takes this much interest in a strangers' life. Except Jane. She takes an interest in anything anyone tells her.

"Oh, well, um, I've got an internship at a publishers in London starting in September, and I'm hoping that will be a shoe in the door. I'm hoping to go into publishing, and one day foster young, unappreciated talent that pushes new boundaries – particularly in and around the LGBTQ community. We've come really far but there's so far to come in terms of representation, you know? I just feel like there's so much we can do."

Okay, I'll admit that I spoke more than I usually do but it was a bit of a test to see how far his genuine interest went. The answer? Pretty far. Most people smiled and nodded up until the internship, then said 'well done!' and changed the subject. Not in this case though. This guy had a massive grin on his face, and – oddly – looked very proud of me.

"That's fantastic! You know, I definitely see where you're coming from. I'm a musician and at the moment I'm just performing, you know? I feel like I could do so much more than play to a concert hall of rich old people. You know, music has a massive positive impact on education, across all the curriculum? I would love to do that one day – work with kids, changing the world one young life at a time. I don't even care about the money, I just want to really make a difference."

He looked exhausted after all this, as if he doesn't usually talk that much about himself – and, given the number of similarities to Jane, it wouldn't surprise me if he doesn't.

Speak of the devil, I thought, *or angel* (quick amendment), as I saw Jane's head at the other side of the room – thankfully, without Sander in tow. I beckoned her over, perhaps with more enthusiasm than was acceptable, but I didn't really care.

"Oh, Jane, over here! Jane, this is Charlie Bingley, he just moved into Netherfield Court. Charlie, this is my sister Jane."

People often ask if you believe in love at first sight, and honestly, up until that moment, I'd have said no. Love is something that is nurtured, that grows out of something wonderful, not something that spontaneously appears. But this was the day I was proved wrong. When Jane and Charlie looked at each other for the first time, they each saw a kindred spirit. Like they were home again with their fellow aliens from whatever planet-of-niceness they came from. I suddenly had the feeling that I was intruding on a very personal moment and hastily stepped back, unfortunately into my brother Mark, who I hadn't realised was coming up behind me.

"Lizzy, what the hell?!" he exclaimed as I tugged him away, leaving Jane and Charlie in their moment. There are only a few truly beautiful things on this world, and I had a feeling that I'd just witnessed one of them.

Chapter 3: Decent Enough

I left the sitting room as quickly as I politely could, grabbing Charlotte's arm on the way out until I had both her and Mark grumbling.

"Lizzy, what's going on?" Charlotte demanded, rubbing her arm where I'd grabbed her as soon as we left the room.

"It's Jane and that new neighbour, Charlie – they're having a Moment."

"What, like a moment or a *Mo*ment?" Mark piped up. He doesn't usually take much interest in our personal lives, preferring to keep himself to himself; obviously, this was the exception.

"A capital M Moment," I hissed; then, "Don't both look at once! You'll disturb them, and they'll know! One at a time, go on! Mark first," Mark stuck his head round the door, then brought it back, looking bewildered, "then Charlotte."

I'll admit it: I had a sneaky peek after Charlotte looked. But they were just so incredibly right for each other! You wouldn't believe that they'd met less than a minute ago; this right here was the scientific evidence for soulmates. And, to be honest, it wouldn't have mattered if we *had* all looked at once – they were so wrapped up in each other that the whole universe could be watching them talk and they wouldn't be any the wiser.

"Let's go see if Dad needs help in the kitchen," Mark suggested, knowing full well that the only person allowed to disturb Dad for anything other than carrying out dishes was me, but looking for a distraction.

We didn't get that far, however, as we bumped into Charlie's friend, Darcy Williams, who was just finishing a phone call. The hallway was quite narrow, so it wasn't hard for the three of us to completely block it. She took a deep breath as if to brace herself for conversation with people she disliked before speaking.

"Excuse me, I'd like to get through?"

Excuse me, but you're in my house. I'll let you through when I let you through.

"Hi, you must be Darcy? Lizzy was just telling me about you." Thank you, Charlotte, for saving the day there.

"Yes, I am. Now, if you would excuse me, I would like to get through to--"

"So what do you do? You mentioned your work?" I tried my best to sound genuinely interested, and not like I was stalling. Which I was. It didn't look like she was the type to respect a beautiful moment between two precious people.

"I'm a manager and editor." Before I had a chance to respond, she had pushed her way through and was stalking back to the sitting room, presumably to interrupt an unsuspecting Jane and Charlie.

We stood there in stunned silence.

"Well, she seems like a bitch," said Mark.

"Mark!" I chastised, but my heart wasn't really in it. It was quite hard to disagree with him.

"Guys! Attention to the issue at hand!" Charlotte snapped her fingers in our faces, grabbing our attention. "So she has a stick up her butt. Got it. But, more importantly, she has just gone to presumably burst whatever bubble Jane and this Charlie guy are in, and we can't let that happen!"

But we had nothing to worry about; one peek around the door was enough to see that Jane and Charlie were still happily in their own little world, practically emitting flowers and cupcakes with every word they spoke, sitting closer to each other than is acceptable with new friends. Darcy was standing next to them, fake texting, looking horrendously out of place next to the almost disgusting display of adorable happening next to her, completely unaware that she was third-wheeling her best friends and his new young lady. (Let's be real; they'd reached that point already.)

"I've never really got the whole… romance thing," Mark said slowly, and I could tell that he was choosing his words carefully, "But those two seem… made for each other. I haven't even met the guy, but he already seems just… so, so like Jane."

I couldn't help but smile slightly, aware that though we were staring at them for much longer than was generally considered acceptable, the couple in question were blissfully unaware. "They are, aren't they? They're just so, ridiculously perfect. Just looking at them makes me feel like all the world's problems can be solved by baking enough cupcakes and smiling at people."

Charlotte poked me in the ribs, earning a loud "Ow!"

"Lizzy," she hissed, ignoring my glare, "your mum's coming! We need to divert her!"

All Mum has ever wanted for us is for us to all be happy, but she's often found it hard striking a balance. She has a tendency of interfering which has never done any of us any favours, and while it's all in the name of love and care, the other people in our lives have sometimes had problems seeing that. Both me and Jane have lost potential partners during the dreaded 'meeting the parents', and it's not like I can really blame anyone for running for the hills when my mother is working full force. The worst part, though, is that she doesn't realise that she's doing it. In her mind, she's simply watching out for her children by forcing them on any suitable partner while simultaneously scaring said partner away.

So if Mum were to find out that the rich, handsome new neighbour could have easily been crafted especially for Jane? She would ruin everything by going in with her matchmaking 'skills' and making everything so awkward for everyone that it would be over within the hour.

Luckily, though, my dad decided that this was the opportune moment to leave the kitchen.

"Joan?" he asked, looking uneasily at the number of people in the sitting room then back to my mum, "We've run out cream, and I can't make the pavlova you wanted without it. Would you be able to pop to the shop to get some more?"

Good one Dad.

"Of course I will! You should have said something earlier! I can't believe we would run out of cream, who didn't put it on the shopping list?! I'll go and get some right now." And with more chuntering about how nobody else does anything around here she was off, grabbing her purse and car keys, now with a completely new panic on her mind.

"Thanks Mr Bennet! That was brilliant timing!" Charlotte grinned and put up her hand to high-five my dad who looked at it suspiciously, already on his way back to the kitchen.

"Charlotte, I've told you before, just David is fine. And I don't know what you three are up to, nor do I really care. Just don't disturb me in the kitchen. Although if Lizzy's with you then I suppose it can't be anything too outrageous."

Something approaching a smile was sent my way, before he shut himself away in the kitchen again.

***

The party went on, as parties do. Mum came back with the cream, noticed Jane and Charlie but – thankfully – didn't interrupt them; I mingled; and after dinner was served people started slowly drifting off back to their homes, until there were only a few of us left.

I had been helping Dad wash up in the kitchen after dinner, and came back out into the hall to find myself behind Charlie and his friend Darcy who both seemed to be getting ready to go. I was about to make my presence known so I could get past (we seriously need a bigger house) when I heard what they were talking about, so I – okay, I eavesdropped. I crept back into the kitchen and ducked behind the wall, just in case they turned around.

"She's really, really wonderful, Darcy, I've never met anyone like her. I know you always tell me that I think too highly of people, and that I'm too nice – which I don't think is even possible – but there's just something about special about her. I can tell you don't like it, but I want to see her again. I can't let her just slip away! I feel… at home when I'm with her. Surely you can understand that?"

Interesting. So, unsurprisingly, Darcy didn't approve of Charlie and Jane's already budding romance. Very interesting.

"It's not that I don't like it, Charlie, it's just that… well, you barely know her. You met her this evening, and I don't want you getting too attached to something that isn't that serious. I'm just trying to look out for you, and I'm glad you're making friends, but I wish you would be more careful."

There was a sigh, and a long pause.

"I can see where you're coming from, but until you've met someone like that, someone who you just… fit with, someone who clicks so well with you, I don't think you're going to understand. Don't give me that look." I could only imagine the look on Darcy's face right now. "We both know that you're the most intelligent of the two of us, by far. But I *do* feel," and I could sense how difficult it was for him to say this, "that perhaps I'm slightly better with people skills?"

Wow. Blunt talk from someone who had just told my mother that teal really was her colour.

He quickly turned the conversation around, however, and this was where things got interesting.

"What about you? Have you met anyone special recently?"

I could practically hear Darcy rolling her eyes, and I have to say I was with her there – I wouldn't want to meet anyone who was a good romantic match for *her*.

"Charlie, you know I would have told you if there was. You're being ridiculous. I have more important things to worry about right now, you know that, so can we please just go?"

"I'm waiting for Jane; I want to talk to her before we go. What about her sister Lizzy? She's really lovely, and very intelligent, and certainly knows her own mind. What do you think of her?"

What?

I was NOT expecting the conversation to go there.

Me? Darcy? Together? Had Charlie lost his mind?!

"Charlie, you are a very dear friend to me, but you have officially gone mad. What on earth makes you think that that is even a remotely good idea?"

For once, Darcy Williams, we were in agreement.

"I was talking to Jane, and she confirmed that Lizzy is gay, so you wouldn't have to worry about that- "

"And that's my only requirement in a partner now, is it?"

"--and she did remind me of you in her determination, her morals, and her ambition."

"There's nothing that special about her. She's decent enough, but nothing really sets her apart from anyone else. Average looks, intelligent but not spectacular mind; not really what I look for, and you know that. This happens every time you meet someone new, Charlie: you try and throw someone at me, too."

"Oh, are you headed off now?" That was Jane, trying not to sound disappointed.

"Oh, yes, really sorry we couldn't stay for longer. We've had a lovely time but we really do have to go. We have each other's numbers, though; would you like to come for dinner tomorrow? You and Lizzy are welcome to come over."

I'm sure Jane must have agreed, but everything from that point on was white noise, blocked out by my silent fuming. Decent enough? Who does she think she is?! She's just a smarmy twenty-something blessed with a stupidly attractive face and far too much money, going around judging the rest of us, like we were below her?! Please.

I must have said goodnight to my parents and to Jane – Mark having gone upstairs as soon as was polite and Sander having drunkenly passed out hours earlier – but I don't remember it. All I remembered were the words 'decent enough' going round and round my head. Decent enough.

Decent enough.

Chapter 4: Two Gooseberries

The next day brought dinner with Charlie and Darcy, which I can't say I was hugely looking forward to. I could see why Jane wanted me there, because it can't be much fun to have dinner with your beau with his moody best friend third-wheeling, but that didn't mean that me being there would make it any better.

Mum was having kittens, of course; Jane had been invited over to dinner with a gentleman friend, and I'm sure if we'd let her she would have held another party to celebrate the occasion, but we kept her from doing anything more than making Jane an extra cup of tea with breakfast. Mark smiled knowingly every time the words 'dinner' or 'Charlie' were mentioned, and Sander spent the morning asking us all to stop yelling, dim the lights and can he please have another paracetamol now. We ended up passing him mints two at a time just to stop him from asking for more tablets before he was allowed another dose.

Dad was happy because his kitchen had been returned to how it was, thanks to my cleaning and washing up – I'm the only one who knows exactly where everything goes – and nothing else really held enough importance to him to influence his mood. He was still good at picking up on the general atmosphere of the house, though, and very occasionally commented on it.

"Everything alright, Lizzy?" he asked, gruffly but not unkindly, over breakfast, ignoring Sander groaning at the other end of the table.

"Yeah," I replied, but not really committing to it as I stared forlornly into my cornflakes, stirring them until they were an orange, milky mush.

Dad wasn't usually one to pry or push at something, but obviously this time was different.

"Are you sure? You're not yourself this morning, and I'm fairly sure it's not because you're on a mission to destroy your liver before you're twenty-five like your brother over here."

Another groan was enough to tell us that Sander had heard and hadn't appreciated the dig.

I looked up at my dad and tried my best at a smile.

"I'm sure, Dad. It's nothing."

He didn't look convinced, but went back to his newspaper.

The evening came faster than I really wanted it to, and before I knew it I was telling Jane that really, she looked just the right level of lovely, and was getting ready to drive us to Netherfield Court.

Netherfield Court was a set of huge new houses that had been built a few streets away, and Charlie and Darcy had to have been at least one of the first to move in. They were the kind of houses that you can usually only afford if you're a dentist or banker or lawyer, or, as I think will be the case here, the children of some of the above.

Even though I'd admired the houses from the main road often enough, seeing how much more had been built every time I visited home for the weekend, nothing could prepare me for driving in there for the first time. There was an ornamental fountain in one front garden, and one of the houses had at least four garages. It wasn't hard to spot which house we were headed to, however, as it was the only one currently being inhabited. It was a warm day, even though it was the evening, and the sounds of a piano playing what I think was Bach drifted out through the open window. There were two Jaguars parked at the front, and a few ornaments on the windowsills.

"This must be it," I needlessly said to Jane, pulling my second hand Ford up behind the shiny, swish cars. I looked over and she was looking surprisingly unsettled. Her cheeks were slightly pink, and she was breathing very shallowly.

"Jane, it will be fine," I tried to reassure her, aware that we were usually the other way round in these situations. "It's just dinner, I will be there, and if it all goes horribly wrong then I'll try to rile Darcy up for some entertainment." I hadn't told her about what I overheard the previous day, but she chuckled weakly regardless.

"Lizzy, that wouldn't be very nice," she said, still smiling – probably for my sake rather than hers.

"Come on, let's go," I said, trying to give her an encouraging grin and half-hug before getting out the car.

We didn't even have to ring the doorbell before the sounds of the piano stopped and the door was opened. Obviously Charlie had been waiting for us.

"Hi Lizzy," he smiled, before turning to Jane, standing just behind me. "Hi Jane," he said, slightly breathless and suddenly grinning. Had his skin not been so dark I'm sure I would have seen a blush.

"Hi Charlie," she replied, all tension leaving her as she smiled back at him. We stood there for a few seconds, the other two gazing at each other over my shoulder before I gave a small cough, bringing them both back to earth.

"Oh, yes, um, of course, I, um, would you like to come in?" Charlie stammered out, stepping back from the doorway to let us in.

The inside of the house was amazing. I was expecting it to be nice – really nice – but this was a whole new level. It was gloriously spacious, and the furniture must have all been either antique or designer – perhaps both. I peered round into the other rooms as we were led through, spotting a room that just held a grand piano and shelves of CDs and sheet music, a large sitting room with leather sofas and wall-mounted TV, and, best of all, a library. I completely stopped in my tracks and couldn't resist at least peeking round the doorway to see what was in there.

There were easily two thousand books in that room. It was a big room to start with, and all four walls were lined with shelves with a couple of sofas in the centre and a coffee table with a few more books on it. The shelves weren't completely full, however, which I liked; I appreciate someone who anticipates their book-buying habits, my own only being curbed by storage space. I tried to take in as many titles as I could from where I was stood in the doorway, and was amazed by the variety. There were classics, anthologies, biographies, books that I instantly recognised as bestsellers, books that I didn't recognise at all – even some that, I suspected, hadn't actually been released yet.

I couldn't help myself; of course I knew I shouldn't be doing it, but I *had* to go in. It was the kind of library that

I had always dreamed of, a collection that anyone should be proud of. Glancing around to check that there was no one there, I padded over to the coffee table and picked up a book that was lying there. I didn't recognise it but flicked through it anyway, skimming over the blurb and reading the inscription inside.

> Darcy,
> *Hope you enjoy! Couldn't have done it without you!*
> Which was followed by the author's signature.

"Excuse me?"

I spun around to see Darcy, arms crossed with narrowed eyes glaring down at me. "This is a private room. I think you should be in the dining room with your sister?"

More annoyed than embarrassed, I closed the book and put it back down on the table. "I'm sorry, but the door was open and I was curious. I wasn't aware that this room was private," I said, perhaps more coldly than I'd intended. Or perhaps not.

"Well, perhaps you should save your curiosity for when you're not in other people's houses," she snapped back. I briefly considered just walking off and not even giving her the time of day, but that would not have ended well as I didn't actually know where I was going. Besides, this did give me an opportunity to make sure that Jane and Charlie had some alone time.

"Well, I apologise if I crossed any boundaries."

That glare somehow became even stronger.

"You have been invited into this house – against my will, might I add – so I suggest that you start to show us some respect," she snapped.

I took a few steps closer towards her, tried my best to look menacing, and lowered my voice.

"You've made it perfectly clear that you don't like me or my sister," I spat out, "but why don't you try being happy for your friend? I believe it's what friends do."

I regretted those words as soon as they left my mouth, but it was too late; I had to deal with the consequences now. I watched apprehensively as Darcy seemingly rose up, breathing in like a dragon about to breathe fire.

"You have every right to be supportive of your sister, and I respect that. But don't I have the right to do the opposite? You don't know Charlie or anything about him, so don't you think *I* am best informed to make decisions regarding whether or not I'm happy for him?! You, who have known him all of twenty-four hours, and have barely had two conversations with him, are telling me how I should treat him?!"

Thankfully, I didn't have to think of a response, as just as she finished, red in the face and breathing heavily, Charlie appeared, practically skipping down the hall, blissfully unaware of what had just happened.

"Darcy, Lizzy, there you are! Dinner's ready, if you want to come through?"
Without looking each other in the eye, like two children who had been fighting in the playground, we followed Charlie through to the dining room.

"Lizzy, I see you found Darcy's library! Do you enjoy reading?"

"Yes, I do," I grudgingly responded, aware of Darcy's eyes burning a hole in the back of my neck at the mention of the library.

"Brilliant! Darcy loves reading as well, don't you?" He turned around and grinned at Darcy over my shoulder. I suddenly remembered his side of last night's conversation, which I had forgotten in light of Darcy's comments about me, and how he thought we would go well together. Looks like he'll be captaining *that* ship all by himself.

"Yes," Darcy said curtly, "You know that, Charlie."

But Charlie completely ignored her, carrying on regardless.

"If you think she has a lot of books here, Lizzy, you should see her house in London!" Seriously, how rich were these people?! "Darcy's an editor-in-chief at a publishing house, right Darcy?"

I could feel her getting pricklier behind me, so diverted the conversation.

"Anywhere in particular we should sit?" I asked, before looking at the layout of the table and realising that it was already completely obvious where I would sit. There were two pairs of places facing each other, and Jane was already sat down. The glass on the place next to her had been drunk out of, and it *would* make sense that she and Charlie would want to sit together. That left me sitting next to Darcy. Joy, oh joy.

"I should think it's obvious where we're to sit?" Oh, thanks Miss Smarmy-pants, for not helping me in my attempt to exchange Super Awkward Conversation for just Awkward Conversation. Not that I would have expected her to.

I sat down opposite Jane (I needed her for moral support), and took a drink of wine that lasted much longer than was socially acceptable, especially considering that I was driving home. But hey, if I finished it quickly, I'd be sober by the time we leave.

Charlie brought through a steaming dish, carefully placing it in the middle of the table before sitting next to Jane, trying to subtly shuffle his chair closer to hers. The moment Jane blushed, I knew that they were already playing footsie.

I took another swig of wine.

"Okay, this is vegetable lasagne, and there's some garlic bread as well – I wasn't sure if either of you were vegetarian, Lizzy, so I hope this is okay! There's more wine if you'd like some, as well." So he'd spotted my already half-empty glass of wine. And yes, in this case the glass is definitely half-empty. Charlie picked up a serving spoon and started serving up the lasagne, checking with us all that the portion sizes were alright. If I'd been in a better mood I might have found Jane's "It's perfect," adorable and sweet, but the simpering happiness just riled me the wrong way.

More wine.

I took a bite of the lasagne, and I have to say it was amazing. I said as much out loud, and got a nervous chuckle from Charlie.

"I'm glad you like it! I, er, have to say that I'm a terrible cook! So I bought a ready meal from Waitrose. I'm glad you're enjoying it though!"

These people were the kind of people who buy ready meals from Waitrose. If there's one thing I learnt as a student, it's to never trust someone who buys ready meals from Waitrose while sober. Somehow, though, I didn't think that rule applied to Charlie. Darcy, perhaps, but not Charlie.

"It would be better if it had meat in it." Darcy being charming as usual. "Lasagne is a meat dish, and to make it with vegetables defeats the object."

"I just thought it would be nice if we had one thing that I knew everyone could have, and I thought you'd like this because you usually like lasagne." Charlie suddenly looked unsure, placated only slightly when Jane took his hand and squeezed it, smiling up at him. It suddenly occurred to me that perhaps Darcy wasn't this awful all the time; obviously Charlie felt she was acting out of character, so maybe something about either Jane's or my presence put her off?

"You can't always please everyone, Charlie." Was it just me, or was she talking about more than just the food?

Jane cleared her throat across the table. "I personally think it's really sweet. I like that you try to think about everyone."

And that was all it took for them to go back to being adorably wrapped up in each other. Somehow they managed to sit there for an hour and talk about politics, women's rights, animal rights, interior decorating, baking and the education system, all while looking at each other with those heart eyes, and planning how to spend their lives as selflessly as possible. At some point they paused for Charlie to get a cheesecake out the fridge before they started right up again where they left off. Darcy and I sat there in stony silence, two gooseberries to what was, essentially, a date. Neither of us made any effort to make conversation with each other, which was fine by me. However, while I spent the evening watching Jane and Charlie interact, I would occasionally catch Darcy throwing glances at me. But not the glaring-daggers-into-my-face kind of glancing. The inquisitive kind, like she was trying to figure me out.

You know what? I didn't care. Let her try to figure me out. It wasn't worth me putting in the effort to try to figure her out, so I wouldn't bother. Back to being a gooseberry.

Eventually, of course, a level of self-awareness kicked in and Charlie realised that they'd been neglecting the other two of us at the table – not that either of us had a problem with that.

"So, you two also have a brother?" he asked awkwardly, vaguely indicating to me and Jane with a hand.

"Two, actually," I corrected him, remembering that Sander had been unconscious in bed by the time Charlie and Darcy had made it to our house. "Mark and Sander. They're identical twins, but only in looks; they're chalk and cheese personality-wise."

Charlie nodded his understanding, smiling out of the sheer joy of getting to know someone. "So who did we meet last night? He seemed very nice."

"That was Mark," I explained. "He's the quieter one – he tends to keep to himself. Sander is louder, more… outgoing. He, um…"

"He wasn't feeling too good last night," Jane interrupted, her sympathetic smile daring anyone to read any more into that. "He went upstairs early, he wanted to get some sleep to recover."

"Oh, I do hope he's alright!" The genuine concern in Charlie's face almost made me feel bad for swapping Sander's paracetamol for mints that morning. "Is Sander short for Alexander?"

He wishes, I thought, before explaining, "Nope, it's short for Lysander. He never really liked the name – none of us are sure where our parents got it from – so as soon as he was old enough he shortened it and insisted we all called him Sander. I don't blame him really!" We all had a little chuckle at the expense of my parents' naming of their children – well, all except Darcy, but that's to be expected.

"Your mother is quite the character!" Charlie laughed, before immediately looking like he'd said something wrong. I felt like this was the most brutally honest conversation he'd ever had.

"That she is," I chuckled. "She's slightly crazy – by which I mean, really crazy. She likes having something to panic about, and that thing tends to be us, so I'm sorry in advance for anything she says!"

"Lizzy, don't be so hard on her!" Jane mock-chastised me. "She just wants what's best for us, and sometimes that gets on top of her. She's always done whatever she can for us." She proudly said this last part to the table as a whole.

I really didn't want to open the conversation up to my fellow gooseberry, but in the spirit of polite conversation I couldn't really ignore her.

"So do either of you have any brothers and sisters?"

Charlie sighed, but still, of course, smiled. "I don't, I'm afraid – I wish I did! I would have loved to have a brother or sister. Darcy has a brother though!" He looked to Darcy, clearly expecting her to elaborate.

"Jordan," she said shortly, before a look from Charlie prompted her to elaborate. "He's nineteen, about to go into his second year at Oxford, studying Chemistry. Queens' College. He's abroad at the moment though."

"He's got an organ scholarship there," Charlie added eagerly, clearly more willing to part with information than Darcy was. "I actually taught him after I finished at the Royal Academy, and he's absolutely brilliant! I've taught quite a few people but none of them have ever been as dedicated as Jordan was. Especially with all that was going on at home, I guess it was a kind of escapism for him."

He stopped suddenly, aware that he'd said too much. Darcy was sitting rigidly in her seat, staring at the wine bottle like she was trying to set it on fire.

"Gosh, look at the time!" I exclaimed, knowing full well that it was obvious that I was trying to escape the sudden awkwardness of the situation. "We've had a really lovely time, but we must be off now. It's been very nice of you to have us, though."

It took Jane a few seconds to catch on before she stood up suddenly. "Yes, we've really overstayed our welcome. Thank you so much for having us over, I've had a – a really wonderful time."

She and Charlie both ducked their heads at the same time, causing them both to giggle.

Darcy huffed, obviously fed up with the amount of loving-up that was happening in her house.

"I'll show you out," she said curtly, before standing, turning on her heel and striding towards the door.

"You should definitely come round for dinner at our house soon – how does Friday sound?" Jane asked Charlie, clearly having not yet thought through the consequences of bringing a young man round for dinner.

"I'd love that!" Charlie replied, and if it were possible, his grin got even wider.

I could sense the cogs turning in Jane's head, and attempted to telepathically say to her *No, don't do it, don't say it, it won't end well!*

"Darcy would be welcome too, of course!"

Dammit Jane! Why can't you hear my thoughts?!

"I'm sure she'd love that." The saddest part was that Charlie obviously believed what he was saying.

"Come on Jane, we'd better head off," I interjected, before she could cause any more damage by just being too damn nice.

It took Charlie and Jane several minutes to get out of the door, as they kept saying goodbye awkwardly to each other, not stopping until Charlie leant down to give her a kiss on the cheek. She blushed and stammered too much to be able to coherently say anything else, so settled for a beaming smile and stumbled towards the car.

"Someone's had a good evening, then?" I asked teasingly, as we drove back out of Netherfield Court.

"Be quiet and drive," she said with uncharacteristic cheek, before looking back out the passenger window and smiling widely, pink still touching her cheeks.

I smiled to myself privately and drove on home, and for once was briefly glad that Mum was as crazy as she was.

Chapter 5: Dinner Again

I had secretly hoped that Jane would conveniently forget to tell Mum about Charlie and Darcy coming for dinner until the last minute – it was certainly what I was planning to do – but, of course, she told her as soon as we walked through the door as we came back from Netherfield Court. Now that we were all older it was unusual for our parents to wait up for us if they knew where we were, but I was not surprised in the slightest to come home to find my mother eagerly waiting by the door, ready to catch us as soon as we got in. She demanded details of the entire evening, which Jane more than happily provided, especially as she had no idea of the… disagreement that had occurred between me and Darcy before dinner. I nodded and smiled in all the right places before slipping off to bed as soon as I could without alerting Jane to the fact that anything was wrong. Despite firmly telling myself that I was not going to lose any sleep over Darcy Williams, I tossed and turned for hours before I could finally doze off, turning the events of the evening round in my head.

I have always thought of myself as being good at judging someone's character, at working out within a few minutes what sort of person they are, looking past the first impression they give to what lies underneath. I know I'm better at this than Jane, for example, who sees the world through wonderfully optimistic eyes. Charlotte used to tell me that I was too judgemental and too quick to make assumptions, but after I correctly predicted the behaviour of her first-year flatmates at university, she's admitted that I'm usually right. Which I corrected to: always right.

Everything I've seen and heard from Darcy is pointing towards an arrogant, self-centred young woman with a superiority complex, who's never known or needed to know what it's like to really work for something, and imposes her opinion on the world without waiting for the world to answer back. Her only friend, as far as I can tell, is lovely and eager-to-please, eternally optimistic and determined to make the world a better place. The only odd thing is that he's seemingly chosen Little Miss Grumpy as his starting point.

I'm sure there's more to her than meets the eye; I gathered as much from the awkward end to our dinner at Netherfield, but that doesn't matter. She's shown me, in private, her true colours, and they were not nice.

I will put up with her for Jane's sake, but that is all.

***

Friday evening came around much, much faster than I'd have liked. My week was spent preparing to permanently move out of my parents' house and into a flat with Charlotte in London, but even the thought of a prospective move wasn't enough to permanently distract me from all of the crazy goings-on at home.

Mum had been grilling me and Jane for Charlie and Darcy's food preferences. I was far too tempted to say, 'vegetable lasagne', but the part of me that wanted Jane to have a really nice evening won out over the part of me that wanted to piss off Darcy. Eventually we just left it to Dad, giving him free reign to cook whatever he liked. He readily agreed; the longer he had to spend in the kitchen, the less time he had to spend talking to other people.

Mark and Sander didn't take much notice of Mum's growing worries as we got closer to Friday. It didn't directly affect them, and so they didn't care. Mark was still taking an uncharacteristic interest in Jane and Charlie's romance, but it was clear that Sander couldn't care less about what was going on. He and Mum spent much of Friday afternoon arguing about what he should wear – or rather, Mum kept yelling at him to change out of that 'obscene' anime t-shirt and into a shirt and tie, while Sander moaned about how it wasn't fair. They eventually compromised on a plain t-shirt, which Mum retrospectively added must be clean, to more grumbling.

By the time it was seven o'clock on Friday evening, I was keeping the wine away from Sander, Dad had locked himself in the kitchen, Jane kept running off to fix her hair, and Mum was dashing around, swapping ornaments over on the shelves, reminding us all to be on our 'absolute best behaviour' and that as far as Charlie was concerned (she didn't seem bothered about Darcy's opinion) we were 'completely normal'.

"Bit late for that," Mark muttered under his breath whilst pretending to polish the door handles, causing me to snort in laughter.

"Elizabeth!" Mum shrieked. It had been many years since I'd heard that. "If you could please *try* acting like a respectable young lady when our guests arrive, that would be *much appreciated!!!*"

Her face was so red by the end of this that she looked like she was about to explode, and the doorbell ringing at that moment didn't help. The colour instantly drained from her face, her eyes widening.

"They're here," she breathed, shakily. "Everyone relax, act normal... they're here."

Luckily, Charlie and Darcy had been saved by Mum's drama by Mark taking the opportunity to open the door and let our guests in. Jane almost ran down the stairs as they came into the hall, her hair back to how it was five hair styles ago.

"Hi," Charlie said shyly, gazing adoringly at Jane. It was so cute I wanted to squash something.

Like Darcy's foul expression.

Jane timidly took Charlie by the hand and led him through to the dining room, where Mum was trying her best to remember how to breathe regularly.

"You're either Mark or Sander," Darcy said curtly to Mark as he shut the door behind her, making it clear by her tone that she didn't particularly care which one he was.

"I'm Mark," came the grunted response, which was promptly ignored as she followed Charlie and Jane through to the dining room.

"Nice to meet you too," he said under his breath, again causing me to snort with laughter.

The conversation over dinner was, as predicted, horrendously awkward and awful – mostly thanks to my mother.

"So, Charlie and Darcy, you two are both single? You're living together... as friends?"

I wish I was lying, but unfortunately my mother did seem to think that this was an acceptable conversation opener. Charlie, however, didn't miss a beat.

"Yes, I suppose I am single, for the moment at least," he said, smiling at Jane for the last part, who blushed and smiled shyly while pretending to busy herself with the salt and pepper.

"And what about you, Darcy? Is there a special young man or woman in your life?"

Unfortunately, the ground did not open up and swallow us all. I couldn't believe where my mum was going with this! They'd been in our house for all of five minutes and Mum was already on the crazy-shipper-train. To make matters worse, Darcy wasn't answering; she'd clearly heard what my mum said, but was deliberating her answer.

"Darcy?" Mum egged her on. Could this get any worse?

"Not that it's any of your business, but I'm single," came her short answer, clearly irritated with my mum's probing.

"Leave the poor girl alone," Dad wisely interjected, indicating vaguely with his fork at Darcy before going back to his meal.

Just as I thought we were safe, though, Sander decided to have his turn.

"So I bet you guys are, like, super rich? And have loads of rich friends, and stuff?"

I realised too late that he'd just downed his second glass of wine; we'd all been so preoccupied that we hadn't noticed.

"I wouldn't quite say that," Charlie responded, at exactly the same time as Darcy flatly said, "Yes."

"You guys must have some *awesome* parties then!" Sander continued, oblivious to Mark kicking him under the table to shut up. "Do you reckon now that you two," he waved his hand at Jane and Charlie, "are all loved up, I could tag along? You know, for the chicks? And the booze!"

"Ignore Sander," I said a bit too loudly, desperate to divert the conversation. "Didn't we, er, have such lovely weather today?"

"Lizzy, stop being so boring!" Sander exclaimed dramatically. "Who wants to talk about the weather? No one! Go back to your books and stupid marches and shit, I'm trying to have a *fun* conversation. More wine anyone? No? Good, more for me. It's a Friday, I could be out having some actual fun but instead I'm stuck inside here, talking to you boring people." There was a deathly silence as everyone stopped eating suddenly with the exception of Sander, who in his tipsy state was completely oblivious to the scene he had just caused. Even Charlie and Jane were struggling to come up with something to break the tension here.

I could feel myself getting hot under the collar. "Pride parade isn't a stupid march," I whispered, aware that I sounded like a child who'd just been told off. By now I was used to people making snide comments and mocking me, but I couldn't help but freeze up when it came from within my own family.

"Have you ever been to the London one?"

The silence in the room shifted from awkward to incredulous. If there was a list of things we weren't expecting Darcy Williams to say this evening, discussing pride parades was at the top.

"No," I replied sheepishly, starting to find my voice again. "I've only ever been to the Birmingham one, I went with the society at university."

"If you ever get the chance, you should go. I make sure to go every year."

This conversation was getting weirder and weirder.

Mum cleared her throat nervously.

"Well… Lizzy's moving to London in September, aren't you Lizzy? So maybe you could go next summer? Wouldn't that be fun?"

…and it just got weirder.

I smiled weakly, though, determined to keep the conversation away from Sander for a little while longer. "Yes, I, um, I'm sure it would be."

We all looked down at our dinners, silently willing someone else to break the tension that had settled over the table. Eventually Charlie and Jane started up some small talk, and despite having an open conversation, no one really felt able to join in. Even Sander sat there quietly, occasionally grumbling about something incoherently.

I was still slightly shaken up from Sander's comments earlier. I had come so far from the scared sixteen-year-old who was trying to figure herself out, and usually I could just shake silly comments off, especially when they're as petty as that. But when it comes from someone you've known your whole life? Sometimes I could just feel myself shrinking back into that shell. Don't get me wrong, I know I've been really lucky; on the whole, my family have been brilliantly supportive and I've never felt like they loved me any less for my sexuality, but that doesn't stop the occasional snide comment from hurting. Sometimes I would feel so ungrateful; there are so many people who have had it so much worse than me, even some of my friends have the most awful coming out stories, and here I am in a loving, caring family who accept me for who I am, whinging about the odd snippy comment from an idiot younger brother.

It felt like we were sat at that dinner table for years, waiting for someone to deem it an acceptable time for Charlie and Darcy to leave. I can't really remember them going. I'm sure I must have stood up and smiled at the right times and wished them a safe journey home, but it was all on autopilot. I could feel myself retreating into my own head again; a combination of Darcy and Sander pushing me back into my shell.

Sleep was a welcome friend that night. I didn't have to think about anything, or worry about anything. I just lay down and let the warmth of my duvet surround me until I drifted off into a heavy, dreamless slumber.

Chapter 6: Friend Requests

I woke up the next morning feeling in a funk. Post-graduation blues, Sander's mood and Darcy's general presence in my life had all combined to leave me feeling dull and lacklustre. It was still a few weeks before I moved down to London with Charlotte so there wasn't enough to do to keep me occupied and to stop me from thinking myself into a hole.

I should have been excited, shouldn't I? My life was just getting started: I'd finished with university, I'd got a (paid!) internship lined up, and I was well on my way to succeeding with what I wanted to do. I just felt like I was moving through fog. I knew which direction I was moving towards, and I could see the things that were close by, but everything else was completely obscured.

I spent the morning moping around the house, not putting any effort into actually doing anything; I couldn't even be bothered to lecture Sander about any of the usual things I have a go at him for. Jane often told me I was too hard on him, but didn't he need to grow up at some point? His constant immaturity was one day going to affect more than just him, I was sure of it, and when it did happen I would be the first to say 'I told you so'.

Usually when I'm in a bad mood, it takes Jane only a matter of minutes to pick up on it, even if she's in a completely different part of the house, but after an hour of being downstairs with no sign of her, I went to check on her to find that she wasn't in her room. I checked my phone to see if there were any messages to find that I'd forgotten to charge it up, and the battery had died while I was asleep. I plugged it in and switched it on to find two notifications.

Charlie Bingley sent you a friend request.

I opened up the notification and was taken to Charlie's Facebook profile. He had all his settings on private, but Jane's posts to him showed up. I distracted myself briefly by scrolling through the pictures of kittens and the music puns, all with some variation of 'Saw this and thought of you! <3 xx' as the caption. I accepted the friend request, thankful that I hadn't had one from Darcy, and checked the other notification.

Jane Bennet: Morning Lizzy! Hope you slept well. I'm out all day with Charlie, he's taking me on a surprise day out! I hope you have a good day, and I'll see you this evening. Keep smiling! X

And then after that,

Jane Bennet: We're at the zoo!!!! Loads of cute animals. I'll tell you all about it later! X

They were going to the zoo for a date?! Too cute.

Lizzy Bennet: Have fun! X

I quickly typed a response, knowing that Jane was the kind of person who worried that she'd said something wrong if someone saw a message but didn't reply.

Another notification appeared at the top of my screen:

Jane Bennet updated her profile picture.

It was a selfie of her and Charlie in front of the penguin enclosure, looking adorable – as usual. I silently thanked Mark Zuckerberg for making Facebook too difficult for Mum to handle past messages and friend requests; if she'd seen this then I dread to think what would've happened.

I refreshed my feed, hoping for an article or quiz to keep me occupied, but really shouldn't have been surprised by what came up.

Charlie Bingley updated his profile picture.

It was him and Jane. In front of the giraffe enclosure.

Was it weird to press Like? I had accepted his friend request less than three minutes ago, was it crossing some sort of boundary to immediately like a picture of him with my sister?

I saw that someone else, aside from Jane, had already liked it, so I hit the button anyway.

Lizzy Bennet, Jordan Williams and 1 other person like this

Jordan Williams? That must have been Darcy's brother. A quick click on his profile showed me that the family resemblance was too strong for him to be anything but. I pressed back as soon as I'd seen his profile picture, more to reassure myself that I wasn't being a stalker than anything else.

My phone buzzed again; this was getting ridiculous.

Darcy Williams sent you a friend request.

What?

WHAT?!

She sent me a friend request? But she hated me, right? I certainly couldn't stand her. I was perfectly happy not being Facebook friends with her, but ignoring a friend request from someone you so obviously know is... well, not the done thing. I couldn't even come up with a crappy excuse like 'It's only for university and school friends' or something, because I had literally just accepted Charlie's request.

Compromise was needed. I accepted the friend request, but changed the settings so she wouldn't appear on my news feed. I didn't want to see any more of her than I absolutely had to.

Just as I was about to put my phone down, it buzzed once more. "Seriously?" I said to an empty room, before picking it up and checking the message.

> Jane Bennet: I already am having fun! Do you have any plans for the day?
> Lizzy Bennet: I was just planning to do stuff around the house. And stop messaging me! Go have fun with Charlie, don't neglect him!
> Jane Bennet: You've just been 'doing stuff around the house' for three days in a row now! Go out for a bit, go for coffee or something! You'll feel better.
> Lizzy Bennet: If I promise to go out will you stop messaging me and enjoy your date with Charlie?
> Jane Bennet: It's not a date! And yes, I will, if you hold up your side of the bargain! And I want photo evidence.
> Lizzy Bennet: It so is a date. And fine, you win! I promise. Now go have fun!
> Jane Bennet: :)

It was a well-known fact that Jane was super-nice and had everyone's best interests at heart, but she could be really crafty at getting you to do things. Of course, she always managed to persuade people to do what she wanted them to do because it was always for a good reason. Like getting me out of the house for the first time in three days.

I waited for my phone to charge before grabbing my book and my bag and heading off to the high street.

The town we lived in, Longbourn, was big enough to have a high street, but small enough to have nothing else. There was a church, a community centre, a couple of small supermarkets, a card shop, a couple of charity shops, a few newsagents and, in what had previously been a bookmakers, a coffee shop.

There were a few people in the queue in front of me, which was unsurprising given that it was a Saturday lunchtime, so I took the extra few minutes to read through all of the menu and choose something different for a change. I noticed that the guy behind me was at least pretending to do the same, but kept throwing me glances which were clearly meant to catch my attention. I determinedly ignored them.

I got to the front of the queue and ordered my coffee and cake. (Cake bought to keep Jane happy doesn't contain any calories. Fact.)

"That will be five twenty-five please," the cashier said as I handed over my loyalty card and fished around in my purse for what remained of my student loan.

"Hey, no worries, I've got it." The guy behind me was leaning in and brandishing a ten pound note that I'm sure he'd got ready in advance for this.

I gave him a withering look as I gave a handful of coins to the cashier, who was trying not to crack up at this guy's cringe-worthy behaviour. I was sure I'd find it funny if it wasn't happening to me, although I had to admit there was an irony to the situation.

(I realised as I headed to a table in the corner that the cashier had once briefly dated Sander – briefly because she's not that daft – and so probably knew the exact reason why I was ignoring this guy.)

I had just settled in with my book when I heard someone clear their throat. I tore myself away from the page to see the same guy standing at the other side of the table, coffee in hand.

"Hi," he said, giving me a crooked smile that was obviously meant to make me swoon. "Is anyone sitting here?"

I couldn't think of an excuse quickly enough, so just said, "No, feel free," before going back to my book, hoping that he would take the hint.

He didn't, of course. He carried on regardless, not put off by the fact that I was blatantly ignoring him.

"I'm George," he said, still trying to look seductive, holding his hand out for me to shake.

I left it long enough to send a message, before deciding that I may as well get some entertainment out of this.

"Lizzy," I said, shaking his hand but trying not to look too happy about it. I gave him the once over. He was very good looking, I'll admit it, if obviously not my type. It was the kind of good-looking that you see on swimwear models, the kind that made you never want to look in a mirror again.

"So, do you come here often?" Seriously, could he have been any worse?

"No," I said, about to stuff some cake into my mouth to give me an excuse to not talk, before remembering my promise to send a picture to Jane. I grabbed my phone and quickly took a photo.

Lizzy Bennet: Photo evidence! Now have fun on your DATE!!!

The guy opposite me – George, I reminded myself – nodded towards my phone. "For Instagram?" he asked.

"Oh no, I was sending a picture to my sister, she was the one who suggested I come out today."

I hadn't thought I was giving him an opening, but he seemed to take it anyway.

"So I have her to thank for seeing such a lovely lady around town today, then?"

I nearly threw up in my mouth.

"Yeah." New plan: just give one word answers. Save this story for the next time I need a good anecdote at a party. Then leave.

"So, you like reading, huh? Books, coffee... anything else you're interested in? What about Netflix?"

The words 'and chill' were hanging on his lips as he finished that sentence.

I suddenly saw my opening, smiled internally, and feigned thought for a moment before answering, "Women."

I tried not to laugh as I watched realisation dawn on his face.

"So... so that's why it's not working! You're gay! Don't take this the wrong way, but I'm actually kinda glad, I was wondering what I was doing wrong! Turns out I just have the wrong plumbing. Not gonna lie, that does make me feel better!"

I couldn't help but laugh now. "It didn't work because you used such terrible lines, not just because I'm gay! But if it makes you feel better, then by all means believe that!"

We stopped laughing, before we caught each other's eyes and both snorted, sending us back into a fit of the giggles.

"Shall we start again," I suggested, once we'd calmed down a bit. "Hi, I'm Lizzy Bennet. One hundred percent gay."

"Hi Lizzy Bennet, I'm George Wickham. One hundred percent no longer hitting on you." We shook hands again, each laughing slightly at the other.

"So what are you reading? Genuine interest this time, not looking for an opening!"

I handed the book over to him so he could read the blurb.

"You really love books then, huh? I've never been a huge reader myself; I've read stuff like *Harry Potter* and I enjoyed most of the stuff we read in school, but I've never really got into reading for pleasure, you know?"

I nodded in understanding. "There are so many people who enjoy reading but don't read on a regular basis, and it's really just because they don't have the right book. It's one of the many reasons why I want to go into publishing; the number of people reading recently has grown enormously, but there's still so many people who could be interested but just... aren't."

"You want to go into publishing? That's so cool!"

My hands flew to my forehead. "I'm so sorry, I'm just sitting here and assuming you know everything about me! I'll, um, stop talking now!"

"Hey, no worries. I think you're pretty cool, Lizzy Bennet, and I think it would be awesome sauce if we were friends. Then we don't have to worry about oversharing and telling life stories and stuff. How does that sound?"

I nodded my agreement. "I do feel like I've known you for much longer than ten minutes – I think we would be pretty cracking friends. So, friend catch-up: what are you doing in life at the moment, or what do you want to do? And what brings you to Longbourn?"

"I've just got a job as a sales person in Meryton, but I didn't have chance to sort out somewhere to live so I'm currently kipping with my friend Denny."

"Oh, I know Denny! He was in my sister's year at school. I'd say they were friends, but she's friends with absolutely everyone, so I'm not sure if it's really a valid statement."

"What's your sister's name? I'll ask if he remembers her."

"Jane. Sorry, I completely interrupted you there, carry on."

"Oh yeah, so I'm currently a sales person, but I'm hoping that if I work hard I can become a manager or something relatively soon. We, er," he started to look a bit sheepish and embarrassed. "We didn't have much money growing up, and I really want to be able to support a family of my own one day. I don't want my kids to have to miss out on stuff because I can't afford it, you know? I know it's kind of shallow. My life ambition is to have money, whoop-di-doo!"

"No," I said, thinking about how, although we weren't exactly rolling in money, my parents had always had enough to make sure we were comfortable with extras for hobbies and holidays and school trips, and how hard it must be growing up in a family that didn't even have that. "I think it's admirable. People say money isn't important, but it is, and there's no use pretending otherwise."

He smiled weakly, obviously glad that I wasn't putting him down for wanting to earn money. "So, what about you? You mentioned publishing?"

We chatted back and forth for hours, until we were politely asked to leave because they were about to close the shop. We just got along so well and chatted so easily; I think Charlotte must have been the last person I'd met that I'd just clicked with so well.

"We should probably go our separate ways now," I said as the coffee shop door was firmly locked behind us. "Hey, before we go, just let me quickly add you on Facebook – how do you spell your surname?" I got my phone out ready for typing.

"George, then W-I-C-K-H-A-M." I quickly found him and pressed 'Add as friend'.

My phone buzzed almost straight away with *George Wickham accepted your friend request*. I dismissed the notification, then looked up to see him staring at his phone screen.

"You're friends with Darcy Williams?" he asked, bewildered.

I laughed nervously. "I wouldn't say friends... more people who can't stand each other but seem to constantly have to put up with each other?"

Obviously my answer had been acceptable, as he nodded gravely and put his phone away.

"Why, do you... know her?" I tentatively asked.

He paused for a moment. "Which way are you walking?"

I indicated in the general direction towards our house – at less than a mile away, I'd felt like I couldn't really justify driving.

"Denny lives that way as well – I'll tell you while we walk."

We walked in a pregnant silence for a few minutes, before he took a deep breath and began talking.

"I've known the Williams family all my life; in fact, Darcy's father was my godfather. My father wasn't around much when I was growing up, and Uncle Henry helped me through a lot of tough times."

He paused again, gathering his thoughts.

"I, um... well, I don't know how much you know, but, um..." he cleared his throat, "There was a car crash, a few years ago now. I was seventeen, halfway through college, and..." he paused again, "I'll never forget that phone call. Being told that the two people you looked up to as your parents were just... taken away from you, in an instant? It's something I wouldn't wish upon my worst enemy."

I couldn't think of anything suitable to say, so stayed quiet. The thought of losing your parents or loved ones like that? Of them just being… gone, with no hint or warning?

"In their will it was specified that, once I had a place at university, I would be given fifteen thousand pounds each September, every academic year until I graduated. That would be enough to cover tuition fees and most of my living costs, and I might have needed to get a part-time job but I would be able to live reasonably comfortably, without getting myself into debt. It's the kind of money that would make all the difference to me, but would barely make a dent in the Williams' accounts."

I nodded sympathetically, suddenly very aware of the forty-grand student debt looming over my head, unlikely to ever be paid off.

"Knowing that Uncle Henry had wanted me to have a future, had wanted me to push myself to be the best person I could be, it motivated me, and I worked so hard in my final year of college so that I could go to as good a university as possible and it paid off. I got a place at Manchester Uni to study Law, following in Uncle Henry's footsteps. He had left me this opportunity and I was going to make the most of it."

He paused again, first under the pretence of crossing the road, then pinching the bridge of his nose, hiding his eyes.

"I had a place, I had everything ready to go, and all I needed now was the funds to make it happen. I asked Darcy if she would be able to pay my tuition fees, my rent, and transfer me the rest of the money for my living cost. And she-" he ran his hand through his hair, breathing heavily, "-she said no." I audibly gasped; I knew Darcy could be awful, but this was another level. "All that work for nothing. I had to withdraw two weeks before starting my course, because it was too late to apply for student finance and I had no other money, and neither did my mother. I've been trying to make my own way ever since, determined to make the most of myself despite the setbacks."

I was shocked speechless. To go against your father's will like that, ruining someone else's life? What would possibly justify such actions?

I said as much out loud. "I guess she has a grudge or something?"

He laughed humourlessly. "I could always tell that Darcy was jealous of how much attention her father gave me; she thought I didn't deserve it. Her parents were on their way to visit me when they crashed. I think she blamed me for their deaths. She was never particularly pleasant to me when they were alive, but I never thought she could stoop so low."

The worst part of all of this was that it was believable. I would never have thought that anyone could do something so awful, but this fitted with everything I had seen of Darcy so far. Her manner, her attitude, the way she treated her supposed friends... I could certainly see her doing something like this. Something that, to her, must have seemed so petty and ineffectual, but in reality ruined someone else's life.

"This is the road to Denny's," George suddenly said, pulling me out of my thoughts. I hadn't realised how far we'd walked; I was only a few minutes from home.

I tried my best at a smile. "Well, it was wonderful meeting you."

He forced a grin back. "Yes – I'll send you a message. We must meet again, Lizzy Bennet!"

I laughed slightly. "That we must! You're a good guy, George. I'm actually kinda glad you started hitting on me."

We both laughed at that, before bidding each other goodbye and going our separate ways.

I let myself in just as Dad was serving up dinner.

"Hey there," he said, grabbing another plate for me as the others started tucking in. I noticed that Jane wasn't back yet. "Had a good day?"

I thought for a minute, mulling over the events of the day, before answering. "Yes. It has been a good day. Very… interesting. But good."

After all, I'd made a new friend. And even if Darcy Williams tried her hardest to destroy everything and everyone that came in her way, she couldn't take that away from me.

Chapter 7: The Worst Road Trip Ever

Jane didn't get home until two o'clock in the morning after her date with Charlie. At least she came home; we had to put up with Sander making lewd comments about it all through dinner. I did wish Mum and Dad would try to talk some sense into him sometimes. Just because he was the youngest, if only by a few minutes, he could get away with almost everything. I was sure they thought that he was just 'sorting out his issues' or something, and that if they just let him do what he wanted now it would all turn out alright in the end. Occasionally I tried to say something, but it always sounded petty coming from a sibling, no matter what age; parental intervention was needed more often than not.

After the zoo closed Jane and Charlie went for dinner, and after the restaurant closed they went to McDonalds and stayed there until, from what I can gather, they were each on their third coffee, and decided to call it a night. I was glad they had a good time though, and I was happy that Jane finally had someone who's constantly on the same page as her, who would talk with her until the early hours of the morning, putting the world to rights together. Of course, the other advantage of them having actual dates instead of awkward group dinners is that they could be as cute as they wanted, without me having to go through either Darcy's presence or being the third wheel. I was so, so happy for both of them, but glad I no longer had to watch them make heart eyes at each other while making what just sounds like puppy noises.

Despite her late night, however, Jane was up first thing in the morning as usual, ready once more to make the world a little brighter. She told me what felt like every last detail of their date over breakfast, right down to how they realised partway through the day that they were wearing the same colour socks, but I hadn't had my morning tea yet, and so was struggling to pay attention.

I had finished my cereal and was just taking my first sip of tea when Jane nervously piped up with another piece of new information, the words rushing out.

"So… Charlie invited me to go on holiday with him."

I spat tea all over the table.

Jane instantly grabbed kitchen paper and started mopping up my mess while I inelegantly wiped my mouth, noting that even though she seemed nervous Jane's eyes had an excited sparkle to them.

"That was, um, nice of him," I managed to get out after the initial shock had worn off. "Just the two of you? Alone? I mean, um, where to?"

"A week in the south of France. And it won't be just the two of us," she looked scandalised even at the thought, "Darcy will be there too." I tried drinking more tea to hide my face. "And you're invited."

This time I choked.

After some (surprisingly strong for someone so small and nice) slaps on the back from Jane, I managed to splutter out, "Jane, why would I want to spend a week being Darcy's fellow gooseberry to you and Charlie? Surely you can see that it's not a good idea."

Her face suddenly fell; I could tell that it hadn't occurred to her that I might say no.

"Please, Lizzy? I can't go by myself, it would be too strange. It would only be okay if you were there too."

I knew as soon as those big, hopeful eyes widened that I was losing this battle, but I was going to go down fighting.

"Let's look at this rationally. When are they going?"

"They're leaving a week on Monday. So in nine days' time."

Thank you, Jane, I can count.

"And they're staying for a week?"

"Yes. So we'll be back in time for Charlotte's birthday."

"And where *exactly* are they going?"

"Darcy owns a holiday cottage on the coast." Of course she does. "It's quite far away from any major towns, and it has four bedrooms, so we can each have our own room." I could tell that she wasn't reassuring *me* for this last part.

"How much will it cost?"

"Nothing except spending money and food contributions, although I'll expect we'll eat out most of the time. I suppose it's the perks of owning the house!"

"And how are we getting there?"

"We're driving."

What.

I don't know what I'd expected. If the house was far away from any towns then plane or train wouldn't be practical, and the only other alternative was getting there by car. Unless we all learnt how to teleport, but I didn't think that would be happening anytime soon.

"Please, Lizzy." Uh-oh. The begging eyes were out. "It would mean so much to me and the other two to have you there." Wasn't sure about that last part. "And it will be fun! Spending all day at the beach, watching the world go by... please come. It won't be the same without you."

There was no use pretending any longer – we both knew how this was going to end.

"Okay," I relented, putting my hands up in mock-surrender. "I'll go."

She squealed and jumped up, grinning and clapping her hands, looking seven rather than twenty-three.

"I'll go and let Charlie know right away!" She threw her arms around me in a suffocating hug. "Thank you so much, Lizzy! We'll have a great time, you'll see!"

***

Monday week came far too fast. I'd got everything ready to go: I'd found my passport and health card, bought a relatively flattering swimming costume, and deliberated far too long about how many and which books to take. Suitcase packed, I went to bed on the Sunday night apprehensive about the week ahead.

Charlie and Darcy were picking us up from our house at five o'clock from our house to drive down to Dover for the ten o'clock ferry. I must admit I was glad we were taking one of their cars; I didn't know who would be driving, but I knew it wouldn't be me so I didn't mind.

At quarter to five, Jane and I were waiting in the sitting room with our cases, groggily poking each other occasionally to keep ourselves awake. I was fully anticipating sleeping for most of the car journey, so had my iPod and a travel pillow at the ready for when I could settle in the back of the car and nod off. Jane, however, seemed to think that that would give a bad impression, and so was frantically trying to down a coffee before they got here, with another in a thermos flask ready to go.

At five o'clock there was a quiet knock on the door from Charlie, who was ready to help us put our cases in the car. I was surprised to see a large 4x4 rather than one of the Jaguars that I had seen outside their house at Netherfield Court, but even in my sleep-deprived state I could reason that there was no way the four of us, plus our cases, could fit in the smaller cars. I briefly wondered quite how many cars they owned, but filed the thought away for another time when I was less sleep-deprived. I must admit that I was relieved when I saw that Darcy was driving. Hopefully, focussing on the road would mean she was less likely to talk.

"Lizzy, do you want to sit in the front?" Charlie asked hopefully.

It was far too tricky a decision to make. On the one hand, it meant that Charlie and Jane would be able to be couple-y and cuddle and talk to their hearts' content together without disturbing us as much, but on the other hand... I'd have to sit next to Darcy. All day. Given, though, that she was driving and I was planning on sleeping, I figured I may as well. I had been hoping that I could sit in relative silence for the whole journey anyway. Now, I'd just be sitting in silence somewhere else.

As soon as I had got into the car and put on my seatbelt, I put my travel pillow behind my head, got a blanket out of my tote bag and got ready to go straight back to sleep. I wasn't going on this trip willingly, and while I would of course do my best to be polite, well-mannered and pleasant at all times, I was still going to sleep whenever I wanted to.

It seemed, however, that some people had other ideas. Jane hadn't been the only one drinking coffee; both Charlie and Darcy were running on caffeine. In Darcy's case it was understandable. She was driving, after all, and needed to be awake for that. Charlie, however? He had no excuse, except presumably wanting to talk to Jane, and talk to Jane he did. Those two could make a conversation out of anything, and with them both on a caffeinated high, they did their usual adorable, made-for-each-other thing only twice as fast.

We had barely left Longbourn when Charlie decided to speak to the car as a whole.

"And we're off! Isn't this exciting? We're going to have so much fun! Only thirteen hours left to go until we get there!"

God help us all.

**

Despite being completely exhausted, comfortable with my blanket and pillow and with sleep-inducing music playing on my iPod, I did not manage to get one jot of sleep on the way down to the ferry. Charlie and Jane were chatting away like there was no tomorrow, which there wasn't going to be if they didn't shut up soon, and Darcy had some weird, abstract music turned up far too loudly, drowning out the flute and harp that were playing through my earphones. I was too tired to really enjoy reading, however, so I spent the journey staring out the window, watching the English countryside whizz by. I was starting to regret not packing some coffee of my own. At least then I could have kept up with the others.

I was very glad that I hadn't mentioned my plan of sleeping all morning to Jane. I could just about cope with her and Charlie's attentions to each other, and didn't need her fussing over me and apologising for being too loud on top of that. This whole trip was going to be stressful enough, and the longer I could stay in my own little bubble the better.

We'd been driving for about two hours when Darcy's music got even weirder. I know enough about classical music to get by, but this was something else. There wasn't really a melody, just a load of notes being thrown around, and something that sounded suspiciously like a vacuum cleaner started making noises. If I hadn't had a headache before I certainly had one now; this was some seriously weird stuff.

"Hey, Darcy, could we put the radio on? How does Radio One sound?" Charlie asked, hopefully.

Darcy huffed at the suggestion. "You know the rules; the driver chooses the music." I wasn't aware of that rule, but this week just got a whole lot less fun. "You know how I feel about Radio One; it's just churned out pop rubbish. This is Art." She said it in a way that made the capital A of Art explicitly obvious.

"Pop music is art too, just a different kind. I agree that some pop music is pretty terrible, but a lot of it's very good." I immediately regretted saying anything. I had to spend a week living with this woman, and the longer we put off the first argument the better. The problem, of course, is that neither of us are the kind to back down; once we start to disagree on something, it could only end in flames. I should have just left her to her hoover music and be done with it.

"Pop music is there purely to entertain, it has no other purpose. This is pushing the boundaries of music, exploring the issues in our society today through the medium of sound," she explained as if to a child. I told myself to rise above it, to only give rational arguments, and I managed it but only just.

"Pop is short for popular, so surely that's where we should be looking for views on society and culture? I'm not saying that your music isn't doing that, but I don't think you should be so scathing about pop music just because its primary purpose is entertainment. Surely that is the point of music? Surely that's what makes music different from just sounds?"

I did a mental self-five at this. For someone who knows barely anything about music – but, admittedly, a fair bit about culture and the arts as a whole – I thought I argued my case very well.

The only response, however, was to have the hoover music turned up some more, and to be ignored all the way to Dover. Which, to be honest, was not entirely a bad thing.

The hour-long ferry journey gave me a chance to stretch my legs and, more importantly, get some space away from the other three. It was a lovely day, so Jane and Charlie headed outside to watch the sea and enjoy the fresh air, I sat on a sofa in the coffee shop reading a book, and I didn't even bother to look where Darcy went; the opposite direction from me was all I noticed and all that mattered.

All too soon, however, we were back in the car, ready to drive all the way through France. Thankfully the hoover CD had come to an end, and Darcy's next choice was something a little more... well, musical. We stopped for lunch at a seafood restaurant, bought some snacks from the 8 á 8 for the trip ahead, and carried on driving.

For about half an hour, we had a relatively pleasant journey. Charlie and Jane had finally stopped talking and were holding hands, we actually had some okay music on, and it had been a couple of hours since Darcy and I had had a disagreement, which must have been some kind of record. It almost felt like we were waiting for the other shoe to drop. It had all been going too well, and something surely had to go wrong at some point.

Unfortunately, the other shoe did drop, and when it did, it happened in the worst possible way.

"Darcy?" Jane asked timidly from the back seat.

"Mm-hmm?" came the disgruntled response.

"Could you pull over quickly?"

I looked over my shoulder to see Jane looking a nasty shade of green.

"Quickly, pull over!" I exclaimed, realising that Darcy wasn't going to do anything. Amazingly she did, and just in time; Jane leapt out of the car and threw up into the bushes at the side of the road.

I love my sister to pieces, I really do, and I would do anything for her. But thank goodness Charlie was there; it was now someone else's responsibility to stroke her back, hold back her hair and clean up any vomit that got anywhere other than on the grass. Like on Jane's shoes.

"I'm so sorry," Jane said, starting to cry a little once she'd stopped throwing up. "I've never been travel sick or anything, I think it must be something that I ate at lunch. I'm so sorry."

She started to cry some more as Charlie pulled her into a hug and gently calmed her down, holding her close and whispering something to her. Whatever he said, it seemed to work. After a few sips of water she was still pale and shaken, but well enough to get back in the car to continue.

Charlie sat in the middle seat this time so that he could still have his arms around Jane while we drove, and I will be the first to admit that it was absolutely adorable. This ridiculously tall, enormous guy with his arms around this tiny, tender young woman, giving her enormous puppy-dog eyes? It was one of the most precious things I'd ever seen.

Usually when someone has food poisoning, the faster they throw up the better, because it gets it out of their system so it doesn't last as long. Not in this case though. It turned out to be a very good thing we'd got snacks from the 8 á 8; the carrier bags came in very useful when we were on the motorway, unable to pull over in a hurry. It was safe to say that we would be avoiding seafood for the foreseeable future.

We made it to Darcy's beach house at nine o'clock in the evening. Jane had thrown up a further six times on the journey back, all the while with Charlie there to look after her and make sure she was okay. Darcy and I carried all the luggage in while Charlie carried a thankfully sleeping Jane and helped me tuck her into bed in one of the spare rooms, overlooking the sea. I tried to look like I wasn't watching as he tenderly brushed her hair off her forehead, letting his hand linger on her cheek for a moment before gesturing to me to go back out into the hallway, gently shutting the door behind him.

"Your room is this one," he whispered, showing me into the room next to Jane's. "I'm opposite you and Darcy's in the other front corner; we each have an en suite so you don't need to worry about sharing bathrooms or anything. I think I'll, er, turn in for the night – Darcy already has."

I smiled and nodded. "That sounds like a really good idea!" Despite it being only just nine o'clock – eight o'clock British time – we were all completely exhausted from the long journey. "Goodnight!"

I slipped into my room and took a moment to admire it. It was absolute enormous. A large king-sized bed was in the centre of the room, a wardrobe that looked big enough to hold all of Narnia, and a bookshelf filled with well-thumbed paperbacks.

Making a mental note to look through them tomorrow when I was awake, I quickly looked through the other door which, as predicted, led to the bathroom. It was the same size as the bathroom we had at home, which we shared between six of us; a bath and shower all-in-one, toilet and sink, and an enormous counter. I wanted nothing more than to sink into the bath and soak off all the day's worries and stresses, but I knew that I would fall asleep, and wake up either underwater or very, very cold, so I settled for washing my face, going through my evening routine, and falling onto the soft, downy covers, letting sleep wash over me.

Chapter 8: An Understanding

I woke the following morning in the early hours with the sun shining brightly on my face. It took me a few seconds to work out why this bed felt different than home before I remembered where I wa:; in the south of France, having driven down with Jane, Charlie and Darcy the day before. I'd been so tired I'd forgotten to shut the curtains, and so woke up with the dawn. I checked my phone to see the time – six o'clock in the morning – and spotted a scrap of paper on the bedside table.

Wi-Fi name: WilliamsOnTour
Password: Jordan_is_gr8

I'm guessing Darcy wasn't the one to set up the Wi-Fi, then.

I logged in, feeling even more perplexed about Jordan Williams. From the little I'd heard about him, he seemed completely different from his sister. While my phone connected I entertained myself by thinking about what Darcy would set as a Wi-Fi password. She'd probably leave it as the default, for 'security purposes'. Or, more likely, change it to something like *KeepOutLizzyBennet*. Yeah, that would probably be it.

I knew the moment my phone connected because it flooded with messages that had all been sent since we left England yesterday morning. I went through them, one by one.

Mark Bennet: Woke up after you'd gone. Have fun. Please come back and save me from Sander, he's already driving me crazy.

I smiled wryly to myself at the thought of Mark having to put up with Sander 24/7; they were usually either at school, which they'd just finished, or had one of us two around. I sent a suitably sympathetic reply, and opened the next message.

> *Charlotte Lucas: Hey Lizzy, hope you and Jane have a totally awesome time in France!! I've just been chatting to Maria, and I think she's going a bit overboard for my birthday party next week... she's planned for me to invite twenty people and so far I've only invited about five!!! So yeah, if you wanted to invite anyone extra that would be fabbity-fab. Maybe Charlie, and your new friend George? And I suppose you'd have to invite Darcy as well. Plus your whole family! Seriously, I saw the shopping list for dinner and we're going to need as many people as possible to eat it all! But have a great time in France, and try not to get food poisoning – you know I've never trusted French cuisine...*

What a brilliantly ironic end to a message! I quickly typed out a reply, knowing I would forget if I left it until later.

> *Lizzy Bennet: Hello from France! :D Funny you should mention food poisoning... poor Jane ate something funny yesterday and was hurling all the way down. Not fun. But hopefully a good night's sleep and she'll be better. And yeah, I'll invite extra people – I'll just add them to the FB event? And check out this awesome room!*

I quickly snapped a photo of the room, the sun beaming through the window, and sent it after the message.

One more message to go.

George Wickham: Hey Lizzy, just wanted to say have fun in France! And don't let a certain someone get you down. I've been to the cottage before, as a kid, and stayed in the front room on the right. It's so beautiful there, wish I could go again! Can't say I envy the company though. Send me loads of pictures! Including any unflattering ones of Williams. Schadenfreude, you know? ;)

I lay back on the bed, deep in thought. I hadn't allowed myself to truly connect George's story with the woman in the room across from me; I'm sure that if I did, there would be no way that I could make it through this week. George wasn't out for revenge, or even an apology. The only thing getting angry would accomplish is to make things worse for Jane. No, I would grit my teeth and pretend that nothing was wrong, if only for her sake.

Now that I was awake, I decided to explore the room a bit more and wait for a more reasonable hour to go downstairs. I padded over to the bookshelf to examine the titles there. In my experience, you can learn a lot about someone from their bookshelf from the genres, how they're ordered, the state of the books themselves. Admittedly a bookshelf in a holiday cottage was slightly different; it was likely to be a portion of someone's book collection, and probably books they enjoyed but weren't necessarily their favourites.

The majority of books on this shelf were YA adventure stories, mostly about cool indie kids who went on adventures and found alien colonies or vampires or dystopian governments. I didn't recognise most of the titles though, which is unusual for me, but I soon realised why after I picked one up off the shelf. A small circle printed in one corner told me that it was a proof copy; I checked the covers of a few more to find the same label on all of them. There were probably about fifty proof copies here, all published in the last two or three years. I remembered that Darcy was an editor, and wondered if that was how she got hold of them all.

I spotted that the top shelf had a different selection of books, most of which I recognised and had been around for longer. I picked one up which had been read so many times that the spine was curved (I appreciate a curved but not broken book spine) and the front cover curled up. I couldn't help but see the corner of a post-it note on the front page, and carefully opened the book to read it.

> Jordan –
> Happy 16th birthday! This was one of my favourite books, and I hope you enjoy it too.
> Lots of love,
> Darcy xxx

That was weird. Like, really weird. Seeing such an affectionate message from... Darcy? This was the same person, right?

This room must usually have been Jordan's, then. It would make sense, if Darcy was in her usual room and Jane was in what was once George's. It was odd thinking that this room belongs to someone I've never met, and that many of their personal possessions are still here.

I know I shouldn't have, but I was feeling nosy, and was I really doing anything wrong? The books were just there, and I *had* been given this room for the week.

I put the back, and picked up the next book along. This one was in a similar state to the other one, and again had a note inside, but this one with different handwriting.

> *Jordan,*
>
> *Merry Christmas! Thank you for being such a good friend to me – you're a really special person, and I know things have been rough for both of us recently. I'm sorry I wasn't able to get you much, especially considering how much you and Darcy have done for me, but with this note I promise to make it up to you in future years!*
>
> *-W*

I had no idea who that was from, but I felt as soon as I finished reading it that I'd stepped over a line. There was far more here than I knew about, and I had no right to go prying. I carefully but quickly made sure all the books were back as they were before getting my own books out of my bag. I carefully piled them up on the bedside table before getting my phone out to reply to George's message.

> *Lizzy Bennet: I'll make sure to get some funny pics ;) I think I'm in Jordan's room? Back right. I've just been admiring his book collection – seems like a family of avid readers!*

I put my phone back down, not expecting a reply anytime soon, but heard it buzz almost straight away.

George Wickham: Wow, you're up early! At least I have the excuse of a commute... And yeah, that's Jordan's room. He's a cool kid, haven't spoken to him recently though. He was always kinda like a little brother to me.

It was now even harder to not let Darcy's actions towards George overcome my emotions. Everything George had said made it sound like he used to be part of the family, close to everyone except her, and she'd gone and ruined his future because of it.

It suddenly occurred to me that perhaps the 'W' in the note I read was for 'Wickham', although it would be odd to sign a note off using a final initial. It would certainly make sense, though – the note talked about close friendship, perhaps close like brothers, about being helped through difficult times, which would certainly describe Mr and Mrs Williams' deaths, and an implication of a lack of financial means, again fitting with George. I couldn't remember all of the specifics and knew that it would definitely be an invasion of privacy to read it again or, worse, ask George to confirm my suspicions. For now? I would content myself with trying to solve the enigma that was the Williams family.

***

Nine o'clock came and went without a sound from anywhere else in the house, so I padded out of my room and knocked lightly on Jane's door, not too loudly in case she was still sleeping.

"Come in," came the quiet reply, and I slipped into the room, shutting the door quietly behind me. Somehow I didn't think waking Darcy up early on the first day of a holiday together would be a great idea.

"Oh, Lizzy, it's you!" Jane looked relieved to see me there. "I wanted to come and find you, but I had no idea which room you were in or anything so I thought I'd just stay put. Did I fall asleep in the car? I must have, I slept in my clothes! I don't remember coming in at all."

I recounted the events of the previous evening, right down to Charlie's tender actions as he tucked her in.

"It was one of the most adorable things I've ever seen," I finished, smiling at the pink in Jane's cheeks. "Are you feeling any better this morning?" I asked, remembering the reason for Jane's exhaustion the previous night.

She smiled weakly. "Lots. I'm still feeling a bit shaky, but I'm sure that will pass. Good thing we're on holiday and don't have to do anything!"

I nodded in agreement. "Yup, good thing indeed! How do you feel about breakfast? I don't know how much food there is here, but I'm fairly sure there's still some biscuits left over from yesterday?"

"Lizzy, you can't have biscuits for breakfast!" Jane said, mock-scandalised, but got out of bed anyway. I sometimes forgot that she'd never got round to actually being a student, and so still thought that certain foods are only suitable for certain meals.

As we tiptoed downstairs, still wary about waking anyone up, I got my first good look around the ground floor of the house.

"Wow," I gasped, looking at the size of the kitchen, dining room, sitting room, then seeing the conservatory and beach deck outside. It was nowhere as big as their house at Netherfield Court, but was still much bigger than our house at home, despite having less rooms.

"This isn't a holiday cottage, it's a holiday mansion," I said to Jane, still in awe of our surroundings. From the enormous window in the sitting room you could see miles of deserted sandy beaches, leading to a magnificent bright blue ocean.

We both spun around as the front door opened. It was Darcy, carrying some fresh bread and a bag of what was, from the smell, French cheeses.

"Good morning," she nodded curtly, before going straight into the kitchen. "I trust you both slept well?"

"Yes, we did, thank you," Jane replied, smiling as always, and saving me from having to find a response.

"Good," Darcy said shortly, before laying out the foods she'd bought. "Jane, I doubt you're completely recovered from yesterday's illness, so might I suggest that you just have some plain bread to start with?"

Wow. I mean, the delivery could do with some work, but it was almost as if she cared about someone else. This was new.

But what about George, an unbidden voice said in the back of my head, reminding me of Darcy's true colours. It's entirely possible that Darcy was a different person from the girl who held such petty grudges, but I'm sure that, if that were the case, George would have had an apology and an offer of forty-five thousand pounds. Neither of which he had received.

"I didn't realise anyone else was awake," I blurted out as I joined Darcy and Jane at the breakfast table.

"I went out about an hour ago," Darcy replied in a flat tone, neither of us meeting the other's eye. I guess I must have been absorbed in my book and didn't hear her leave.

We ate in an uncomfortable silence until Charlie came down, still slightly bleary with sleep.

"Morning!" he said, heading straight over to make a coffee, oblivious to the mood of the room. After putting the kettle on to boil he joined us at the table, kissing Jane on the cheek chastely before sitting down. "How are we all this morning?" Darcy and I made noises that vaguely resembled 'good'.

"It's so beautiful here," Jane gushed. "I'm almost glad I was asleep when I got here, because I woke up in this beautiful place!" She turned to Charlie, taking his hand. "Thank you so much for caring for me yesterday. It meant so much to me," she said with sincerity, looking him firmly in the eye. Darcy and I both looked down at our plates; I could tell she also felt like we were intruding on a private moment.

He brought his other hand to cover their interlocked fingers. "It was a pleasure. I'm so sorry that you were ill, and I'm only glad that I was able to look after you."

I bolted down what remained of my breakfast before mumbling something about a shower and dashing upstairs. This why I didn't want to go on this trip in the first place at least in part. It was a bonding experience for Jane and Charlie, and they didn't need me in the way.

I showered and got dressed for the day, putting my swimming costume on underneath my clothes. I could hear the others getting ready in the rooms around me, and so packed a bag with my towel, sun cream and a book, ready for a day spent on the beach.

Within half an hour, we were all settled outside. Charlie and Jane were in the sea, Darcy was working on her laptop, and I was lying back on the sand, reading a book. We were in a surprisingly companionable silence. Perhaps she had also decided to try and get through the week with as few disputes as possible.

"What are you reading?" she asked after a while. At first I was surprised by her genuine interest, before remembering the library I'd seen at Netherfield Court.

I passed her the book, briefly explaining the premise as she glanced at the cover.

"I've read that, it's absolutely brilliant. The ending was not what I expected at all – I won't spoil it for you, but it's really wonderful."

I sat up, curious all of a sudden.

"You've read it? But it only came out the other day. I was really worried the book shop in Longbourn wouldn't have any and I'd have to wait a week before I could find it anywhere else. She's one of my favourite authors, I've read all her books."

Darcy lifted up my copy and pointed to the small logo at the bottom of the spine. "I published it. I'm the editor-in-chief at Pemberley Publishing House."

I was used to being rendered speechless by Darcy Williams, but this time was completely different.

"You – but you – you published this?!"

She raised an eyebrow. "That's what I said. We've published all of her books; she was one of my father's first authors, back when he started the company. Now that I have a lot more responsibilities I obviously don't get to read as many of the books, but I always make sure to read her manuscripts. She's a very talented woman."

Well, would you look at that. Darcy and I agree on something.

She looked at me inquisitively; not as if she was interested in what I had to say, more like she saw me as some sort of specimen.

"What would you say makes a good book? I'm sure you have an opinion." She sounded slightly scathing at the end there, but I was going to take it regardless. This was serious progress. If we could agree on something, even just one thing, it would make things so much easier for Charlie and Jane.

"The most important thing in a book is that it has to move you," I started. I could talk about this in my sleep. I actually had done in the past, back when I was filling out applications for internships. "It doesn't really matter what emotion it makes you feel, but it has to make you feel *something*. The reader has to feel involved, has to feel like they're a part of the action. The best books are where you desperately want it to have a particular outcome; where it moves you so much that you don't think you can bear much more of it, but you keep going because you have to know what's going to happen." I cleared my throat, mildly embarrassed by my short speech. "What about you? What do you look for in a book?"

I met Darcy's eyes, and she was giving me a very strange look: a look of almost... respect?

"I completely agree with you. If a story doesn't influence the reader... then it's failed in its purpose as a story."

There was a strange tension between us suddenly. After all, we'd only disagreed about anything before, and here we were, completely on the same page.

All of a sudden it was broken, as Darcy looked back to her laptop. "I still have a few sample chapters left to approve; none as good as what you're holding in your hand, of course."

I nodded and went back to lying on the sand, opening my book once more. We didn't talk again for the rest of the day, but in a strange way we were comfortable in our silence, two introverts who had let each other into their spaces. For the first time, I hadn't got to the end of a conversation with Darcy feeling resentful and angry. Instead I felt... well, I felt like I'd had an intelligent, mature conversation, no matter how brief.

But what about George, came that unbidden voice once more.

For a few minutes, I'd forgotten what Darcy was really like. And that's not to say that you can't have an intelligent conversation about literature and not also be an awful person, the two aren't mutually exclusive. We could have civil conversations until the cows came home but we would never, and I mean never, be friends. That much is for sure.

Chapter 9: An Ideal Spouse

The rest of the day passed in very much the same way. I spent the day reading, Darcy spent the day on her computer, and Jane and Charlie spent the day being their usual adorable selves: playing in the sea, cloud-watching together, even building sandcastles together. I was very glad I had a large stack of books with me; Jane and Charlie are a lot easier to put up with when you have something there ready to distract you should they cross the boundary and become just *too* cute.

Jane finally managed to persuade me to go into the sea when Charlie started setting up the barbecue in the evening. At first I protested – a lifetime of British beach holidays had taught me that the sea was only warm for about an hour in the mid-afternoon – but, after assurances that the sea was much warmer here, I relented, if only to chat with Jane for a bit without the other two around.

As promised, the sea was the perfect temperature; warm enough that I felt as if I could stay there for hours, but cool enough that it was refreshing after a hot day spent lying in the sun. As soon as we got in deep enough I splashed Jane, who shrieked with laughter.

"Lizzy!" she exclaimed, pretending to be annoyed. "How dare you!" And she splashed me back, grinning mischievously.

I tumbled into her, laughing, and we both careered into the water, each trying to get the other as soaking wet as possible. I was grinning so hard that it hurt, and Jane was soon out of breath from laughing so much. I couldn't remember the last time we had so much fun, even if just for a few minutes. I was finally glad that I came here in the first place. Sharing this moment with my sister, feeling that childlike joy once more, was worth any number of days in sour company.

And perhaps that company is becoming slightly less sour, I thought fleetingly, quickly glancing over to the beach where Charlie was attempting – unsuccessfully – to pry Darcy away from her computer.

As we got too deep in the water to really play around much more we calmed down, slowly swimming and enjoying each other's company. The sea was bright blue and crystal clear underneath the cloudless sky, which was touched with pink hues as the sun began to set. There was something so beautiful about the sea; being surrounded by both everything and nothing, feeling its endless expanse and its immediate presence.

"Lizzy," Jane piped up unsurely, seeing me lost in thought. "Are you happy?"

I smiled at her in return, knowing the answer.

"Yes," I replied. "Very."

She beamed back at me, as if my happiness was the only thing that mattered to her, and I suppose, in that moment, that that was true.

"What about you?" I asked. "Are you happy?"

She looked wistfully back towards the beach and smiled.

"Lizzy? I'm the happiest I've ever been."

***

It seemed that Charlie's lack of cooking skills extended to the barbecue, because it took him an hour to get it ready to cook anything on. When he finally did beckon us in from the water there was a chill in the air as evening began to set in.

"Dinner is served!" Charlie announced as Jane and I quickly towelled off and threw our clothes on over our swimming costumes. "Freshly barbecued sausages for the two wonderful Bennet sisters." He made a show of serving up our slightly-burnt sausages in a bun with ketchup on them. I looked over at Jane's, and noticed that the ketchup had been squirted on in the shape of hearts. Jane turned the same red as the ketchup and I pretended not to have noticed anything, and that the coughing fit was thanks to the saltwater from the sea and not the saccharine display that had happened right in front of me.

"So, Lizzy," Charlie started as we settled down on the sand with our food, Darcy having finally put away her laptop, "I saw that you and Darcy were chatting about books earlier. You know, I'm so glad that you too have something like that in common. I get the feeling you're both obsessed. I'm sure by the end of the week Jane and I will be fed up of you two chatting away!"

I looked at him like he'd grown a second head. He obviously so genuinely believed everything that he was saying, but how could he be so deluded? Did he have actually no idea that sometimes two people just don't really get along? He seemed on a mission, though. He was going to get us talking to matter what it took.

"What would you say your favourite ever book is?"

"Charlie! You can't ask someone that! What an awful thing to make someone decide!"

I was stunned into silence by these words from a scandalised Darcy. I completely agreed with her, of course; you can't expect someone to just choose a favourite book, it would be like asking them to choose their favourite child or something, but that didn't make the words any less shocking. I completely expected her to sit there in silence, internally revelling in my discomfort as I was thoroughly quizzed on any topic Charlie came up with, so this was a complete surprise.

"Okay, then!" said Charlie, looking mildly surprised but taking it in his stride. "Well… what else are you interested in, Lizzy?"

"Oh!" I could feel my cheeks getting pinker as the focus remained on me. "Well, I write a bit – of course I write all the time, but, you know, sometimes just for fun. And I played hockey for a bit, I guess. The biggest thing in the last few years has been the university LGBTQ society. I was a member from my first year, and by my third year I was the president; that took up most of my spare energy!"

As always, Charlie looked unnervingly interested in what I had to say. "Wow, that's really impressive! So, you reckon you'll carry on with that sort of thing now that you've left university?" I didn't miss that he glanced towards Darcy, who was trying her best to look like she wasn't really listening.

"I'd like to," I shrugged. "Hopefully once I've moved to London it will be easier to find things to get involved in."

"Well, maybe Darcy could help you with that!" Charlie looked eagerly towards Darcy who glared back at him. Sorry, Charlie; time to hang up that Captain's hat. This ship is going nowhere. "Or, um, well," Charlie stumbled under the ferocity of Darcy's glare. "I think it's all wonderful; really wonderful! I love hearing about different people's hobbies, skills, interests. It never ceases to amaze me!"

It almost hurt how genuine he was being, but Darcy made a small scoffing sound that I didn't think any of us were supposed to hear. When she realised we were all looking at her, she gave that awkward fake-smile that means that she knows she's about to say something rude, but she's going to pretend she's none the wiser.

"Well, Charlie, you've always been, er, easily amazed."

Charlie looked taken aback, and I didn't blame him. This was his best friend criticising him in front of his new girlfriend. "I don't think that's a particularly *bad* thing; if anything, I think it's good. Finding happiness in small things."

"I agree," chimed in Jane, and she and Charlie shared a sickeningly sweet look before Darcy spoke again.

"That's very well, but I don't want you lowering your standards because of it. Not everyone is as spectacular as you think they are."

She didn't look at anyone but Charlie as she said it, but it was more than obvious who the comment was aimed at.

"Everyone's different, Darcy," Jane said, in a neutral tone that was almost reproachful coming from her.

"Just because you can't see the point of something – or some*one* – doesn't mean that no one else can."

Jane and I shared a glance which we both knew meant that we were mentally sharing a high-five.

"Just leave her alone," Charlie said softly to Jane, and I could tell that it was more for Jane's sake than anyone else's. "Darcy has an impossibly high set of standards for *anyone* to live up to." Although he teased, it was clear that there was some sincerity behind what he said.

"They are not *impossibly high*!" Darcy said. "Besides, that was a private conversation and I'd prefer it if you didn't repeat it."

"Private?" Charlie said, his tone the closest to mocking that he could ever get. "If I remember correctly it was New Year's Eve, you'd had, what was it, two drinks? And Jordan got us all playing truth or dare."

"Charlie –" Darcy warned, but it didn't bother him. Perhaps he'd known her for too long.

"Come on, Darcy. Enlighten us."

She sat up haughtily, shaking out her shoulders. "It's quite simply, really. They should just be accomplished."

I wasn't exactly sure where this was going, although I had some not-so-great feelings about it.

"And how would you define 'accomplished'?" Jane asked, curious.

The look Charlie gave her told me that she'd just made a huge mistake.

"An accomplished person should, first, know their own mind, but be open-minded enough to consider other opinions, and should not be averse to changing their own." Wasn't sounding too bad so far, but little did I know where this was going to end up. "They should, of course, have certain skills; they should speak at least two languages apart from their own, although only one needs to be completely fluent. They should have a good musical knowledge and a good knowledge of literature, and have a degree from a Russell group – or international equivalent – university, preferably Oxbridge. They should be financially independent within, rather generously I must say, two years of graduating university, and should be well on their way to being successful in the field of their choice. They should take a general interest in politics, culture and the environment, and be aware of how these things are linked, and must possess an air of elegance and grace; after all, someone who is accomplished should know that they are, and be proud of it."

She finished proudly. Jane and I were in stunned silence, and Charlie began to laugh.

"You and your list, Darcy! And I suppose they mustn't be allergic to peanuts? Because then you wouldn't be able to eat peanut butter?"

Darcy glared at Charlie, who still looked amused.

"I'm not sure what you find so funny; it's perfectly rational to have a list of things to look for in a potential partner. And if someone was truly accomplished? I'm sure that, was the relationship going well, I would give up peanut butter for them."

Her complete sincerity made Charlie laugh some more.

The whole thing was the most ridiculous thing I'd ever heard. To have a list like that for potential partners? Sure, everyone has things that they look for in a romantic partner, but it's usually just a couple of things that tend not to relate to someone's academic achievement. It's not like it's common to turn someone down because of their A-level results.

"Darcy, how many people do you know who you would think of as being accomplished? According to your description, of course." I was determined to make her see how ridiculous this whole thing was.

"Well, myself of course, and my brother; and I can think of about half a dozen others off the top of my head. It's not as restrictive as you might think."

I raised an eyebrow. "Are you sure? Because I can't think of anyone – apart from yourself, of course – who fits all the things on that list."

Jane desperately tried to intervene. "How about we--"

She was ignored.

"I expect we move in quite different circles, Lizzy, and I would not expect you to know the same kind of people. I'm sure you also have a list for what you look for in a partner, yes? And I'm sure I might find it equally unrealistic?"

I looked straight into her eyes, determined to show her how outrageous she was being.

"What do I look for in a partner? Of course, we must be well-matched in personality – not the same, not at all, but of matching strengths. She must be honest. Caring. Loyal. Trustworthy. Moral. And, most importantly, we must love each other. That's all that really matters; everything else comes after. What does it matter if she has more or fewer qualifications than me? Or if one of us earns more money than the other? Or if one of us is not completely sure in who we are, and needs a bit of help with it? All of that can be worked through, but those key values? They must be there from the start. And I have to say that I didn't notice any of them on your list."

There was stony silence. A storm passed over Darcy's face, but she wasn't truly angry; I could tell that I had hit a nerve, but also that she was thinking about what I was saying. I looked around to see that we were alone on the beach; Jane and Charlie must have slipped off without us noticing. I stood up, gathering my things.

"Goodnight, Darcy," I said, and it came out much more warmly than I'd intended it to. It was only as I was lying back in that enormous bed that I remembered Charlie and Darcy's conversation that I'd overheard back when we first met them, at my graduation party. Charlie had been suggesting that perhaps Darcy and I were suited to each other, that perhaps there could be something between us.

I dismissed the thought immediately. There was nothing between me and Darcy except animosity and annoyance. It certainly explained, however, why Charlie and Jane kept leaving us alone together. After all, they had shown no issues with being openly loved-up around other people. It also explained why Charlie had kept pushing at the conversation earlier, desperately trying to get me and Darcy to find some common ground.

Charlie was certainly sneakier than I gave him credit for, but it wouldn't work. Yes, I would admit, Darcy was physically attractive. *Very* physically attractive. But, as that nagging voice kept reminding me, I knew about things she'd done in the past, things that maybe Charlie didn't know about. After all, would Darcy really tell him that she'd gone against her parents' last wishes? I doubted it; she's too proud to admit to something like that. We were now getting along well enough that I thought we could probably survive this week, and that was all that mattered; getting back to Longbourn in one piece.

My final, slightly odd thought before I drifted off to sleep, though, was that I sort of hoped that Darcy would one day find her accomplished person. Apart from anything else? Someone that similar to her deserved to be stuck with her for the rest of their life, and I couldn't say I envied them.

Chapter 10: Home Again

Although I did, in the end, have a nice time in France, I won't pretend it wasn't lovely coming home. Sleeping in my own bed, eating Dad's food, even putting up with Mum's panics and Sander's antics, were all things I hadn't realised I'd miss. It was odd. I'd been away for months at a time over the last three years, but something about the prospect of moving out permanently in the near future made me appreciate home all the more.

The next big thing, however, was Charlotte's twenty-first birthday party, which was happening at the end of the week. Charlotte wasn't massively enthusiastic about going out or having a huge party, but her sister was, and so there was a party being thrown at her house. As per Charlotte's request, I had invited as many people as I could. I think she was hoping that if enough people came, she could slip away and stop being the centre of attention. It amazed me that both Charlie and Darcy had accepted the request straight away. It wasn't like either of them knew Charlotte at all well, having only met her the once. It was more likely that Charlie wanted to go as Jane's date and Darcy was tagging along, either because she wanted to keep an eye on him or because she had nothing better to do.

George, however, had yet to respond, and so I asked him about it when we met up for coffee in the week.

"Oh, yeah, about that," he said as we settled in some big armchairs in the corner of the coffee shop. "Are you sure your friend really wants me there? I mean, she's never actually met me, wouldn't it be weird?"

I shrugged. "I think she wants to meet you. Both of you are my friends, so it makes sense to her that you two should get on, at least. I also think she just wants to have loads of people there who won't make a fuss over her. Her sister's planning it and apparently has gone a bit overboard with the catering, so I think she's hoping that if enough people come then the food will all be eaten and she'll be able to slip off while everyone else is occupied. It's guaranteed to be good food now that my dad's going though, he won't let anything leave the kitchen unless it's perfect! Even if it's not his kitchen."

We both laughed lightly at the thought of my dad commandeering the Lucas' kitchen.

"I also saw that, um, Darcy's going," George mumbled, swilling his coffee around in its cup, not meeting my eye. I put my head in my hands at the realisation.

"Of course! I'm so sorry; Charlotte asked me to invite her, she didn't want to invite Charlie and not Darcy, and I didn't think about... well, you know. You two. I completely understand if you don't want to come, and I'm sure Charlotte will too."

George sat up straight in his seat, shaking his hair slightly out of his eyes in a motion that I was sure he'd practiced in front of the mirror. "You know what? I have nothing to be ashamed of. I shouldn't be scared to bump into her. I've done nothing wrong! I should show her that I've come back stronger, that I'm making something of myself on my own."

I grinned wildly. "That's the spirit! You show her and her ridiculous list of accomplishments. So, I'll see you on Saturday?"

He bowed his head in mock-defeat. "You persuaded me! I'll be there on Saturday. And what was that about accomplishments?"

"Oh, nothing," I waved him off, "Let's not talk about Little Miss Grump anymore."

"Good plan," George agreed, chuckling slightly at my nickname for Darcy. "In fact, let's make a pact. From here on out, neither of us will let one Miss Darcy Williams get us down. She is of no consequence to us, and we will continue on with our lives regardless of anything she does or says that makes us either want to punch something or curl up in a sock drawer and stay there for days. Deal?" He held out his hand.

"Deal," I affirmed, shaking it. We met each other's eyes and sat in sincerity for a moment, before we couldn't hold it in and started laughing, not even caring that all the other customers were staring at us.

***

"Happy birthday!"

Charlotte jumped as she opened her front door to see me yelling at her on the doorstep.

"Lizzy, don't scare me so much next time! And is that – oh, you know I don't like people making a fuss! Really, you didn't have to get me anything." She looked at the large helium balloon I had in one hand and the even large bag of gifts in the other.

"Don't be silly, you're twenty-one! I had to get you a present – and don't worry, I didn't spend *too* much. Are you going to let me in or shall I watch you open these in the porch?"

Charlotte rolled her eyes at my sarcasm, but opened the door to let me through.

"Come on in. Mum and Maria are busy getting everything ready but they won't let me help, so I'm at a bit of a loose end."

"Good thing I brought you lots of presents to open then!" I grinned, holding up the gift bag. Charlotte peered in the top apprehensively, sighing.

"Every year I tell you not to get anything and you always do! I don't need anything new." I'd heard the same spiel on every birthday and I always ignored it, buying her a present regardless.

"And every year I tell you that it's what best friends do. You always buy me a present for my birthday, yes? So, I'll get you something for yours."

We headed up to her room, which seemed to be the only room in the house not covered in streamers and balloons. As soon as the door was shut behind me I shoved the gift bag in Charlotte's face until she took it off me, her withering look telling me that she had relented and was going to open them.

"Okay, before you start," I said, sitting down cross-legged on her floor opposite her, "everything is useful. It all has a purpose, and I will explain as we go along." She looked at me with anticipation. "Okay, go now!"

The first present she took out was the largest by far. She carefully slid her fingers under the tape, folding the wrapping as she went. "A blanket? With... are they sleeves?"

"Yup, a blanket with sleeves! We're about to live in London with not much money to our names, and I know you won't let me put the heating on until we start to get frostbite because of the cost, so I bought you this to keep warm! Especially if you're up late working or something."

She looked up from the box with a grin on her face. "Thanks so much, Lizzy! This will be great. I can't even stay mad at you for buying me presents anymore!"

"That was the idea!" I replied cheekily, getting a whack on the arm in response as she pulled the next parcel out the bag.

"Okay, this one is actually loads of small things, but I didn't think it was worth wrapping them up separately," I explained as she once again began carefully prising away the tape, folding the wrapping paper neatly to use again.

"...kitchen scales?"

"That's just the box I used – look inside."

I could see her gasp as she opened the lid. "Wow, Lizzie, this is... there's so much here!" She pulled out an hour-by-hour year-long planner, a pack of coloured pens, a pack of whiteboard pens, a set of notebooks and some blu-tack.

"Well, you're going to start teaching soon, and I wanted you to have a kind of classroom starter pack, you know? Some stuff to kick you off. I just know you'll be a brilliant Miss Lucas!"

She was still admiring the pages in the planner; it's almost sad how excited she gets about stationary, but what can I say? I know my best friend well.

"If you can pry your eyes away from the entire stock of Longbourn's only stationary shop, there's still one more present in the bag."

She reached inside the bag and brought out the last gift, which was much smaller than the others. I could feel myself start to get nervous; I had been very worried, buying this present, that she wouldn't like it. It wasn't quite as practical as the others, and more personal.

I could tell that she sensed my trepidation as she opened the parcel, and unfolded the grey t-shirt that was lying in the wrapping. Her eyes grew wide as she read the slogan, and when she lowered it I could see that she had a huge grin on her face.

"Lizzy, I love it! Thank you so much! Here, I'll put it on now." She pulled off the shirt she was wearing, and tugged the new one over her head. "How do I look?"

I looked her up and down, from the huge grin on her face to the rainbow-coloured slogan reading 'Ally And Proud'.

I nodded, not trusting myself to speak. She leaned forwards to give me an enormous hug.

"I'm so proud to be your best friend, Lizzy Bennet," she said, her voice choking up, "and I'm so proud of how far you've come."

I knew that we were both remembering sixteen-year-old me on my first day at a new school, timidly admitting during a conversation about celebrity crushes that I was gay. She let go of me and passed a box of tissues, taking some for herself while I loudly blew my nose. I gave her a watery smile before standing up. "Come on," I said. "Let's go and celebrate!"

And as we trudged back downstairs, her grumbling all the while, I couldn't help but reflect on how lucky I was to have such a brilliant best friend.

Chapter 11: A Night To Remember

Over the next hour guests slowly started to arrive at Charlotte's house. I recognised almost everyone; Charlotte's extended family, some old school friends, a couple of uni friends who lived within driving distance and, of course, my own family. As soon as they walked through the door my mother marched straight up to me and demanded to know if Charlie had arrived yet. Jane shot me an apologetic look from over Mum's shoulder; I could tell that she'd been interrogated in the car all the way down.

"No, he's not here yet Mum, but I'm sure he will be soon. How about you get a drink or something?" Charlotte successfully managed to persuade her to go and choose a drink so that I could quickly talk to Jane.

"What's Mum bothered about now?" I asked her, slightly worried that I would have to spend the evening doing damage control.

Jane sighed heavily. "She really wants Charlie to be here because she wants to be able to show off about how he and I are… you know."

It occurred to me then that I didn't actually know. What were Jane and Charlie? Affectionate friends? Dating? Exclusively, or not? Were they officially together, boyfriend and girlfriend? Engaged?

Okay, I was fairly certain it wasn't that last one, but the point still stood. What, exactly, were they? Not that I wanted to put pressure on them to figure it out, that's the last thing I wanted. I just don't want Mum to ruin whatever it is they have because she got it wrong.

Jane was being so uncharacteristically pessimistic about Mum's motives that Mum must have really been going on about it, which didn't exactly bode well.

I looked back at Jane's worried face and tried to look comforting. "Don't worry. Charlotte and I will do everything we can to keep her occupied for as long as we can."

She didn't look convinced, but didn't have time to worry much more as Charlie and Darcy had arrived.

Ever since Charlie and Jane have met I had never seen them be anything but completely wrapped up in each other, but something this time was different. She gave Charlie a strained smile as he greeted her and leant down to kiss her on the cheek, squeezing her hand, and as they went into the sitting room – thankfully in the opposite direction from Mum – I could see that Jane's shoulders were tensely raised.

I started slightly when I realised that rather than follow her friend through, Darcy was still standing with me in the hallway, which was now empty apart from us. She was giving me a very odd look, as if I was some kind of puzzle that she couldn't solve. She quickly looked away once she realised I had spotted her, and I saw out of the corner of my eye her hand brush against her pocket as she went to get her phone out but thought better of it.

"Hi," she said, still looking anywhere but at me.

"Hi?" I replied, trying and failing to make it sound casual. "Um, ahh, are... how are you... doing?"

"Verywellthankyou," she said as one garbled word, still not meeting my eye. She cleared her throat and took a deep breath before speaking again. "Are you, are you well?"

"Yes," I nodded, trying to find a way out of the conversation, if it could even be called that.

"I saw that you invited George Wickham to this party." Oh. That was this where this was going. "I'm sorry to say this," I scoffed internally at that, "but I don't think he'll be showing his face. He and I have… history."

"He told me," I said icily. I'll admit that I was intrigued as to what Darcy had to say for herself on the matter, but she didn't seem overly concerned about defending herself. She raised an eyebrow, meeting my eyes again.

"He told you? So, you'll understand that it's better if, for his sake, we don't have to as much as look at each other?"

"I don't blame him for not wanting to come," I said, trying my best to keep a cool head. "He told me exactly what you did to him, and while I'm happy to look past it and at least be civil, I completely understand if he couldn't bring himself to do the same."

She looked at me incredulously. "What *I* did to *him*?!"

"Yes, what you did to him," I snapped. "And he will be here. He told me as much just the other day."

She barked out a scornful laugh. "You really think that? Trust me, George Wickham knows better than to show his face here. I don't know what he told you, but given that you so readily believed him I doubt I'll be able to change your mind."

"I have no reason not to believe him," I countered, but there was no point; she had already gone to join the others in the sitting room.

I felt my phone buzz in my pocket.

George Wickham: Hey, I'm so sorry but I can't go to the party. The thought of facing her is too much, I'm sorry. Wish your friend a happy birthday for me.

I hastily tapped out a reply.

Lizzy Bennet: It's okay, I completely understand! Hope you have a good evening

The reply came almost immediately.

George Wickham: I knew you'd get it – thanks for being cool with it! You're a good friend :)

I put my phone back in my pocket and headed through to the sitting room where everyone was gathered. There were a few nibbles on the coffee table and a playlist Maria had made playing quietly in the background, but Charlotte was nowhere to be seen. Neither was my mother, so Charlotte was probably keeping her occupied elsewhere in the full knowledge that as soon as she was unleashed she would wreak havoc. Jane and Charlie were chatting to a couple of Charlotte's cousins (of which there were many) and Darcy was, once again, standing in the corner typing away on her phone. Sander and Mark seemed caught up in a rather animated discussion that bordered on argument, so I quickly headed over there to break it up before they caused a scene.

"Look, Mark, it's easy. What about Maria? You know her, and she's basically our age, so it will be fine. You just go up, start chatting, ask her how she's doing, pay her a couple of compliments. You've seen me do it so many times, you know it's not hard."

"But Sander, I don't want to, okay? It's not about being scared, or not wanting to embarrass myself, or not knowing what to do. I just don't want to."

"Hey guys, what's going on?" I asked, quickly intervening. They turned to look at me at exactly the same time, each with the same disgruntled expression, and for once I was struck by quite how similar they were.

"I'm trying to get Mark to go and chat to some girls, ask someone out or chat her up or something, but he won't because he's too chicken."

"I'm not chicken!" Mark snapped back indignantly. "I just... I just don't want to. I can't explain it. I just... I just can't." He choked slightly and looked down at his fingers which were white from how hard he was gripping his hands together.

"Leave him alone, Sander," I sighed, hoping that Sander would give in without a fight and go make trouble elsewhere. I should have known better.

"I don't get it, Lizzy. He just won't! I don't get it. What's the big issue? Afraid of rejection?"

I went to say something but Mark beat me to it, suddenly angry. "Why can't you understand that I just don't want to?! I know that you've always thought with your dick rather than your brain but don't assume that the rest of us are the same. I just. Don't. Want. To."

Sander put his hands up in defeat. "Chill, dude. Just tryna look out for you." He looked uncharacteristically concerned for his brother, and I knew why. Mark hadn't just acted like Sander was being his usual annoying, pushy self. He'd acted like it was a personal attack, and something had clearly touched a nerve.

"Sander, why don't you, um, go and mingle for a bit?" I suggested, trying to keep my tone neutral to maintain the fragile equilibrium that had just been reached. He nodded and slipped away, obviously happy to leave me with Mark.

"You okay?" I asked him, concerned. He nodded solemnly, looking at the ground, his arms wrapped tightly around himself. "Do you want to talk about it?"

He briefly looked up to meet my eye, before ducking his head again and mumbling a quiet "No". I slowly pulled him into a hug, and his arms cautiously moved to wrap around me. Even though he'd overtaken me in height a few years ago, he suddenly looked and felt incredibly small.

"Don't let anyone boss you around," I said, desperately hoping that these were the right words that he needed to hear. "You do what you want to do, yeah? There's no pressure, at all." I heard him sniff quietly and stepped back from the hug, handing him a tissue from my pocket.

"Thanks Lizzy," he said weakly, wiping his eyes.

"No problem," I smiled, but Mark wasn't looking at me anymore; he was looking at something going on behind my shoulder.

I whipped around to see my mother making her way across the room, Charlotte right behind her.

'Sorry Lizzy,' she mouthed at me, as Mum marched straight up to Jane and Charlie.

"Hello again," she said loudly to the two people Jane and Charlie were talking to, even though I'm fairly sure she's never met them. "I see you've met Jane, my daughter! And this is Charlie, her wonderful young man. They really are a beautiful couple, wouldn't you agree?"

I pushed through the small crowd of people as fast as I could, diving forward to pull my mother back by the elbow.

"Mum, what the hell are you doing?" I hissed at her. She pulled herself away from my grip, making a show of dusting herself off and adjusting her shirt.

"Excuse me, Lizzy, for being happy for your sister and wanting to tell people about it," she huffed, and marched off before I could say a single word about how inappropriate she was being. Charlotte, however, quickly filled the space that my mother had just left.

"I'm so sorry Lizzy," she started, looking distraught. "I tried my best, but she just wouldn't listen! I had no idea she would make such a scene."

I did my best to smile at her. "It's not your fault, not at all. Thank you for holding her off as long as you did!" I glanced over to where she was now chatting with some of her friends from book club, who inexplicably managed to be at every social gathering within a mile radius.

"At least she's out the way now," I said. "Now she can gossip to her heart's content and no one else will hear."

The atmosphere in the room slowly started return to its usual level, the low-level chatter being punctuated by the sounds of the crisps bowl being refilled against Maria's alarmingly large indie rock collection. I did notice, however, that Jane hadn't quite recovered from Mum's outburst. She was making small talk with anyone who came her way, and for the first time since my graduation party three weeks ago she and Charlie weren't joined at the hip. He was tagging along with whatever she was doing, nodding and smiling whenever necessary, but they weren't tucked away in a corner, off in their own little world. I won't pretend it didn't bother me a little that Jane was acting distant, but nothing had phased them before; I couldn't see how that would really change now.

After another half-hour or so, Maria stood on a chair and cleared her throat. She was so small to begin with that standing on a chair didn't put her much above everyone else, but it had the desired overall effect.

"Food is ready!" she announced. "There's a buffet ready in the kitchen, so if you would like to take a plate and help yourself! And while I'm here with everyone's attention... Happy twenty-first birthday Charlotte!" There was a round of applause as Charlotte turned beetroot red. "Do be sure as you go through to have a look at the slideshow that's running for a selection of Charlotte's most embarrassing photos, from infancy until now!" With a cheeky grin, she hopped off the chair just as Charlotte grumbled "Just you wait until *you're* twenty-one" under her breath.

We hung back as the group of people slowly migrated through to the next room, not wanting to get caught in the crowd, and joined the back of the queue.

"So," came a smug voice from behind me. "Looks like someone still hasn't shown up."

"No thanks to you," I said, still facing forwards, not wanting to give her the satisfaction.

"You have a very high opinion of George Wickham," said Darcy, and I was surprised by the softness in her voice. "Your loyalty does you credit. I'm sure you have your reasons, but take it from me. He's not to be trusted."

This time I did turn around, looking her straight in the eye.

"Darcy, I don't know why you seem to think that he's at fault here, but whatever it is, surely you can forgive him? People change, and George is making a huge effort to make the most of himself."

She looked at me shrewdly. "Forgiveness sometimes has to be earned, and so far, George has done nothing to earn my forgiveness. I'm sure you can understand that."

Everything that she was saying suggested that perhaps there was more to their history than George had told me, that something else had happened. I didn't want to believe it, and believing it would mean trusting Darcy over George, which was something I never thought I'd do.

"You must be very proud, Joan," came a loud voice walking past us. My mother and her friends had, somehow, been first in the queue for food, and were now walking back past us with full plates, oblivious to us being there.

"Oh, I am," Mum gushed, pausing in eating her mini-quiche to elaborate. "They're so wonderful together, aren't they? And I'm so glad Jane's happy!"

"And it can't hurt that he's rich, can it?" One of her friends laughed. "She's done well for herself there!"

"Oh, that she has!" Mum replied as they all started giggling. I couldn't have been more grateful that the line moved forward at that moment, moving us out of earshot.

I was mortified. How could she act like this? Parade her daughter's relationship around that way? I absolutely could not let Jane find out. She would be even more embarrassed than she already was, and with how she was acting from Mum's earlier outburst I could only imagine what knowledge of the most recent conversation would do.

I could almost hear Darcy thinking behind me, but I didn't dare turn around. All I knew was that, just as she might have been starting to accept Jane's presence in Charlie's life, my mother had sent her right back to the start. My mum has always been overenthusiastic in her involvement with our lives, but this was the first time that I was truly embarrassed to be associated with her.

I had no idea how long it took for us to get to the food table, as I was too busy stewing in my own thoughts to keep track of time. Charlotte asked if I was okay a couple of times, but I couldn't bring myself to give more of a response than a shrug. I hated that her birthday celebrations, which she wasn't feeling hugely optimistic about to start with, were being dampened by my family's drama. The food was as good as I expected what with my dad helping with the cooking, but it didn't really register with me. I was worried about Mark, I was worried about Jane, and I was even worried about whatever Sander was up to, as I couldn't see him anywhere.

After I had finished my food and left my plate on the table, I went outside for some air. There were so many people inside, and usually that doesn't bother me, but I just couldn't bring myself to really talk to anyone. I went out through the back door into the Lucas' small garden and took some deep breaths, enjoying the cool evening air, before I heard someone else talking.

"I tried, I tried doing what you suggested, but I just – I just froze up. And then I brought up something I really shouldn't have, and it all went to hell from there." I couldn't believe this. I'd come outside to get away from people only to interrupt Darcy on a phone call. "No, I'm not telling you what the subject was! What? No, it's just – that doesn't matter. The point is, I screwed up. Again. I... I can't do this." As I peered round from the side of the house I saw her sitting on the bench, head in her hands. "You're right, as always. I just wish I was better at this kind of thing. Mm-hm. Yeah. Jordan, I – I would be myself. Except I'm not entirely sure I know who that is."

Okay, so this was personal. Really personal. Once again, I was eavesdropping on something I definitely shouldn't be hearing.

"Yes, of course I'll keep you posted, and I'll see you in a few weeks anyway! You have fun, right? Don't go worrying about me. I'm fine, honest! Yes, I know you don't believe me. Okay. Okay. Bye."

Don't think about it, I told myself as I went back inside. *Whatever it is? Don't think about it. You're moving away in less than two weeks. Chances are you'll never have to see her again.*

That's right. I was moving to London in less than two weeks, and we were going to have the time of our lives. There was no point in spending any more of my time worrying about Darcy Williams; she was of no consequence to me anymore. All that was left to do now was to pack up, get ready and go. I could leave all of this behind: all this stress, all this worry, everything that was going on here. I was going to Rosings Publishing House to work for a year, and I would meet new people, see new things, and start a whole new chapter of my life. A life with no room for worries about Darcy Williams.

Chapter 12: Decluttering

Preparing to move to London was a strange experience. I'd lived by myself before, but university wasn't quite the same as going off to get a job; it all felt a bit more grown-up. Even though I was moving out permanently, I wasn't able to take very much of my stuff with me. The size of London flats meant that I would be taking the bare minimum, and leaving the rest here for when I eventually got somewhere bigger a few years down the line.

I woke up the day after Charlotte's birthday feeling the need to declutter, and I'm sure it was not unrelated to having so much on my mind. It was strangely therapeutic, stuffing bin bags full with old clothes and even some books, ready to be donated to the charity shops on the high street. Having something mundane to focus on stopped my head from running in circles, helped to distract me from thoughts that didn't lead anywhere.

Even though I'd sworn off thinking about some… people… I still had to think about (and worry about) those nearest and dearest. After dallying outside Jane's room for a few minutes, I decided to see if she had anything that she wanted me to take to the charity shop for her. I knew that even if she didn't she'd find something she wasn't too attached to; she could never resist donating to charity.

She opened the door as soon as I knocked, giving me an enormous grin as soon as she realised it was me.

"Morning Lizzy!" she said brightly. "How are you on this beautiful morning?" Her grin was still unwavering, but her eyes were darting nervously. Even by Jane's standards, this was far too cheerful.

"I'm great, thanks! I was just about to head to the high street to give some stuff to the charity shops, do you have anything you want me to take?"

She nodded frantically, her huge grin still in place. "I'm sure I do somewhere! Let's just see..."

As predicted, she started rifling through her things, determined to give me something.

"How are you doing?" I asked tentatively as she searched.

"I'm absolutely brilliant!" she replied, and to her credit her voice shook only slightly at the end.

I knew Jane well enough to recognise her mood. Nothing I could say would get her to tell me what was wrong, but I didn't think I really needed to ask. Just as Mum overcompensates, so does Jane. When she's really, really happy, that probably means that she's covering up a worry about something, and it didn't take a genius to guess that she was still upset about what happened at Charlotte's birthday party.

"Here you go!" She handed me a butterfly notebook that Sander bought for her about ten years ago, still grinning far too widely.

"Thanks," I said. "Look, Jane, if you ever want to talk about anything... I'm here, okay? Even when I'm in London. I'll always be able to make time for my number one sister."

Her smile started to falter. "I'm your only sister," she giggled weakly. "But thank you, Lizzy. It means a lot."

The next room along was Mark's, and I had a feeling that he, too, would be out of sorts after the previous evening. I knocked and waited for him to grunt "Come in," before I opened his door. He was still in bed even though it was nearly midday, lying under the covers and looking up at the ceiling.

"You okay?" I asked, concerned.

"I guess," he responded, still staring up at the ceiling. I padded into the room and slowly sat down at the edge of his bed.

"Just know that... you can talk to me about anything, okay? And it will be fine. Whatever it is, it will be fine."

I seemed to be saying that a lot today.

He turned his head to look at me. "Thanks, Lizzy," he said sincerely. "I... I'm not sure what there is to talk about right now."

I gave him a small smile, trying to be as comforting as I could. "That's fine."

He didn't look like he felt much better, but he nodded anyway. "Okay." His head turned back to look up at the ceiling. He didn't say anything, but I'd known him his whole life. I knew when he wanted me to leave.

"I'll see you at lunch, yeah?" I phrased it as an expectation rather than a question. He gave an imperceptible nod, not turning his head again. I knew that I could stand there all day and not get anything else out of him, so I quietly slipped out of the room, clicking the door shut behind me.

I love all of my siblings equally, but I couldn't deny that I much favour the company of Jane or Mark over that of my youngest brother. This time, however, I was almost skipping for joy at the prospect of talking to Sander. I could always rely on him to be full of himself, immature, and infallibly more cheerful than he should be in any given situation. Today was no exception.

"Who is it?" he called out as I knocked on the door.

"It's me, Lizzy," I replied, and I heard him moving around before he opened the door, still pulling on his shirt.

"Hey Lizzy! What can I do for you?"

Wow. I was expecting chirpy, but not helpful and optimistic. I looked at him suspiciously.

"I was just about to take a load of stuff down to the charity shops, and I was just wondering if you had any stuff you wanted to donate?"

He shrugged. "I don't think I have anything, but I can come and help you take it if you like?"

"Who are you and what have you done with Lysander Bennet?" I asked incredulously.

"What, I can't be helpful once in a while?" he replied, only slightly indignantly, as he stepped out of his room and shut the door behind him. "Fine, I'll admit that I don't have the greatest track record. Now are we going or not?"

Still completely baffled by what was going on, I led the way downstairs and into my car, ignoring Sander's indignant, "Hey, isn't that the notebook I bought for Jane, like, ten years ago?"

"Right then, what's this really about?" I asked as soon as I'd pulled out of the driveway.

Sander shrugged in the passenger seat, fiddling with the seatbelt that I'd insisted he put on.

"I'm turning over a new leaf, right? I didn't even have more than one drink last night at the party. And you're about to move away, so I figured I may as well kill two birds with one stone. Do something helpful while spending time with you."

Well, it was certainly logical. I said as much out loud.

"What brought this on?" I asked.

He started picking at a thread on his jeans. "I'm fed up of being the irresponsible one. Jane's the kind one, you're the smart one, Mark's the sensible one and what am I? I guess I just want to match up to you guys for a change."

I decided to ask Charlotte to have twenty-first birthdays more often if it brought out all these underlying issues in my family.

"Sander, while I completely respect and appreciate you trying to become more responsible – which is definitely a good thing, by the way – you shouldn't compare yourself to us. We're all different people, and I know it must be harder with you and Mark being identical twins, but you've got to be yourself." I looked at him as we stopped at a red light. "Does that make sense?"

He nodded. "Yeah, it does. It's a good thing we've got you, Lizzy, you keep us all sane!"

The words *But you're leaving soon* were left unspoken between us.

It hadn't occurred to me before now that Sander possessed the self-awareness enough to realise that perhaps a change would be good. It felt quite sudden. Not two weeks ago, he was getting tipsy at the dinner table. Perhaps him trying to throw Mark at women was his way of trying to bond? This was certainly the nicest he'd been to me without wanting a favour in a very long time. He definitely seemed genuine; I think he really did want to make a change.

"Here we are," I announced as I pulled into a parking space. "Let's go. I reckon between the two of us we can drop these off in one trip." I was right. We managed to carry everything between us (I was amazed at how much stuff had come out of my room) and dropped it off at the nearest charity shop, helping the tiny old lady at the door carry it all through to the back room.

"How about I treat us to coffee?" I said to Sander as we stepped back out onto the street, suddenly feeling the need to spend more time with my brother.

He grinned back. "Only if you're paying!"

It was amazing. Over a matter of days Sander had really turned around; he was polite (most of the time), he was making an effort to talk to me, and for the first time in years I felt like I was really getting to know my brother.

As soon as we stepped into the coffee shop, I heard my name being called from the other side of the room. I looked around to see George smiling and waving me over. I gave him a thumbs-up to show that I'd seen him, before turning back round to order.

"Lizzy," he said as we went to sit down at the table with him, "I'm so sorry about yesterday. I just... I couldn't face it, and I know we'd said that we wouldn't let her bother us, but it was just… it was just too hard. I'm so sorry to have let you down."

"I completely understand," I reassured him. He didn't look completely placated, but he seemed to have got the hint that he could stop apologising. "George, this is my younger brother, Sander."

"Pleasure to meet you," George said, smiling and shaking Sander's hand.

"And you," Sander replied, throwing me a quick glance that told me he was unsure with this slightly more civilised way of introducing yourself to another person.

"George is living with Denny, you know, Jane's old classmate?" I said.

"Oh, right, yeah, I remember him!" Something odd dawned on his face. "Are you guys, um, you know, yeah?"

George burst out laughing. "No, we're friends! Heterosexual, separate bedroom friends. You'd think with a sister like yours you'd have a better gaydar!"

Everyone has one problematic friend, I was sure of it. Mine was George Wickham.

"It doesn't *quite* work like that," I said patiently, but I couldn't really get a word in edgeways.

"Did Lizzy tell you how we met a few weeks ago? It's a great story. I was here, in this coffee shop, and in front of me in the queue was this beautiful woman. I could tell that she was super smart, way out of my league, but I figured what's the harm in trying, right?" I put my head in my hands in despair at the ridiculousness of this story. "So I'm there desperately hitting on Lizzy, and she's just completely ignoring me, not giving me the time of day."

Sander started chuckling in his seat. "I can bet that went down really well! Wow, you tried to pull the moves on my sister? Talk about *me* having a bad gaydar!"

Okay, Sander did have a point there.

I should have known that these two would get along like a house on fire; they were so similar in so many ways.

"So she tells me she's gay, we have a good laugh about it, and start again as friends." George was finishing his story. "Turns out we get along really well, and the rest is history!"

I chanced a glance at Sander who was looking rather in awe, and I wasn't surprised. Here was this cool, attractive guy, who just exuded brilliance and perfection; the kind of person Sander had always wanted to be.

"I bet you have a really cool job or something, right?"

Yup. There was some serious hero worship going on here already.

George shook his head. "I wish I could say I did! Unfortunately I'm just working as a sales person at the moment. Pretty boring, run-of-the-mill stuff at the moment, I'm afraid! But I'm hoping that if I keep at it and work hard I can get something better. What about you, what are you doing at the moment?"

It occurred to me then that perhaps George would be a good influence on Sander. Despite being a bit of a womaniser and party-boy, and despite certain setbacks, George was working hard to get his life on track and to make something of himself; something that it seemed Sander was now also aspiring to do. I was suddenly glad that we'd bumped into George. It seemed that already he was taking Sander under his wing, giving him tips on everything from writing a good CV, to which beers are the easiest to down in one. I don't know why I hadn't thought before to introduce them. Probably because, I realised with a pang, I hadn't thought about Sander much at all recently, or what might be good for him. I was moving away in less than two weeks and I was only just getting to know my youngest brother. Pretty crap timing if you ask me.

George and Sander exchanged numbers as we left the coffee shop, Sander and I heading home for lunch and George going to take an afternoon shift.

"How is it that for someone so bookish and indoors-y you have such cool friends?" Sander asked as we drove back home.

"I can't help it," I laughed in reply. "I'm glad you and George got on, though. He should be around for a while, I'm sure you two would be great friends!"

"George said he'd try and get me a job at the shop he works at," Sander pipes up, as if I hadn't been there for the entire conversation. "That would be really good. It would be great to have a job."

"That would be nice of him," I said, unable to think of anything better to say while I was concentrating on the roundabout. We soon stopped at another set of lights, though, so I was able to talk to him properly.

"I'm sorry I won't be around for long," I said, turning slightly to look at him better. "I had fun this morning."

"Me too," he replied, smiling. "Oh, the light's green! Go!"

"Don't tell me what to do," I huffed, pretending to be annoyed as I drove on.

Yes, it would be hard moving to London just as things are starting to fall into place with my family, but I knew I had to go. I had a great job lined up, I had a flat ready to move into as soon as I got there, and I had my whole life ahead of me. They would be okay without me, I was sure of it. Jane had Charlie, Mark would, I'm sure, be okay soon enough, and Sander seemed determined to get his life on track.

Things were starting to look up for the Bennet family.

Chapter 13: London

It's a funny feeling when you've been looking forward to something for so long and it finally arrives. It all felt slightly anti-climactic. We'd spent weeks packing, planning, getting everything ready, and now we were packing our bags into my car, ready to go.

We'd managed to find a flat two or three miles out from the centre that was relatively cheap – at least, cheap by London standards. Being in a more residential area meant that there would be space for me to keep my car, but I didn't plan on using it for anything except trips outside the city. We were each going in different directions every morning: me into the city centre, Charlotte further out into the East End, but neither of us had a commute that would take us more than about forty minutes.

It was strange leaving home again. There were hugs all round, and Mum even cried a little bit, but really it wasn't anything that hadn't happened before. I'd even be back for Christmas. There was just something about getting a proper full-time job that made moving out feel a bit more final than it did when I was going off to university.

Eventually though, after accepting a tin of home-made biscuits from Jane, an 'awesome road-trip playlist' CD from Sander and a tight hug from a still quiet Mark, we headed off down to London. It was wonderfully mundane for something that felt so significant. We were taking another step into the perilous world of adulthood, a step which was most easily taken by driving down with your best friend.

The drive took us less than two hours, so by the time we'd picked up our keys and brought our things into the flat there was still time for a late lunch. The only food we had with us was the biscuits Jane had given us, some tea-bags and some milk, so after hunting round to find our kettle and two mugs we sat at the kitchen counter, drinking tea and eating shortbread.

"I don't think I've ever felt so British in my life," Charlotte said, laughing slightly. "What a way to start our lives in London, eh? By having tea and biscuits."

The flat was small, but that was to be expected in this area and at the price we were paying for it. Our rooms each only had enough space for a bed and a wardrobe, with just enough floor space to stand and open the door. The bathroom seemed to have formerly been a cupboard that they had squeezed a toilet and shower into, and the only other room was the kitchen, but it was more than enough. it was clean, well-kept, and had just enough space for us both to get by.

We were each unpacking our things in our separate rooms when there was a buzz from the door; someone was ringing our doorbell downstairs. We dashed down the stairs, wondering who it was, to see a supermarket delivery man, his lorry pulled up on the pavement behind him.

"Delivery for Lizzy Bennet and Charlotte Lucas?"

We looked at each other, but Charlotte seemed just as confused as I was.

"Um, we haven't ordered anything," I explained. He looked down at the order sheet in front of him.

"It definitely says Lizzy Bennet and Charlotte Lucas here. Oh, but the order was placed and paid for by Jane Bennet."

Yes, my sweet, wonderful older sister had done our first supermarket shop for us, and there was so much of it! It took us four trips to take it all up to our flat between us. There was everything from bread and cereal to fresh fruit and vegetables to toilet roll and shampoo, and even a plaque that said 'Home Sweet Home'.

"Jane has to be the sweetest person I've ever met," Charlotte commented as we tried to fit all that food into our tiny kitchen. Of course, it was nearly all store cupboard things; Jane had thought ahead and not bought us too much that could go off.

"You don't need to tell me that!" I replied as I tried to fit all the cans of soup onto one shelf, but I knew that even Jane wouldn't do something like this unless she was trying to cheer herself up. This certainly qualified as extra-nice. We had enough food that we could be under siege for months and wouldn't notice. I worried briefly at how much money she had spent, especially as she doesn't really have a reliable income, but a glance at the receipt told me that she'd been hoarding loyalty card points for months and used them all in one go.

I sent her a message of thanks as soon as we'd finished packing away the sixth bag of pasta, and she replied almost immediately.

> *Jane Bennet: I'm glad it got to you okay! Hopefully it should keep you going for a while… how's London? :D*

Lizzy Bennet: Good so far, although we've only just finished unpacking. Hope you're all okay at home!

I pocketed my phone again just as Charlotte handed me a piece of paper and a pen.

"Right," she said. "We have a few weeks before we start working, and I think that we should do as many tourist things as possible in that time. I thought that we should each make a London Bucket List; a list of things that we want to do and see in London."

It was all starting to sink in now; we were in London! We had the whole city just waiting to be explored, and it was time to make the most of it.

"That sounds like a great plan!" I said, grinning. "Okay… so we each write our own lists and then compare?"

Charlotte nodded enthusiastically. "That's the plan! Okay, you're ready? And… let's go!"

I leant against the kitchen counter, pen poised, thinking of things to write. I've always lived close enough to London that I'd seen a fair few of the tourist things, but we hadn't come down often enough to have seen everything by any stretch of the imagination. We'd been round all the museums and seen a couple of other famous spots, but there were plenty of places that I had yet to go.

First up: books.

British Library
Foyles bookshop
Kensington Gardens (Peter Pan statue!)
Southbank book market

Next? Satisfying my inner fangirl.

Platform 9 ¾
Baker Street
One (or more!) shows

And a few tourist-y places that I hadn't been yet.

Buckingham Palace
Big Ben
London Eye

"Finished?" I asked Charlotte as I wrote down the last item on the list. She nodded, handing me her sheet of paper. I handed mine to her, and looked at her list.

Trafalgar Square
London Eye
Any show! Don't mind which one
Science museum
Big Ben/Parliament
Oxford Street
Hyde Park
Buckingham Palace
Tower of London

"Between us I think we've got a fair chunk of London covered!" Charlotte laughed, as she stuck both of our lists on the fridge. "Where shall we start?"

I looked down both lists, comparing them.

"You know what Charlotte? I think tomorrow we should go and meet the Queen."

She grinned back at me, laughing. "Brilliant! First stop: Buckingham Palace."

Chapter 14: Bucket List

The next day we woke up early, unused to the sticky, grimy air of London that was exemplified in the July heat. We breakfasted, opening the first box of cereal (courtesy of Jane), and headed downstairs and outside, searching for the nearest Tube station. I'd been on the Tube before but not in a while, and it took us a few goes. We almost got the wrong train twice, *actually* got the wrong train once, and had a brief panic when Charlotte couldn't find her oyster card on the way out. Something about the exhilaration of being away from home, that feeling of adventure, meant that we found all these mishaps hilarious, causing some of the other passengers on the train to give us some very odd looks as we collapsed into hysterical giggles once we finally got on the right train.

It was almost lunchtime by the time we successfully made it to Buckingham Palace, and after some cliché selfies with the guards we queued up to look around. It was everything we had expected, and more. With grand, gilded rooms and sweeping staircases, it was both the most impressive and the most extravagant house I'd ever seen.

Over the next few days, we saw more of London than I thought possible. We went round the Science Museum, Hyde Park (including Kensington Gardens and the Peter Pan statue), Baker Street, Kings Cross Station and, when we got lost once, the National Gallery. There was no rhyme or reason as to where we went when, and we kept revisiting certain patches many times, but we didn't mind. We said that we were getting to know the city – we were certainly getting to know the underground – and as we didn't really have a set number of days in the city, we went at a leisurely pace, or as leisurely as you can in London.

On our fifth day we went to the Houses of Parliament and Big Ben, admiring the spectacular buildings that housed the government. The weather had been – amazingly – nice all week, and once we got used to the humidity and that feeling of never quite being clean that comes with being in London, we were happily enjoying the outdoors. We finished going around Parliament with time to spare so went to St Paul's cathedral for a couple of hours in the afternoon, before going to the London Eye. We queued for hours, as expected, but once we finally made it on? It was worth it. The view of the city was unbeatable, and the summer weather was giving the city a certain romance; the Thames glistening in the sunlight, the skyline lit up by the sun beaming down from a bright blue sky.

Most people don't know this, but Charlotte is a surprisingly crafty person. If she wants something from someone she won't just spring it on them. She waits until the time is right, engineers the situation in her favour, and then waits until you have no choice but to give her what she wants.

I had thought that five years of friendship meant that I could spot whenever Charlotte was planning something; I was wrong. As soon as she started to speak I could tell that she had been wanting to bring this up all week, but had waited until I was in a locked pod on a large metal spinning wheel with no escape before she said anything.

"What's going on with you and Darcy?"

I looked at her in bewilderment; this was certainly not on a list of things I was expecting her to bring up this week.

"I don't know, what is going between me and Darcy? We don't get on? She's just a person I don't agree with."

"Can you honestly say that you haven't thought about her at all while we've been here?"

"Yes." That was a lie, and we both knew it. She'd been acting so weird the last time I saw her, I couldn't help but try to work out what was going on. Don't get me wrong; I didn't care about her or anything. I was just... trying to figure her out.

"Why are you bringing her up?" I asked Charlotte, huffing and folding my arms as I looked out across London.

"So it bothers you?" There she goes, answering a question with a question.

"Of course it doesn't bother me. What should be bothering me?"

"Lizzy, are you completely oblivious to everything?"

I whipped my head round to look at her. "What's that supposed to mean?"

She sighed. "How do you and Darcy feel about each other?"

I snorted derisively. "We don't like each other. We can agree on very few things, we're rarely so much as civil as each other. What else would it be? You've seen how we are together."

"Yes," mused Charlotte. "I have."

Something about the way she said it told me that she knew more than she was letting on.

I cocked my head to one side, examining her. "What are you thinking, Charlotte?" I could usually read her like a book, but this time...

"So you feel that way about Darcy. Does she feel the same way about you?"

"Of course she does! I told you what happened when Jane and I went round for dinner that time, and the way she was when we were in France. What are you..." She had a very odd expression on her face. "What's that face for? What on earth is going through your head?"

She sat in silence for a few more seconds, enjoying my discomfort, before putting me out of my misery.

"Perhaps... perhaps Darcy's feelings towards you aren't as cold as you think they are."

I laughed scornfully. "What the hell is that supposed to mean? Are you saying that... No. No actual way. Surely you can't believe that... Are you insane?! Bloody hell! You've really lost it, Charlotte Lucas. Like really, really lost it."

She sighed patiently, as if talking to a child. "Maybe Darcy's attitude is a bit of a front, you know? And I'm not saying that's okay," she put her hands out to stop me interrupting, "but maybe she just doesn't really know how to express herself."

I gave her a withering look. "That is the most ridiculous thing you've ever said. Now, I was actually having fun. Can we drop the subject of Darcy bloody Williams?"

She gave me a far too knowing look, but dropped the subject anyway.

"I've got something to cheer you up," she said, now smiling cheekily.

"What now?" I sighed, but my eyes grew wide as she pulled two tickets out of her pocket.

"Some shows have discounted tickets for students and young people every day. You spent so long in the queue at Starbucks this morning that I managed to nip down to the box office and buy two."

"You... you got us tickets for a show?!" I flung my arms around her, knocking her off her balance slightly.

"Thank you! Thank you thank you thank you! Charlotte, you're the absolute best, I – I can't believe it! We're actually going to a show?"

She nodded, obviously pleased at my excitement.

"It starts at seven, so we have time to grab some dinner beforehand. What do you think?"

I grinned. "Sounds like a plan!"

Charlotte may have been off her rocker when it comes to analysing the behaviour of one Darcy Williams, but she certainly knew how to cheer me up, and two tickets to a West End musical were exactly what I needed.

Buoyed up from the atmosphere from the show and the excitement from a few days of being tourists, we spent the whole bus journey back loudly singing the songs from the show we'd just seen, ignoring the looks everyone else was throwing at us. Or rather, I was; Charlotte was doing her best to look disapproving. She tried to look annoyed but couldn't hold it for long and spluttered out a laugh, which set me off.

"You're going to have to work on that when you start teaching," I said as I wiped tears of laughter from my eyes.

"Crap, this is our stop!"

We jumped up, slamming the 'Stop' button and running down the stairs, leaping off the bus still laughing away. There was a short walk from the bus stop to our flat, and now that we'd been here a few days we could do it at any time of day without getting lost.

"What shall we do tomorrow?" Charlotte asked.

"Well, in terms of things on our buckets lists, we haven't done any of the book things that I wanted to do. And before you say anything, I know that it's not really your thing, but… can we at least do one of them? If it's nearby somewhere else?"

"Go on then," she replied, pretending to be annoyed but smiling too much to really pull it off. "Where would you like to start?" she asked, as we walked up the pathway to the front door.

"Lizzy?"

I whipped round, hearing my name. I saw someone sitting on a wall on the other side of the street; as they stood up and came closer, I realised who it was.

"Jane? What are you doing here?"

As she came closer, I realised that she had been crying, her eyes red and puffy.

"Lizzy, I'm so sorry, but I didn't know what to do so I just got on a train and came here to see you. I'm so sorry," and she set off in another round of tears. She was shaking, unable to keep the composure that she always had. I gently put one arm around her and led her towards our building.

"Come on, let's get you inside and have some hot chocolate, yeah? And then you can tell me what happened."

The three of us slowly trudged upstairs to our flat, the only sound our footsteps and Jane's sniffles. Once we were inside I sat her down at the kitchen counter and made up a hot chocolate in my biggest mug and gave it to her.

"What happened, Jane?" I asked gently. While I didn't want to push her, it must have been bad if she turned up here without giving us any notice, and the situation – whatever it was – might have worsened if we didn't do something about it.

She sipped her hot chocolate, wiping her eyes. "I'm so sorry for dropping in on you Lizzy, but I didn't want to talk to anyone else, and I meant to ring you, I honestly did, but my phone battery died on the train and I didn't know your number by heart so couldn't use a payphone, and I came by your flat and you weren't answering the doorbell but I couldn't ring to find out if you were in or not so I just waited for you in case you were out and I'm so sorry."

"Calm down, Jane," I said, gently rubbing her back. "Take deep breaths. It's okay now, you're here, I'm here. Tell me what happened."

Another loud, agonising sob broke out.

"Charlie left me."

Chapter 15: No Such Thing As Love At First Sight

I couldn't believe it.

I actually couldn't believe it.

Jane? Charlie? Broken up?!

This was not how things were supposed to go. I mean, sure, things weren't one hundred percent, especially when I left, but bad enough to break up? I'd had no idea.

It was already eleven o'clock and I couldn't think of what we could do that late in the evening, so I suggested that we all got some sleep. Jane crashed out straight away in my bed, exhausted from the emotional turmoil of the day, so I gathered together a couple of spare blankets and cushions and made a sort of nest on the small floor space in my room. I put my biggest jumper on over my pyjamas and curled up, waiting for sleep to wash over me, but my mind was too busy whirring around for me to relax.

Why would Charlie leave Jane? Yes, they hadn't been together long, but anyone could see that they were perfect for each other. All I knew so far was what Jane had told me, which was only that one, heart-wrenching sentence, but you didn't have to know Charlie very well for this to seem massively out of character. Anyone could have seen how much he cared for Jane. Something must have happened, and I had to get to the bottom of it.

Maybe it was as simple as there being no such thing as love at first sight after all.

I somehow drifted off eventually, but woke at the crack of dawn, a crick in my neck from sleeping in an odd position. For a split-second I wondered what I was doing on the floor before the previous evening's events came flooding back. The sun was shining through the thin curtains enough that I could see my book by the light, but I couldn't focus on the words, my mind swimming with disconnected thoughts.

When it got to six o'clock, which I felt was an acceptable time to get up, I slipped out of my room and grabbed a clean set of clothes before having a shower, letting the warm water relax my muscles as I realigned my body, ready for the day. I lost track of how many times I shampooed and conditioned my hair, still stuck in my thoughts. Once my fingers started wrinkling I got out, drying myself off and getting dressed, giving myself a quick pep talk in the bathroom mirror.

"Pull yourself together," I said to mirror-Lizzy. "Jane needs you. She needs you to be rational and caring and to help her get through this. Get out of your funk."

My monologue was interrupted by a banging on the door, followed by Charlotte's voice calling through the door.

"Get on with it! Some of us need to pee!"

"Sorry," I said quietly as I slipped out the bathroom.

Charlotte tried to smile, but it came out as more of a grimace. "It's fine – how's Jane?"

I shrugged. "I don't know, I haven't seen her so far today. I think it's probably best if we just leave her to sleep."

She blearily nodded in response. "Sounds like a good idea. Could you put the kettle on for me? I'm going to need a cup of tea before I even start thinking about facing today."

"You and me both," I replied, walking to the kitchen as Charlotte went into the bathroom.

"It just doesn't make sense," I said to Charlotte ten minutes later over our mugs of tea. "I haven't the faintest idea as to happened, but I thought that those two were it, you know? I thought... I genuinely thought they'd be together forever. God, I'm naïve."

"Lizzy, we all thought that," Charlotte said. "None of us had even the faintest idea... no one saw anything like that coming. Have you heard from anyone at home?"

I shook my head. "I haven't checked my phone yet. Not since... crap, not since Jane got here. I'd better let Mum and Dad know."

I grabbed my phone to check for messages. I had eleven missed calls from the home phone, a message from Mark and an email from Dad.

> *Mark Bennet: Lizzy, is Jane with you? None of us have seen her since yesterday afternoon, she seemed really upset before she left and we're quite worried. No idea what's happened.*

> I hastily tapped out a reply.

> *Lizzy Bennet: Jane's here, sorry I didn't let you know last night, she was really upset and it slipped my mind. She said something about Charlie breaking up with her? She hasn't woken up yet, going to try to get to the bottom of it today*

> I pressed send and opened the email from my dad.

I've rung you a few times but I don't know if your phone's off or something. Jane's gone missing, and we wanted to check if she was with you? She was very upset about something yesterday but wouldn't tell us what. If you could just let me know that she's safe. Your mother is, as expected, beside herself with worry. As am I.
Love from
Dad

Jane hadn't even told the others that she was leaving? Jane never wanted anyone else to worry about anything, she was the kind of person who left notes if she went to the corner shop. She must have been distraught.

"Everyone at home is really worried, she didn't let them know she was leaving," I said to Charlotte, filling her in. "I'm gonna ring home, talk to Dad. It sounds like Mum's a bit hysterical, I'd better let them know." She nodded her agreement and stood up to get breakfast ready.

The phone was answered after the first ring. Dad had probably slept by it.

"Dad, it's me, it's Lizzy."

"Lizzy, is Jane there? Is she okay?"

"She's here, she's safe. She was really upset when she arrived yesterday and I haven't gotten to the bottom of it yet, but she's sleeping now so I was just going to leave her until she woke up."

"Sounds like a good idea. Obviously, it wasn't the best idea to just get on a train and go to see you, but I'm glad she's with you, Lizzy. You're sensible enough to help her. I'm glad she's in safe hands."

I know my parents don't have favourites, but I often get the uncomfortable feeling that if my dad had a favourite, it would be me.

"Lizzy, I have to ask... do you have any idea what happened? Even the slightest inkling?"

Really, it was Jane's news to tell, I knew that. But the longer I put it off the worse it would be, and she wasn't going to be in any state to let anyone else know for a while. If I told Dad now, he could calm Mum down enough for it to not be too hard on Jane when she went back home.

"I think... I think she and Charlie have broken up. Or he broke up with her, or something."

I wouldn't have expected Dad to be particularly affected by this news – he prided himself on taking minimal interest in gossip – but he gasped audibly over the phone.

"That's... that's the last thing I expected. Oh, poor Jane, no wonder she was so upset. I'll tell your mother, let her recover from the initial shock before Jane comes home." The similarities between my dad and myself sometimes alarmed me; we were almost always on the same page. "You look after her, okay? Make sure she's okay."

"I will, Dad, don't worry. I'll do everything I can."

"That's my girl. And say hi to Charlotte for me."

"My dad says hi!" I said, still talking at the same volume as Charlotte was now sitting next to me again, eating her toast.

"Hi Mr Bennet!" she called, loud enough for it to be picked up by my phone's microphone.

"I've told you to call me David!" He called back, loud enough for Charlotte to hear.

"Okay Dad. I'll speak to you soon, keep you posted. Love you."

"I love you too Betts. Speak to you soon."

I sat in silence for a few seconds after he hung up. It had been years since I'd heard his childhood nickname for me; hearing it again brought back so many memories of both the happiest and the hardest times of my life, and was a harsh reminder of how much this was all affecting my dad.

Jane didn't wake up until half past eleven, and I tried my best to keep myself occupied until then. I wasn't very successful. I didn't have any work to do yet, the flat was already pretty clean, and I couldn't focus on anything like reading. In the end, I sat in the kitchen binge-watching a BBC drama from twenty years ago while playing mindless games on my phone.

"Lizzy?" came a quiet voice. I turned around to see Jane standing shyly the doorway.

"How are you doing?" I asked, quickly putting the kettle on to make her some tea.

She shrugged. "I'd say I'm okay but I'm not. Thank you for letting me stay here."

"Hey, it's fine! You're my sister, you're always welcome here."

She gave me a teary smile that didn't quite reach her eyes.

"Thanks Lizzy. Oh, I'm such a mess..." she looked down at the floor as tears started to come thick and fast once more.

"It's okay, it's okay, I'm here. It's alright, you can cry, it's fine." I pulled her into a tight hug as she shook with sobs. "The kettle's just boiled. How about I make you some tea? The world looks a whole lot better after tea." We both knew that that wasn't true, but she nodded and sat down anyway.

"Here you go, one enormous mug of tea. Medium strength, milk and no sugar, because you're sweet enough already." She smiled weakly as I brought back Mum's old joke, and started slowly sipping her tea.

"What do you want to do today? We can do anything. We can go shopping, we can go to a park, we can go sightseeing, we can go to the cinema, we could sit here and watch TV all day. Your call."

She shrugged again. "I'm really sorry Lizzy... I'd love to do all those things but I just can't. I'm sorry. I don't know what to do."

I waited a few seconds before replying. "Do you... want to talk about it?"

She reached into her pocket and pulled out an envelope.

"Here," she said, handing it to me.

I pulled out the sheet of paper inside. It was very good quality writing paper, the kind that your grandparents get you for Christmas, but it was soft and crumpled from having been handled so many times. As I unfolded it, I saw Charlie's neat hand-writing on the page.

"Jane, I don't think I should read this, this is personal."

She shook her head. "That's the thing – it's not. You read it."

Dear Jane,

I am writing to tell you that I am leaving Hertfordshire to go and live in New York for a few months. I have a number of engagements there over the coming weeks and so will be staying there for the foreseeable future.

It was lovely meeting you and spending time with you, and I wish you the best for the future.

Yours sincerely,

Charlie Bingley

"This is ridiculous," I said as soon as I finished reading this. "What the hell? He's just… left? And told you by *handwritten letter*?! What is this, the 18th Century?!"

"Lizzy, don't be so harsh. He might have just-"

"Might have what, Jane?" I stuffed the letter back in the envelope unceremoniously. A glance at the other side told me that he'd at least hand-delivered it rather than sent it by post. "You know what? He doesn't deserve you. Any arsehole who thinks they can treat my sister like this, well they've got another thing coming."

"Your defence of me is admirable, Lizzy, but it's no use. He's probably in New York by now, and I'm… I'm here. Without him. Alone." She determinedly wiped the tears from her cheeks. "There's no point. He's gone."

I couldn't believe the cowardly way he'd behaved. Not wanting to maintain a long-distance relationship is one thing, but to not tell someone face to face? To send them a letter?! That was a whole other story.

Something about the whole situation just didn't feel right. Jane and Charlie, while not necessarily in love, were certainly on their way to it, and until recently had been as happy as could be. There was something else going on here, and I was going to get to the bottom of it. Obviously, though, Jane didn't know what it was either. If things had really been going badly between her and Charlie she wouldn't have been this surprised, surely?

"What do you want to do now?" I asked softly.

She shrugged in response, which was a very un-Jane-like action. I put my hand on her arm in what I hoped was comfort.

"How about you stay here for a bit? There's still a week or so before Charlotte and I start work, and I saw that you brought some clothes. It will be good to get away from home for a bit, clear your head."

She nodded, attempting a smile before she broke down in tears once more.

"Why does it hurt so much, Lizzy?" she cried, and I pulled her into a hug, hushing her and rubbing her back. It's been a very, very long time since I've seen her this upset, and I didn't really know what to do. She was usually the one making sure other people were okay, and helping other people though their problems. What was I supposed to do when she was the one who needed looking after?

One thing was for sure. Charlie Bingley had a lot to answer for.

Jane didn't cheer up enough for the next couple of days to really do much. I made sure she left the flat each day, if only to go and buy more milk or post a letter that didn't really need sending, but it didn't seem to help. We shared my bed, top-and-tailing because Jane has cuddle tendencies, but Jane would sleep for twelve hours at a time when I slept for six.

I spent a lot of time trying to find some information on what was going on. According to Mark, who also seemed surprisingly upset at the turn of events, neither Charlie or Darcy had been seen by anyone, including Mum's nosy friends. All evidence pointed to them leaving town, but it was certainly odd given how they only moved in a few weeks ago.

I took to social media stalking to try and find something out, but there was neither hide nor hair of them. Darcy had unfriended me (not that I was complaining), and Charlie had not only unfriended but also, seemingly, blocked me, and it would not be an unreasonable assumption that the same had happened to Jane.

Sander seemed to be having fun with George, though. Every time I opened Facebook there was a new picture of their latest shenanigans. It all seemed fairly safe; well-known clubs, pints at the end of the day, going to the football. At least, I thought, Sander was be safe with George, and hopefully would learn that you can have fun and be responsible at the same time.

I looked at Darcy's Facebook profile, hoping to find some hint of what had happened, but her privacy settings were all on and her profile picture hadn't changed. I tried to think about where else I could find information when it came to me: her brother.

I searched *Jordan Williams* and went onto his profile. His profile was also private, but he'd updated his profile picture since I last saw it. Not that I'm in the habit of looking at the profile pictures of the brothers of people I barely know.

The picture was a photo of him and Darcy smiling (which was a weird look on Darcy) in front of the Royal Albert Hall.

> *Great to be back in the UK, and reunited with my awesome sister! – with **Darcy Williams**.*

So, Darcy was in London, and Charlie was in New York. Well, it was a start.

Wait a minute. Darcy was in London?!

But London was a very big place – surely we wouldn't bump into each other? Of course not. Don't be ridiculous.

Except that we were in the same profession. Admittedly at very different levels, but still. All it took was one conference...

I couldn't think about that now. The chances of us meeting were miniscule, there was no point worrying about it. I'd got this far in my detective work; I may as well keep nosing around. Giving up on Facebook, I opened Twitter; I doubted Charlie had blocked us on there.

I was wrong, of course; his personal account had been made private. If there's one thing I know about artists, however, it's that they have two Twitter accounts. All I needed to do was find the other one of Charlie's.

It didn't take long. A quick search of *Charles Bingley* brought up what I needed.

Charles Bingley @cbingleypiano

The profile picture was a headshot and the header was a picture of piano keys. I scrolled down his most recent tweets.

> *@cbingleypiano Very excited to announce that for the next few months I will be based in #NYC*
> *@cbingleypiano Looking forward to meeting all you talented folks at #Julliard*
> *@cbingleypiano Carnegie Hall here we come! Or the audience at least... definitely one for the bucket list!*

So, he genuinely was in New York. That was a small comfort, at least.

I didn't tell Jane about any of this. All I'd done was confirm what we already suspected, and there was no point in bringing everything up again more than was absolutely necessary; we didn't want to upset her any more. It was my job now to try and take her mind off things, which was easier said than done when she didn't want to leave the house. Eventually, though, we persuaded her that there was no point in being in London if she was going to spend all her time indoors, and that she should do at least a few tourist-y things while she was here.

So off we went again; back round Buckingham Palace, back round the Houses of Parliament, back round the museums. It worked its magic, though. While she was by no means completely happy, her smile could sometimes be caught again and she had managed to go twenty-four hours without crying – at least, as far as we were aware. I decided to ignore the sniffling that came from the bathroom every couple of hours.

By the time we were saying goodbye to her at the station, she had some of her Jane-ness back. She was fussing over me once more, making friends with strangers, planning on changing the world. Her eyes still looked sad, and she sometimes took a double take at things, but that was to be expected. What she and Charlie had shared, while short-lived, was special. It took time to move on from these things.

I hadn't realised how much of my worry-capacity had been spent on Jane until we got back to our flat that evening and I started to think about what happens next. With all that had been going on, I had completely forgotten to get worried about starting a new job. I'm sure that while that's a good thing in many ways, I did not appreciate the last-minute panic of ironing my shirt, making my lunch, double-checking Tube times, polishing my shoes.

This was it. This was my fresh start: the start of something enormous. Today, I was Lizzy Bennet, but tomorrow? Tomorrow I would be Elizabeth Bennet: Intern at Rosings Publishing House.

Chapter 16: Rosings

Isn't it funny how nervous we can get before big events? Starting a new school, starting university and, today, starting a new job.

At some point midway through my first year of sixth form I decided to stop letting my nerves get to me. Easier said than done, of course. Now, though, when I feel nervous about something, I tell myself I'm not nervous and it does kind of help.

I've always liked to be in control of my life, and that included my emotions. Sometimes I would tell myself that if I could control the outside, I could control the inside.

Now was one of those times.

I allowed two hours to get ready on the morning of my first day at Rosings, which involved getting out of bed a six o'clock. I have previously mastered the art of rolling out of bed and being ready to go within ten minutes, having had breakfast and made myself presentable enough for a lecture. Lectures and the work-place, however, are two very different things, and I was about to make my first impression. I had to look immaculate, and be focussed and ready to work.

A longer shower than usual as I'd felt the need to wash my hair twice, a breakfast that would keep me going until lunchtime but wouldn't make me feel full or bloated, and dressed in my brand-new outfit that I'd bought for the occasion. Skirt, shirt, jacket, and some comfortable but smart flat shoes. I made an effort with my make-up for once, but not being in the habit of putting it on meant it took me three goes to get my eye-liner right.

My early start in the name of not rushing meant that I had half an hour left before I needed to leave so I set to distract myself until I could justify leaving to go and get the Tube out.

I got my phone out, ready to waste time on whatever the latest mindless game was to see a message from Jane.

> *Jane Bennet: Good luck today Lizzy! I know you'll be brilliant. Thank you for letting me stay with you the last few days xx*
> Oh, Jane! Bless her.
> *Lizzy Bennet: Thank you!! And it was lovely to have you. Can't believe I won't see you for a few months now! Hope you're doing okay x*

She hadn't been online since the previous evening so I didn't wait for a reply and put my phone away, knowing that nothing would really be able to distract me. Charlotte didn't start work for another week, so she was still fast asleep; I settled for making sure I'd packed everything I might possibly need, unpacking and repacking my bag over and over.

As it got closer to eight o'clock I decided to slowly start making my way down to the Tube station. There weren't too many commuters this far out from the city centre, or at least few enough that I could choose my own walking pace without being swept away in the crowd.

Stopping to buy myself a coffee on the way, I arrived with twenty minutes to spare. It felt like a good time to arrive: not too early that I was in the way and overly keen, but early enough to show that I meant business.

I paused in front of the building, taking a moment to admire it. I'd been here once before for my interview, but hadn't taken the opportunity then to really take it in. It was incredibly grand, even by the standards of London city centre; the building itself must have been at least two hundred years old. I was sure that the old chimneys, still there but no longer in use, must have cost more than my family's house.

I gave a brief glance to the plaque on the outside of the building:

Rosings Publishing Houses
Est. 1813

This was it. Here I was, about to start an internship at one of the oldest and largest publishing companies in the country. And I was standing at the door like a lost puppy.

Taking a deep breath, I pushed the door open and stepped inside.

While the building looked old on the outside, the inside was much more modern. The foyer was large and spacious, with a reception area on the left and sofas on the right. There were pictures of book covers dating back to when the publishing company began on the white walls, and large archways leading off to different parts of the building. At the back of the foyer, behind a small seating area, was a grand staircase, with a subtle sign indicating that the lifts were behind it.

I stepped towards the reception desk, trying my best at a smile when the receptionist met my eye.

"Hello, I'm Elizabeth Bennet, I'm the new intern?"

He nodded, and indicated towards the sofas across from the entrance. "If you'd like to take a seat over there, someone will be with you shortly."

I nodded my thanks and gingerly sat on the edge of the big leather sofa, poised and nervously smoothing down my skirt.

I had been sat there for what felt like hours but was only about five minutes, watching as a steady stream of people made their way through the front doors and towards their offices, when a young man, no more than two or three years older than me, also stopped at the reception desk. He was fairly short, not much taller than me, and of medium build, with blond hair, a short, thin beard and, as I saw when he turned around, bright blue eyes.

"Hi," he said, giving me a nervous smile as he came to sit next to me after talking to the receptionist. "Are you my fellow new intern?"

"Guilty as charged," I replied, also trying my best at a smile, but resulting in something more resembling a grimace. "Lizzy Bennet." I stuck my hand out.

"Will Fitts," he replied warmly, shaking it. "This is a pretty impressive place, right? It looks amazing."

I nodded enthusiastically. "Yeah, it's gorgeous! I can't believe I'm going to be working here for a year!"

"I know, right? That's a totally crazy thought. So, are you fresh out of uni or what? Tell me about yourself. If we're going to be working together for a year I need your back story!"

He seemed like the kind of person I wouldn't mind working with; he was nice, genuine, and had a sense of calm about him, even with the inevitable first-day-nerves.

"Yeah, I've just graduated from Birmingham. This is kind of my first real job!"

"Oh, cool! Are you from Birmingham then?"

I shook my head, laughing slightly. "No, I'm from Hertfordshire."

He laughed with me. "I thought you didn't sound like a brummy lass! You're far too well-spoken for that."

"What about you, have you come straight from uni?" I asked.

"Yup! Fresh out of Kings College London," he replied. "I took a couple of years out, though, so I'm actually twenty-three."

We spent a few more minutes getting to know each other: nothing too personal, just chatting about university and hobbies before someone came to speak to us.

"Hello, hello, hello!" A small, beady-eyed man with what looked like a pudding-bowl haircut had come out from one of the corridors leading off from the foyer, and was scuttling towards us. We both stood up, correctly assuming that he was there to talk to both of us.

"You two must be…" he made a show of checking our names on the clipboard in his hands. "…Elizabeth Bennet and William Fitts?"

"Yes," we chorused, not sure what else to say.

"Very good, very good." He looked rather odd. While he was wearing smart clothes, all of which were clean and well-ironed, none of them quite matched. His three-piece suit was three slightly different shades of brown, set against a patterned grey shirt and a bright green tie. I glanced down and noticed that his black shoes had bright red laces. The whole effect was... interesting. "I have lanyards for you both. They have your ID cards attached so don't lose them, as they also function as your key card."

A lanyard was pushed into my hands, and I quickly looked down at it before doing a double-take; apparently, I was called William Fitts now. I glanced out the corner of my eye to see that Will had also noticed that he had the wrong card.

"My name is Colin Collins, and I will be your supervisor while you're here at Rosings. Now, if you'd like to follow me?"

He led the way into the offices. As soon as his back was turned Will and I quickly swapped cards. Colin Collins had not stopped talking all the while. It was almost as if he didn't need air.

"I'm sure you will enjoy your time working here; every day I come in here more grateful than I was the day before that I work for such a wonderful establishment. If you ever do meet Miss de Bourgh, who is an absolutely marvellous woman, I must add, then you should make the most of the occasion. There is so much you can learn from such an esteemed businesswoman; it is truly an honour to be her employee. Ah, here we are."

There was a small alcove between what seemed to be the ladies' toilets and the photocopy room, and in it was crammed a desk with a chair at either side. Colin

Collins continued to chunter on, giving us excessive detail on every feature we passed.

"This will be your desk. I know it's small, but you won't be at it very much; I daresay you will spend most of your time in other parts of the office. I'm sure you understand that you hold an integral role in the running of this company by supplying everyone with the correct sheet of paper at the correct time, so I trust you will make it a priority to familiarise yourself with the photocopier. It is a very impressive photocopier, I must say; Miss de Bourgh does not cut corners, especially on something as important as the photocopier. As your supervisor, I will give you sufficient notice whenever there is a particular event that you are required to be at, be it either because your assistance is needed or because I consider that observation of such an event would contribute to your knowledge of this profession. At all other times, you are simply to get on with whatever tasks your colleagues may set you, be it administrative or fetching them a hot beverage. Now, any questions?"

I really wanted to ask him what possessed his parents when they named him Colin Collins, but felt that that would be inappropriate, so settled simply for a "No," which was echoed by Will.

"Very well then," Colin Collins said. (What should I call him? Mr Collins? Colin?) "My office is down the hall and around the corner should you need anything; I will come and check how you're doing in a few hours. Usually I would give you a tour of the whole building, but I have a very important meeting that I absolutely cannot rearrange, so that must wait until tomorrow. Your lunch break is from half twelve until half one, and I suggest you take it; you may not have time for one as your responsibilities build up. For now, I suggest you settle in and get to know the area; I'm sure it won't be long before someone needs some assistance."

We stood in bewildered silence as Colin walked back down the hallway and into his office. As soon as the door had clicked shut behind him, Will and I exchanged looks and immediately started giggling.

"He's quite the character!" Will laughed loudly. I quickly hushed him, not knowing how many offices were within earshot, but carried on giggling all the same.

"Okay, come on. We're professionals now. Let's be professional." We managed to stop laughing for a few seconds, but a relaxation of the morning's nerves combined with the experience of meeting Colin Collins meant that we couldn't keep straight faced for long.

We calmed down eventually, of course, before debating who would get which side of the desk (I won the coin toss and so was furthest from the toilets) and setting up our things. As recommended, we worked out how to use the photocopier, and set up our email accounts ready for when someone needed to contact us.

"Looks like it's going to be a slow morning," I said to Will, coming back to the desk after my first task: fetching coffee for a meeting upstairs.

"How about we carry on getting to know each other?" he suggested. "How about truth or dare?"

I snorted with laughter. "Truth or dare? What are we, twelve?" He raised an eyebrow, challenging me. "Okay, but truth only, no dares. We don't want to get fired on our first day for abseiling somewhere we shouldn't be or something. Keep the questions PG rated, and nothing too personal; I've read enough YA novels to know that chances are at least one of us has a tragic backstory."

He nodded his agreement. "That sounds like a good plan. Save the none-PG questions for when we inevitably become lifelong friends and get pissed one night."

"Fair enough," I laughed. "Do you want to go first? You lost the coin toss earlier, it's probably fair if you get to find out my secrets first!"

"Okay," he said. "Have you ever..."

Both of our laptops went off at the same time with a message.

"Hold that thought," he said, as we both opened the email.

"Someone wants this manuscript printing and it's too long for the printers upstairs. I'll send it to print, could you take it up?"

I heard the printer whirr to life in the room behind me.

"Sure, that's fine as you took the coffee earlier," he replied. "Gets you out of spilling your secrets though!" he joked as an afterthought.

I collected the papers from the printer and settled in to read my induction booklet as Will took them off upstairs. He seemed like a great, funny guy, and if the morning so far was any indication, we were going to get on brilliantly.

Half a day down. Another three hundred and sixty-four and a half to go...

Chapter 17: Unexpected Acquaintances

Will and I went out for lunch that first day on the principle that we should make the most of as many lunch breaks as we could before our schedules were filled up. We were expecting a long queue – after all, it was lunchtime and we were in London city centre – but it took even longer than usual thanks to the old lady in front of us who was struggling to get her change out of her purse.

I didn't mind waiting if it took another couple of minutes to serve someone, but I *did* mind what happened next. She turned around with her tea in hand, saw us standing there and, glancing between us, leaned closer to me, lowering her voice to a stage whisper.

"He's a keeper, he is - you're a lucky girl!" She winked at me, and I could feel my face going red with equal parts embarrassment and anger. How dare she?! This old lady who I'd never met before in my life just came up to me and made a completely uninformed comment about my life!

"Ugh, why do people think that it's okay to do that?!" I fumed after we'd sat down with our food. "She just looks at us and... assumes. It just... gah, it infuriates me so much!"

Will looked at me across the table with anticipation. "Rant over?"

I flopped back in my chair. "Only because I don't have the energy to carry on being angry. I'm just... fed up of people seeing a guy and a girl and assuming they're together."

"This is more than that though, right?" he said. I looked at him, surprised. "What? I'm good at watching people."

I took a deep breath. One of the odd things about coming out was that it was something you never stopped doing. While it got easier over time, there was always that fear when you had to tell someone new, especially someone you didn't know very well.

"It's the fact that I have to correct people. They assume I'm straight, I have to tell them otherwise and I don't like that. I wish... I wish people assumed nothing until you told them, you know?"

He nodded sympathetically. "I can get that. I guess I don't mind it so much myself. When people assume that kind of stuff, you know? And especially in that old lady's case. I mean, she just turned around and saw a normal guy and girl. I find it hard to get angry at that."

"I guess so," I replied noncommittedly, fiddling with the edge of my coffee cup. He had a point, even if it wasn't one I particularly agreed with.

"It sucks when someone thinks they know all about you, though," Will said, obviously attempting comfort.

"Yeah," I sighed. "I'm just... fed up. I came out six years ago, you know, and every day I still have to pluck up the courage to tell someone new."

Will leant forwards slightly, his face filled with sincerity. "Thank you for having the courage to tell me. I can get how hard it must be to be constantly battling with the world to be seen for who you are."

I smiled weakly. "You know, I feel like I could have done a lot worse when it comes to colleagues!"

"Well, don't speak too soon! You haven't seen what I'm like on Thursdays yet..." He paused as I laughed, both of us more at ease. "Tell me about yourself. Any tendencies to go after your colleagues with a stapler if they forget your coffee?"

"I don't think you'll have to worry about that," I grinned. "Well... as you know, Birmingham University, living in Hertfordshire. What else do you want to know?"

He shrugged. "I don't know... hobbies?"

"You know," I said, "you never realise how few hobbies you have until someone asks you that question! I don't know... is it cliché to say that I like learning new things? Museums, books, BBC documentaries. That's my jam, right there."

"I don't think that's cliché," said Will, sipping at his coffee. "I'm a bit of a movie buff myself. And board games – the more expansion packs, the better."

"That's awesome!" I replied. "We used to play board games at home sometimes, but we haven't in years. I have two brothers and a sister, so anything competitive tended to get a bit intense," I added at his look of confusion.

"Wow, three siblings? I wish I had a brother or sister. I mean, my flatmate and her brother are kind of like my family, but it's not the same, you know?"

I nodded in agreement. "Yeah. I get mad at them sometimes, but I wouldn't have it any other way. Being an only child must have its perks, though?"

Will only shrugged, not quite meeting my eyes. "It had its moments, I suppose." It was clear that he was uncomfortable with the topic, so I moved on swiftly.

"So, er, what do you think of Rosings so far?"

I was grasping at straws, trying my best at small talk.

"It's great!" Will replied perhaps too enthusiastically, clearly grateful for the change in subject. "Colin's an interesting one, I have to say."

"He's completely nuts!" I exclaimed. "I've known him all of four hours but I can definitively say that there is something very, *very* strange about that man."

"I'm glad it's not just me that thinks so," Will chortled. "Maybe that's why he's stuck managing interns: no one else can bear to share an office with him?"

"Wouldn't surprise me! And the way he goes on about Catherine de Bourgh, it's worrying to say the least."

"Have you ever met her?" Will asked. I shook my head. "She's... formidable, to say the least. Meeting her is certainly an experience you won't forget in a hurry."

I gulped at his description of our new boss, making a mental note to avoid her at all reasonable costs.

Glancing at my watch, I saw that our lunch break was unfortunately almost over. We were sure that by now most of the office would have realised that there were new interns and piled up plenty of work for us, and we were proven right when we saw the long to-do list that had been left for us by Colin on our desk.

I felt much more like an intern and less like a hanger-on in the afternoon once I had things to do, and every spare minute was spent trying to work out how to get around the rabbit warren that was the Rosings offices. Not only was it one of the oldest publishers in the country but it was also one of the biggest. There were constantly people coming in and out with all sorts of things that needed doing. The afternoon passed quickly and before I knew it, it was five o'clock and Colin was coming to see how we'd got on.

"How was your first day here at Rosings then? I trust that you are suitably impressed and awed by the publishing empire that the wonderful Miss de Bourgh has built up here! I know that I am every single morning when I come in to work!" Luckily, he didn't seem like he wanted an actual verbal response, so we nodded in the right places as he continued to talk. "I am sure that you now fully appreciate what an honour, what a prestige it is to be working here under Miss de Bourgh! There is no better way to introduce yourself to the working world. Why, just a few years ago, I myself was an intern here and look at me now!

"Now, here are your schedules for the next few days – oh, they're here somewhere," he rifled through the bundle of papers he was holding and pulled out two slightly crumpled pieces of paper. "You each have some meetings that you will need to help prepare for and to sit in should you be needed for anything, while also giving you a chance to observe how the beautiful machine that is Rosings runs. I trust you will make every effort to look your best." He gave us something that I think was supposed to be a smile, but just made his mouth look even smaller. "I will also be giving you both a tour of the offices first thing in the morning; I can only apologise for not doing it sooner, but if Miss de Bourgh asks me to do something else then I'm sure you understand that that must take priority! Now, if there is nothing else that you wish to ask then I will see you on the morrow! Good day to you both!" And with that he went back down the corridor and into his office, with the kind of walk that school children do on their way to lunch; as fast as possible without actually running, in order to get to the intended destination quickly but without breaking any no-running rules or, as I expect is the case here, lowering oneself to such an activity as running indoors.

"He certainly is an odd little man," I commented once he'd left. Will and I both laughed weakly, but were too exhausted from the day (which was really only an afternoon) to put much effort in.

"Right, home and a nap," I said, gathering my things.

"That sounds like such a good idea," Will agreed wearily as we headed out the offices together.

"Which way are you going?" he asked as we walked back out the front door.

I pointed right in the general direction of the Tube. "That way."

"Oh, I'm going this way – I live just down the road. Well, I'll see you tomorrow!"

"Yeah, have a good evening!"

It was almost six o'clock by the time I got home to find Charlotte cooking a stir-fry for dinner.

"Hey!" she said as I came in to the kitchen. "I figured I'd make dinner for us both tonight, celebrate your first day in a new job!"

"Thank you, that's so lovely of you! I'm just going to get changed, I'll be back in a jiffy."

I quickly changed out of my suit into a t-shirt and an old pair of jeans before re-joining Charlotte in the kitchen.

"So how was it then?" she asked as she served up.

"It was… interesting. The place itself was, of course, wonderful. It's such a beautiful building, and it's brilliant being in the middle of all the excitement, and I'll happily sit and work surrounded by books all day… My supervisor's interesting. He's called Colin Collins."

Charlotte snorted into her glass. "Colin Collins?! Poor guy. Sorry, continue."

"Well, he's a bit… eccentric. He's always going on about how wonderful the company is, and how amazing Catherine de Bourgh is – she's the boss – but he just sort of bumbles around, completely disorganised. He could do with some tips from you, Miss Colour-Paper-And-Pens!"

She nodded, laughing slightly at the description. "Well, he certainly sounds like a character!"

"That's exactly what Will said!" I saw her look of confusion. "Will's the other intern this year, he's a pretty cool guy."

"And does he know that you're about as straight as these noodles? Remember what happened the last time you met a 'pretty cool' guy."

I sighed. "He does know, and he was cool with it – much like George was once he'd stopped flirting."

"Just looking out for my bestie" she said, pointing her fork at me.

"Well, bestie appreciates it," I replied, before concentrating on my dinner.

The week passed in a blur of meetings, photocopying and coffee runs. We'd seen a fair bit of the offices on the first day but Colin still took us on a tour on Tuesday morning. I must admit that I didn't really pay attention to most of what he said; I think about ninety percent of it was about the brilliance of Catherine de Bourgh and how wonderful Rosings was thanks to her. Any time that wasn't spent in meetings or running around after other people was spent getting to know Will. The more we chatted, the more we realised had in common, and I had a feeling that he was going to be a good friend.

Friday was the first time we managed to get a lunch break since that first day, but rather than go out again we just sat in the coffee shop off the foyer, eating our sandwiches.

"If I have to spend any more time alone with the photocopier I think I'll have to propose for decency's sake," Will grumbled through a large mouthful of his sandwich. "At least I'm nearly done for the weekend. What about you, busy afternoon?"

I nodded, pointedly swallowing the food in my mouth before replying. "Yeah, it's a bit of a jam-packed few hours, I've got a couple of meetings and a load of things I need to get ready for Monday morning. What about you, busy fetching coffee for the third floor again?"

"Oh god, not the third-floor coffee run! But undoubtedly yes, they said that I make better coffee than you. They obviously don't realise that we don't actually make the coffee, but that there is a machine that does that for us!"

"Sounds like they've got a bit of a thing for you! Wouldn't be surprised. It is the office that deals with the, er, romantic literature, and you do bear a slight resemblance to a blond James McAvoy," I said.

"Wow, you really think so? You think they have, you know a crush on me?"

He seemed astounded. Was he not aware that he looked like the kind of person who would ride miles across the wet and cold English countryside in a billowy shirt to find his true love?

"Of course they do! I mean, I can see that you're a very attractive person. The only problem for me is that you're a very attractive manly man. Those ladies in the third-floor office, however, see that as a good thing."

A look of comprehension dawned on his face. "Oh. Oh. That, er, actually makes sense. You know what, I should go. And deliver... coffee. To the, um, third floor."

I laughed slightly to myself as he rushed off, his face bright red. The way he was blustering about, you'd think no one had ever had a crush on him before, which I found very hard to believe.

The afternoon dragged on and five o'clock came and went, but I was determined to finish everything that needed to be done before Monday. Will brought me a coffee just before he left at five o'clock on the dot, and by half past six I'd managed to get everything done. I'd nearly finished packing up when I noticed something under Will's chair. It was a half-empty blister pack of tablets that I didn't recognise – clearly prescription.

I took a picture and sent them to Will.

Lizzy Bennet: Are these yours, and will you need them over the weekend? They were under your chair.

The reply was almost instant.

Will Fitts: Yes, thank you so much!!! I hadn't even noticed I'd lost them, I'll come and get them now. Shall I meet you outside the front door?

Lizzy Bennet: What's your address? I know you live nearby, I'll meet you there.

Will Fitts: Are you sure? You're a lifesaver, I swear.

A few more seconds passed before another text arrived with his address, and I was right; he lived a stone's throw from the office. He must be living with his parents or something, because there's no way he could afford that on our salary.

The walk to Will's front door took all of three minutes, and when I reached the front door to his building he was in the lobby waiting for me.

"Thank you so much, you're a star," he said as he opened the door to let me in, taking the pills from me. I'm so glad you found these, I'd be a monster by Monday otherwise."

I jumped as the lobby door opened again behind me, a blast of cold air hitting the back of my neck.

"Oh, hey, Darcy!" Will waved, and I felt a rock hit the pit of my stomach. "Have you met Lizzy? Lizzy, this is my flatmate, Darcy."

Shit.

Bloody hell.

Why is this happening?!

Darcy Williams. Darcy. Bloody. Williams.

On the bright side, she looked as shocked as I did. She obviously had no idea I even knew Will, let alone that I had any reason to be in the building where she lived. Not that I had any idea that *she* knew Will.

Darcy was standing rigidly, a suitcase in her hand, breathing shallowly.

"What is *she* doing here?" she asked Will, shaking slightly trying to control her emotions. Yes, I was surprised to see her and the feeling was mutual, but surely this was a bit of an overreaction.

"Darcy, this is my friend Lizzy. Do… do you guys know each other or something?" He was stood stock still, his eyes glancing between our faces.

"Yes, we, er, met over summer. I'm sorry Darcy, I had no idea that you lived here. I should, er, probably be going."

I quickly turned to leave, but Darcy was blocking the only door.

"No, Lizzy, it's okay, you don't have to go, right Darcy?" Will was desperately trying to salvage the situation, but it wasn't going to work. "I don't know anything about how you guys know each other, but…"

I was suddenly aware of a silent conversation happening across me. I glanced over my shoulder to see Darcy giving Will a Look; the kind that said that he should know exactly why she was Looking at him. His expression was one of confusion, until it finally morphed into one of realisation.

"Oh! Lizzy's… Lizzy's the girl you told me about."

"Wait, what?" I was really confused now.

Darcy exploded at Will. "Why would you… why did you say that?! You have no subtlety at all! Why would you…"

I didn't hear the rest because I grabbed my bag and ran out the front door.

"Lizzy! Wait!" Will was running after me. "Lizzy I'm sorry, you don't have to go! Please, can I just talk to you?" He finally caught up and leapt around me, blocking my way on the street.

"Lizzy, I'm so sorry. I don't know exactly what's gone on between you two, but don't run off because of her."

I sighed, trying to figure out what to say. "Nothing… nothing terrible has happened between us. We met over summer, and we didn't really get along, but I thought we were starting to be civil towards each other. Obviously not, judging by her reaction when she saw me."

He looked sorry for me. I hate it when people look sorry for me. "You can come up, though; don't leave on her account. I'm sure she'll stay out of the way if you don't want to see her, and I expect she was just a bit shocked, that's all." He paused, looking awkward for a few seconds. "I don't have that many friends, and I just… it will be really hard if you two can't be in the same room."

He looked so beaten down that I almost relented, but I just… I couldn't. Maybe another time, but everything had changed so suddenly and I needed to clear my head. "I'm sorry, but I really should go. I – I was just coming to drop something off, anyway. I'll see you on Monday, okay?"

He paused before nodding and passing to one side to let me pass.

"Thanks," I whispered as I walked past him. I took a few steps before I suddenly remembered something.

"Will?"

"Yeah?"

"You said Darcy told you about me. I just... what did..." I swallowed, trying to find the words. "What exactly did she say about me?"

"I'm so sorry," he said, and I could tell he meant it, "but I can't tell you. It's not my place."

"If it's about me then you should be able to tell me!" I stormed back towards him.

Will sighed heavily, rubbing his forehead with his hands and dragging his fingers through his hair. "I... just don't worry about it. Nothing that Darcy has said will make me like you any less. If anything, it's the opposite."

I nodded, letting out a breath that I didn't know I'd been holding.

"Thanks," I said, giving as genuine a smile as I could muster. "See you Monday."

The journey home was a blur. I don't remember walking to the station, or finding my platform, or getting on my train. All I could think about was what had just happened. So, Will lives with Darcy. Didn't see that one coming. And neither, apparently, did Darcy. The way she had looked at Will when she saw that I was there, as if it was some kind of... betrayal of trust?

As soon as my phone connected to signal after leaving the underground, it buzzed with a new message.

Will Fitts: Hey Lizzy, I just want to say that I'm so so sorry about what happened. I had no idea that you guys knew each other or that Darcy would have that reaction, or even that she would be there at all. I'm really sorry if I upset you in some way, I never wanted that to happen. I completely understand if you don't want to be friends anymore. Will.

I paused, standing out the way of the station exit to reply.

Lizzy Bennet: Of course I still want to be friends! I get that it was all just an unfortunate coincidence, and I'm sorry that I reacted how I did. I'll see you on Monday, yeah?

I wasn't sure what else to say, so I pressed send and pocketed my phone.

It took Charlotte one look at my face when I walked through the door to guess that something was up.

"Why the long face? What happened?"

I sat down in the kitchen, went to make myself a cup of tea, then thought better of it and went straight for a beer.

"It's a long story, but... okay, you have three guesses as to who Will's flatmate turned out to be. Go."

Charlotte looked at me like I'd gone mad. "How am I supposed to guess that?! Just tell me."

I didn't have the energy to carry on playing games, so I told her.

"Darcy freaking Williams."

Her face was a picture. "Darcy Williams? As in, bitch-face friend to adorable puppy Charlie Bingley?"

I nodded. "The very same."

She looked at me, agape. "Well? What happened?!"

"Long story short? She saw me, she freaked out, Will said something he shouldn't've, I freaked out, I left."

She gave a low whistle. "That... wow. That really sucks."

"Tell me about it! This was not how I was expecting the day to end." I took a long drink of my beer. "The week was going so well, you know? And then she just... showed up and ruined it all. And it's not like I'm going to be able to avoid her, or even the topic of her very easily, as she's my colleague's flatmate!"

"I wish there was something I could do to help," Charlotte said. "Tell you what. How about I take you out to lunch on Monday? I'll get to have a nosy peek at your office, you get a distraction from things. How does that sound?"

I smiled at her. "That would be really lovely!"

It wasn't long before I surrendered to the exhaustion the day had left me with, sleeping as soon as my head hit the pillow. The weekend passed far too quickly, and soon enough it was Monday morning and I was back off to my second week at Rosings.

"Morning," I said to Will as I set my bag down by our desk, slightly apprehensive at seeing him.

"Morning," he said in return, obviously feeling the same way.

I straightened up, filled with sincerity as I said, "Listen, Will... about what happened on Friday. Let's just forget it happened, yeah? Carry on as normal?"

He gave me a relieved grin. "That sounds like a great plan!"

Thankfully, the morning passed mostly as normal. We got on with our usual jobs, occasionally sharing small talk. Colin had come around in another flap about something or other that he had lost. We helped him find it, heard about how wonderful the company we worked for was, and then he went on his way.

Lunchtime came faster than usual, but I was absolutely starving.

"Any lunch plans?" Will asked as we started to finish things up for the morning.

"My flatmate and I are going for lunch," I said apologetically.

"Cool," he smiled. "Sneak her in to meet me after, right?"

"Sure," I agreed. "Don't get in too much trouble while I'm gone!"

"Don't count on it!" he called back as I left.

Charlotte was waiting outside the front of the offices when I stepped outside.

"This is an amazing building," she said as soon as she saw me, gesturing to the ornate stonework surrounding the door. "I can't believe you actually work here!"

"I know, it's pretty impressive, isn't it?" I agreed, looking up and down the front of the building. "Come on, let's go get lunch!"

Charlotte was, as usual, completely right; lunch out was exactly what I needed to get my mind off things. At quarter past one we went back to the office, allowing some extra time so that Charlotte could have a sneaky look around.

"Hey Will!" I called as we came down the corridor. "Will, this is Charlotte Lucas. Charlotte, this is Will Fitts."

"Lovely to meet you," Will said as they shook hands.

"Likewise. I've heard so much about you!" Charlotte replied.

"All good I hope!"

"Elizabeth! William! I have some papers here for you!" Colin had come bustling down the corridor, frantically searching for the correct papers. He stopped short as he realised that there was another person there. "Hello, can I help?" he said to Charlotte.

"I'm, um, Lizzy's friend," Charlotte said. Strictly speaking she shouldn't have been there, and I hadn't counted on Colin having an emergency. He looked at her inquisitively before carrying on with his paper-induced panic.

"I put it here somewhere... schedules... schedules... ahh, here they are! Oh no... Aha! Got it!" He flourished a piece of paper at both Will and I, once again handing us each the wrong one. "These list all the events you're expected to attend this week. Now, if I can just find that to-do list... Miss de Burgh would not approve of this disorganisation! Oh, why do pieces of paper all look the same?"

"You should try coloured paper."

We all stopped in dead silence and looked at Charlotte, who looked slightly embarrassed at having spoken out of turn. "Well, if you used, um, coloured paper, then you could find a particular sheet much more easily. It's more expensive, but as long as you only use it for, say, schedules and to-do lists, things that are essential but don't use too much paper, you will barely notice the cost difference."

Colin looked gobsmacked. "By Jove, you're right," he said. "That's... that's ingenious! I can't believe I've never thought of it before! What's your name?"

Charlotte looked at me awkwardly before answering. "Um, Charlotte Lucas."

"Pleased to meet you, Miss Lucas. I'm Colin Collins." He shook her hand enthusiastically. "Miss Lucas, you seem very wise in the way of organising one's papers and office supplies. Would you care to advise me on my use of Post-It notes?"

Of course Charlotte went with him – she's too polite to say no, especially as he was my supervisor. I just wasn't expecting her to go so... willingly.

"What just happened?" I asked Will as soon as they were out of earshot, who was struggling to contain his laughter.

"Your flatmate just got a stationary date with Colin Collins, that's what happened."

They were in his office for an hour. A whole. Hour. How anyone could put up with him for that long, I have no idea.

They were both laughing when they came out.

"So you see, Colin, Google calendars really are useful, because they can link between all your devices, and you can edit it much more easily than you can do a paper calendar."

Seriously? Colin still uses a paper calendar?

"You certainly put forward a very convincing case, Charlotte; perhaps you could explain it all to me some more over dinner tonight?"

Wow. That was surprisingly smooth for a man called Colin Collins.

"That would be lovely. I'll meet you at six o'clock then?"

Wait.

No.

She accepted?!

I didn't hear the rest of their conversation, as Colin went back into his office and Charlotte came over to me.

"I'd better be off Lizzy, but it was so lovely seeing the offices! And lovely to meet you two, Will," Will nodded in return, "but I'd best be off. I'm going out tonight; don't wait up!" And with that she left, all but skipping down the hallway.

"That's really cute," Will said dismissively, before going back to his computer.

"It is not cute!" I hissed. "Charlotte deserves so much better than stupid Colin Collins. She's just settling for him. I'll have to talk some sense into her."

"Whatever you say," said Will, still looking at his computer screen.

"This is serious," I snapped, determined to get him to see sense. "Colin is awful, and he can't be allowed to seduce Charlotte. That is not okay."

"Lizzy, they're grown adults. This is the twenty-first century. If Charlotte didn't want to go out with him, she would have turned him down." He looked across at me, exasperated. "I think you're going to have to leave them to it."

I went to bed early that night, and heard Charlotte come in at about eleven o'clock, but didn't get up to greet her. As happy as I was that she'd gone out on a date, I couldn't quite summon up the excitement that was needed to be a supportive best friend. Will was right, she was allowed to date whoever she wants. That didn't make it any easier to be happy for her, though.

Luckily, as Charlotte wouldn't be starting work for another week, I was able to leave in the morning without seeing her. I needed a few more hours to muster up the energy to be pleased and excited before I could let myself have a conversation with her, or things would turn nasty very quickly.

Once again, I had a standard morning; Will was still fetching coffee for the ladies on the third floor, I was still bringing information packs to meetings and printing off manuscripts. Will had seemed rather subdued all morning, which combined with my own dampened mood meant that we sat in a not uncomfortable silence.

It wasn't until lunchtime that we really had a conversation.

"Will, can I ask you something?"

"Yeah, sure. What is it?"

"Well..." I took a deep breath. "I wanted to ask you about Darcy. But I know she's your friend, and I'm afraid that you won't like what I say."

"Okay." He set down his sandwich. "First, let's set the record straight. Yes, Darcy's my friend; one of my closest friends. But I *do* know that she can come off as...

well, I know that she's not that great at leaving first impressions. Or second impressions, for that matter. So, I'm sure I will completely understand anything you have to say. I gather that you two... didn't really see eye to eye?"

I nodded. "You could put it that way! We were just very different people who disagreed on basically everything. Neither of us are the type to back down, so things often got... tense."

He laughed at this. "I can imagine! Jeez, I was with you two in the same room for all of two minutes and you could have cut the air with a knife!"

"I guess what I wanted to ask was..." I paused, working out exactly what I wanted to say. "You're a cool, nice guy. Why are you friends with her? I can't really see why you two would end up such close friends."

"Right, here's the thing about Darcy," he said, looking me straight in the eye. "Yes, her social skills are basically shot. Yes, she has a habit of insulting people as soon as she meets them. But that's because she's scared. She's scared of getting close to people, and she's scared of letting other people get close to her. It's like she has an elite group that only certain people are allowed membership to, and if you're not in it then woe betide you."

That made sense. It certainly fit with everything else I knew about her so far, including the way she'd treated me. "So, what, you're in this kind of exclusive group?"

"Yeah," he shrugged. "It takes a lot to get close to Darcy, but once you do? It's worth it. She's one of the most protective people I know when it comes to those closest to her, she'll do anything for them. Do you know her brother?"

I shook my head. "No, but I've heard a lot about him."

"There you go, example number one. She cares about him so much. Since her parents died she's sort of taken over that role for him, and she'll go to the ends of the earth to make sure he's okay. She has done in the past, too. And – okay, so she has this friend, and he was seeing this girl. It wasn't really serious, but this guy had it bad, he was completely obsessed. She wasn't that into him, though. She had basically no money, and it was obvious that his money was a huge thing to her, or at least her family. Yeah, apparently she had a completely crazy family who were awful. He got an offer to move to New York, and we're talking crazy opportunities, life-changing kind of deal here. He almost turned it down to stay with this girl, or was going to try long-distance, but she kind of started losing interest at about the same time. He was so besotted though, and Darcy managed to talk some sense into him. Made him realise that she wasn't worth it. It wasn't easy, to tell this guy that the woman he's head over heels for is probably using him and that it would be best to leave straight away, but she went and did it anyway because she couldn't bear to see him get hurt further down the line."

I couldn't breathe.

I... how did you breathe? Something about in and out, in and out? Taking air in, letting it out again.

"Who was the friend?" I asked, my voice surprisingly steady given that the rest of me was trembling.

"Charlie Bingley. They just bought a house together a couple of hours outside of London, been friends since they were kids. Have you ever met him?"

"Yes," I whispered, not trusting myself to say any more.

He looked at me, concerned. "Lizzy? Are you alright?"

"Yes, thank you. If - if you'll just excuse me." I jumped up and walked as quickly as I could, trying my absolutely best to give off the impression of calm as I darted round the small, shared desk to the toilets. As soon as the door swung shut behind me I heard a sob, and looked around before realising it had come from me.

How dare she.

She... she split up Jane and Charlie.

She split up. Jane. And Charlie.

Sweet, caring Jane and kind, lovable Charlie, who looked at each other as if they were the sun and stars.

No wonder she freaked out when she saw me; she thought I knew. She ruined my sister's happiness, and I daresay the happiness of her best friend too, over what? Her pride? Her belief that there actually wasn't anything good in the world?

I leant on the counter, breathing heavily, and realised that my whole body was shaking. Looking in the mirror I saw that my face was as white as a sheet except my eyes, which were red and bloodshot.

Everything that I had previously guessed about Darcy was right. Everything. She was as arrogant, obnoxious, and as awful as I had imagined, if not worse, and she had ruined everything for my sister.

I hoped, for her sake, that I would never have to set eyes on her again. There was no telling what I would do.

Chapter 18: The Last Woman on Earth

My mood did not improve as the day progressed. I did my best to avoid Will, not ready to deal with his inevitable questions about my reaction to our conversation at lunch, and bolted off as soon as it was five o'clock, determined to go straight home.

As soon as I stepped through the front door, I was confronted with a beaming, excited Charlotte, but I couldn't think for the life of me what there was to be so happy about.

"Hey Lizzy! How are you doing today? The kettle's just boiled, do you want some tea?"

I looked at her suspiciously. "Why are you so cheerful?"

"Well, I had a brilliant date yesterday, didn't I? Now, normal tea or herbal tea?"

Oh, yeah. In the... excitement... of today's new revelations, I'd forgotten why I'd been avoiding Charlotte last night and this morning. Now that she mentioned it, Colin had also been unnervingly cheerful today, trying out his new colour-paper system.

"A wonderful date? With Colin Collins? I find that hard to believe. Look, I've just had a really bad day and I'm really sorry but I'm just not in the mood." I realised that I was raising my voice. "I'm sorry, Charlotte. I just really want to just eat dinner and sleep."

I looked up, expecting her usual comforting smile as she asked what was bothering me and together we would make it all better. Instead, though, she looked hurt and insulted, and when she spoke it was with an uncharacteristic ice in her tone.

"I'm sorry, Lizzy, for having fun. I'm sorry that the whole world does not revolve around whatever drama it is you've got yourself into this time. But just because you've had a bad day doesn't mean that you shouldn't be happy for me, or at least force yourself to sit and listen while I talk about my date." Her eyes were fiery in a way I hadn't seen before as she spoke. "In fact - you know what, Lizzy Bennet?! You're such a hypocrite. You were the first person to criticise Darcy for not being supportive of Jane and Charlie over summer, and now here you are doing the exact same thing." She looked like she regretted her words, but did nothing to take them back. "I really thought you were better than this." She choked up at the end of the sentence, before stalking out of the kitchen and slamming the door shut behind her.

I sat in stunned silence. Charlotte and I *never* argued, not ever. She must really, really like Colin to defend him so readily.

I realised with a start that she had a point. I was doing the same thing that I had criticised Darcy of doing not two months ago.

But there's a difference, I thought fiercely. *I would never intentionally break them up.*

What had I done? The thought alone was like a slap in a face. I'd been rude to my best friend, causing her to storm out for the first time ever, and by extension had insulted my supervisor. I couldn't look at my only friend at work in case I said something awful about his flatmate, and

I couldn't talk to Jane in case I blurted out what Darcy had done.

If there was one thing I was sure of right now, it was that there was no way that Jane could find out.

Charlotte and I had not been talking for all of ten minutes and already it was awful. Deciding to make amends, I knocked on her door quietly.

"Charlotte?" There was no response. "Charlotte, I know you're in there. I just… I'm sorry. I'm really, *really* sorry. I… you know that I just want you to be happy, and if Colin makes you happy… then I'm happy for you. You were right. I'm sorry, Charlotte. I'll do anything to make it up to you."

After a few seconds, my phone buzzed.

Charlotte Lucas: I'm not going to yell at you through the door because I'm not seven. But I don't want to see you right now. Thank you for saying sorry. I forgive you. I just need some time.

I'd take that, for now. This was all my own stupid fault; I would put up with the consequences.

We didn't talk for the rest of the evening, but I left her some dinner outside her door and received another message in thanks. All I could do now was go out of my way to be as nice as I could, and hope that Charlotte would forgive me.

For the first time in years, I cried myself to sleep that night. I felt so helpless; between Charlotte, Jane, and Darcy, all these things were happening and they were all out of my control. The enormity of being properly away from home, of being an adult, hit me full force, and there was nothing to distract me from it. I'd upset Charlotte and

Will in the matter of a few hours; was this what I did now? Did I just ruin things for other people?

I only slept for a few hours before the morning came, and it was time to get ready to go to work. I firmly put the previous day's conversation with Will out of my mind, determined not to let my opinions of Darcy Williams affect my life any longer.

***

Sometimes, even if you feel completely and utterly prepared, even if you feel completely in control of a situation, you can be blindsided. Something can happen that you never could have predicted, and it brings everything crashing down around you.

Today was one of those days.

It started as a normal day. Will and I once again went back to being chatty and smiling, forgetting any previous conversations or awkwardness. Once again, we fetched coffee, did the photocopying, attended meetings. A normal day. Nothing unusual.

Lunchtime came, and Will went to go and buy a sandwich from the coffee shop just off the foyer. I started to eat my lunch while he was gone, enjoying a few minutes of peace and quiet while he was gone.

I heard the click of a pair of high-heels walking along the corridor, but didn't think anything of it; after all, our desk was next to the ladies' toilets, so it wasn't something particularly out of the ordinary.

At the clearing of a throat, however, I looked up and started. Darcy was standing there.

"Lizzy," she nodded stiffly, completely different from how she'd been acting the last time I'd seen her.

"Hi, Darcy," I said, forcing a smile. If she could make an effort to be civil? So could I. No matter how difficult it was. "Will's just getting some lunch, he shouldn't be long. You're, er, welcome to wait for him here, if you want?"

"Actually, I wanted to talk to you," she said, her words calm and measured.

"Oh!" Was not expecting that. "Of course, that should... be fine."

She had better be here to apologise, to explain what on earth she was thinking when she persuaded Charlie to leave Jane.

"May I?" she asked, indicating towards Will's chair. I nodded, still confused as to what was going on.

She took a deep breath as she sat down, preparing herself to speak, and paused for a few seconds, gathering her thoughts.

"I have been... thinking a lot since I met you. There is something about you that I haven't been able to work out." She paused again, before recomposing herself back into her usual haughty self. I got the impression that she was about to give a rehearsed speech.

"Gender has never held any significance to me in choosing a partner; there are more important things in a relationship. I have, for reasons that I cannot explain, been attracted to you from the moment I met you. The behaviour of your mother, your youngest brother, and your poor financial conditions make you the kind of person that I would normally never associate with, let alone dream of something even resembling a friendship. However, against my better judgement, despite all of you and your family's shortcomings, the feelings I have for you have forced me to come to the conclusion that I am in love with you."

What.

Did – did Darcy Williams just... confess her love for me?

This... no. Just, no. This wasn't happening. I would have known, surely? Had some indication, something other than glares and hatred? How could she... how could she know that she loves me? My brain couldn't work its way around it; this wasn't something that was possible.

"So? Do you feel the same way about me?"

"No!" We both jumped at my outburst, and I'd spoken far too quickly. But did she... did she seriously think that there was any possibility that I might feel the same way about her? How did she even think that she felt that way about me?!

She looked at me incredulously. "You – you don't? But I thought that-"

"What? You thought what?" I spat out. "I have never given you even the slightest hint to indicate that I might perhaps have feelings for you, and that's because they're not there. I thought... I thought that we shared a mutual dislike. Obviously, I was wrong."

"And may I ask why you don't return these feelings?" she asked, her eyes like lasers.

"You actually have to ask?!" I scoffed. I didn't hold back. All that anger, all that rage that I'd been holding back ever since I first met her let loose in one go. "You're rude, arrogant, conceited; even now you can't tell me that you lo-- that you care for me without simultaneously insulting me and my family. You ruined the happiness of my sister, my sister who I love so much, and you *ruined everything* because of your own selfishness! You couldn't bear to see someone else happy, so you just had to go and squash it, because God forbid someone have a better life than you!" At some point I'd stood up. I paused, breathing heavily. "Well? Do you deny it?!"

Her voice was quiet, filled with barely contained fury. "I can't deny it. But it was not all my doing. Charlie was unsure about what to do with the relationship. I simply pointed him in a particular direction. And what choice did I have? She had no significant feelings for him, and it was made very clear by your mother that Jane would be benefitting financially from the arrangement. You would have done the same in my situation."

With a pang, I remembered Charlotte's words to me the previous night, but that didn't mean that I could forgive Darcy for what she'd done. If that was her only explanation, the closest thing she had to an apology? It wasn't good enough.

"George Wickham," I said, my voice now dangerously low. "Nothing excuses what you did to him. You ruined his entire life over some... petty childhood grudge."

My anger only grew as she laughed humourlessly. "So, you just take his word at face value? Here's some news for you: People lie. People can be manipulative. The world isn't just made up of nice people who are good and mean people who are bad. Grow up." By now she was standing up as well, towering over me.

There were a few seconds of silence as her words hung in the air. She showed no sign of wanting to take them back.

"Do you remember when I first visited you and Charlie in Netherfield Court?" I asked, suddenly filled with a strange sense of calm.

"Of course I do," she said, clearly wondering where this was going.

"You told me to have some respect. Now here's some news for *you*: respect goes two ways. I will respect you when you start to respect me." My voice started to get louder once more. "You come in here, insult my family, insult me, patronise me, confess to *ruining the happiness of my sister and my friend* and have the nerve to say that you are in love with me!"

I leant forwards over the desk, glaring daggers into her eyes. For the first time since she came in here, she looked nervous.

"That, Darcy, is why you are the last woman on earth that I could *ever* fall in love with."

Chapter 19: Reconciliation

Will reappeared from his abnormally long trip to the canteen just as Darcy was leaving. At first she stormed off, but halfway down the corridor her posture sank in on itself and she ran the rest of the way, running into Will at the end. He stopped her and I couldn't hear what they were saying, but he didn't seem at all surprised to see her. He had his hands on her shoulders and had angled his face so that he could try to look her in the eye, even if she was trying to look anywhere but.

I couldn't hear what they were saying, and I didn't even pretend not to watch as she stepped back, taking a moment to compose herself. She tossed her hair out of her eyes, rolling her shoulders back and adjusting her suit jacket before stepping purposefully out of the office building.

Will turned once she'd left and saw me sitting at our desk, bewildered.

"Lizzy, what happened?" he asked as he strode down the corridor towards me, both concerned and shocked.

"You knew," I said flatly, struggling to summon much emotion. "You knew she was coming to talk to me. That's why you left, that's why you were gone for so long."

He ran his hands through his hair, leaning backwards in his seat. "I did. I didn't know exactly what she wanted to talk to you about. I still don't, though I can guess. I just reckoned that she wanted to... reconcile. Have a fresh start. Make things better."

"You were wrong," I said, though it lacked any bite. He looked too hopeful and optimistic for me to really be angry at him. "What she told you, about me – it was that she..." My mouth went dry at the thought; my brain was completely refusing to supply the words. "She loves me. Is in love with me. Or so she says."

Will immediately buried his face in his hands. "Oh, god..." he groaned. He dropped his arms to the table. "Lizzy, I'm... I'm sorry. She wanted to talk to you, and I said that maybe she should just... try and be friends. Settle any differences. I told her that telling you all of that would be too much, and she..." his voice had started to tighten. He took a few deep breaths, composing himself. "I know that you don't like her, and I know that she probably hasn't done anything in the last hour to change that. But please... if you could at least find some way of seeing that she's not the person you think she is? That she can redeem herself somehow? I'm not saying that you need to... return her feelings, not at all, I would never push you to do that, or even be her friend. I just... could you find it in you to forgive her?"

His pleading eyes almost persuaded me to say yes, that for the sake of our friendship, I would be able to do that. But I couldn't bring myself to.

"I'm sorry Will," I whispered, choking up as I spoke, "but I can't. You... you told me about Charlie. About how Darcy... encouraged him away from a relationship that was bad for him. That relationship wasn't bad. It was one of the most wonderful relationships I've ever seen. The girl was my sister, and Charlie's feelings were returned in full force from her. She was heartbroken when he left, and I don't know if I'll ever get my sister back as she was before. She is so, so dear to me, and Darcy... Darcy ruined her happiness, ruined the best thing that's ever happened to her, without as much as a second thought." I shook my head, tears now spilling out of my eyes. "That's why I can't forgive her."

Will looked at me gravely, sadness filling his eyes. "I understand," he said, and I could tell that it hurt him to say it.

I drifted through the rest of the day, not smiling, barely talking, unable to take in anything that was happening around me. Will walked me to the Tube station, worried that I was too out of it to make it safely there by myself.

"I'll see you tomorrow," he said softly at the entrance. "I would go home with you, make sure you're okay and everything, but I think I should probably see how Darcy's doing."

I nodded, still numb.

He rested his hand on my shoulder in what I think was meant as a sign of comfort. "See you in the morning."

I was still in a daze as I walked through the front door, and for a second I wondered why Charlotte was sitting waiting for me, looking so nervous, before remembering our argument the previous night.

"Hi," she said, slightly on edge.

"Charlotte, I..." The words came flooding out all at once. "I'm so sorry, I was such an idiot! You were right, you're always right, I was being stupid and a hypocrite and I hated that we were fighting. I'm so, so sorry, and I will do anything to fix it."

For an awful moment as we stood there, just looking at each other, I thought that she might still be angry, that I'd screwed everything up for good. As Charlotte pulled me into a gripping hug, though, I felt the worries and panic wash right off me.

"I hated fighting too," she said over my shoulder. She let go and looked me straight in the eye. "Everything is forgiven. I know that you know what upset me, and I know that it won't happen again. How about you cook us dinner and we just... forget about it?"

I smiled for the first time since the morning. "Of course! Curry night?"

"Sounds perfect!" Charlotte said, smiling back at me as I started to get the saucepan out of the cupboard. "How was your day?"

I shuddered involuntarily, busying myself with getting things out for dinner. "It, er, wasn't bad."

"You're a terrible liar, Lizzy Bennet," Charlotte sighed, but she didn't push me for any more details, instead joining me and chattering on about a new TV show she was watching. It was easy to distract myself now that I had mindless conversation and something to do with my hands. The more we talked about whatever came into our minds, be it comments on the latest political news or trying to work out whether or not our out-of-date milk was still safe to drink, the more I could feel myself relax, the stresses of the day not disappearing but certainly finding somewhere to hibernate.

We had just finished dinner and were washing up the dishes when my phone buzzed on the table. Quickly drying and putting away the plate in my hand, I went over to check it.

1 new message from Darcy Williams

She had better have something good to say for herself.

"Anything interesting?" Charlotte asked from the kitchen sink.

"Nothing," I said vaguely, pocketing my phone. Darcy could wait.

As much as I wanted to put it out of my mind, the thought of the message left on my phone bounced around the back of my brain until I gave in to temptation. I made up a pathetic excuse that I know Charlotte saw straight through and shut myself in my room, taking a few deep breaths before taking out my phone and opening the message.

> *Darcy Williams: Lizzy, I know that you don't want to hear from me right now and I understand if you do not respond to this. However, I believe that we could perhaps benefit from a conversation together. Rest assured that I will not bring up the feelings that I spoke of earlier unless you wish to discuss them. Rather, I feel that I do need to set the record straight on at least one count, and perhaps also owe you an apology of sorts. Of course, you are not obliged to agree to this. Yours, Darcy.*

I lay back on my pillow, contemplating what she'd said.

It seemed like it might not be a bad idea. We certainly did need to find a way to agree on at least some things, and she seemed to be aware that, perhaps, she hadn't behaved quite as she should have done. However, there were two major flaws in this plan. The first was that for us to have a conversation I would have to see her again, and the second was that if I saw her I would have to be civil to her. Neither of them seemed like particularly attractive prospects.

Meeting her would probably, in the long run, be a good thing, but I didn't want to see her for at least a few days. Things had changed so fast, and I was feeling the need to take a few days to let things sink in and have some breathing space – breathing space that it looked like she was willing to give me.

It took me several attempts to compose a reply, but eventually I managed it.

> *Lizzy Bennet: I think it would be a good idea if we talked some things through, but I need a few days. I hope you understand. I could meet you on Saturday afternoon in Hyde Park?*
>
> Only a few seconds passed before I got a reply.
>
> *Darcy Williams: Okay. I will meet you at two o'clock by the Peter Pan statue? And don't worry. I won't try to be in contact from now until then.*
>
> *Lizzy Bennet: Thank you. I will see you on Saturday.*

That hadn't been so bad. We'd managed to communicate efficiently and civilly using virtual means, so now all we needed to do was somehow manage to transfer that to an actual conversation.

My phone buzzed once more and I briefly panicked, thinking that she'd already broken her promise to leave me alone until Saturday, before seeing that it was from Will.

Will Fitts: If Darcy's improved mood is anything to go by you two seem to have reached some sort of agreement! I'm glad.

Lizzy Bennet: Yeah, Darcy invited me to meet with her to talk things through. I agreed, it seemed like a good idea.

Will Fitts: I know! Darcy got me to check her message about three times before she sent it. I didn't change anything, but she was really worried about it coming off wrong.

I couldn't really think of what to say to this; clearly Darcy put more thought into what she did and said than I'd previously assumed, but I didn't think saying that to Will would be a great idea. I was saved, however, by Will sending another message.

Will Fitts: How are you holding up?

Lizzy Bennet: Feeling a fair bit better now, thanks :) I'll see you tomorrow?

Will Fitts: I'm glad to hear it. See you tomorrow!

Three days. Three days, then Saturday.

It couldn't come soon enough, and it couldn't be far enough away. All I knew was that it would be sure to change everything.

Chapter 20: Never Growing Up

I woke up on Saturday to the bright end-of-August sun beaming through the thin curtains. I could feel a strange ball of anxiety in my stomach as soon as I woke up but it took me a few moments to remember why; I was meeting Darcy today.

I lay in bed for half an hour or so, contemplating what I should say to her. I didn't want to antagonise her at all; I just wanted answers, and if I upset her they would never come. Making a mental list of what I wanted to know helped me to organise my thoughts, and get ready for the inevitable awkwardness that would be happening in the afternoon.

I lay in bed until I heard Charlotte moving around. Stretching and rolling out the stiffness in my shoulders as I got up, I went to the kitchen to get breakfast.

"Morning!" I said, sounding chirpier than I felt. "How are you this morning?"

"I'm very well!" she replied as the kettle boiled and she began to make some tea. "I'm going out with Colin today. We're, um, going round the museums." She looked at me cautiously, as if expecting me to make a comment. When I smiled, however, she relaxed, and continued to get breakfast out.

"I'm really happy that you two are going out," I said, surprised at how much I meant it. "You're really good for each other."

She started turning a subtle shade of pink. "You think so? I mean, obviously I think so, that's why I'm going out with him... we just kind of complement each other, you know? He gets excited about the mundane things in life, he's eccentric. I like that."

She shook herself slightly, recomposing herself. "What about you? Any exciting plans for the day?"

I paused in my tracks. I hadn't told Charlotte about Darcy – at least, nothing past her being Will's flatmate. I hadn't told her about Jane, and I had certainly not told her about Darcy's... confession. I had an awful feeling that if I did, her response would be 'I told you so'.

"I'm going to Hyde Park this afternoon," I settled for. After all, it was the truth.

"Lovely day for it! Meeting anyone there?"

I was silent for too long. Charlotte whipped around, her face excited at the notion of some sort of secret. "You are meeting someone! Someone special? Are you – are you seeing someone? And haven't told me?!"

"No!" I quickly interrupted, desperate to stop the look of betrayal that was rapidly falling over Charlotte's face. "I, um..." Now I had to tell her. "I'm actually meeting Darcy. You know. Darcy Williams." I wish I could have sounded less embarrassed.

"Of course I know!" Now she was looking positively gleeful. "You are seeing someone! I knew it!"

What?!

"No, Charlotte, I'm not seeing someone! Not in any sense other than the literal," I said, firmly putting the record straight.

She looked utterly confused now. "Why on earth are you meeting up with Darcy if you're not dating her?"

Was I the only person who understood that I didn't like Darcy? Did I miss some sort of memo?

I sighed heavily, exasperated. "If you must know, we're... talking things through. Setting the record straight. We're going to have to be civil to each other at some point, so we're... clearing the air. A fresh start."

Charlotte nodded, looking far too much like a proud parent for my liking. "That's brilliant, I really hope you find some common ground! Do you have some idea of what kind of things you're going to talk about?"

Yes, but I hadn't told Charlotte about them.

"Um, sort of. I have some general ideas."

"What sort of--" I was saved by Charlotte's phone going off. "Colin's outside!" she said, a huge grin suddenly bursting onto her face. "I'll see you later!" She gave me a quick one-armed hug before running off to go downstairs.

Now I had to keep myself occupied for a few hours. Easier said than done.

I decided to call home. The last time I had spoken to anyone at home for anything more than a couple of exchanged messages had been when Dad called me to see if I was with Jane. If nothing else, it would distract me from the right here, right now.

The phone rang a few times before it was picked up with a sullen "Hullo?"

"Mark? It's Lizzy!" I said, trying and probably failing to sound cheerful.

"Oh, hey Lizzy," he said, sounding marginally perkier. "Did you want to speak to Jane?"

I shook my head, but remembered that he couldn't see me. "No, not particularly; I just fancied ringing home, seeing how you were all doing! How are you?"

"I'm okay. Better since Sander became friends with your friend George, because he's stopped bugging me all the time. Now he only bugs me some of the time. And he has a job now, so he's out a lot more."

"Sounds good! What about you, anything going on with you?"

He paused for a moment before continuing, his voice having an edge of trepidation. "I... I was thinking about maybe applying for uni next year. Take this year as a gap year, but a proper one, not like Jane's gap years. What do you think?"

"I think that sounds great!" I enthused. Going to university was by no means an expected thing in our family, but I was glad that Mark was considering it. "What did you want to study, psychology?"

"Yeah," he said, sounding surprised that I'd guessed. "How did you know that?"

I laughed slightly. "It's all you ever talked about while you were doing your A levels, makes sense you'd want to study it! If you need any help with your application, you know where to find me!"

"Thanks Lizzy," he said shyly. "Do you want to speak to anyone else? Sander's at work and Jane's off volunteering somewhere new, but Mum and Dad are about."

"Is Dad there?" The thought of having to get through a conversation with Mum right now made my head hurt, but I was sure that talking to Dad would be comforting.

"I'll go find him," Mark said, pausing before adding, "Thanks for calling, Lizzy. I miss you."

"I miss you too!" I replied. Mark was the one of my siblings who I worried about the most. He struggled to see eye to eye with the other two, whereas we often saw kindred spirits in each other.

"Hi Lizzy!" My dad had taken over the phone.

"Hi Dad!" I replied, again forcing more enthusiasm than I was actually feeling. "How are you?"

"I'm alright," he said, without much feeling. "I've been trying out some new recipes. Your mother's still recovering from Charlie leaving, and so I've been keeping to myself, out of her way."

It said a lot about my mother that she was more upset at one daughter's boyfriend of six weeks leaving than she was at her other daughter moving away.

"How have you been, anyway?"

"I've been good, Dad, work's going really well."

"And how are you really?" Of all my family, even Jane, my dad was the best one at spotting when I was hiding something.

"Honestly, I am... I am okay. Things have been fairly eventful here and I've been trying not to let it get on top of me, but it feels a bit like I'm... I don't know, like I'm fighting all the time? I'm just... tired."

He sighed, obviously worried. "Will you be okay, Lizzy? And answer me honestly, don't try and say what you think I want to hear."

"Honestly, Dad, things are on the way up. I'm doing pretty well overall; I'll be fine. I've been worse."

"Good." He didn't sound convinced, but I'd take it. "I'm afraid I have to head off now. I'll speak to you soon?"

"Yeah, Dad," I said. "Love you."

"Love you too Betts."

I took a deep breath as I hung up, wiping away a tear that I hadn't realised was there. It would be so easy just to go home, pretend that none of this happened and just be safe, but I couldn't do that. Instead? I had to go to Kensington Gardens.

I left early and sauntered as slowly as I could through Hyde Park, reaching the Peter Pan statue ten minutes early, but Darcy was already there. She was sat on a bench with her back to the lake, studiously gazing up at the statue. I slowly approached her and sat down at the other end of the bench, not saying anything.

We sat in silence for a few minutes, neither of us acknowledging the others' presence, before one of us spoke.

"J. M. Barrie never liked the statue," Darcy said, breaking the quiet. "He said that--"

"--he said that you couldn't see the devil in Peter," I finished. "I know."

A few more moments of silence. "He never grew up," I continued, the words feeling oddly heavy in my mouth. "He never learnt, never understood. That's why dying is an awfully big adventure. Why he killed without a second thought. He didn't know what death was. To him, everything was a game."

We still weren't looking at each other, both of our gazes fixated on the statue in front of us.

Yet more quiet.

"I envy him," Darcy said eventually, her voice so quiet that I had to strain to hear it. "He never knew what pain or death truly were."

I turned to look at her, knowing that she was thinking about her parents. She didn't meet my gaze, still staring resolutely ahead, but for the first time I felt like I was actually seeing her.

"What happened?"

Now her head whipped round, her face puzzled at my question.

"What do you mean?"

I felt the urge to look away, to fiddle with a loose thread on my jeans, to kick the ground, but I held the eye contact.

"With George Wickham. What happened?"

She turned away again, but I was glad; the atmosphere between us was too charged to keep it up much longer. She sat, again in silence, one hand gripping the other so tight that her brown skin was turning white.

"George Wickham was one of my closest friends growing up," she said, her eyes fixated on the ground a few metres in front of her. "My father was his godfather, and he was always around. He'd go on holiday with us, he'd come for dinner a few times a week. He was like another brother to us. Jordan, especially, looked up to him a lot. Jordan's only a couple of years younger than George, and honestly he was much closer to George than he ever was to me."

She swallowed, blinking heavily before continuing. "My parents died four years ago, in a car accident. I... it was the hardest part of my life. I had just graduated with my masters, and here I was, in charge of all the family's finances and possessions and guardian of a fifteen-year-old brother. Honestly, Jordan was the only thing that kept me going most days. George was wonderful, as well; he was over every day, making sure we were alright.

"My parents had specified in their will that, upon acceptance to a university, George was to be given fifteen thousand pounds, annually, from his first to his final year, paying for his tuition fees and covering the majority of his living costs. George got into Manchester University, and so I arranged to transfer nine thousand pounds from my parents' old account to the university in September, and to transfer the rest, two thousand pounds per term, to George's account. He, however, refused. He wanted to be able to handle his own finances, to be able to sort out his own money. He said that he didn't want the burden on me, that I could transfer him forty-five thousand pounds in one go and he would ensure that the university would be paid what they were due, and he would have just enough money to live off."

Darcy's back was slowly becoming more rigid as she tensed up, her voice almost unwavering as she told her story. So far, this was matching with everything George had told me. The biggest change was that, in this version, Darcy and George had once been friends.

"You have to understand, George had been like a brother to me. I had no reason to believe that he would do anything with the money except what it was originally intended for. So, I gave him the money. All in one go, I transferred the money over to his account. Forty-five thousand pounds." She scoffed slightly at herself. "How could I have been so stupid? I should at least have said I'd give him fifteen thousand each year, but no! Everything was still so… fresh, so new, and I just… didn't have the energy for a discussion. So, I agreed. I thought I was doing us both a favour."

She put her head in her hands. "I… You know, I almost pity him. I certainly blame myself, at least in part. He had not, by any means, had an easy life, and perhaps when he needed our support the most, all he got was cash. Maybe if I'd… maybe if I'd stuck with him, tried to get through to him, this wouldn't have all happened.

"He came to stay with us at Christmas that year, and in the evening, he explained to me that… he said he'd spent all the money. All forty-five thousand. Yes, nine thousand had gone to the university, and he'd spent some on rent and food. But the rest… he wouldn't say what he'd done with the rest. He was so desperate, though. He had no money, none at all, and quite frankly the amount we'd given him made a miniscule difference in our bank balance. I said that I'd give him the money, as we'd originally planned, term by term. He could have another two thousand pounds, and at Easter he would get another two thousand. As long as he passed his first year of university, he would get the nine thousand for the following year.

"The day after New Years', however, he came back. Asking for more money. He'd spent it again. I refused. There was a limit to my charity, and I felt that he was taking advantage of me. Lots of... unkind words were exchanged that night. Jordan heard the whole thing, and sided with George; he didn't speak to me for weeks after that.

"We didn't hear from George for months. I assumed that he'd gone somewhere else, found another way to get what he wanted, and frankly I wasn't in a fit state to care. Although, of course, I missed him, and wished we hadn't parted on such terms, I was glad that it was one less thing for me to deal with. I – well, I – looking back, I was depressed. My parents were gone. I'd been thrown into a new life filled with responsibilities, suddenly the owner of a company, of multiple properties, and I had to somehow be a parent to my teenage brother. There wasn't much space to worry about my own mental health."

I saw that her hands had started shaking. This was obviously something that she still didn't talk about, perhaps not to anyone.

"Jordan was growing up, and started going out with his friends more. I tried to keep track of where he was going, who he was going with, but as long as he was happy I didn't dig deeper. I thought that just letting him do his own thing would be the best thing. The last thing I needed was for him to resent me, and I thought that trying to control him would do just that.

"He had an allowance, but over the summer he started asking for money and I gave it to him. I wasn't around much, and I didn't want him to be missing out on having fun with his friends because he didn't have the money. We both went to private school, separate boys and girls, and so money was an expectation; yes, some of our classmates were given allowances, if rather generous ones, but many also just had to ask their parents and money would be given.

"At first it was twenty pounds here and there for dinners, trips to the cinema. Then it started becoming fifty pounds for a train somewhere. Then a few hundred for weekends away that became more and more frequent. When he first asked me for a thousand pounds, I knew I had to intervene. We sat down, I asked why he needed the money, and he kept insisting that he was going away with his friends but they were flying so it would cost a lot more this time. It was only when I went to call one of his friends that the truth came out."

She took several deep, shuddering breaths. I still watched from a few feet away, a silent observer.

"He was giving the money to George. Almost all of it. George had... contacted him. Started spending time with him, but told him to lie to me, knowing that I would want to keep tabs on what was going on. George had... George had completely alienated Jordan, convinced him that I didn't care and that I was too busy to really spend time with him. I don't think it took much to convince Jordan to stop spending time with his own friends in order to go out with George more often; George was like an older brother. He was cool, and he... he did things, and let Jordan go to places that no one that was any good for him would.

"George had been gambling, drinking, and smoking far more than just tobacco. I think – no, I know that it had only really started after my parents died. He had no one to turn to, so he found his solace elsewhere. He'd somehow convinced Jordan that the only way they could remain friends was if Jordan gave him money, that Jordan was somehow obligated to provide it."

Although her voice had stopped shaking, there were a few tears on her cheeks.

"Friendships can be just as abusive as relationships. George was… *is* manipulative and calculating. He'd become the only thing in Jordan's worldview, and again I blame myself for not seeing it sooner. Jordan had no idea how much he'd been played and manipulated; he kept telling me that George would pay him back as soon as he got the money, and George had made sure that he kept a strict account, and George was the only person who really understood him.

"I couldn't believe it. I still can't quite believe it. My sixteen-year-old brother, caught up in George Wickham's mess? The only thing I could do was ground him indefinitely, only letting him go out when I knew that he was with friends and I knew exactly where they were going. Just thinking of the things he might have been exposed to… I made him promise a lot of things to me. It was… I will never forget that conversation. I made him swear that he hadn't done anything illegal himself; that he hadn't had any drinks, that he hadn't smoked anything, that he hadn't bet on anything. He admitted that he'd had the occasional drink, but never more than one, but that was it. I believed him, and still do. But that whole incident damaged our relationship almost irreparably. It took over a year for us to really get along again, and that was mostly thanks to Will."

She sat back, turning to look at me at last.

"There you go. There's the story of George Wickham. Happy?"

My head was spinning; this did not match up, at all, with my friend. Yes, people can change, but there was no way this could be the same person. Surely?

"The George Wickham I know... is very different from the one you described," I said, trying to put it as tactfully as I could.

Darcy raised an eyebrow. "Really? Describe him to me."

"Well, he's... hard-working, honest. A bit of a player and a flirt, but he's a good friend. He listens well. We agree on almost everything, and we get along brilliantly. When he's not chatting me up."

"Tell me how that differs from the George Wickham I described."

I looked at her quizzically. "What do you mean?"

"The person you described is your ideal friend. He gets on with you. He agrees with you. He listens to you. George Wickham is a mirror. He looks at what a person wants, and he gives it to them."

I shook my head. "No, that can't be right. The first time he met me, he was flirting with me. He was trying to hit on me."

She shrugged. "He got it wrong. Happens to the best of us. He saw you, and misjudged it, but he got it right the second time, didn't he? Apologised with enough sincerity for you to believe him but not too much that you felt he was annoyed at you. Made a genuine attempt to get to know you, to get to know more about you than your sexuality. Took an interest in your interests."

I sat there, stunned. "How do you know all that?" I whispered.

"Because I know George Wickham," she replied, her tone matter-of-fact.

Everything was starting to make sense. George's refusal to show up when Darcy was there, his manner when we first met... it all fit with Darcy's story. And honestly? Right now, George had more of an incentive to lie than Darcy did.

I was almost surprised at how calm I was at this revelation. Yes, of course I was angry; angry at George for lying, angry at Darcy for hiding the truth from me for so long (although I understood why), but I was mostly angry at myself. If I was so good at seeing who a person is, who they really are, in a matter of seconds... how did I miss this?

I glanced over at Darcy again, expecting her to look smug, but if anything she looked sorry for me. As if she hadn't wanted to be the one to break the news of the truth about my friend.

Or ex-friend, I suppose. I wasn't planning on maintaining contact.

"That's awful," I said eventually. "I... I'm so sorry that you and your brother had to go through that. All of it."

It didn't really feel like the right thing to say, but I couldn't think of anything better.

"Thank you," Darcy murmured, meeting my gaze, and I could tell how much she was swallowing her pride to say that.

So now I knew the truth about George Wickham. It was certainly not what I expected, but I had to admit that, in this case, Darcy was certainly not in the wrong. I had a feeling, however, that that was not going to be the case for the next thing I wanted to talk about.

"Jane and Charlie," I started, Darcy's head whipping round at the rapid change of subject. "You broke them up. And," I saw that she was about to start speaking, "We're here to talk things through. Nothing else. As much as I sympathise with you about George – and I really, really do – I'm putting that to one side for now. I want – no, I need – to know why on *earth* you interfered with their relationship."

Any trace of tenderness was instantly gone, as Darcy snapped up to the defence.

"I did what I thought was right. You cannot criticise me for that."

"Yes, I can!" I said, exasperated, desperately trying to make her see sense. "Jane and Charlie's business is just that: *their business*. There are only two instances when anyone else is allowed to interfere: one, when we're asked to; and two, if we genuinely think that one of them is unsafe."

"I was concerned for my friend's feelings," she said, coldly. "He was fast falling in love with a woman who didn't love him back, and her circumstances were less than ideal. I won't repeat what I said the other day on the matter; you heard me then."

"And did you ever bother to find out how Jane felt?!" I asked, almost shouting now.

There was no answer.

"Exactly. You had no idea how Jane felt, because you never bothered to find out. You never bothered to get to know her. You spent a week living in the same house as her, and never even made the slightest effort. Did you even have a conversation with her? You saw that she was acting as if she didn't really want to talk to Charlie at Charlotte's birthday, but did it ever occur to you that perhaps she was embarrassed at our mother's behaviour? That she wasn't sure how to talk to Charlie about anything that wasn't *directly related* to either making the world a better place, or fluffy animals?! Jane's feelings for Charlie were just as sincere as his were for her. I can guarantee you that."

She turned back to looking at the statue, sitting up and throwing her shoulders back haughtily. "Charlie didn't take much persuasion to leave. His feelings for Jane can't have been as strong as we perhaps thought."

I barked a humourless laugh. "That's complete bull, and you know it. Just a minute ago, you were saying how much Charlie loved her and you wanted to spare him the heartbreak, and now you're saying that he can't have been that attached after all?!" I threw my hands up in the air in despair. "I'm not going to get through to you, am I? You're too proud to admit that perhaps, you might have done something wrong, so now my sister and your best friend are going to have to live with the consequences."

I looked at her, willing her to turn around to face me, breathing heavily.

"Is this the end of our conversation then?" she asked, her voice cutting.

I threw myself back against the bench, looking forward once more. "There's one more thing I want to ask you about."

She turned to look at me, genuinely puzzled. "What's that?"

I took a deep breath. "How did you... why do you say you're in love with me?"

She looked taken aback; she hadn't been expecting the question.

"Isn't it one of those things that you just... know?"

I swivelled round so I was sitting sideways, facing her. I was determined to make her see reason.

"You don't know anything about me. You barely know me. How can you... how can you come to the conclusion that you're in love?"

"But I do know you," she said, her voice tender and vulnerable. "You're passionate. You're caring. You're loyal. You're moral. You're logical. You're brave. You're intelligent. You're strong."

"I'm not strong," I said, my voice barely a whisper, cracking dangerously. "I'm not strong at all."

"But don't you see?" she leant forward, narrowing the gap between us for the first time since we had arrived at the park. "That's what – that's what makes you so strong."

Those piercing eyes, which had unnerved me from the day I met her, met mine which were on the verge of tears. "I still don't understand," I said, voice wavering. "I thought... I thought those things didn't matter to you."

She smiled, and I realised that this was the first time I'd ever truly seen her do so. "Someone showed me that those things do matter. More than anything."

Our eyes were still locked and we were frozen still, breathing in unison, when I felt her hand brush against mine.

I jumped up as if burned, alert and shocked. I didn't know what to do. Apologise? Stay? Leave?

I went for the latter, instantly turning on my heel and walking as briskly as I could, not worrying about which direction I was going in.

"Lizzy, wait!"

I stopped, but didn't turn around.

"I'm sorry. That was… I shouldn't have done that. It was… it was unsuitable. To the situation."

I didn't say anything, but stayed where I was, standing stock still.

"Are we… are things better now? Are we getting somewhere?" She pleaded with me from where she was stood, not coming any closer.

I turned around, slowly.

"Things… things are getting better," I said, trying a smile.

"Good." She looked relieved, giving me a smile that was far wider than the situation called for. "I'll see you around."

I nodded. "See you around."

And I walked home, leaving Darcy Williams alone, on a bench, by the Peter Pan statue.

Chapter 21: The Top Floor

As the weeks went on, my new life started to finally settle down to something resembling normality. I went back to fetching coffee and photocopying, Charlotte started her new job, Will and I continued to be friends. Darcy was never mentioned except in passing mundanity – usually Will quickly ringing her to ask her to buy milk, or complaining that she hadn't done her washing up the evening before. He never asked me about what had happened when Darcy and I spoke; he had either gotten all the information he wanted from Darcy, or had decided not to pry.

It was very strange, having your best friend date your supervisor. Most of the time it was just in the background. Colin had yet to set foot in our flat, let along stay the night, so in my head I usually tried not to make a connection between Colin-Charlotte's-boyfriend and Colin-my-supervisor, or between Charlotte-Colin's-girlfriend and Charlotte-my-best-friend. Don't get me wrong, I was happy for both of them. I just hadn't quite got used to the thought of Charlotte's boyfriend being the rather eccentric man I shared offices with. They were, certainly, better together than anyone could have expected, but I still struggled to get it straight in my head.

Occasionally, however, it was unavoidable.

"Lizzy, may I have a word?" Colin asked me one morning. He had started calling me Lizzy after a very embarrassing incident when he called me Elizabeth and I didn't realise, and he kept calling my name until I eventually twigged. It had been so long since anyone had called me Elizabeth that I usually didn't respond.

"Of course," I said, putting aside the stapling I was doing for the fifth-floor offices.

He looked slightly embarrassed, rocking back and forth on his feet. "Well, as I'm sure you are aware, this weekend will mark a month since Charlotte and I first went out together, and I wanted to get her a gift. I wanted to know if you had any ideas."

Hmm. This would be an interesting conversation.

"Well, er, Colin, I think it might be nice if you got something that... represented your relationship. Maybe a reminder of a date you went on, or something that referenced an in-joke."

His whole body lit up at the thought, making him seem about three inches taller. "That's a wonderful idea! Such as a poster from a film we saw? Or a voucher for a restaurant we go to? Or a scrapbook of all our meetings so far?"

"Maybe something between the first two and the last one," I quickly intervened. "Maybe save the scrapbook idea for a whole year. But yes, something along those lines."

"Brilliant! I'll get thinking right away," he said, practically skipping off down to his office. "Oh, I forgot!" he called down from the end of the corridor. "Miss de Bourgh wants to see you as soon as possible!"

Hang on a second.

"Colin!" I called back. "What do you mean?"

"Miss de Bourgh would like you to go to her office! A very high honour indeed, I should say!"

You could put it that way. "Right now?"

"Yes, right now!"

This could either be very, very good or very, very bad.

I contemplated this prospect while I was stood in the lift, going all the way up to the top floor. I'd never met Catherine de Bourgh, but she had a fairly constant presence in my life as the one person that Colin talks about more than Charlotte. I couldn't imagine what she might want to talk to me about. Bosses of huge companies tended not to invite interns up to their office for a cup of tea and a chat.

As the lift went higher and higher, I could feel my nerves begin to itch. By all accounts, Catherine de Bourgh was a very domineering person, and she had an impressive influence. You could certainly feel her presence throughout the building, even though she rarely left her office.

I cautiously stepped out of the lift at the top floor, taking in the lavish furnishings and the patterned wallpapers. It felt like it was my first day all over again as I approached the secretary at her desk.

"Hello, I'm here to see Miss de Bourgh?" I said, trying to sound more confident than I felt. The secretary looked at me coldly over the top of her glasses, assessing me.

"Name?"

"Elizabeth Bennet."

She nodded, then went back to her computer. "Please take a seat."

I gingerly sat on the edge of one of the big armchairs, feeling underdressed in my high-street-store dress next to the designer décor. I held one hand down with the other, knowing that now was possibly the worst time to resurrect my habit of biting my nails.

There was a large antique clock on the wall across from me that ticked loudly, counting down the seconds. I watched the hands slowly make their way around the clock, occupying myself by doing the mental maths to work out how many degrees each hand moved in any particular time period. Maths had never been my best subject, but there was something oddly calming about running the numbers through my head.

After what the clock told me was only half an hour, my calculations were interrupted.

"Miss de Bourgh will see you now."

I stood up, smoothing down my skirt, and followed the secretary to Miss de Bourgh's office. My steps felt far too loud, even on the soft carpet, interrupting the air of mindfulness that the walls seemed to emit. We stopped abruptly at the end of corridor at a mahogany panelled door with a small gold plaque on it, announcing who was inside.

The secretary knocked three times.

"Enter." A carefully measured tone spoke from within the office. I hung back as the secretary opened the door.

"Elizabeth Bennet is here to see you," she said, before giving me a pointed look that clearly said that I should be going inside.

"Send her in. Thank you, Anne."

I slowly stepped inside the office, trying to hide my jump when the door clicked shut behind me. The room was enormous with wooden-panelled walls, one of which was lined with book cases. The desk was the same wood as the walls and the chairs were all large and coated in leather. The thing that was most out of place was the Mac computer on the desk; the rest of the room could have easily come straight out of a Dickens novel.

Even the woman sitting behind the desk blended in with the ambience of the room. Even sitting down, she seemed like an incredibly tall person, her presence reaching every crevice of the room. It was like seeing a monarch, seated upon her throne. She knew that she was superior. It wasn't something she thought, or an impression that she tried to give; it was simply a fact.

"Please take a seat, Miss Bennet," she said, every syllable carefully placed. I perched on one of the leather armchairs nearest to her desk, trying my best to look calm. She busied herself briefly, moving a few sheets of paper on her desk.

"I've had very good reports from Collins about you," she said, sounding impressed if grudgingly so. "He's been very pleased with everything you're doing so far. He says..." she referred back to the top sheet of paper. "He says you're a great asset to Rosings."

I wasn't sure what to say to that and I didn't really trust myself to speak, so I didn't make a sound.

"Well? What do you think about that?"

"Oh, I..." I stammered out. "I think it's very kind of him to say so." A diplomatic answer, though I say so myself.

"I meant, do you agree with him." Her voice had taken an odd edge.

I looked at her for a moment, trying to hide my bewilderment. "I, well, I try to do everything I can to, um, contribute to the company."

I could see by her face that she wasn't hugely impressed by my response, but couldn't see any reason to call me out on it.

"Tell me, Miss Bennet, are you familiar with Pemberley Publishing House?"

Immediately my brain transported me back almost three months to a beach in the south of France.

"I have heard of it, yes. And I've read quite a few of their publications. They're a relatively new company, is my understanding." I couldn't see where this was going, but I wasn't sure I liked it.

Miss de Bourgh placed her hands, fingers interlocked, very deliberately on the desk in front of her. I'm sure she would have leant forward had she not been dignity personified.

"A few days ago, I spoke to their head of recruitment. This time of year is a very busy time for them, and they're vastly understaffed. As you said, they're a relatively new company; there's a lot of money going around, but not quite enough to support an internship programme. As such, we have an unofficial agreement of sorts. In return for favours when I need them, Rosings' interns sometimes go to Pemberley for a few weeks when they're needed more there. Now is one of those times."

Now I could see where this was going. Couldn't say I liked it.

"Are you aware of Pemberley's history, Miss Bennet?"

I shook my head, my brain still reeling, before realising that a verbal answer was needed.

"No, I'm afraid I'm not."

"Pemberley used to be an imprint of Rosings. My cousin and I both worked for Rosings when our grandfather died, leaving us the company. We wanted different things for the company, so my cousin took the Pemberley imprint as his own and set it up as an independent publisher. When he unfortunately passed away a few years ago, the company was passed to my niece."

I nodded my understanding, thinking this all through. I amazed me how, even in the twenty-first century, companies were still passed through families like that. I suppose it made sense. If you'd spent your life working in the family business, then when your parents died it would make sense that it would go to you, and that you would take charge. While it was still a common model in small businesses, it hadn't occurred to me that it would happen on this scale. It would certainly explain the 'unofficial agreement'; when family interests were involved, all kinds of business rules and ideals were put to one side.

It took my brain a few moments to catch up with the rest of this explanation, however. According to what Miss de Bourgh was saying... that would imply that Darcy was her niece.

Was there anyone in this world who was not somehow connected to Darcy Williams?!

I was torn out of my thoughts as Miss de Bourgh continued.

"As I'm sure you've guessed by now, what I am asking is that you would consider spending perhaps four weeks at Pemberley, as an intern. Your wages would remain unchanged, as you would still be officially employed by Rosings, and you would gain invaluable experience in the field. You may be wondering why I am asking you to consider this, and there are two reasons why I would prefer to send you than Mr Fitts. Firstly, although you are both more than competent, I have received slightly better reports – from the office as a whole – on you. It seems Mr Fitts has a tendency to spend a lot of his time on the third floor. Secondly, I don't know if you're aware of this but Mr Fitts is close friends with my niece; it would be inappropriate for me to suggest that he work under her."

So she had no idea that I knew Darcy. Interesting.

She was still sitting still, her eyes analysing my every feature, storing the information away for future use. I don't think she took my silence as indecision, but she decided to act that way regardless.

"If you would be so kind as to give me your answer by the end of the week, if not earlier; ideally, you would start next Monday."

I nodded, glad to be given something that it was easy to agree to. "Of course, Miss de Bourgh. Thank you very much."

She didn't as much as move a muscle on her face as she dismissed me. I had barely stood up from my chair, however, when she stopped me.

"Miss Bennet," she said, still carefully placing every syllable, "do I gather that you and my niece have met?" Her shrewd eyes told me that she had deduced this from the things I had not said as much as the things that I had.

I thought for a moment, trying to pick the most suitable words. "Our paths have crossed," I settled for, mentally kicking myself afterwards. I'd made it sound like we were Tolkien characters.

"I see." There was still no change in her face, and I suddenly got the feeling that she knew a lot more than she was letting on. "I hope you know that you are very unlikely to be spending time with her during your time at Pemberley. Should you choose to go, of course."

I couldn't quite tell in which direction she was encouraging me in this statement, so I decided to take it as the one that best applied; that I shouldn't let the prospect of Darcy Williams influence my decision.

"Good day, Miss Bennet," she said, in a tone that left no room for argument – not that I was in any hurry to stay. I nodded my thanks and went straight for the lift back down the ground floor. I'd survived my first (hopefully not of many) experience with Catherine de Bourgh, and felt stronger for it. It wasn't hard to see how she'd become so successful; no one would dare refuse her anything. Just by sitting there, she'd managed to get me to seriously consider going to work with *Darcy*.

Despite what Miss de Bourgh said, Darcy really was the deciding factor. Working at Pemberley would be incredible. The pay and commute were the same, so I wouldn't have to worry about that, and I'd get to see a whole new side of publishing: the small, independent publishers, who stood in complete contrast to the grandeur of Rosings, while still being incredibly successful. I wouldn't lose my internship here at Rosings but it would add so much to my experience and knowledge of the field that it really was a no-brainer.

Except for Darcy.

I knew that it was unlikely that I'd ever have to really see her, but she'd always be... there. There would always be that possibility of her just appearing, and there would be nothing I could do about it. My feelings towards her had been a lot less cold in recent weeks, and I certainly understood her a lot more now that I knew more about George Wickham. His actions had obviously had a profound impact on Darcy, big enough that both of them in their own ways tried to hide what had happened. But that didn't change what she did to Jane. Yes, perhaps I understood her better: her need to protect her friends, her want to keep those close to her safe. But that didn't mean that what she did was okay, or that I was ready to put it all behind me.

Forgive and forget, they say. I was sure, by this point, that I'd almost completely forgiven Darcy. I wasn't going to hold her actions against her. That didn't mean, though, that I could forget.

One thing was for sure; I would have a lot to think about. The prospect of Pemberley was on the horizon. All I had to do now was have the confidence to reach out and take it.

Chapter 22: Will

"What did Iceberg want with you this afternoon?" Will asked through a mouthful of spaghetti, perched at my kitchen counter.

"Don't call her that," I said, gently chiding him for the nickname he'd given our boss a few weeks ago. I now corrected him out of habit, rather than with any sincerity. "She wanted to ask if I'd transfer to Pemberley for a few weeks."

Will was suddenly alert, turning slightly so that he could face me as I busied myself in my dinner. "What did you say?"

I shrugged, trying to maintain an air of nonchalance. "I said I'd think about it. Or rather, she told me to think about it and get back to her by the end of the week. There wasn't much talking done on my part."

He looked at me expectantly for a few seconds more as I pretended not to notice. "Well? What are you *going* to say?"

I set down my fork and leant back in my chair. "I don't know. Working at Pemberley, even for just a few weeks, would be brilliant. It's much more the kind of company that I'd like to work for eventually. I just... I'm not sure."

"Why not?"

"You know why not."

"Yes, but I want to hear you say it."

"I'm scared, okay?" I ran my hands through my hair. "I'm scared... I'm scared that things will be weird.

Really weird. Yes, we probably won't be working together at all but she'll be around, and it's a smaller office than Rosings; it will be much harder to avoid her." I laughed slightly to myself. "You know, the whole thing's kind of ironic. She asked me instead of you because apparently it would be inappropriate for you to work for your flatmate. Because I'm such an appropriate choice. Also, she said you waste too much time on the third floor."

My distraction tactic worked. Will went bright red and started spinning his fork round in his spaghetti.

"What's all that about," I said playfully, gently nudging his arm.

He murmured something under his breath.

"Sorry, I didn't quite catch that!" I sang, teasing. "Come on, you get to grill me on girl stuff. That goes both ways."

"There's no one in particular," he said defensively. "It's just... they like me. They like spending time with me. And it's not like when we're downstairs, and if you're idle for more than thirty seconds Colin appears with a whole new list of things to do. Is that so bad?"

"No," I said, shaking my head, surprised at how personally he'd taken my question.

"Can we go back to you and Darcy now?" he asked quietly, and he sounded so dejected that I agreed.

"Okay. Back to Pemberley."

"Why are you so scared of her?" he asked, his eyes searching desperately.

"I'm not scared of her," I said, painfully aware that I was sounding like a child. "I'm just... scared of the unknown. Scared of what might happen."

We sat in quiet, each concentrating on our own dinner to avoid conversation. I had yet to discuss mine and Darcy's conversation with anyone, even Charlotte, but it felt like I needed to bring it up now. I could tell that Will was waiting for me to say something, and I didn't blame him. I didn't have a history of reacting well when it came to surprise Darcy conversation.

"Did you know that Darcy's secretly a hopeless romantic?" I started, laughing as Will snorted into his glass.

"Of course! Don't act like that's brand new information," he said, chuckling. "She likes to think that she sees love as some sort of exact science, it's either there or not. Just as you think she's some kind of ice queen… bam, here comes Shakespeare with more sonnets!"

"Yeah," I laughed, glad that he also saw the humourous side. "Will, I – I don't know what to do. She says she's in love with me, and I think that even if she's not then she thinks she is, which in this situation equates to the same thing. I feel like we reached some sort of strange compromise when we last spoke, and… and I guess I don't want to jeopardise that."

"Lizzy, if I ask you something will you promise to answer me honestly?" Will asked, his face heavy.

Taking a deep breath, knowing what was coming, I nodded.

"How do you feel about Darcy now?"

I took a moment to plan what I was going to say before I said it. As much as I knew that Will wouldn't repeat this to Darcy, I still wanted to get it right first time.

"I… I don't know. I can sort of see why she did what she did to Jane, but that doesn't really make it okay and it has certainly not improved my opinion of her. George Wickham on the other hand – everything makes so much more sense. The way Darcy is, the way Darcy was, the way George was… I feel like I understand her a lot more now. And I think… I think I'm starting to respect her, if not like her. She does what she thinks is right to protect the people she loves. I can't fault her for that."

"She's always been like that," Will said, nodding. "Even when we were at school she tended to be obnoxiously righteous about things. It was annoying that she usually had a point."

I nodded my agreement as I ate my spaghetti; it was easy to imagine Darcy being like that at school. Something I remembered Darcy saying made me curious, and I voiced my question to Will.

"I thought Darcy went to an all girl's school? Unless it was different for sixth form."

There was a long silence, longer than was normal for such a question, and I turned to see Will staring into his plate, resolutely not looking at me.

"Everything okay?" I asked, concerned.

"I thought Darcy told you?" he said in a hollow voice. "She – she was supposed to tell you."

I was really beginning to worry now. I thought it had been such an innocent question.

"Tell me what? You – you don't have to tell me, if you don't want to."

"I told Darcy," he said, voice shaking and barely audible, "to tell you. She was supposed to tell you, and I knew that she didn't want to but I wanted her to because it's important and... I needed you to know." He turned to face me, his eyes dry but on the verge of crying.

"Will, what's wrong?" I asked, getting more concerned by the second. "What was she supposed to tell me?"

"I wanted her to tell you about me, and about how me and her became friends, because you needed to know. I wanted you to know. And you'd think differently of Darcy if you knew, I know you would, and I also just needed you to know because it's still such a big thing and I wish it wasn't but it is."

"You know you can tell me anything?" His body language was becoming more and more closed, his shoulders curling in, his legs slowly rising up closer to his chest. "You don't have to. But you can."

He nodded frantically, still not turning to look at me.

"I... I can tell you? And you... we won't stop being friends?"

"Of course we won't!" I said incredulously. "Whatever it is you want to tell me, I'll still be here afterwards. I promise."

He nodded again, determinedly wiping his eyes and sitting up straight.

"Right, okay. Well, here goes... I, um, usually don't talk about this. At all. And I don't tell people unless they need to know. It's not that I'm... ashamed. At all. Okay, maybe a little bit. It's just a thing that I don't like to think about. And... although you don't *need* to know right now, I think you will soon, and I'd rather you hear it now. Also, with you and Darcy as you are... yeah. I'll tell you now."

I was more confused than ever, but sat quietly, giving Will space to sort out his thoughts.

"I went to school with Darcy, she was a couple of years above me. It was a small school, so everyone knew everyone else, and gossip spread round like wildfire. Everyone knew who Darcy was. She isn't the kind of person you forget in a hurry. She was a model student, top of the class, good-looking enough to be considered cool, but... well, you know her. You couldn't really call her popular."

I nodded my agreement at this, smiling slightly, which seemed to set him at ease.

"Darcy was in her first year of sixth form when she set up an LGBT awareness group to tackle bullying. She'd never come out, as such, but she was never particularly quiet about being attracted to women as well as men. I still don't know all the details, but I think that over the summer some of our peers had been pretty awful to her. Being Darcy, though, she didn't take this lying down.

"That was how I met her properly, rather than just a quick conversation in the dinner queue or something. I was one of the two other people who attended that meeting. Even her own brother didn't go. They didn't see eye-to-eye about anything, really, until fairly recently."

"She did mention that," I said, interrupting for the first time since he'd started talking. "When she told me about George Wickham... she mentioned that you had helped her and Jordan repair their relationship."

"She did?" He looked so surprised at that news that I was instantly glad I'd said that. "That's... wow. That's so *nice* of her." He shook his head quickly, shaking himself out of his thoughts. "Sorry. Yeah. So... there were three of us at this meeting. That's how I met Darcy.

"At the time, I was... questioning some things. Lots of things. Nothing felt right, and I wanted to know why. I was so far from talking to anyone about it, though, and honestly, I went because I was... curious. While she'd been very clear that it wasn't a 'club for gay people' or something, and that everyone was welcome to attend because it was about anti-bullying, going to the first meeting wasn't something most people were keen on doing. And this was about six or seven years ago. As I'm sure you've noticed, attitudes are so different now from then, even though it was just a few years ago.

"Bloody hell, I'm beating around the bush," he suddenly exclaimed, again putting his head in his hands. "Get to the point," he said, more to himself than me.

I noticed that his breathing was becoming erratic, so I carefully put my hand on his shoulder. "It's okay," I said quietly. "Take deep breaths. It's alright, you don't have to tell me."

Once he'd calmed down, he shook his head before continuing. "I know I don't have to," he said slowly, eyes wide, "but I... I want to."

I smiled and nodded in return, indicating for him to carry on once he felt comfortable.

"I wasn't always... me," he said, stammering slightly. "I mean, Will wasn't the name I was given. At birth. I won't tell you what it was. You don't need to know, and I don't want to ever have to say it again. But... it was a girl's name. My... body. Doesn't match. You know, in my head.

"When I first went to that meeting... I didn't know what was wrong. I knew *something* was. I looked in the mirror every day and didn't feel like I was really seeing me. I thought that, maybe, I was gay. That's why I went to that meeting; I think I'd naively thought that walking through that door would give me the answers. I'd had crushes on girls, and I knew that that meant that I was gay, right? I didn't know any more than that. My family were very conservative, I'd never even heard the phrase LGBT before that day.

"Darcy didn't know it at the time, but in that first meeting she did do what she'd set out to: she spread awareness. We must have looked ridiculous, three of us sat around this huge table for a meeting, but we had the meeting anyway. The first thing Darcy did was explain what LGBT stood for, what it meant.

"I remember the moment she explained what the T stood for; it stands ingrained into my mind. The moment she explained what it meant to be trans, I remember thinking: that's me. That's what I am. That's what's wrong, that's what the problem is.

"At first I felt euphoric. I'd done it! I'd worked it out. But then reality came back. I had to go home, daughter to my conservative parents, and pretend that nothing was wrong. I spent the evening online, looking up people's stories, any information I could find, going on forums, reading medical sites. Finding out that I was not alone.

"It was almost a year before I really came to terms with it. It was a year of hiding, lying, pretending. I remember being constantly paranoid that somehow my parents would find out, even though I was so careful to delete my internet history and make sure that there was no way they'd even guess. I couldn't help but start some things, though. I cut my hair, refused to wear skirts for anything but school. I bought a sports bra, in the hope that it would make me look just a little bit less feminine. I... I did some things I'm not too proud of. To myself."

His eyes were fixated on the wall in front of him. I couldn't help but gasp almost inaudibly at the last comment, and he winced as I did so. I put my hand on his, trying to comfort him, not saying anything. That he'd gone through this... it was awful. I couldn't imagine what he'd gone through just to get to this point.

"Darcy was the first person I came out to," he continued after a few minutes, wiping a tear off his cheek. "It doesn't take much imagination to think of how that went. She was cool, as always, but accepting and a surprisingly good listener. We'd got to know each other over the year, and I honestly don't think she was particularly surprised. She talked me through what to do next. She sat with me in the doctor's waiting room when I first went to see the GP, she persuaded her parents to pay for private counselling sessions. I don't think they took much persuading – they were always great, with... with everything."

There was a long silence, long enough that I could hear that Will wasn't breathing.

"I told my parents," he said, his voice constricted from the tension his body. "A couple of years later. It wasn't long after Darcy's parents had died, and I... I guess I wanted to make sure there weren't any secrets between us. Parents suddenly seemed like such a temporary thing, and I wanted to make the most of having them there. I was too optimistic. They... they didn't take it well. I... I haven't seen them. Since that day. They... made it very clear that I wasn't welcome at home anymore. So, I... left.

"I lost track of how many months it was. I could have worked it out afterwards, but I didn't want to know. I... it was awful. I – I don't want to talk about it. I... I nearly..." He gave out an awful sob, the kind that shook you to the core. I instantly put my arms around him, holding him as he shook against my shoulder.

It was a few minutes before he was calm enough to speak again. "I'm sorry, it's just... talking about it..."

"It's okay," I said, rubbing his shoulder with my hand. "You don't have to talk about it anymore if you don't want to."

"No, I want to finish," he said tearfully. "I... Darcy found me. She realised I was gone, and I think she must have been to my parents' house to find me. She hunted for me for months, spending every spare second looking. She found me, eventually. She took me in. Insisted I live with her. Helped me go back to the doctors'. She was there when I made the decision to start transitioning, helped me through the hormones and the surgery. I owe her everything. If she hadn't found me... I don't know what I'd have done."

He let out a deep breath, and turned to look at me. "There you go. Now you know." His eyes were filled with sadness, and in them I saw someone decades older than he should be.

I looked him straight in the eye, with all the sincerity in the world.

"You're the bravest person I've ever met," I said, and his breath hitched as the tears started falling again. "And I'm... I'm proud to call you my friend."

We hugged again, and I could feel him smiling despite the tears.

"So, the ladies on the third floor, huh?"

We both laughed despite the situation; or perhaps because the situation needed it.

"You're pretty cool, Lizzy Bennet," he said, the twinkle returning to his eyes.

I smiled. "You're not so bad yourself, Will Fitts."

Chapter 23: Eye to Eye

I went with Will on his way home that evening. Despite having cheered up slightly as the evening went on, I was still worried about him and wanted to make sure he got home safely. He almost nodded off on the journey, drained and lacklustre from the emotion of earlier.

As he dozed, I mulled over everything that he'd told me. Will's story had surprised me, certainly, but hadn't confused me. As I thought back over the week's I'd known him, conversations that had previously puzzled me made more sense. No, once again, the subject of my confusion was Darcy Williams.

Honestly, I no longer felt confused by her actions. She was making more and more sense as a person. Her motivations, her weaknesses, everything was starting to fall into place. I was more concerned with my thoughts towards her. I was beginning to realise that the more I found out about her, the more there was still to know – and, I grudgingly admitted to myself, the more I wanted to know.

Oh, I didn't *like* her – I think – I just... wanted to know more about her. She intrigued me. She almost drew me in. All those weeks spent avoiding her, avoiding the subject of her, when really, I was just too stubborn to admit that my opinion *had* changed, and certainly for the better. Let's face it – it couldn't have gotten much worse.

Will and I were both pulled out of our thoughts when the voice on the intercom announced that we were at the right stop. We walked in comfortable silence back to his flat, enjoying, for once, the slower pace of London life in the evenings.

Will turned to bid me goodnight when we reached the door of his building, before realising that I was following him in. I hadn't planned on going in, but once I was there it suddenly seemed like the most obvious thing in the world.

"Lizzy, are you sure?" Will asked disbelievingly.

I shrugged, pretending I didn't know what he was worried about. "Yeah, of course."

He looked at me like I'd grown wings. "You know... you do know that Darcy will be there, right? Darcy Williams? Who you refuse to talk about or think about ever? That Darcy?"

"Yes," I said, as if it was the most obvious thing in the world. "Now, lift or stairs?"

Shaking his head at me in disbelief he went into the waiting lift, still confused when I got in with him.

I kept smiling nonchalantly in an effort to hide my nerves. Last time I'd been inside this building, it had ended with me running out while Darcy stood in the lobby as Will went after me. Hopefully, this time would be less dramatic.

I'd never visited Will's flat – Darcy's flat – before, and I wasn't sure what I'd expected. It was enormous, that was for sure, with a large, open plan kitchen, sitting room and dining room. My first impression was that it looked like it could have come from a catalogue. The furniture was well proportioned for the room and complimented the walls and floors perfectly. Only a few things gave away that people actually lived here: the photographs lined up on the mantelpiece; the piano in the corner with music haphazardly stacked on top; the bulging bookshelves, a few books stacked up at the side where they wouldn't fit.

And in the middle of the room, her back to the door as she sat on the sofa reading a book, was Darcy. She looked round when Will opened the door, her brow furrowing with worry when she saw Will's downtrodden, pale face.

"Will, are you okay? What happened?"

I could tell the exact moment she noticed me. The colour rushed to her cheeks, her eyes widening as her breath hitched. I was still pretending that everything was fine, that nothing out of the ordinary had just happened. Even if I was starting to panic inside, my first priority was making sure that Will was okay, and that wouldn't be accomplished if I stood there awkwardly. Thankfully, Darcy seemed to catch on, and quickly diverted her attention back to Will.

"Will, are you okay? What's wrong?"

He shrugged and gave me a pleading look which I knew meant that I should explain everything to Darcy.

"I'm just going to go to bed," he said. "Thank you for everything Lizzy." He gave me a quick but strong hug before morosely traipsing off to presumably where the bedrooms were.

"What happened?" Darcy asked, instantly defensive. I reminded myself that, as I now knew, it wasn't personal. Her hackles were raised as soon as she suspected a threat to one of her friends.

"Will told me," I said bluntly, still having not moved from my place in the doorway. "He told me about his past. And how you helped him."

She looked taken aback by my answer, and froze for a few seconds as she let it process. When she finally spoke, her tone was firm and even. "Would you like to come in and sit down?"

She phrased it as a genuine question. Not the kind that people use when they're being polite, or when they want you to know that you mustn't refuse. I nodded, gently pushing the door shut behind me and going to sit on the sofa. The sofa was so big that to sit at the opposite end would be very obviously rude, so I sat slap bang in the middle, still just out of Darcy's reach.

Darcy waited until I was settled before speaking again. "Lizzy, I'm sure you know that I wouldn't expect any less from you, but I have to ask – you took it... well? You did the right thing, said the right thing?"

"I think so," I said, still not entirely sure what 'the right thing' was. "I told him that he was brave, which is true; I've never met someone with so much courage. I hugged him, let him cry, told him that of course we would still be friends. Of course, also true." I ran my hands through my hair, laughing humourlessly. "This coming out stuff doesn't get any easier, does it?"

I saw that Darcy was staring intently at me, a very odd look on her face.

"What?" I said.

"Nothing," she replied. "It's just... I've seen you angry. I've seen you insulted. But I think this is the first time I've seen you truly sad."

Her words hung in the air for a few seconds; I felt like my skin was on fire. My head suddenly went numb;

she had seen so much of me in that second. How much more did she know?

Did she know more about me than I did?

"I'm glad Will has a friend like you, especially at Rosings," she said, clearly intending for the conversation to move swiftly on.

Well, it was now or never.

"Actually, now you mention it…" I started, suddenly feeling out of place – or at least, more than I already was. "Miss de Bourgh asked me today if I'd consider transferring to Pemberley for a few weeks. I, um, don't know if you were aware; she only mentioned that she'd spoken to the head of recruitment."

Darcy's face shut off, betraying no emotions.

"Oh… oh. Well, I was aware, of course, that we have previously taken some of Rosings' interns for a few weeks at a time; I wasn't aware of it being planned again. I don't usually get hugely involved in it, however; although I notice the difference whenever there's an extra pair of hands, I know that those, er, lower down, are much more directly influenced." She paused for a moment, thinking. "What did… what did you say?"

I shrugged in response. "I haven't decided yet. I think… I think I will take up the offer. If that's okay with you at Pemberley, of course. I think… well, you needed to know. Given our… circumstances. And as I was headed here anyway with Will… yeah. Now you know."

She gave me a small but genuine smile.

"Well, it will be a pleasure to have you there. I look forward to seeing you." She went bright red again, and stammered incoherently. "I mean… I mean, um, it would be good. Having you. I mean, working in the office. Office. Work. Colleague. Yes, that would be... good."

I couldn't help but giggle slightly, and she threw me a look that I think was meant to be reproachful, but looked more pleased. Obviously, I would need to laugh more often around her if it had this reaction.

"I'm afraid I should probably go home," I said, realising that I almost didn't want to leave. It was a slightly uncomfortable feeling.

"I'll call you a cab," Darcy said, taking out her phone.

I stood up, picking up my bag and coat. "Oh no, it's fine. I can get the Tube."

"No, it's late; take a taxi. I wouldn't want anything to happen to you."

In the few seconds that it took me to process the last comment, she was almost on the phone to the taxi company.

"No, Darcy," I interrupted, feeling my face start to heat up. "I – it's quite a way. I... I can't really afford that. I'll get the Tube."

She wasn't listening, however, booking a cab over the phone.

"It's booked in my name," she said once she'd hung up. "It will be added to my account. You don't need to worry about that."

She did have a point about safety. If I got the Tube it would be well past midnight when I got home, and I didn't want to be walking back by myself at that time.

"Thank you," I said, smiling slightly. "I'll, um... I'll go outside and wait for them."

"Okay," Darcy replied, clearly happier now that she knew I'd be safe. "I'll see you on Monday, I suppose."

I paused on my way out, trying to think of something to say.

"I'm glad Will has a friend like you," I said, and she nodded as our eyes met. I could feel a mutual respect growing between us, and for the first time I felt that we were on some kind of equal footing.

I got back to the flat just as Charlotte was arriving back from her date with Colin. She glanced over, curious as to who was leaving the taxi right outside our building (we were still getting to know our neighbours) before looking utterly baffled when she realised it was me – and that I hadn't paid.

"Lizzy, what's going on?" she asked determinedly as we trudged up the stairs to our flat. I hadn't even had a chance to ask if she'd had a good evening, and I could tell I wouldn't have a chance until I gave her answers. "You've been hiding something recently, there's no use in denying it, and now I want to know."

I sighed. I hadn't told her anything about Darcy since I saw her at her and Will's flat weeks and weeks ago; Charlotte didn't know about Charlie and Jane, about George, about Darcy's feelings for me. There was no way I could tell her most of that. A lot of it was private, either my secrets or someone else's, and I knew that nothing good would come out of telling her. This was all stuff I needed to figure out on my own, and as much as Charlotte would want to help I knew that it would be easier to keep things to myself, at least for now.

"Darcy booked the cab," I said, knowing that at least some explanation was needed. Charlotte turned to look at me, speechless.

"Darcy Williams, you know?" I clarified.

"Of – of course I know!" Charlotte spluttered. "But what the hell is Darcy Williams doing paying for you to be chauffeured about?!"

I shrugged, trying to downplay it as much as possible. "We decided to, um, bury the hatchet. Act like mature adults. I, um, well, as of today, it looks like I'm going to be working at her company for the next few weeks. We had to at least be able to get on for that to work."

Charlotte looked at me suspiciously, but seemed to deem it an acceptable response.

"Alright. That will do. For now. But I know you're hiding something, Lizzy!"

I gave her my best winning smile in return. "I'm an open book! You know everything about me!" I felt an awful twinge of guilt as I said it; I hated lying to my best friend. "Now, tell me all about your date!"

And she did. I heard absolutely everything: from Colin's cufflinks to the breed of pigeons that they ended up feeding.

I sent a quick message to Will before I went to sleep that night.

> *Lizzy Bennet: Hope you're doing okay. You're so brave, and I'm so proud of you, and I'm proud to call you my friend. Hopefully tomorrow will look a little brighter :)*

He didn't reply, but my phone said he'd been inactive for an hour now; chances are he was asleep.

It took a matter of seconds after I shut my eyes for me to drift off into sleep, thoughts of Will and Darcy lazily lingering in my mind. As much as I hated to admit it, there was more to Darcy than met the eye; more than I'd thought possible. There was something about her, something that I couldn't put my finger on. She infuriated me so, so much, and I knew that that would never change, but I also knew that I couldn't wait for the next time that I would see her smile.

Chapter 24: Welcome to Pemberley

It was a strange sort of nervousness that I felt as I started at Pemberley the following Monday. I wasn't nervous about the work itself. I wouldn't be doing much different from at Rosings, and by now I was more familiar with the inner workings of a publishing office.

I found myself worrying instead about the impression I'd make. It certainly wasn't the usual first-day-at-a-new-job impression that I was worried about, but I couldn't put my finger on what exactly it was that I was concerned about. I stood there in front of the mirror, determinedly trying to get my eyeliner just right, worried that I'd either over or underdressed.

The building itself wasn't hard to find. I just had to turn the other direction when I left the Tube station and walk a short way down the road. While the actual building was nothing compared to Rosings in grandeur, I could sense the difference in atmosphere as soon as I walked in. The offices seemed to be bursting at the seams; no space had gone unutilised. There were stacks of books everywhere you turned, and desks crammed into every corner, but everything seemed organised, like a well-oiled machine that was always just on the brink of collapse.

I couldn't see anyone to make my presence known to so I loitered in the entrance, hoping that someone would take pity on me and take me to where I needed to be. I wasn't waiting long; a familiar face arrived within a matter of moments, the smiling face less comforting than it should have been.

"Hi!" said the face that I'd only seen in photographs. "You must be Lizzy Bennet? I'm Jordan Williams."

"Hi," I replied, shaking his hand.

"Welcome to Pemberley!" he said, but his cheerful manner couldn't completely mask the way he was examining me as he spoke. "If you want, I can show you around?"

I nodded my agreement, and he led me round to go and see the offices.

"I'm sure you know that I don't actually work here," he said, bouncing slightly with eagerness as we walked. "Of course, I know my way around enough, with this being the family business. I should really be at uni today, but I didn't have any lectures so I hopped on a train and came down. Darcy hated that, you know how suspicious she is of public transport, but I'm here now! I had to meet the famous Lizzy Bennet."

I stopped in my tracks. "Wait, what?"

He faltered as he realised he'd said something he shouldn't have.

"I – I'm sorry, I didn't mean to... well, it's just that I've heard so much about you. It's nice to finally meet you."

"Don't worry about it," I smiled, "and the feeling's mutual. I've heard a lot about you too!"

I was hoping that that would comfort him, and dispel any awkward feelings in the air, but I couldn't have been more wrong. He tensed up, lowering his gaze to the ground.

"Oh. Well, I know that Darcy told you about... stuff. You know. Involving... other people."

"Oh, no – I mean, yes she did – but that wasn't what I was thinking about. Darcy, Charlie and Will have all spoken very highly of you."

"Really?" His eyes rose to meet mine, questioning what I'd said.

"Yep!" I said, trying my best to look reassuring. "Now, shall we continue on looking round?"

It wasn't hard to see why everyone got along well with Jordan. He was funny, witty and utterly likable. It took us half the morning to get around the whole offices, as everyone wanted to stop and say hello, catch up with Jordan and see how he was doing.

"The business has grown enormously in the past few years," Jordan explained in the relative quiet of the stairwell to the second floor. "That's why we're so crammed in, trying to keep up with the rapid expansion and make the most of it. Darcy's been looking to expand physically for a year or so now, but so far no luck. There's not much room for expansion in central London!"

"I can imagine," I said, amazed at how they'd managed to fit bookshelves in the stairwell to make more space elsewhere. "You have a very good taste in books, by the way. I, er, stayed in your room in France."

"Oh, of course, I'd forgotten you stayed there! Not sure how I managed to forget that really, I heard about it for weeks afterwards from Darcy!"

I stayed silent at that, not sure what to say. He glanced at me sideways, as if unsure about asking me something.

"So… you. And my sister. That happened." He was watching me out of the corner of his eye, judging my reaction.

"I wouldn't go as far as to say something happened," I replied, feeling my cheeks start to redden. "We… had a conversation. Then we had another conversation." I wasn't sure why I was telling him all this; it seemed likely that he already knew it.

"Do you wish something had happened?"

I whipped my head round, alarmed.

"Sorry!" he instantly said, looking on edge once more. "I… that was out of line. I'm sorry."

We finished walking up the stairs in silence. Jordan reached for the door that led to the rest of the offices, but let his hand rest on the handle, making no move to open the door. He stood there for a few seconds, and I could tell that he was carefully selecting his words in his head before saying them out loud.

"If you… just, please don't hurt my sister. Whatever happens." He looked at me pleadingly. I felt an unpleasant sensation, like icy hands had gripped my lungs.

"I think – I think it might be too late for that," I breathed, unable to get the words out properly.

He sighed, obviously frustrated. I think that perhaps he felt he hadn't made his meaning clear.

"No, what I mean is… well, lots of people are rude to Darcy. Always have been. And, yes, while what happened between you two might have been a step above… just, please don't lead her on. Please don't let her think she can get close to you and then change your mind. And – and I know you wouldn't do that on purpose. But my sister's not a curiosity. Not something to entertain yourself with until something better comes along. She's not a puzzle to get to the bottom of and then leave alone."

His face as he spoke told me that he was speaking from experience. Relationships, friendships; I already knew that they weren't Darcy's forte, and it didn't take such a stretch of the imagination to see that she could be taken advantage of, however unintentionally. No wonder her walls were so high.

"Jordan, I..." I wanted to tell him that I had no intention of pursuing a relationship with Darcy, because I didn't. I wanted to tell him that we were nothing but acquaintances with mutual friends, because it was true. But I couldn't quite get the words out. "You have my word."

He nodded solemnly, and it would have been amusing if it hadn't been so sincere. "On with the tour?"

I smiled in agreement. "Yep. On with the tour!"

We had barely gone a few metres down the second-floor corridor, however, when we stopped again. This time, however, was because Darcy had just emerged from an office on the left.

She stopped when she saw us, assessing the situation before saying anything.

"Lizzy! It's lovely to see you. I mean..." When had she become this floundering idiot that I'd seen over the last few days? It was sort of... endearing. "It's, er, hello. Hi. Welcome to Pemberley." She relaxed once more. She was on safe ground now. "How are you liking it so far?"

"It's great," I said, with no need to fake enthusiasm. "It's... well, it's amazing! I'm so glad I agreed to come here," I gushed.

"Me too," she said, and I could see in her face that she wanted to try and correct herself but managed to be restrained. I was glad for it. The last thing either of us needed was for her to panic about everything she said.

She turned to her brother. "Jordan, could I... could I have a word?" she asked curtly, her tone suddenly changing. Jordan looked at me slightly sheepishly before going up to Darcy, who led him a short way down the corridor before stopping and talking in hurried, hushed tones.

I told myself that it wasn't really eavesdropping, as such. After all, they were the only other people in the room besides me, so it didn't take *much* straining to hear what they were saying. So definitely not eavesdropping.

"Jordan, what the hell are you doing?" Darcy hissed. "I didn't even know you were in the city, let alone showing people round the office."

I could see him shrug, feigning nonchalance. "I was just popping by, and someone needed showing round. So, I showed them round."

It was obvious from her face that Darcy didn't believe him, and I was fairly sure that Jordan didn't expect her to.

"Next time tell me when you're here, okay? And I'd already arranged for someone to show her round, so you've just caused confusion. And--" her voice was lowered even more. I pretended to read the notices on the wall so that I could turn one ear towards them. "I know what you're trying to do, and it's quite frankly immature. It's not okay to just check up on people's personal lives like that, especially when it involves other people."

I could feel the awkwardness between them from where I was standing, that odd balance between a sibling and a parental relationship that threw things off-kilter.

"I just... I worry about you. And I wanted to make sure that... things were good. Between you two. And that... and that she was good enough for you."

I could see Darcy's expression melt, and she spared me a glance before pulling him into a hug. I'd never seen her display this much emotion before, and I could tell that it wasn't something that she was comfortable with in public. The glance she'd given me, however, told me that she knew I was listening, but would play along with me ignoring them. I decided, however, to give them a moment of privacy. I was sure that their relationship was still slightly shaky, no matter how much improved, and the least I could do was genuinely distract myself.

Darcy dispatched Jordan off somewhere else a few minutes later, and came back up to me.

"Would you like me to finish showing you round?" she asked, her eyes hopeful.

"I've only got to this floor to see, and I think I should probably get on with some actual work," I said, half joking, but regretted it once her face fell. "But obviously, it would be good to see the rest of the offices first! You know, for... efficiency. Later on."

We walked slower than we needed to down the corridor, Darcy pointing out various offices on the sides.

"These are the meeting rooms here... originally we just had the two, but we recently converted some offices into a third one as we were getting too many scheduling conflicts. You will be based here..." She indicated so one of a number of desks crammed in a corner opposite from the further meeting room, next to a vending machine. "I know it's not much, but I'm afraid it's all we've got space for!"

"That's fine," I quickly reassured her. "It's bigger than my desk at Rosings, and I have to share with Will there."

"I imagine he's a bit of a desk hog?" she asked, a twinkle in her eye.

"You have no idea," I said, as we both laughed. "I even put a strip of tape down halfway, and he'll pile things up on my side! I've taken to using his staples and tape if he does it too much. Small pleasures, but worth it!"

Darcy nodded in agreement, smiling knowingly. "I know what you mean! He's finally learnt to stop leaving his worn socks in my library but I still keep finding his plates everywhere!"

"That does not surprise me at all!" I replied, still laughing lightly. "So, what kind of stuff will I need to be doing here?"

"Whatever you're needed for, really. I'm sure that it will be very much the same as at Rosings, so hopefully you'll know what to expect."

"Brilliant," I said, putting my bag down on my desk chair. "I should probably get started then! Unless there's anything else?"

"No, that should be all," Darcy replied, before catching herself. "Well, now you mention it..." she looked embarrassed all of a sudden, looking down at her shoes. "There is one thing, and I'm not going to be in the office for the rest of the week so I would like to mention it now. But... don't feel obliged. I know this puts you in an awkward position given that we're colleagues now, and at very different, ah, in very different levels of employment. I don't want you to feel like you have to agree; I won't hold it against you if you don't. I just..." I looked at her expectantly, wondering where on earth this was going. "I wondered if you were free at the weekend. To spend the, ah, afternoon with, well, with... me. Just me."

That was not where I thought this was going, at all. (Although where else could it have been going, really?!)

Darcy... wanted to spend time with me. With just me. Just the two of us, together. Like a date.

Was this a date?

No. It wasn't a date. It couldn't be. We weren't even friends, not properly anyway. It could be a... friend date.

Because maybe being her friend wouldn't be the most awful thing in the world after all.

I'd been silent for too long. Darcy stammered out, "It's fine, I... I understand! I was out of line asking you, it's... it's fine. We can just forget about it."

"No!" I said, and we both looked surprised at my outburst. "I mean... I would, er, like to spend time with you. At the weekend. On Saturday. Which is a weekend day."

I could see the corners of her mouth curl up in that smile people did when they were trying to hide how completely over-the-moon they were about something, and were trying to appear cool about it.

"Okay. It's a... thing. Saturday."

"Yeah," I said, still unsure as to what I'd just agreed to, or why I'd just agreed to it. "It's a thing."

She nodded, and slowly backed towards her office, stumbling over a chair that was behind her. "Saturday. Thing on Saturday."

She kept walking backwards, keeping my eye contact, before she reached her office door. She lingered there for a second before dashing inside.

For some reason that I couldn't get to the bottom of, my cheeks were feeling stiff and aching, and I realised with a start that it was because I was grinning.

I had a... thing. With Darcy. And I wasn't even mad about it.

Chapter 25: London Town

Working at Pemberley was a world away from working at Rosings. The most noticeable difference was that I was actually needed. People did their own photocopying, fetched their own coffee, and although I wasn't doing anything much more exciting I certainly felt like I was making a bigger contribution.

Having Darcy out of the office also made things a lot easier. Even though we were getting along a lot better, I still didn't really fancy having every day consist of a string of awkward encounters. It was one less thing to worry about; I could simply get on with whatever I needed to do.

Darcy being out of the office didn't mean that I didn't hear from her, however. She had added me on Facebook once more, and had sent me a couple of messages. Nothing huge, just... stuff.

I had got home on Monday evening to find one waiting on my phone.

> *Darcy Williams: Hello, I just wanted to say that I hope you enjoyed your first day at Pemberley!*

I'd replied instantly.

> *Lizzy Bennet: I did, it was wonderful! I'm looking forward to the next few weeks.*

I heard from her again on the Wednesday lunchtime, when she sent me a photo attached to the message.

> *Darcy Williams: I was walking through Hyde Park and had time for a detour.*

There was a photo of the Peter Pan statue attached.

I wasn't sure what to make of that. Why was she telling me this? Why was she letting me know? And why wasn't I more annoyed by it? Why was I annoyed at all?

In the end, I just resolved to ignore the message. I couldn't think of anything to say in response, and regardless of this strange friendship we seemed to have struck up, I wasn't obliged to reply to any messages that she sent.

I didn't hear from her again after that until Friday evening. I felt a strange kind of trepidation in the run-up to Saturday. I wasn't entirely sure what I was nervous about, but there was definitely something bothering me. I just couldn't quite put my finger on it.

She sent me a message clarifying plans.

Darcy Williams: I just wanted to double check that you're still okay for tomorrow?

Lizzy Bennet: Yes, of course! Did you have anything in particular in mind?

Darcy Williams: How about I pick you up from your flat at about one o'clock?

I sent a message with my address and my agreement to the plans.

Lizzy Bennet: So do I get to know what these mysterious plans are?

Had it been anyone else I would have sent a flirtatious wink-face, but it just... it just seemed wrong somehow.

Darcy Williams: It's a surprise! You'll find out tomorrow

"Who're you messaging?" I jumped as Charlotte came into the kitchen.

"No one!" I said quickly, throwing my phone onto the kitchen counter. She gave me a sceptical look.

"Yeah, that was really convincing. Come on, it's okay if you don't want to tell me, but... is it someone special?" She looked at me far too knowingly.

"It's no one special," I argued back. "It's... if you must know, it's Darcy."

Wow. That felt surprisingly good to get off my chest.

"So, it *is* someone special!" Charlotte said smugly, seemingly growing in pride.

"No!" I insisted. "We're just... meeting up. Tomorrow. A thing."

She sighed despairingly, and reached for my phone. "Give me that," she said as we both attempted to grab it at the same time.

"What are you doing?" I said, trying to sound like I was keeping my cool.

"Looking out for you. That's what besties do, right?" She started typing the passcode in. "Your birthday... no. My birthday... no. Really, I'm hurt! Jane's... damn, I'm locked out for thirty seconds."

I took the opportunity to grab my phone back.

"What's the big issue?" she said. "Okay, so I shouldn't have taken your phone without asking, but... if it's nothing, why are you hiding? What kind of messages have you sent?"

Okay, she had a point. It's not like there was anything particularly personal, and if I refused to tell her she'd assume something very, very different, although heaven knows why.

"Here you go," I grumbled, after I'd eventually unlocked my phone.

"What was the code?" she asked as she read the messages.

"Harry Potter's birthday."

"I should have known! Now, let's have a look... okay, Lizzy, you have to face facts. This is flirting."

"What?! No it's not!" I went to snatch my phone back but she pulled it out of my reach.

"This is definitely flirting, there's no two ways about it."

I sighed, and gave her my best puppy-dog eyes.

"Charlotte... you're my best friend. But can you please accept just this once that I will tell you about that stuff if it happens, and not before?"

Even after years of friendship she fell for it, but we both knew that the discussion wasn't over.

"As long as you tell me as soon as you're ready," she said, handing my phone back.

"Thanks," I mumbled, pocketing my phone once more.

Saturday afternoon came far too quickly for my liking. Before I knew it, I was waiting in the kitchen nervously, my knee bouncing up and down, tugging at my jumper. I couldn't even remember why I'd agreed to this. Why on earth had I decided that spending the afternoon with Darcy would be a good idea?

At exactly one o'clock the doorbell rang. I dashed down the stairs and out the front door to where Darcy was waiting.

She smiled at me slightly awkwardly and we stood there for a second, neither of us sure what to do.

"Hi," I said eventually. "How, um, how are you?"

"I'm very well thank you," Darcy recited. "You look... you look lovely."

I willed myself not to blush, but I could feel my cheeks turning pink anyway.

"Thank you," I said, bashfully.

"Should we get going?" she asked, indicating towards the taxi that was pulled in at the curb.

"Okay," I nodded, and she dashed forward to open the door for me.

"So where are we going?" I asked as the taxi drove off, leaning back into my seat.

"I thought I'd take you to some parts of London that I thought you might enjoy. Some of my favourite spots that I think you'd also like. If that's okay?" She looked so earnest and desperate to please that even if it had sounded like the worst possible way to spend a day I would have said that it was a good plan.

"So it's a surprise?" I asked teasingly.

She shrugged, failing to hide that her cheeks had coloured slightly. "Of sorts. I'm sure you'll be able to guess the theme fairly quickly!"

I nodded, intrigued. "Is that a challenge? 'How quickly can I guess the theme'?"

"If you want it to be," she said coolly, but I could see in her eyes that she was joking. "I… I do hope you'll like it."

"I'm sure I will," I reassured her.

"Good," she smiled. "Have you enjoyed your first week at Pemberley?"

"I've loved it," I said, aware that I sounded like I was sucking up, but I didn't really mind. I was, after all, telling the truth. "I'm really looking forward to the next three weeks. It's so different from working at Rosings, it just feels that bit livelier. Everyone's so lovely and wonderful, and you get much more of a sense of people caring about their work, you know?"

I looked over and saw that she had a small but proud smile. "I'm glad you enjoyed it. And I certainly agree with you; it's why I also love working there so much. Oh — we're here!" she said suddenly, and I looked out the window of the taxi to see the British Library. I gave an audible gasp as I scrambled out the cab, admiring the enormous building in front of me.

"You brought me to the British Library?!" I exclaimed, clapping my hands excitedly. I turned around to see her watching my reaction, looking pleased. "I'm going to go ahead and guess the theme now; is it books?"

"If it had been a challenge, then full marks!" she said, laughing. I realised that this was the first time I'd heard her laugh, but somehow the thought buoyed me up even more. Her laugh was gentle and light, worlds away from the cold demeanour I'd grown used to.

"Shall we go in?" I asked, still barely containing my excitement.

"Of course! I didn't bring you here to admire the architecture!"

The library was incredible. As a working library, it wasn't realistic to really explore the whole thing, especially as you needed a pass to access most of it. There was an enormous glass bookcase spanning several stories down the centre of the building that was filled with old leather-bound volumes as far as the eye could see. After admiring the beautiful antique books, I was dragged to the exhibition.

As soon as you walked into the room, you could feel the weight of the history contained within it. We spent what felt like hours poring over the documents, pointing out anything of interest, discussing what we saw. Darcy explained the significance of all the musical scores that were on display, and we both admired a manuscript of Jane Austen's *First Impressions*, comparing our handwriting to hers. I was speechless as I saw the original Beatles' lyrics, written on pieces of envelopes and postcards. We marvelled at the details on the ancient maps, and admired the beauty of the ancient religious tomes.

"So, what did you think?" Darcy asked as soon as we were out of the door and able to talk at full volume.

"That was... incredible!" I said, still reeling. "To see all of those amazing things... I have a whole new respect for composers. And authors. And anyone born before the typewriter!"

"I know what you mean," she replied as we walked back towards the street. "But it's a whole different attitude to the arts really, isn't it? I mean, you had to put in hours and hours of work that would have undoubtedly ached and been uncomfortable, so you would only do that if you really believed in what you were doing."

"Definitely," I agreed. "It just... it adds a whole new level to these things really, doesn't it? The lengths people go to produce excellence. It's something you don't see often now."

I was surprised to see that the taxi was still waiting for us outside the library.

"Are we just being chauffeured round all day?" I asked, ignoring Darcy's attempts to get me into the taxi.

"Of course," Darcy said, as if it were the most obvious thing in the world. "It's the most efficient way of getting about, and it's no trouble; the charge will just be added to my account at the end of the day."

I walked to the passenger door, indicating for the driver to roll the window down.

"Apologies for having you wait so long, but we won't be going any further," I said, deliberately not looking at the charge that had already clocked up on the meter. "We'll be fine from here on!"

The driver just nodded and drove off, obviously looking for clients that actually needed driving round.

"What did you do that for?" Darcy said, flabbergasted. "How will we get around now?"

"Using public transport, of course," I said, rummaging in my bag. "Have you got your oyster card with you?"

She mumbled something incoherently, and I had an awful feeling I knew what she was trying to say.

"Sorry, I didn't catch that," I said, only slightly patronisingly as I found my oyster card at the bottom of my bag.

"I don't have an oyster card," she said, sighing.

"You don't have an oyster card!" Even though I was expecting it, it still shocked me. "How do you get around?"

Again, I had a horrible feeling as to what was coming next.

"I take taxis," she shrugged. "I can afford it, and I can walk to work so I don't use them that often. It's so much more efficient and pleasant than public transport."

"Okay, I will buy you an oyster card," I said, leading the way down the street. "The nearest station is Euston, it's not far from here! Why don't you use the Tube or the buses?"

"There's just so many people," she said haughtily. "I don't see why I should use them when I have alternatives. It's seems so grimy, and so cramped, and I'm sure it must smell. It's never appealed at all."

"Just for today, let's get the Tube," I suggested. "See how the other half do it. Or other ninety-five percent, I suppose. Besides, you're missing out on so much! There's something weirdly wonderful about disappearing underground in one part of the city and popping up a few minutes later in another! There's a strange energy behind it, you really can't experience London without taking the Tube at least once."

"Well I don't have much choice now, do I," she grumbled, but followed me regardless.

"Here we are!" I said as we reached the station. "Okay, I'll buy you an oyster card... and before you say anything, I'm fairly sure just the cab so far today was more than an oyster card will be. Let me pay this once. How many more stops do we have today?"

"A few," she said, feigning nonchalance.

"I'll get a five pound one for now. You can always top it up later if need be."

"So I just... what do I do?" She looked so out of her depth, I almost felt sorry for her.

"You just put it against the sensor on the way in, and again on the way out. It's not hard. Now, where are we going next?"

"That would ruin the surprise," she said indignantly.

I sighed impatiently. "Well, what's the nearest Tube station? That's all we really need to know."

Her face told me instantly that she had no idea, so I told her to go and look at a map on the wall and tell me.

"Waterloo," she said as she came back.

"This way then!" I guided her through the ticket barrier as we joined the rush of people.

On a Saturday afternoon in London, the Tube is more filled with families and tourists than commuters. A usually quiet train was filled with screaming children who were hot and tired, arguments about which stop to get off at in every language under the sun, and teenagers trying their best to appear cool by loudly playing music on their phones. In short, Darcy's idea of hell on earth.

There were no seats left, as usual, so we were crammed between a very loud American family and a small old lady grumbling about 'young people these days'. We were old enough (just) to be considered comrades in this opinion, and in the interest of keeping the journey away from just unpleasant, I didn't disagree with her. Darcy was stood to attention for the whole trip, her eyes anxiously flitting from the route map and the screen displaying which stop we were at.

'*The next stop is Waterloo*'.

As we pulled into the station I practically dragged Darcy off the train, unsure whether she was used to the speed needed to navigate the underground. Once we were off the train, however, she relaxed, admiring the posters for shows that were lining the walls, gently running her fingers over the tiling in the tunnels.

"We're... we're here," she said, surprised, as we stepped out of the station.

"I told you we would be!" I replied. "It's the magic of the Tube. So, where are we going now?"

The autumn sun beamed down on us as Darcy led me down the street, and before long I could see the London Eye in the distance.

"Welcome to Southbank book market," she said as we reached the river's edge. I practically ran up to the first table of books, running my hands along the spines.

"There's so many," I gasped, pulling some out to have a look.

"We have all day," she said, smiling at my excitement. "Well, actually, we don't. But take your time!"

And take my time I did. We looked at every single book that was there, pointing out our favourite titles to each other, playing at who could spot the most Pemberley and Rosings logos.

"How does this sound," I said, after we'd looked up and down all the tables. "We each spend… let's say, ten pounds. That should buy about three books. And we buy three books that we think the other would enjoy."

"It's a plan," Darcy agreed, and we each set off down the tables, hunting for good books to swap.

Every time I spotted a title I knew I pulled it out, considering if Darcy would enjoy it. It occurred to me that I didn't really know what sort of books she was interested in. I watched her at the other end of the market, methodically going through the lines of books on the table, her eyebrows tight in concentration. From what I'd seen of her book collection there was no theme or focus, just a very large collection of very good books.

When I looked up again she had a pile of books in front of her which she was attempting to sort through, scoffing at some, holding two others up as if to decide between them.

I decided to find three excellent books that had, for whatever reason, at whatever point in my life, really resonated with me. Something was telling me that that was the sort of thing she'd enjoy. It only took me a further ten minutes to find three books that fit that criteria, but Darcy was another half an hour, painstakingly combing through her shortlist trying to work out what to get.

"Here you go!" I said as we finally sat down on a bench overlooking the Thames, presenting her with the stack of books. "I wasn't sure what sort of thing you like, so I chose three that meant something to me."

It sounded ridiculous once I said it out loud but she smiled as she took the books, running her fingers over the spines.

"I can't wait to read them," she said, smiling genuinely before nervously handing me her own pile. "Now that you say it I wish I'd done the same as you, but, er, these are all books that I own but haven't read yet so I thought we could, um, read them at the same time."

I couldn't help but grin at that. "Wow, I – that's such a good idea! I can't wait."

Her eyes flitted around as she smiled shyly. "I just hope you enjoy them."

"I'm sure I will!" I said as I read the blurbs before putting them into my bag. "So, where are we headed now?"

"Charing Cross Road," Darcy said, "which isn't far from here; we could walk?"

"Sounds good," I said, going to gather my things.

"Oh, I just remembered something! Being here at the Southbank reminded me."

"What is it?" I asked, confused.

She reached inside her bag and pulled out an envelope, handing it to me. I looked inside to see two tickets.

"There's a concert here in a few weeks," she said. "It's performances from some of the Royal Academy's most distinguished alumni from recent years. I thought you might like to go."

"Oh, you mean... with you?"

She shook her head. "I already have a ticket. You can choose who to give the other one to. Although, given who's performing, I think we both know who should have it."

I looked at her suspiciously for a few seconds, trying to fathom what she was trying to say.

"Is Charlie performing at this concert, by any chance?" I asked quietly after a few moments.

She only nodded in response. "I'm sure you'll know what to do."

With that, she stood up and dusted herself off quickly. "Shall we get going? There's not much afternoon left, and we have to be somewhere for seven o'clock."

Seriously, how much had she planned?!

After a twenty-minute walk spent discussing the books we'd bought each other, we found ourselves at Foyles book store; the biggest independent book shop in the country.

"Welcome book lover, you are among friends," I read from the wall as we went in.

"Well, what do you think?" Darcy asked eagerly.

"It's amazing!" I said, before rushing off to go and browse.

We spent over an hour in the shop; they were basically pushing us out when we left. I'd been uncontrollable, grabbing anything off the shelves and piling them all up. In the end, we managed to keep each other in check by agreeing that we should each pay for the other's stack. I couldn't help but feel that the fact that we both drastically reduces our piles after that was to both of our credits.

"Where now?" I asked as they locked the door shut behind us, exhausted from the high-intensity book shopping. "Surely everywhere must be shutting soon?"

"I tried to think about things that you could only do in London that you probably hadn't done yet – I, er, looked quite a way back through your Facebook – so I bought us tickets for the Globe's production of *The Tempest*. If – if that's okay, we don't have to go."

"That's fantastic! Thank you so so so much!" I immediately went to give her a hug, but froze at the last second, realising what I was about to do. We both stood there awkwardly for a few moments before Darcy cleared her throat.

"It's, um, quarter past six now. So, shall we go?"

Nodding enthusiastically, I led us back towards the nearest Tube station, checking the map on my phone as to which line to get. The Saturday evening Tube was full of people like us: people on their way home after a busy day or just on their way out for the evening.

I had never so eagerly swiped my way through the barriers, a bemused Darcy entertained at my excitement. Even knowing that it wasn't the original theatre, or that it wasn't even on the original site, didn't make me any less excited when I saw it ahead of us. While the Shakespeare purist in me was disappointed at not having standing tickets, my aching feet from the day of exploring London were more than grateful for the chance to sit down.

As was to be expected, the show was brilliant. We were in fantastic seats, and although I dread to think of the cost, I had a brilliant view of the stage. We laughed, we cried, and I think I even spotted Darcy mouthing some of the famous speeches along with the actors.

We got our ice creams in the interval and sat back, discussing the first half, swapping ice cream flavours. As the second act started we settled back into our seats, ready to enjoy the rest of the show.

We could have only been about ten minutes into the second half when I noticed something strange. At some point, Darcy's arm had shifted so that her hand was on the armrest between us. While it was clearly meant to look casual, it was obvious from her posture that it wasn't.

I don't know what possessed me; whether it was the atmosphere of the theatre, the buzz still left over from the wonderful day, or some kind of strange, inexplicable force. Regardless, I found myself gently shifting my arm up slightly so that my hand was resting in a similar position. A few centimetres away from Darcy's, not so far that I was out of reach, but not so close that we could accidentally touch.

I told myself to focus on what was happening on stage but I couldn't; I was hyperaware of every move Darcy made, of everything that she did. I was very deliberately not looking down at our hands but forward at the stage. I still couldn't help but sense her presence, though, and there was a strange feeling in the air between us.

It was another fifteen minutes before I felt something on the edge of my hand. Darcy was, like me, looking straight forward, but her eyes were slightly glazed, like she was concentrating on something else entirely. I spared a quick glance down and saw that the edge of her hand was ever so slightly overlapping mine; so little that it could have been an accident, that it would not be odd for me to pull away, but enough for her intention to be obvious, should I wish it to be.

I felt like there were two very separate parts of my brain at war with each other. One side was telling me that this was ridiculous. How did I even get into this situation? I was with Darcy Williams for Pete's sake, and despite all her redeeming qualities, she still broke up Jane and Charlie and she was still awful and rude.

The less articulate side of my brain, which unfortunately was the side that controlled my movements, had different ideas. I couldn't help it as I shifted my fingers an infinitesimal distance towards her, feeling her hand gently curl around mine.

We stayed like that for the whole of the second half, neither of us drawing attention to it. As soon as the play was over we each brought our own hands back, applauding the performance and standing up.

Even though we didn't bring up the hand-holding incident (if you could even call it that) the air between us was much more relaxed as we left the theatre as we chatted about the show we'd just seen.

"I've had a really lovely day," I said as we slowly sauntered back to the Tube station. "Thank you. I... I really enjoyed it. All of it."

Just as I said that, my stomach gave an enormous rumble; loud enough to be audible to the both of us.

"I completely forgot to schedule in dinner!" Darcy said, and we both laughed at the mishap. "Do you reckon we still have time for it?"

"Of course," I said happily, not quite ready to go home just yet.

"Could we... could we maybe get the Tube again?" Darcy asked, slightly shy.

"Are you asking if we can take public transport as opposed to a taxi?" I said, feigning shock and causing her to roll her eyes. "Of course we can. London Bridge station isn't far, I think it's this way."

In the end, we picked up pre-packed sandwiches, looking slightly sorry for themselves at the end of the day, and stowed them in our bags until we could find somewhere nice to eat them.

"This is our stop," Darcy said as the train, now virtually empty, ground to a halt.

"This is by Hyde Park," I commented as we stepped onto the escalators.

Darcy shrugged in response.

"It's a mild evening."

I should have guessed, really, where we were going. We sat down to eat our sandwiches on that same bench where we'd sat and talked over a month ago, looking up at Peter Pan. This time, however, we were sat close together, keeping warm from the autumn chill. We ate in a comfortable silence, each lost in our own thoughts.

As we stood up to leave, Darcy took my hands in hers. It was odd. It felt simultaneously like a bizarre turn of events and the most natural thing in the world.

"I've had such a nice time," she said, looking into my eyes with complete and utter sincerity. "I wondered if you would be... happy to do this kind of thing again. Maybe not exactly the same, maybe not as big, but, I don't know, lunch or something."

"Lunch sounds good," I said, smiling and squeezing her hands. "Lunch on Monday?"

"Lunch on Monday," she agreed. "Now, will you please let me pay for a cab to take you back?"

I rolled my eyes. "Only because it's so late. And just this once."

"Well, actually it's just this twice," she said teasingly.

And we walked together through the park, our fingers interlocked, lit only by the streetlamps and the moon frowning down on us.

Chapter 26: Next Time

I spent most of Sunday thinking over Saturday's events. I'd had a nice time, I really had; much nicer than I'd been expecting. Not that I'd known exactly what I to expect.

Maybe… maybe Darcy wasn't so bad. I felt like I was getting to know the real her: who she was beneath the scowl and the callous exterior. I'd had glimpses of someone very, very special, but I wasn't sure if it was enough to balance out the things she'd previously done and said.

The biggest thing that had changed was that for the first time, I was getting the impression that she felt bad for splitting Jane and Charlie up. If Charlie was in this concert in London, and she'd given me two tickets with the deliberate instruction that she already had one… there could only be one other person she intended that ticket for. If only she hadn't been so proud; maybe she could have told me outright what her plans were. As such, I just had to assume that she intended the other ticket for Jane, and wanted her and Charlie to see each other again.

At least, I really hoped that that was her intention.

By the end of the day, I'd resolved to dwell on the matter no longer. My head was just going round in circles, and I wasn't getting anywhere. Whatever this weird relationship between us was, I would have to wait for further clarification to find out.

I didn't have to wait long, though. Monday morning came soon, and with it the promise of lunch out. I hadn't thought much of it until Charlotte brought it up over breakfast.

"You're looking worryingly cheerful for this early in the morning," she said, dashing round to finish getting her things ready for work. "What's up with you? Any special plans?"

I carefully sprinkled some extra sugar on my cornflakes, and said, "Nothing special. I'm going for lunch with Darcy, but that's nothing to get particularly excited about. Today's just a good day."

It took a few moments of silence for me to realise that she'd paused her frantic packing in exchange for raising an eyebrow and looking at me with disbelief.

"*Nothing to get excited about?!* You've got a face that's lit up like the London Eye at night. Nothing to get excited about, my arse."

"I'm not going to dignify that with a response," I sighed, going back to my breakfast.

"You do know that you're completely and utterly hopeless?!"

"And what's that supposed to mean?"

Charlotte shook her head. "Nothing. I've got to dash, and I'm going out with Colin this evening – don't wait up for me!"

By the time I'd thought of a suitably witty response she was already out the door.

Within the hour, I was at my desk in the office, getting my things ready for the day. As I'd promised myself the day before, I wasn't dwelling on the mess that was my feelings. Instead, I was getting on with the day, taking things as they come, and waiting for something new to happen before reconsidering.

"Good morning, Lizzy!"

I looked up to see Darcy coming towards me, her coat still on and her bag on one arm.

"Good morning," I replied, suddenly unsure of how to deal with the situation. She stepped a few feet closer to me so that we could talk without having to call to each other down the corridor.

"I had a really nice time on Saturday," she said, with an uncertainty that told me that she was unsure whether or not it was the right thing to say.

"Me too," I reassured her, smiling back awkwardly.

She nervously adjusted her unfairly stylish pea coat. "Are we… are we still on for lunch today?"

"Sure," I said, relieved that she'd brought it up rather than me. She nodded awkwardly before heading back down the corridor to her office.

Barely two minutes had passed when my phone buzzed with a message.

Will Fitts: So, a week at the new job and you're already dating the boss, huh? ;)

What? How did he know?! And we weren't – never mind. That wasn't important right now.

Lizzy Bennet: WE'RE NOT DATING. And how do you know these things?

Will Fitts: I live with Darcy, remember? I had to put up with her constantly worrying if you were going to like what she had planned. And I had to put up with her happy giddiness all yesterday. I say you're dating!

Lizzy Bennet: Well, we're not. I don't even like her like that.

There was a pause of a couple of minutes before another message came through.

Will Fitts: Sure. Whatever you say.

I couldn't think of a reply to that, so I just ignored it. The last thing I needed right now was other people getting involved; things were confusing enough already.

The morning passed much faster than I'd hoped, and before I knew it, it was lunchtime. Darcy met me at my desk, coat in hand, asking if I was ready to go.

The restaurant we went to was posh. Like, *really* posh. The kind of posh where a meal cost something close to my rent. Darcy saw my expression as soon as I saw the prices on the menu, and I could tell that she was almost embarrassed.

"Don't worry about the price – I'll pay. My treat."

I sighed, setting down my menu. "I've been hearing that a lot recently. I don't like that you seem to be spending a lot of money on me, it's not fair on you."

"But I can afford it," she said, clearly confused. "There's nothing wrong with that."

"At least let me pay for drinks or something," I pleaded, instantly regretting it upon remembering the prices of the wine list.

She conceded that. "Okay. Now, what food were you planning on ordering?"

I returned my attention to the menu, glancing down the list of options.

"Nothing that takes too long to cook, we only have an hour," I said, thinking out loud.

"We can spend longer if you like," Darcy said, earnestly. "Don't feel the need to restrict your choice based on that."

"Perks of being the boss, I guess," I joked, still looking down at the menu.

"Don't say things like that." Darcy's frown was evident in her tone and I looked up, alarmed.

"What's wrong?" I asked.

She sighed, leaning back in her seat. "I can't help but feel that you're... obliged to be here somehow. That you only agree to spend time with me because I'm your boss, and you feel like you have to do what I say. I... I don't like that."

I raised an eyebrow. "Do I really come across as someone who does things just because they're told to?"

She laughed at that.

"Tell you what," I said, "next time I'll take you out. I'll pay, I'll organise it. I can't promise anything swish, but I promise I'll find a really upmarket fast food place, one where they sweep the floor and everything!"

She laughed again, elegantly brushing her hair out of her eyes.

"So... there'll be a next time?" she asked, equal parts teasing and nervous.

I felt myself go beetroot-red as I realised what I'd said. "I mean... if you want. You don't have to."

I jumped slightly as she reached across the table to take my hand, but left it still all the same.

"I'd love to," she said, holding my gaze.

The moment only lasted a second before the waiter cleared his throat, standing expectantly with a notepad. "Excuse me, may I take your order?"

Even after ordering our food, however, the moment couldn't be brought back, and I oddly found myself wishing that it could.

"So, um... your brother plays the piano?" I started, desperately looking for something to start a conversation with.

"Yes!" Darcy seemed to swell with pride at the mention of her brother, and I gave myself a mental pat on the back. "And the organ, although he prefers the piano. He's absolutely phenomenal, a far better musician than I could ever be. Charlie taught him, although it was our mother who started teaching him; she was a musician too."

"Really?" I couldn't help but jump at this new information. So far, I knew so little about Darcy's home life with her knowing so much about mine, that I couldn't help but get eager at the slightest thing.

"Yes, she was a violinist." As she began talking about her mother, Darcy broke eye contact with me, instead staring at where she was running her fingers over the rim of her glass, smiling in sadness at the memories. "She used to play for us all the time, she – she was incredible. I still have her CDs at home, I – I play them sometimes. When I miss her. I didn't play them for a year after she'd – after she – it was Jordan's idea, one evening, to put one on, and I'd run out of excuses to say no. I'm glad he suggested it, though." She trailed off, lost. "Sorry, I

– I shouldn't be talking about this, I didn't want to bring the mood down."

"It's fine, I reassured her, smiling when she looked up at me for reassurance. "If you want to talk about it, then that's completely fine. Or not. It's completely your decision."

She paused for a few seconds before continuing on. "That's how she and my dad met. He went to one of her concerts and visited her afterwards to congratulate her, and the rest is history. I suppose I've always envied them, knowing straight away that they'd found the person they wanted to spend the rest of their lives with."

There was another silence, this one more awkward. Darcy seemed to sense that she'd said something that wasn't completely appropriate, but couldn't seem to find a way to fix it. I stepped in, guiding the conversation away from such difficult waters.

"What were their names?"

I'm not sure why I blurted it out; maybe I was just realising quite how much more she knew about me than I her.

"My father was called Robert, my mother was called Amanpreet," she replied. "I remember once, when I was very young, overhearing my mother arguing with my grandmother. My grandmother was very loving, and always wanted the best for us, but – but she never really understood why my mother married someone who was white. She seemed to think that my mother was ashamed, especially when she gave me and Jordan English names. I asked my mother about it, afterwards, and she said that she never wanted either of us to have to worry about our names, to be teased or to have to spell them out or anything." She shrugged, although I could tell it bothered her. "Our middle names are our grandparents' names, so there's that, I suppose."

I wasn't sure what to say to that, but before the lack of response became too obvious I was saved by the arrival of our food.

"That's enough about me," Darcy asked as we began to dig into our meals. "Any childhood memories you're burning to share?"

"There was this one time," I started, determined to lighten the atmosphere, "that I threw away all of my Barbie's clothes except the skinny jeans and the plaid shirts."

Darcy snorted into her glass as I said this, recomposing herself, then bursting into giggles once more as we made eye contact.

"Jane was distraught," I continued. "I think there were a couple of miniature dresses she'd had her eye on for weeks, only for them to be gone!"

I felt my phone buzz in my pocket, but ignored it. If it was important they would ring again, or leave a voicemail.

"I was a bit of a prankster a kid." Darcy looked at me with disbelief, and I nodded. "Yeah, I got my brothers – especially Sander – into trouble a few times. It was usually Jane who told on us, and she often managed to wheedle the truth out of Mark, but not until after Sander and I had put flour in mum's hairdryer, or switched the salt and the sugar in the kitchen. There was this one time--"

But I was interrupted by my phone ringing once again. Whoever was calling was still trying to get through.

I sighed apologetically. "I should probably answer," I said. Darcy nodded as I pressed the green 'answer' button and held the phone to my ear, glancing at the caller ID.

"Hey Mark, what's up?"

I heard a loud sniff on the other end of the phone, and my heart skipped a beat.

"Lizzy? It's… it's Sander. Something's happened, or is happening, and I don't know what to do. I don't know what to do, Lizzy." He broke off into noises that sounded far too much like sobs.

"Mark? It's okay, I'm here. What… what happened with Sander?" Darcy was looking at me across the table, clearly worried.

"Lizzy, I… I don't want to tell you over the phone. I just don't know what to do. Just please, you have to come home, you have to help him! He won't listen to me, and I can't tell Jane or Mum or Dad. Please, Lizzy."

"Mark, it's not that simple. Look, if you can give me some kind of idea as to what's wrong, I might be able to come home, but I can't otherwise. Please, Mark. Tell me what happened."

"I…" More sniffs. "I don't know exactly what's going on, he won't listen when I ask him about it, but… well, I think he's been stealing money from me, and Mum and Dad as well, and I was really worried, so I went to his room and he – he had this stuff, Lizzy, in his drawers, and I don't think it was legal stuff. I don't know what he's doing, but you need to stop him. Please. I… I tried talking to him, and he told me it was for a friend and that I shouldn't have been looking which I know I shouldn't, but..."

My blood ran cold; I suddenly knew what had been going on.

How could I have been so stupid?!

"Mark? Mark, this friend, do you think... do you think it might be George Wickham?"

I heard Darcy's sharp intake of breath from across the table but I didn't dare meet her eyes.

"I think so," Mark said weakly. "I think it is. I'm sorry Lizzy, I know he was your friend, I didn't want to suggest anything but... he's the only person Sander's been hanging out with lately, and I can't think of anyone else it could be."

"It will be okay, Mark," I said, trying to reassure him but feeling hopeless myself. "I'll come home, I'll help you sort this out. We'll get through this. I'll be home by the end of the day. Will you be okay until then?"

He didn't say anything, but I knew he was nodding.

"I'll be fine," he said, voice trembling. "Thank you for coming, Lizzy. I know you'll be able to help."

I said goodbye and hung up, my heart rapidly sinking lower and lower. Mark may know that I'll be able to help, but I didn't. How could I help? What could I do? This was all my fault.

"Lizzy?"

I jumped. I'd forgotten that I was with company.

"Lizzy, what's going on?"

Darcy's question triggered off something in my brain as I grabbed my bag and coat, getting ready to leave.

"Something's happened, my brother... he's been spending time with George Wickham. And now... now things are bad, and my other brother thinks I'm the only person who can help."

I let out a small sob, covering my hand with my mouth, as the enormity of the situation hit me.

"This is my fault," I cried, oblivious to the fact that we were in the middle of a restaurant. "I... I knew. I knew and I didn't say anything, because I... because I was too bloody self-righteous. I told myself I was doing the right thing... but I couldn't have been more wrong."

Within a second, Darcy was around my side of the table, wrapping her arms around me.

"It will be okay," she murmured into my hair as I cried onto her shoulder. "It will all be okay; we'll make sure of it. You go home right away – don't worry about work or anything, I'll say I sent you to a conference or something. I'll take care of that. You go home and be with your brothers. It sounds like they both need you."

I pulled away, wiping my eyes and nose inelegantly.

"Thank you," I sniffed. "I... I'm sorry, but I think I should go right away."

"I'll book you a cab to the station." I went to disagree, but Darcy held up a hand to stop me from saying anything. "I mean it. It's not far, but will save you time. I assume you have enough clothes and things at home that you don't need to go via your flat?" I nodded, dumbstruck. "Then I won't hear another word about it. Let's get you to the station, you're needed at home."

The journey home was a blur. I remember Darcy being in the taxi with me, making sure I was alright, reassuring me and telling me that it wasn't my fault, even though we both knew it wasn't true. She bought me a train ticket because my hands were trembling too much to operate the machine, and got a sandwich from the station shop for me to eat on the train. I remember her waving me off at the platform, her face crestfallen.

And I remember firmly blotting her from my mind, because I had more important things to worry about now. Any business I had with Darcy Williams could wait, for hours, days, months; as long as it took. Right now, my family needed me and I was going to be there for them, no matter what.

Chapter 27: Mark

"Sander, is that you back? I was just wondering--"

My dad froze in his tracks as he realised that the front door had been opened not by Sander, but by me.

"Lizzy? What are you doing here?" He took in my tired, ashen face, my office clothes and no luggage except my bag and coat; not the image of a planned trip home. "What happened? Is everything okay?"

I didn't answer, but let myself be pulled into an enormous hug. There was something so comforting and marvellous about being home, but it jarred. My reason for being here was far from relaxing.

"Lizzy, I'm worried. What's going on?"

So, he had absolutely no idea what was going on, and I was going to have to tell him at least part of the story. Otherwise, how would I explain my being here?

"Mark was… worried about Sander," I said, carefully choosing my words. "Really worried. It sounded pretty bad over the phone, so I came straight back. And before you say anything," I could see him open his mouth to start to talk, "It's all sorted with work. I can definitely stay for a few days, and longer if need be, it's all sorted out. I just… I just needed to be here."

"Lizzy?"

I turned around to see Mark standing on the stairs, concealed slightly by the shadows. "Lizzy, is that you?"

I nodded, not trusting myself to say anything and he flung himself at me, flying down the stairs. He felt so small and my heart ached with responsibility as I felt that, without a doubt, I'd failed in my duty as an older sister. I should have been there, I should have been protecting my brothers and looking after them, and I'd only made things worse.

My dad quietly slipped away, mumbling something about being in the kitchen. I think he knew that we weren't going to tell him more, at least for the time being.

"Mark, what's going on?" I asked in hushed tones, not wanting my parents to hear. Dad was in the kitchen but chances are he wouldn't be opposed to eavesdropping, and who knew where Mum was hiding.

"Come and look," he said, his face dark.

We dashed upstairs and slipped into Sander's room. It was tidier than it had been, and a lot cleaner than when I last saw it.

Mark crept nervously up to Sander's chest of drawers, pulling open the top one. I could tell that he hated doing it, that he hated the invasion of privacy, that he hated betraying his brother's trust. He moved a few things round, and beckoned me over.

He pointed into the drawer, his voice barely a whisper. "Look."

I looked over into the drawer. Mark had moved aside the various pairs of socks and boxer shorts that were on top, and my breath caught at what was underneath.

What Mark had described over the phone couldn't have prepared me for this. I'd been a student, I'd watched crime dramas, and I knew that those packets didn't contain anything that you'd find on Dad's spice rack. I couldn't name it for certain, but I knew it wasn't legal.

Besides the packets were stacks of cash; ten and twenty pound notes rolled up, some even inside socks. There must have been a few hundred pounds there, at least.

"This drawer has the most," Mark said, his voice flat and devoid of all emotion. I could tell that he was only just holding it together. "But nearly all of them have something in. I reckon there's a couple of grand in here in cash. Plus whatever else he's hiding." He turned to me, tears starting to roll down his cheeks, too tired to shout or get angry. "How could he do this, Lizzy? He's my brother! He's my brother, my twin, we're supposed to be the same, we're supposed to be friends, how could he?! How could he, Lizzy, my brother, it's Sander, why did he..."

He trailed off into sobs and I held him close, the need to help my brothers the only thing stopping me from breaking down in a similar fashion.

"Come on," I said quietly, determined that, whatever happened, we needed to get to the bottom of this and sort it out. "Let's go to your room, and let's talk about this and work out what to do, okay? I know it's hard, I know it's difficult, and it's completely okay to be upset, but right now we need to focus. Okay?"

He nodded, sniffing, and quickly rearranged Sander's sock drawer to how it was before following me back to his room.

"What happened?" I asked as soon as Mark had shut his door, perching on the edge of his bed. "How did... you did you find out?"

He gingerly sat next to me, looking at his hands which were shaking slightly.

"I... I kept noticing that money was going missing from my wallet. At first I thought I was just going mad, that I kept thinking I hadn't spent money when I had, so I started to keep track of my spending. I'd go out, take some money out from the bank, come home. Then the next time I went out, I'd go to pay for something and it'd be gone. So, I kept track of how much money was there at what times of day, checking it every hour or something. And I started to notice that the only times that money went missing was when Sander was in the house. And it's not just me; I overheard Dad the other day on the phone to the bank, trying to explain that he didn't make all these transactions that have come from his card.

"Once I'd figured out that it was Sander, I tried to catch him at it, and I did see him once or twice. I tried to talk but he wouldn't listen. He kept telling me that I was being ridiculous and that I didn't have better things to do. So, I looked in his room."

He looked back up at me, tears once again coming full force.

"I know I shouldn't've, Lizzy, I swear – but what else could I do?! I never expected... I never expected it to be that bad, I just thought that maybe... maybe he was short on cash or something, I don't know, maybe there was a perfectly reasonable explanation."

I rubbed his back, not sure what else to do that would help. "Of course you thought that. We all knew Sander was... wild, but none of us saw this coming."

"But I should have!" Mark shouted, making me flinch. "I... I've been so wrapped up in my own stupid stuff, trying to figure all this crap out, I should have noticed that something was going wrong. I should have seen it coming, but I didn't because..."

My heart filled with dread; something else was going on here, and I was sure it wasn't going to be good from the way Mark was talking.

"Because what?" I asked gently, trying to coax it out of him.

He shrank into himself, picking at his fingernails. "We had a huge row," he said, so quietly that I could barely hear him over the sound of the rain pouring outside. "You remember at Charlotte's party, when we argued then. That... that got worse. He kept pushing, and pushing, and he tried to get me to go out with him and this George guy once or twice and it was okay to start with, but..." he shook his head, his whole body trembling. "We both said some awful things. To each other. About each other. I tried to explain, I really did, you have to believe me Lizzy, but he just didn't get it! He just... he wouldn't get it. He said that... He said that I, I didn't work. That I was broken, that there was something wrong, and I wouldn't let him fix it. I said some pretty awful stuff back, and we haven't properly spoken since. It was weeks ago now, but... every time I think about what he said? It hurts more and more and more. Because there's nothing wrong with me. It's okay, right? To... to not want to... to not like... girls and stuff?"

He looked at me so earnestly, as if I held all the answers to his problems, as if I could take all his cares away. I couldn't help but feel slightly relieved. This was familiar ground, this was the sort of thing I was actually able to help him with.

"I'm the last person who's going to judge you for that," I said softly. I tried to put an arm around him but he jumped up immediately, looking destroyed.

"No, no! You don't get it either! It's... no one. There's no one. There never has been, and there never will be. No girls, no boys, no anyone. Is that..." His face crumpled as his whole posture sagged. "Is that so bad? Why am I not allowed that? Why is that not okay?"

I stood up and held him once more, breathing an internal sigh of relief when his arms came around me in return.

"That is more than okay," I said, and I could feel his body shaking. "Of course it's okay. You're you, and that's what matters. You have to be *you*. And sometimes there are people who make you feel like you're not okay, like you're not valid, like you're not important. Those people are wrong. If that's all you remember, Mark, remember that they're wrong. You have every right to be who you are. It will take courage, it will take pride, but you can do it. Don't let anyone tell you otherwise."

He pulled away from me, his expression unreadable. I wasn't sure what to say. Had I said the right things? Was that what he had needed to hear?

He took several deep breaths, steeling himself for something.

"Lizzy," he said, in a voice that left no room for argument. "I know you've probably inferred this from what I've said already. But I want to say it. I..." His poise was lost for a moment, as he took a few more breaths. I squeezed his hand, letting him know that I wasn't going anywhere.

"I'm ace," he breathed out, his voice catching. "I'm... asexual. And I – I think I'm aromantic, as well, although – although I'm not quite as sure on that one. And oh god, it feels so good to say it out loud!"

He was laughing and crying at the same time, his hands going to his head to tangle in his hair. "I... I did it. I said it."

"I know," I said, and it was only at that moment that I realised that I, too, was crying, "and I'm so proud of you!"

I hugged him tightly once more and already he felt lighter and taller and just... more *Mark*. There was something different that hadn't been there before: an understanding, a level of comradery that hit me like a tidal wave. We'd each had that monumental moment. That first time you say something out loud, that deep-set fear that maybe it wouldn't end as you'd hoped, that maybe it would all go wrong. We were by no means the same, not at all, but we shared being different. We'd taken that isolation and we'd turned it against itself, inviting the whole world in. Even if the whole world was only one person.

"Thank you, Lizzy," Mark said against my shoulder, his voice still thick with emotion. "You're brilliant."

"What can I say, it comes naturally," I joked, and we both giggled, giddy as our emotions gradually balanced out again.

I wanted nothing more than to sit with Mark and talk for hours on end, setting aside one by one the heavy weights that we each carried round with us, but there was a reason why I was here at home and I couldn't neglect it for much longer.

"You mentioned George Wickham," I said tentatively, kicking myself for bringing us both back to earth. "Do you... do you think that he had something to do with what's going on? With Sander? Only..." It was now or never. I had to come clean at some point. "While I was in London, I... was told some more about him, and he – he's not all he seems. Or at least, not all I thought he was. What I've heard of his past matches quite closely with what's going on with Sander right now, and I just... I need to know, Mark. I need to know if you think he has anything to do with this whole mess."

"I think he's certainly involved," Mark said darkly. "I don't know exactly what's going on, or to what extent he's involved. But I don't trust him. He's too changeable; he's always exactly the kind of person he needs to be at that moment."

"You're a much better judge of him than I am, then," I said, unable to completely take the bitterness out of my voice.

Mark shrugged in response. "That's the thing about being in the background. People don't know I'm there. And then I can observe, and make a more informed decision about someone. Works out pretty well really. As to exactly how he's involved in all this, though--"

He was interrupted by the front door opening and shutting again.

"Looks like you can ask Sander that yourself."

Chapter 28: Richer or Poorer

Sander went straight up to his room when he came in, not even calling to announce that he was home. We heard him as he ran up the stairs and slammed his door behind him, Dad calling up from downstairs to no response.

We sat in silence, not knowing what to do or say. I glanced over at Mark, his tear-stained face frozen with a fear I hadn't seen before. Counting the seconds on Mark's clock on the wall, I measured two minutes before we heard Dad's gentle footsteps purposefully climbing the stairs before he knocked on the door.

He came in, slowly taking in Mark's red, puffy eyes and my downcast face, and I could see the uncertainty flash across his face. It must be the hardest thing, as a parent, to have grown-up children. They have secrets that they can't tell you and problems that you can't help them with. Dad hardly knew any of what was going on and he already looked helpless and lost.

"I'm glad you're here, Lizzy," he said in a low voice, and I could tell that, for our sakes, he was trying to keep himself together. "Things have been... rough recently. It's good to have you back, if only for a little while."

I nodded, desperately wanting to go and give him a hug, but I knew that right now I needed to stay close to Mark. Everything else could come later.

I settled for a weak, "Thanks Dad," giving him my best attempt at a smile. He grimaced back and padded out of the room, the door clicking shut quietly behind him.

"Shall we go and talk to Sander?" Mark asked, his voice the quiet of an empty house.

"Only if you're sure you're okay," I said, determinedly. "You've had a tough evening already, you don't need to make it any harder if you don't want to."

He shrugged, but there was no real intent behind it.

"I want to," he said, the forced confidence straining his voice. "If we don't, I'll just end up worrying about it and it will all get worse."

I nodded slowly in understanding. "Okay. Do you want to go now? Or wait a bit?"

"Now." He stood up, determined, and strode purposefully towards the door. I followed, trying to imitate his feigned bravado. All motivation seemed to leave him, however, when he reached Sander's door. He turned to face me, eyes wide and questioning.

"Maybe it's best if I do this by myself," I whispered, frantically trying to make an action plan in my head. "You know what he can be like when he feels like he's being ganged up on."

Mark nodded reluctantly and turned around as I knocked, but rather than go back to his room he stood a few steps down the corridor, where he'd be out of sight from Sander. I couldn't send him back, though, as Sander opened his door.

There was a beat as he took me in, clearly surprised. "Lizzy? What are you – what are you doing here?"

I don't think that it would have been unreasonable to hope that he'd be happy to see me, maybe even bordering on excitement, but he sounded more guarded and suspicious than anything else.

I couldn't think of a good answer to the question, so I just shrugged. "I'm just... here. How are you doing?"

"Well enough," he grunted, his eyes flitting from my face to the hallway behind me, as if expecting something to happen.

Eventually I stuttered out, "I'm glad. How is the... how is the job?"

"Can't complain."

I stood in silence once more, and it went on just a second too long.

"Mark set you up to this, didn't he?"

"What?" I was genuinely shocked – not from the accusation itself, but from how quickly he'd reached that conclusion. Mark hadn't been exaggerating, not at all. "Why do you say that?"

He pushed me out the way with an anger-fuelled energy and looked down the corridor to where Mark was still listening in on our conversation.

"Ha! I knew it! Typical Mark, going and crying to big sister when he doesn't get his way. I'm a huge bloody disappointment, aren't I? You want me to be just like you, don't you, you think that because we look the same we are the same and that I'm the problem here! Well maybe, Mark, just maybe, maybe *you're* the problem. I'm sorry that I'm such a huge disappointment, but let's face it, it's not like you really exceeded my expectations either. Of all the brothers I could've had, I got stuck with *you*. You think that you can make everything exactly how you want it but you can't, and it's time you just accepted that."

Mark and I were both stunned into silence. I hadn't spoken to Sander in so long, and this... this was not the brother I remembered leaving behind way back in August.

I only had myself to blame.

Sander looked at us both expectantly, as if challenging one of us to say something, but when we remained speechless he turned to go back to his room.

"Sander--" I called out as he stepped through the doorway.

He paused in his tracks as if contemplating something before speaking, not even turning around to look at me.

"Screw you, Lizzy."

And he slammed the door shut behind him.

I turned, shocked, ready to make sure that Mark was okay, but I didn't need to ask. He was barely breathing, his eyes open wide and his skin tight across his face.

"Mark," I said tentatively, "Are you – what can I do to help? Speak to me. It will be okay, we can fix this. Please. Let me help."

I was aware that I was rambling, unable to control the words that came out of my mouth, but I was desperate to fill the silence.

Mark shuddered in a breath, looking like a spooked animal. "I'd like to be alone right now," he said, constricted.

"Mark, I... as long as you're sure it's for the best. Not what you want to do the most, but for the best."

I don't think he really understood the distinction between those two things, but he nodded anyway.

"Yes. I... I have to go."

He hadn't even shut his door behind him when I saw him collapse in silent sobs, unable to hold himself up any longer. I felt more lost than I'd ever felt before. what could I do? What was there to do? What did my brothers need me to do?

I couldn't go to Dad, or Mum; it seemed that I knew more than they did put together, and I didn't feel like it was my place right now to divulge the story to them. Besides, if Sander found out that I'd told them, any hope of regaining some of his trust would be lost. The only other person who did know what was going on was, I expected, George Wickham, and there was no way I was contacting him. Not at all.

I went back to my room, getting out my phone, and before I knew it I had rung someone. It took me a few seconds to work out who my subconscious had deemed worthy; the few seconds which it took them to answer.

"Lizzy?" the voice said on the other end, and it was a voice that I never thought I'd need, or want, to hear. "Lizzy, is that – is that you?"

I felt my breath hitch as everything caught up with me, and I could barely get the next word out. "Darcy?"

I heard her sigh in relief down the phone. "Lizzy, thank goodness! Are you home, are you alright?"

I nodded, then remembered she couldn't see me. "I – yes, I'm home. And I... I think I'm alright. No, who am I kidding, I'm not. I just... I didn't know what to do," I could hear the tears in my voice, "and I... I rang you. I'm not sure why, really. I just..."

"I understand." She saved me from having to finish that sentence; I honestly don't know what I was about to say.

"It's… it's George Wickham. He's turned my brothers against each other, although I doubt it was particularly hard, but… he's got Sander stealing money. And hiding… hiding things for him. Darcy, I don't know what to do, I can't do it! I can't help him, I can't, I don't know what to do, I don't know where to start! This is all my fault, I should never, I shouldn't have kept this from them. I… I can't."

I don't know exactly when but tears had started falling, and they were streaming down my cheeks. I inelegantly rubbed my nose and sniffed, feeling the weight of the afternoon's events crashing down on my head.

"Lizzy, listen to me," said Darcy, her voice leaving no room for argument. "This is not your fault. This is George's fault. Take it from someone who knows; you can't blame yourself for someone else's actions. The responsibility lies with him. All you can do is learn from it."

"We both know that's not true," I said hollowly. There was no response. "It may not be my fault. But it's my responsibility."

"Regardless of all that," and I could hear her beginning to choke up, too, "I believe in you. The most important thing right now is to help your brothers repair their relationship, and I know you can do that. You have a way of making people see things not in the way they want to, but the way they should. If anyone can help them, it's you."

"You really think so?" I hated how pathetic I sounded.

"I know so."

I wasn't sure what to make of that, but right now I wasn't in the frame of mind to worry about it.

"Lizzy, if there's anything I can do to help – anything at all – then just tell me. I can be there in an instant, if there's even the slightest chance that I could help."

"You're giving me time off work, that's help enough," I said earnestly. "Thank you for the offer, but I don't see how anyone could help. Not really. Things are looking... pretty hopeless around here."

"I think we both know that even the most hopeless situations have a tendency of working out," Darcy said, and I felt an unexpected weight behind her words. She took a deep breath, audible even over the phone, before saying her next words and I could tell that she was steeling herself up for them. "I will always be there for you. Know that. I will be here."

I could feel my voice constricting again as the tears sprung up once more. "Thank you," I managed to squeak out, not trusting myself to say more.

"You're welcome," she said, barely more than a whisper, and for just a moment it was as if she was there, right by me, and we were sharing this intimate moment together.

"Lizzy, promise me that you'll let me know if I can do anything to help. And promise me that if you need me – for anything – you'll ask. It's all you need to do."

I nodded again before remembering once more that she couldn't see me. "I promise."

"Okay. I will... speak to you soon, then, okay?"

"Okay." I couldn't quite bring myself to say goodbye, and the tone in my ear told me that she'd felt the same.

I cradled my phone gently in my hand for a few moments longer, pretending that she was there and that it was all going to be okay. That I knew what was going to happen, and that it would all be alright.

I curled up on my old twin bed, not even changing into my pyjamas or getting under the covers, and lay on my side, facing the wall. Drifting off into something resembling sleep, the world around me gently shut off.

A few hours later, after it had gone dark, I was pulled out of my doze by a knocking at the door. I blearily called out a "Come in," sluggishly sitting up and adjusting my clothes.

"Hey Lizzy."

It was Jane. Wonderful, sweet, lovely Jane, with that caring, loving smile, and that soft voice that made you feel like all your troubles would just drift away.

"Dad said you were back. How are you doing?"

I shrugged, unable to summon the energy to say anything. She came and sat next to me on my bed, gently resting an arm around my shoulders in comfort.

"Have you seen Mark?" I asked.

"Not since I got in this evening. Is he in his room? Is he alright?"

I knew he wasn't, and frankly I didn't expect him to. He'd come out, one of the scariest things you could ever do, and then immediately been insulted and snubbed by his identical twin brother, the one person who was meant to be closer to you than anyone in the world.

Jane sensed that I wasn't going to verbalise an answer, so pressed on.

"How about you? How are things in London?"

I didn't mean to. I honestly had no intention of it, but I couldn't help myself. I told her almost everything; about Darcy, about her apparently loving me, about how we'd been seeing each other since. I told her everything Darcy had told me about George, and how I felt like such an idiot for ever believing him. The only things I didn't tell her about were Will's past, and how Darcy broke her and Charlie up. One wasn't my story to share, and the other was not something that Jane needed to hear, at least until I knew more about her current feelings on the matter.

She stayed silent throughout the whole thing, letting me speak, not interrupting, listening intently to every detail. The most surprising thing, however, was the first thing she said after I'd finished.

"And how do you feel about Darcy now?"

The question hit me like a ton of bricks. "What, no shock or confusion at the turn of events? Jane, I literally told you that a woman who has spent all summer insulting our entire family claims to be in love with me, and that's your first question?"

She sighed, as if having to explain something to a child. "Lizzy, the only person surprised by that confession was you." She looked far too knowing as she said this. "Now, answer my question. How do you feel about her?"

It was a question I'd been avoiding, I'll admit. How did I feel? Really?

"I... I feel like there's a Darcy in my head, a Darcy who resembles the person who yelled at me for looking in her library back in June. That Darcy, the one that I think of when I think 'Darcy Williams'? Her, I don't like. She's awful. But..."

"But what?"

I sighed, ignoring Jane's expectant look.

"That Darcy doesn't match up with the one in real life. The one who takes me to the theatre and to lunch and to the library and who lives with my friend. I like spending time with that Darcy. I like... I like that Darcy. And I guess... I guess I'm just having issues replacing the Darcy in my head with the one I know. The one that I... the one that I like."

I knew what Jane wanted to ask, but I also knew that she wouldn't ask it. I resolved to answer it anyway; it would keep her happy.

"I'm not sure what kind of like it is. But when I'm with her I feel... safe. Cared for. And I feel... I don't know. Comfortable but on edge at the same time. Does that make sense?"

There she was with that knowing face again, nodding and giving a smile that on anyone else would have been smug.

"That makes perfect sense."

Chapter 29: Sander Speaks

Being at home was infinitely better than the alternative, but that didn't mean it wasn't awful. There was nothing I could do. Sander wouldn't talk to anyone, and without his input there wasn't anything else *we* could do. The daytime was easier, because I was kept occupied. Anything that could be done without being in the office was being emailed to me, so I managed to be relatively productive while feeling better about not being at work. I didn't know if I could justify staying at home much longer, though. By Wednesday afternoon, I had resolved to return to London the following week if no more progress was made.

Sander was hardly ever in, and when he was he shut himself away in his room. He didn't eat dinner with us, he wouldn't acknowledge that we were there if he walked past us. Mum and Dad pretended it didn't bother them, but it wasn't hard to see that they were faking. Mum, especially, had taken to lamenting about how we 'all went through this phase' and that 'he'll come around soon enough'. Mark came downstairs often enough but barely spoke, his eyes swimming in sadness. Jane was the only one who could convincingly pass off as being alright, but when she thought no one was watching you could see her face sink slightly.

Dinner every evening was an awkward affair. Dad would make enough for six, lay the table for six, and after half an hour take the last plate up to leave outside

Sander's door. Inevitably, though, it ended up being thrown away; Sander wouldn't touch it.

By Wednesday night I'd realised that someone had to do something. It was obvious that Sander wasn't going to come to us so we had to go to him, before the situation or the mood in the house got any worse. Mark was struggling, it was plain to see. His eyes were red-rimmed every time I saw him, and he was barely eating. He and Sander had never got along brilliantly but their fights were rarely anything serious, and they'd never gone for more than an hour or so not talking to each other. They'd never even gone to sleep on an argument before. You could always hear one of them tip-toeing to the other's room to reconcile because they couldn't sleep.

That wasn't what clinched it, though. Hearing my parents' conversation over dinner confirmed for me that something had to be done.

"I went to the bank again today," Mum said once we'd settled into our meal. "Oh, David, this tastes wonderful! Anyway, I know you say I'm being paranoid, but there's definitely money coming out of our account somehow, and the bank won't do anything about it. They say there's nothing suspicious about it, and that as it's a joint account we just need to communicate more about taking money out. But I know there's something going on, some money gone that we didn't take out."

My dad sighed. I could tell they'd had this argument before. "Joan, it's completely possible that someone has taken some money, but I highly doubt it. I've had a look and I think we just need to be more careful about how we spend our money. As they said, there's nothing suspicious about anything, they're all perfectly valid transactions. We just need to spend less of it."

Mum huffed and I could tell that she wanted to say something more but held herself back, probably from some daft British opposition to discussing finances at the dinner table. Mark, however, was giving me a pleading look, and I could tell that we were thinking exactly the same thing. Mum and Dad had a family account to which we all knew the account details, the idea being that, should there be an emergency, we would be able to access the accounts. It wasn't an ideal solution, of course, but Mum and Dad trusted us not to take money out from it except for in emergencies, and up until now it had worked fine. That trust had now, however, been broken. It was my task now to fix this, preferably with my parents being none the wiser, at least until it was over. As estranged as Sander seemed to want to be right now, I was sure he wouldn't want that forever.

Thursday afternoon, about an hour before Sander was due to return home, I put my plan into action. Even though I didn't really feel that I was doing anything wrong I still glanced each way down the corridor before slipping into Sander's room, mentally apologising to him for what I was about to do. I opened every drawer, the doors to his cupboards, displaying everything that he'd hidden. The only relief came when I didn't find anything in my look behind all the furniture, glad that there wasn't more than I'd already found. Glancing at the clock, I saw that it would be at least another half an hour before he came home so I sat stiffly on the edge of his bed, running scenarios around my head. I determinedly didn't look at the clock. Counting seconds wouldn't help anything.

I jolted as I heard the front door go. My body was ready for a flight or fight response but I forced myself to stay where I was, my brain registering somehow that Dad had tried to say hello to Sander, Sander was coming upstairs, Sander was nearly by his door –

To my credit, I managed to keep stock still as he opened his door and did a double-take as he saw me there. He glared at me, angry, but I could see the moment that he saw the open drawers, the exposed wardrobe. His eyes drifted just the slightest amount, and in the deathly silence of the room I heard his breath hitch.

"What the hell do you think you're doing?" He asked in what was clearly supposed to be a menacing voice, but it came off as scared.

"I don't think I'm the one who needs to answer that question," I replied, surprising myself with how level I managed to keep my tone. "How about you sit down, and we can talk about this."

He slowly shut his door behind him, threw his bag into the corner, and slunk into his desk chair.

"Are you threatening me?" he said, his voice wavering.

I shook my head, trying desperately to lower the tension in the room. "No. I'm not threatening you. I want to talk to you. I want to get to the bottom of this. And I want to fix this."

"You mean you want to fix me," he said scornfully, throwing his head back. "That's what you want, isn't it? You want me to be part of some picture-perfect family, you want me to be more... more like you. That's what you want, that's all you've ever wanted!"

"That's not true," I said, feeling my temper already beginning to bubble, but not getting much more of a chance to speak.

"It is true!" His voice was rising rapidly. "It's all any of you want. You're all embarrassed by me, you all wish that I wasn't like this. There's nothing wrong with me, nothing wrong with what I do, and now I have friends who appreciate that. You don't get to tell me what to do anymore, Lizzy!"

He leant back in his chair, panting slightly.

"That's not true," I said, putting every effort into keeping my voice quiet and calm. "I love you, Sander. You're my brother. But this *isn't you*. When I left... you were really working on turning things around. Becoming more responsible. But I think... no, I *know* that I blame myself for all this."

He scoffed. "You blame yourself? Of course you're finding a way to make this about *you*. There's nothing to blame yourself for, Lizzy. You need to accept that I am who I am, even though I know you've never liked it. You're so high and mighty, you know? So full of it, you just thought 'oh look, Sander's getting a job, oh goody now he'll be more like me'. You don't understand me, Lizzy, accept that."

"Who told you that?" I asked, my voice dangerously low now. "Who told you that we didn't care, that we don't understand, that we want you to change?"

"No one had to tell me, it's plain to--"

"It was George Wickham, wasn't it?"

He froze, and I could see that I'd hit the nail on the head.

"George didn't tell me anything," he said, his voice barely a whisper. "He helped me to see things for how they really are, that's all."

"Is that who all this is for?" I didn't need to explain what I was talking about. His eyes had glanced back to his stash as soon as I'd mentioned George's name.

"I'm not doing anything wrong," he said instantly, and I could tell that his resolve was beginning to crumble. "You got it all out to scare me, didn't you?" I couldn't deny that. "I'm just holding on to some stuff for him. Until he gets his own place. It's not like I've ever taken any of it, I've just been looking after it."

"Don't you get it?!" I was starting to get more and more frustrated now. "This is illegal. This is against the law. This is trouble, Sander, serious trouble, and you're right in the middle of it. And don't tell me that this is all of George's hard-earned money, I know you've been taking it from Mark and Mum and Dad."

"George is my friend," he said, and it was painfully obvious that he believed it, that it was the only thing he was convinced of. "The best thing you ever did, Lizzy, was introduce me to him. He likes me for who I am, he looks out for me. I'm helping a friend; that's all."

He finished talking, but I could tell that there was still something he wanted to say. He looked worried and anxious all of a sudden, words on the tip of his tongue.

"Sander?" He didn't respond. "Sander, what is it?"

"Nothing." He shook himself out of it. "It's what friends do. Help each other out."

Something about these words, the way he said them, felt rehearsed, as if he was repeating something someone else had said.

"Friends don't do *this*, Sander," I urged, desperate to make him see sense. "Friends don't put friends in danger, or in bad situations. This isn't asking for a friend's help. This is asking for your friend to be your scapegoat."

"George said you wouldn't understand," Sander said, his anger rapidly melting as he became more and more upset. "He said that... he said that none of you would understand. That you don't appreciate me. That you don't care. And he was right. He was right about everything."

"I do care about you." I went to take his hands, but he jerked them away. I ignored the sting it left, continuing on. "I know I haven't been the best at showing it, and for that I'm genuinely sorry. But you're my brother, Sander. I care about you so, so much. George..." I took a deep breath. "George has a history of being manipulative. Of getting people to do things for him, of isolating people, hurting people, and I should've told you as soon as I found out the truth about him."

Sander flinched, and I saw his right arm subconsciously move so his hand was covering his left wrist. I could hear alarm bells going off in my head, but I couldn't work out what they were telling me to do.

"What do you mean, hurting people?" He said, and I could barely hear him over the noise of the rain outside. "Where did you get that from?"

Things were starting to fall into place, and it was awful. I felt a chilling realisation pass over me and I looked up to see Sander's fear-filled eyes. "There's different kinds of hurt, Sander. Right now, though, I want to look at your arm."

He shook his head so hard that it almost rattled, his eyes growing even wider. "No, it was an accident, he didn't mean to, he was angry, he just grabbed my arm too hard, that was all. I hadn't managed to get him the money I promised him and he was drunk, he didn't mean to, he was so sorry as soon as he realised the next day, he kept apologising. It's nothing, Lizzy, really, it's nothing."

"If it's nothing," I said, struggling to keep my voice calm, knowing that if I got angry right now it would ruin everything, "you could show me and it would be fine."

I know that wasn't why he slowly reached his arm out to me. I suspect that, somewhere, he knew that this wasn't right, that friends *don't do that*. His whole hand was shaking. I gently held his fingers still before delicately rolling up his sleeve.

There was a purple bruise all the way around his wrist, with clear marks where the tips of fingers had been. I gave an inaudible gasp as soon as I saw it; I had known that things were bad, but I had no idea how much.

I didn't want to dwell on the injury; Sander had to be my focus right now. I looked up at his face, where a few tears were waiting in the corners of his eyes.

"He didn't mean to," he whispered, still sitting with his arm cradled in my hands. "It was an accident. It was only the once. And I've got the money for him now, he won't do it again."

"This is abuse, Sander," I said, my voice trembling, with no hope but to make my brother see it for what it really was. "That's not okay, not ever. You know that."

"It's not abuse," he said, giving a short, forced laugh. "We're friends, Lizzy. Straight, male friends. It's not abuse."

"It doesn't work like that. Please, Sander," I begged, "Please, just... he's hurting you. He's supposed to be your friend, and he's hurting you. Surely you can see that's not okay?"

"I'd like you to leave now."

"No, Sander, I can't!" There was no way that I could just walk out now. This was far, far worse than I'd imagined, and leaving now would only make everything worse.

"Leave." I opened my mouth to say something, beg him to see what I was trying to tell him, but I didn't have the chance. "Leave! Just go!"

He was shouting, and I couldn't see what else to do if not leave. I hated myself more for every step I took towards his door, not daring to look back at his tormented face.

As soon as the door was shut behind me, I leant back on it and slid down the floor, unable to stop the tears. I'd made everything so, so much worse, and I wasn't sure if this was something that I could fix. This was all my fault, and all I'd managed to do was alienate my brother even more, make him feel like he didn't have anyone at all. I'd failed.

I could hear him crying on the other side of the door and wanted more than anything to go back in there and wrap him up with blankets and pillows, protect him from the world and all the awful things in it, but I was unable to.

I had never felt so helpless before. My brother was hurting, a lot, and had been hurt by someone that I'd introduced him to, and there was nothing I could do. I'd run out of options, I'd played my last card.

All I could do now was wait for a miracle.

Chapter 30: Progress

"What do we do now?"

It was Friday afternoon. While Sander was at work, Mark, Jane and I had gathered in the sitting room to work out what to do next. I'd told them everything that had happened so far, and it wasn't hard to see that we were all equally affected by it. Mark had curled up on an armchair, rubbing at his tear-stained face, but Jane – who usually remains so calm – was pacing stormily up and down the room.

"We can't let him spend any more time with George Wickham, that's for sure," said Jane angrily. "We need help, Lizzy. We can't do this by ourselves, this is serious. Do Mum and Dad know?"

I shook my head. "They know something's up, but not what."

"Why on earth haven't you told them?!" I had never seen Jane acting like this, and honestly it scared me.

"You heard what Sander was saying! He thinks that we all hate him, that we all want to change him into the person we want him to be." I recited the explanation that I'd been telling myself in my head constantly over the last few days. "You know they'd make a fuss. It would only persuade Sander that George is right, and the last thing we need now is for him to feel like we've all turned on him. I do... I do think we should tell Dad at least part of it though. Especially now we know the full extent of it."

"Is that really the reason?" Mark said weakly from where he was curled up in one corner. "I understand, and I agree with you – we should let Dad know part of it, but giving him and Mum the whole story would make things worse for Sander, and we should wait. But… is that the real reason that you're not telling them?"

"Of course it is!" What other reason could Mark possibly be thinking of?

"I know you, Lizzy," he said coldly, his eyes dull and lifeless, "And I know that you're blaming yourself for everything that's happened. I think that you feel that because this is your fault you have to fix it before anyone finds out. It's too late for that, Lizzy. Stop wallowing in guilt, this isn't about you."

"There's no use arguing," Jane butted in, trying to diffuse the situation. "Arguing about motives right now won't help anything. We need to decide what's best for Sander, not what's best for our egos."

Harsh words coming from Jane, but I couldn't blame her; I'd realised with a jolt that Mark was right. I was blaming myself, and it wasn't helping anyone; my own doubts could wait.

"So we're going to tell Dad part of the story, but not all of it," Jane continued, still pacing up and down. "I hate to say this, but do you think we should involve the police? This is serious stuff here. There are levels of illegal and thankfully he's only just over the line, which is a small mercy, but he's also been physically assaulted. This is serious, Lizzy, really serious."

"You think I don't know that?" I snapped. "I'm well aware of how serious this is, but if we call the police… I don't know what would happen. I say we talk to Sander when he gets back today, give him an ultimatum. We'll go to the police if he doesn't do anything, say, by the end of the weekend. If nothing else, it will make him see how serious this is."

"I don't want to threaten him," Mark piped up quietly from his armchair.

I sighed, my head in my hands. "Well, what else do you suggest we do? I don't like it any more than you do, but I think it's our best option. What's most important right now is that we keep Sander safe, but something needs to persuade him that that is really all we want. Quite frankly, I'm not sure what else we can do."

I stood up slowly. "I'm going to go and talk to Dad while Mum's still at work. He should be in his study right now, I'm sure he won't mind me interrupting if it's important."

Jane nodded to me gravely. I didn't know what else to say. After all, what else was there to say? I could keep apologising, but that would only make things even worse than they already were. Mark and Jane were right. We had to focus on fixing things, not dwelling on what-ifs.

I knocked on my dad's study door, almost wishing that he would have gone out or just be too busy to talk. The thought of telling my dad even a fraction of what was going on right now... I already knew that this was going to be one of the worst conversations I'd ever had with him.

"Come in," he called out so I pushed the door open, letting him into the study. "Lizzy! How can I help?"

I stood there for a few seconds, trying to order my thoughts, before blurting out all in one go, "IwanttotalktoyouaboutSander."

I could tell he hadn't been able to make the sentence out but had picked up the word 'Sander' at the end, so he gestured for me to sit down. I perched on the edge of the spare chair in his study, preparing for the worst.

"You know… you know George Wickham?" I started, unsure as to exactly what I was going to say.

Dad nodded, and I could tell by his face that he wasn't surprised at the story starting here.

"George… George has been manipulating Sander. He's been… persuading him that we don't really care about him. That George is the only actual friend he has. George has been… purposefully isolating Sander, trying – and succeeding – to pull him away from us."

I looked down and my hands were shaking.

"George… hurt Sander. He hurt Sander, my baby brother, and I couldn't… I should have been there to stop him."

Before I knew what was happening Dad was there, he was hugging me, and I was crying into his shoulder, unable to hold it back. "It's all my fault, Dad. I should have been there. I should have warned him. I just assumed… I thought he wouldn't do this, I hoped he'd changed, I thought that maybe he wouldn't… maybe he would be a better person than he'd been given credit for. I was wrong, Dad. I thought I had him figured out, but I was wrong, and she kept telling me I was wrong but I ignored her, I just carried on and now Sander's hurt and it's all my fault…"

I cried and cried, hating myself for still getting upset about my own actions when I needed to focus on my brother, but unable to stop it.

"I'm not going to pretend I understood most of that," said Dad once I'd calmed down enough for us to continue with a conversation, "but I think I got the gist. Whatever happened, there is no point in blaming yourself now, Betts."

"You're not the first to tell me that," I mumbled. "Dad, you should know... you should know that Sander's the one who's been taking the money out of your account. George has been... persuading him that it's the right thing to do. I'll do everything I can to make sure you get it back, I promise, I swear."

"The money's not important," said Dad wearily. "I mean, obviously it is, but what's more important is Sander. We can cope without the money. I can't cope without my son."

I nodded, unsure of what to say.

"Lizzy..." He sighed, looking utterly defeated. "I know you're not telling me everything, but... promise me that you will tell me? If I need to know?"

I nodded again. "I promise."

"That's all I ask."

***

I wasn't aware of Sander having come home that evening until there was a knock at my door. I couldn't help but be surprised when I saw who was there.

"Lizzy," Sander said in greeting, not meeting my eyes. "Can I... come in? I want to talk to you."

He looked and sounded so small, as if he wanted to just shrink and hide away.

"Of course you can," I said as tenderly as I could, holding the door open for him.

He waited until I'd shut the door before speaking, not bothering to sit down or make himself comfortable. "Lizzy, I... I've been thinking a lot. About what you said. I don't think George is capable of everything you accused him of. I know he's not. He's my only friend, and I hate that you can't see that. But..." I could tell that he was struggling to get the words out. "But I realised that you were right about some things. And he was wrong about some things. I think... I think you care about me, a little bit, and so I really thought about what you said. Most of the things you said about George I know aren't true, but... I know he shouldn't have hurt me. And I know that all day at work I was worrying about whether or not we'd bump into each other. And I think you shouldn't be scared of your friends. So I'm going to think about things, seriously, and make sure that it doesn't happen again. I'm... I'm not going to keep helping him all the time, either. I'm sure he'll understand I can't keep looking after his... things for him. So yeah. That's it. I thought you ought to know."

Wow. It's not what I expected and not what I'd hoped for, but it was something in between, which was better than nothing.

"I'm... I'm glad you're thinking about those things," I said, choosing my words very carefully. One wrong step could undo everything. "And you should know that I care about you a lot – so, so much. You're my little brother, and I will always want the best for you." I didn't say that I doubted George would understand, and that really, I didn't think he should remain friends with George at all. I knew that if I said those things it would all get worse again.

"Thank you, Lizzy," he said stiffly. He sounded like he was reciting from some sort of script. "You helped me see that one of my friendships wasn't as it should be, and now I'm fixing it. So thank you."

As he left the room, I realised that the worst part of all this was how much he believed the words coming out of his mouth. At least now he knew that what George was doing, what George was persuading him to do, was wrong; it was a start, at least. Now what was left was to persuade him that George really was bad news, and to make Sander see him for who he truly was. Easier said than done, though. I had first-hand experience in being lured in by George's façade.

I realised too late that I hadn't given Sander the ultimatum that I'd agreed on with Mark and Jane but it was clear that Sander had no intention of keeping George's stash, and that was good enough for me. To confront him with an ultimatum now might put us all back to square one.

For the first time all week, I went to sleep that night with a weight lifted off my chest. We were finally starting to make progress. Sander was starting to come around, and we were tentatively making baby steps towards fixing this. I'd arranged to stay at home until the end of the weekend, and we even managed to have the whole family – Sander included – down for dinner. Sander had gone out straight afterwards, I think to talk to George, but hadn't stayed long enough for me to insist that someone go with him. It wouldn't have made any difference, though, and I fell asleep happy in the knowledge that perhaps things weren't quite as hopeless as they seemed.

I should have known, however, that things couldn't have stayed looking optimistic for long. I didn't hear Sander come home, so he must have been out late, but the next morning he came downstairs for long enough to make some toast, not looking at or speaking to anyone, before taking it back up to his room.

By mid-morning I'd managed to talk myself into knocking on his door to try to find out what had happened. It had seemed that he was starting to realise that things weren't as they should be, but had George Wickham managed to undo that in one go? It honestly wouldn't surprise me, but the thought filled me with dread.

I tried to ignore the sting I felt when Sander opened the door. "Oh. It's you," he said, clearly attempting derision. "Come to preach some more about my poor choices in friends?"

"What happened?" I asked, almost certain that I wouldn't like the answer.

"You tried to end the only friendship I have, that's what happened!" he shouted, but it lost its bite under the tears that were beginning to appear. "I tried to follow your advice, and all it did was make him angry. I'm his friend, and I tried to say that I wouldn't help him anymore! I tried to give him back all his things, and he got angry. Because I'm not a good enough friend, Lizzy! I'm a bad friend and I nearly lost everything. He was so angry, just because I tried to do what you told me to." All the rage had left him now. He'd deflated, openly crying. "I tried, Lizzy, I tried, because

I don't want to do it anymore! But he got angry, he kept getting angry, so I said I'd carry on, I'm sorry Lizzy, I didn't want to, I'm sorry..."

As he curled in on himself I went to give him a hug, and tried to ignore my surprise when it was returned. As he moved his arms, I could see a large purple mark just under the collar of his loose pyjama shirt, and I instantly knew what had happened.

There was more to talk about, much more to talk about, but now was not the time. He'd started dozing off, exhausted from the emotional turmoil and sleepless night, so I carefully helped him to his bed, making sure he was comfortable and staying there until he slept properly. It was only then that I left his room, taking my phone out and dialling before I'd even shut the door behind me.

It was answered after the third ring.

"Lizzy?"

"Darcy? Thank goodness, I... I don't know what to do, Darcy, I have no idea what to do anymore. I'm, I'm sorry, I know you have your own things to worry about, but I just... I didn't know who else to call."

"It's fine, I'm here. I'll help, I'll do everything I can."

I never thought it would be so comforting to hear her voice.

"I just, I don't know what to do. Things are bad, really bad, and--"

"Wait just a moment. I will help you, I will, I promise. I just need you to do something first."

"What is it?" I wiped at my cheeks, frantically trying to mop up the tears that were staining my face.

"Open your front door."

I ran down the stairs as fast as I could, nearly tripping partway down, wrenching the door open with all the strength I had left in me, desperately hoping that it would be what I wanted it to be.

But all the hoping, all the wishing in the world could not have prepared me for that moment; for that feeling, when I saw her on the doorstep, that feeling that everything was going to be alright. She was still holding her phone up to her ear, and I realised that I was doing the same, but I didn't even hang up before throwing my arms around her.

"I'm so glad you're here," I said, breathing deeply with her hair pressed against my face.

"Me too," she said, her arms wrapping round me just a little bit tighter as she said it.

And for the first time since I'd left London, I truly felt like I was at home.

Chapter 31: Touching Distance

I couldn't believe it. She was here. Here, with me, and I didn't realise until that moment how much I'd missed her, how much I'd needed her.

I don't know how long we stood in the doorway just holding each other, but it felt like an age wrapped up in a matter of seconds. I never wanted to leave, never wanted to move. I just needed to be held, to be safe, and I'd never felt safer than I did in that moment when she was there.

It was only when I felt her start to shiver slightly that we quickly pulled apart, not quite breaking physical contact but putting more distance between us.

"You must be freezing!" I exclaimed, suddenly realising quite how cold the autumn air was. "You should come inside, warm up. I'll make you some tea or something? I, um, I'm not quite sure exactly how you like it, or if you do like it, we have coffee and hot chocolate as well-"

I was floundering, desperate to do everything right.

"It's okay, Lizzy," she said, gently placing her hands on my arms. "Don't worry, I'm fine. I hope you don't mind – Jordan's come too. He waited in the car though, he, er, wanted to leave us to it. I thought that maybe he might be able to talk to Sander?"

I nodded, at this point agreeing with everything she said. I felt so overwhelmed just by her presence that I couldn't think of what to do or say. She was right, though.

The only person who really understood exactly what Sander was going through right now was Jordan, and right now we needed all the help we could get.

Darcy turned slightly to where her car was parked and I saw that Jordan was waiting in the passenger seat. I could tell that he was pretending not to look at us, but he let himself out when Darcy nodded towards him.

"Hi Lizzy," he said, smiling weakly as he tugged his jacket further around him. There was a strange tension between the three of us. The woman who was sort of my friend and sort of something more if I wanted it, and her overprotective but supportive younger brother, here to help me and *my* youngest brother. Between us we made an odd crowd.

I invited them both in and we sat awkwardly in the sitting room for a few moments, none of us entirely sure what to say.

"Would you like a cup of tea?" I asked again, looking for something to do. The only other time Jordan and I had spoken had been when he gave me his protective-brother speech, and it was whirling round and round my brain, clashing with my desperate relief at Darcy being there. If nothing else, I just needed to get out of the room for a few seconds, if only to clear my head.

Darcy seemed to pick up on my unease. "That would be lovely," she smiled reassuringly. "Milk and no sugar for me, please."

I could tell that she was about to give me Jordan's tea order as well, but paused at the last moment to let him speak for himself. It occurred to me that Jordan was probably also suffering, if only from the resurfacing of memories he'd hoped to move away from.

"Milk and two sugars please," he said distantly. I nodded and slipped out of the room as quickly as I politely could, hurrying into the kitchen.

I took a few deep breaths as the kettle boiled, carefully counting the seconds between breathing in and breathing out.

Darcy would know what to do, I'm sure of it. She'd known, without me having to say anything, she knew before I did that I'd need her and here she was. I somehow just knew that everything would be okay now, because we had help. We would be able to get through this. Darcy would help. With her... with her I could do anything.

The door to the kitchen slowly creaked open. Torn away from my thoughts, I looked up to see Darcy standing there, concerned. My brain threw forwards the memory of the last time we were in this spot; me standing behind the door listening in, her telling Charlie how awful I was. Those two images of then and now collided and I suddenly saw before me a young woman who was scared, who was anxious, who was trying to find her place in the world, who tried but panicked. Someone whose walls were up so high that every compliment, every smile, anything that could be perceived as a weakness was surrounded by thorns and barbs.

"How are you doing?" she asked tenderly, as if knowing that I was okay was the only thing in the world that mattered.

I shrugged. "I've been better. Things are... things are bad." I shuddered slightly. "What George has done..." I sniffed and before I knew it the tears had started up again, my hand coming up to cover my mouth.

"Oh, my darli-- Lizzy, it's alright, it will be alright." She strode over to me and hugged me once more. "It's okay, shh, it's okay, we'll get through this. I promise." She waited until my breathing had calmed down again before loosening her hold slightly, but not enough that we'd broken physical contact. "What happened?"

I took a deep breath. "George hurt him," I whispered, my voice trembling in repressed anger. "He... he hit Sander. Pushed him. I don't know exactly, but I know that now my brother's hurt and I want George to pay for what he's done."

My eyes met Darcy's. Her face held a mix of bewilderment and rage.

"I didn't..." she swallowed audibly. "I didn't know he was capable of something like that, but now you say it I'm barely surprised. I can only... I can only apologise. If I'd done something differently, if I'd said something different years ago, this wouldn't be happening."

"There's no use playing the blame game," I hushed her, firmly taking both of her hands in mine. "Believe me, I know. All we can do now is... try to help Sander. And I think with you here, and Jordan here, we can do it. We'll deal with George afterwards."

She looked at me, her eyes filled with the weight of the world. "I know. I just... I wish I could make it all go away. For you. I wish that you didn't have to go through this."

She was looking at me so earnestly, with such desperation, and I just wished for a second that we could leave. Go somewhere far away, where we had no worries, no problems, and could just enjoy each other's company.

"Just you being here is enough," I breathed, holding her gaze in mine, surprised to find how much I meant those words. She was here, she was so close, she was so present. I gently pulled her hands towards me until there was only a few inches between us, desperate to be closer to her and her comfort. I stretched up, going onto my tiptoes, holding her gaze until the last second when our eyelids fluttered closed. Her lips were so close, all I wanted to do was to meet them, to feel that intimacy and that spark with her. I could feel her warmth, it was within my reach, all I had to do was lean in and –

"No."

A river of ice ran over my body at the utterance of those two letters, that one word that I could never ignore. My eyes flew open, both of us breathless as I lowered my heels back down to the floor. I didn't know what to do; nothing I could say right now would make things better.

Daring to look at her face I saw that her deep brown eyes were wide, trying to process what had just happened. I could feel her hands shaking slightly in mine, but I couldn't bring myself to move, to do anything. I had done the damage. I had to wait now, wait for her to say or do something, say or do anything.

"You know – " Her voice was trembling as she spoke, and I could hear her breath catching, "You know that I want that. More than anything. But not... not like this." She was pleading, begging for me to understand, but I was frozen where I stood, unable to show any reaction. I was still processing what had just happened. I needed to focus though, I needed to listen, I needed...

What did I need?

She took a deep, shuddering breath before continuing. "You know how I feel about you. But... I want, I want you to want me. For who I am. Not need me, not need the person who's there for you. I don't want to just be... there. I can't do this. I'm sorry, I'm so so sorry, I wish I could..."

A single tear escaped from her eye; I slowly lifted my hand up to wipe it away with the pad of my thumb. "I'm sorry," I whispered. "I shouldn't've... this, this isn't, we can't – "

"We can," she said, breathless now, panicking. "Kiss me. Now. I'm sorry, I shouldn't have – I shouldn't have said to stop, we can, it's everything I want, I just..." She leant down ever so slightly, just enough so that she was in reaching distance. "I'm sorry. I screwed up. But we – we can, if you want to, because I want to, so much. Please, Lizzy, please."

I slowly reached behind me to get a tissue, and I delicately wiped the tears from underneath her eyes.

"You were right," I murmured, looking down at my one hand which was still holding hers. "This... this isn't right. This isn't the right time. And you don't need to be sorry. I should be sorry. I shouldn't have... I shouldn't have tried that. I shouldn't have done that, shouldn't have put you in that position."

She thought for a few moments before saying anything, her breath catching as she spoke. "Lizzy, I... I want to be with you. So, so much. But I... I want to know that you've thought about it. Rationally. That it's a conscious, deliberate decision. I can't... I can't spend my time wondering if in a few months, you'll realise that it was a moment of weakness, a moment of wanting comfort from the only person who was there. I want this so badly that it aches every time I look at you, but I can't live with that doubt. Please, promise me that. That if you... if you decide, once this is over, that this is still what you want, that you'll... that you'll be sure. And I know that things don't always work out, and that things can still go wrong, but I don't want to be an impulse decision. I can't be an impulse decision."

I squeezed her hand once, meeting her eyes.

"I promise."

Her eyes flickered back and forth, not holding onto my gaze for more than a second at a time. She glanced at the kitchen counter behind me, smiling weakly. "Looks like you'll have to re-boil the kettle now!"

I laughed despite myself, finally letting her fingers slip from my grasp as I turned to go and make the tea. We worked in silence as she got out the teabags and I got the milk from the fridge, I got the teaspoons out of the drawer and she stirred in the sugar. There was a palpable tension between us but not an uncomfortable one; a strange bond that you only get from mutual rejection.

As I carefully carried two of the three mugs back out of the kitchen, I desperately tried to make some sort of sense of what had just happened. I... I had just tried to kiss Darcy Williams. We had been so close, and I had...

She was right, at least to an extent. I'd needed her, and she'd been there. I was almost taking advantage of her, taking her comfort when it was needed but who knew how I'd feel in a week, a month, a year?

As to wanting her? I wasn't sure about that. I didn't think that I *didn't* want her, but I wasn't sure if I did, either. She... she was beautiful. I'd appreciated her looks before, of course, it was obvious that she was an attractive person. But I was struck suddenly by her beauty; not just in the way she looked but in the way she was.

"Lizzy?"

I heard my voice being tentatively called as I walked past the bottom of the stairs and looked up to see Sander standing at the top. He looked like he had just woken up and, judging by his confused expression, had just seen Darcy walk past.

"Hey," I said, as caring as I could in one syllable. "Do you... do you want to come down?"

He slowly and unsurely made his way down the stairs to where I was standing.

"What's going on?" he asked quietly. "Why is... why is Darcy Williams here?"

I realised that he had no idea; he didn't know any of what had happened between Darcy and I since I had left for London, and (understandably) assumed that she and I were still at odds.

"I'll explain all that later, just know that..." I glanced briefly at her, "we've put aside our differences. Things are better between us. But Darcy... she knows George. From years ago. She and... she and her brother are here. I thought... I thought maybe we could talk to them?"

I saw his stance change as soon as I mentioned George's name, but I kept talking. The fact that he hadn't shouted, run off or denied everything I was saying spoke volumes to how much things had changed in a matter of days. First and foremost, we needed to get Sander back. We needed to persuade him that we were genuine and that all we wanted was his happiness and safety. Everything else would follow on.

He nodded imperceptibly, and I gave him what I hoped was a reassuring smile.

He stood awkwardly in the doorway as we went into the sitting room, and I saw him try to tug the shoulder of his shirt up higher so that it completely obscured his collar bone.

"This is Jordan, and you've met Darcy," I said, trying my best to make it sound like a normal introduction of friends. "This is Sander."

"Hi," he grunted, looking down at the floor.

I could see that Jordan was trying to say something, but he was looking nervously from me to Darcy and back. Whatever it was he wanted to say, he clearly thought it would be better without an audience.

Darcy stood up suddenly. "Lizzy, I... you said you had a... book. To show me. Yes?"

"Yes!" I cottoned on quickly, and although we weren't fooling anyone, I could see that Jordan and Sander appreciated the effort. "I'll just go and show you that, then."

I indicated for Darcy to leave the room ahead of me and briefly looked back to see Jordan giving me a very odd look. I didn't know what Darcy had said to him while I was out of the room, if anything, but it was clear that while he pitied me, he didn't like the change he'd seen in his sister. There was a warning in his stare, one which I attempted to acknowledge wordlessly before going out into the hallway and shutting the door behind me.

In the end, I did end up showing Darcy my bookshelves. We couldn't find much else to talk about with the tension still so high between us and our worry for our brothers. Comparing books seemed to be a safe subject. There was a distance between us, both physical and otherwise, a chasm that we were both too scared to cross. For just a moment, as she deliberately pulled her hand closer towards herself to prevent it from brushing against mine, I hated myself for making things between us become this way.

I took every moment I could to look at her, to try and separate the strands of thoughts that were tangling in my head. In the end, I came to the inevitable conclusion that, of course, she'd been right; there was no use in trying to work it out now. At this moment, I couldn't differentiate between needing her and wanting her, and I couldn't tell the difference between wanting Darcy and just wanting *someone*.

***

I'll never know exactly what Jordan said to Sander, and I never really want to find out. These were two young men who had been through the same ordeal and were helping each other through it. It wasn't my place to know what they'd said to each other.

"Thank you," I said earnestly to Jordan after Sander had gone back upstairs, announcing determinedly that he'd be down in five minutes. "Whatever you said... thank you."

Jordan looked at me oddly and I realised that I recognised the expression; it was the same one that Darcy had when she was trying to figure me out.

"Will you do something for me in return?" he said, and there was a strange softness to the way he said it.

I nodded instantly. "Of course! Whatever you've said has had a profound effect on my brother, and I'd be more than happy to repay you in any way I can."

He glanced behind me to where Darcy was on her phone.

"Remember what I said," he whispered. It didn't sound like a warning, more like advice. "I... I think you two are wonderful together, I won't deny that. But please, whatever you do, don't break my sister's heart."

I tried to say something but a sudden lump in my throat made it impossible to get words out. I nodded instead, and I could tell that he sensed my sincerity.

"We'd better be getting back to Netherfield Court," Darcy said behind me, back in matter-of-fact, getting-things-done mode, and I knew that she'd been pretending not to be listening in to our conversation. "Send me a message later to let me know how you're getting on. Shall we come and see you again tomorrow?"

"That would be good," I managed to force out, as they pulled on their coats and went out to Darcy's car. "I'll see you tomorrow, then."

Jordan briskly stepped out of the porch, and I could tell that he had every intention of leaving us for a moment.

"Tomorrow," Darcy said, so quiet that only I could hear it, and gently squeezed my hand before going out to the car. I could feel the heat rising to my face as I waved them off, trying to figure out what on earth was going on.

I'd been confused before, of course, about my feelings for Darcy, but everything had been fairly simple; did I like her or did I not like her? Somehow that seemed a much easier question to answer than whether or not I liked her in the right way or for the right reasons.

I jumped as Sander tapped me on the shoulder. He was looking oddly confident despite the shaky smile, with a satchel slung over his coat.

"I'm going out," he said, and I could tell it was more for himself than for me. "I'm... I'm going to the police station. And," he held up a hand to stop me from interrupting. "I'll drive. It's not far, and I don't want to involve anyone else. Apart from... apart from anything else, this is something that I have to do for myself."

I nodded. "I'm proud of you, Sander."

He paused for a moment. "I'm proud of me too."

And with that, he stepped outside, shutting the front door behind him. All I could do now was wait.

Chapter 32: Family

As Sander left the house, the full impact of the events of the last hour or so hit me full force. Everything had happened so quickly. Darcy and Jordan were here, and then…

And then…

I threw myself down on the sofa in the living room, too exhausted to stay upright for much longer. As I lay, there, looking at the ceiling, I tried to get my head around whatever the hell was going on. Jordan had somehow managed to persuade Sander to go to the police, something which I didn't think I'd ever have been able to achieve. I assumed that, by telling his side of the story, Sander had realised quite how much George was manipulating him. And Darcy…

Darcy had turned me down, and rightly so. I was forced, now, to come to terms with the fact that I was attracted to her. But how much, and in what way? That had yet to be seen.

I absentmindedly reached for my phone as it buzzed with a message. It was from Will.

> *Will Fitts: Hey Lizzy! I'm presuming that by now Darcy's got to you – she wouldn't let me tell you before because she wanted it to be a surprise! But it took her long enough, I couldn't put up with her worrying and moping anymore – she's all yours! I hope things are all okay at your end, let me know how you're getting on.*

I started to type out a message, but there was so much that I wanted to say that I rang him instead.

"Hey Lizzy," he said, answering almost as soon as I'd dialled. "How are you holding up?"

I tried to come up with something to say, small talk, but before I could think I blurted out, "Darcy and I nearly kissed and I don't know what to do."

"Finally! Holy crap, you guys take a while! Charlotte owes me twenty quid – wait, nearly? What do you mean *nearly*?!"

"What do *you* mean 'Charlotte owes me twenty quid'?" I asked back, indignant and frankly stunned by his response.

He coughed awkwardly. "Well, you know… Charlotte and I were talking about you two the other day after she'd finished work and came here to meet Colin, and we started a little… bet. Nothing to worry about. Now, what do you mean *nearly*?! Don't leave me hanging, Bennet."

I sighed heavily. "Okay, but I wish you wouldn't sound so… emotionally involved in this."

"Lizzy, out of all the people we know, you and Darcy are the least emotionally involved in your relationship."

"Whatever. Basically, I… I tried to kiss her. And… and she wanted to, I could tell that she wanted to so much, but she said no, because she didn't think I was doing it for the right reasons. Which is true, I wasn't. I just… I'm scared, Will. What if I've screwed everything up? What if I've ruined everything, what if I've made it worse? I can't deal with that. I'm not sure what I feel, but I know… I know that I want her in my life. It's just the 'how' that I'm having issues with right now."

"Did she give you any indication that things would be worse? That she wouldn't want to talk to you?"

"No, but... well, I'm just feeling a bit on-edge at the moment, and she's not known for being particularly easy to read, so..."

There was a beat's silence before he realised that I wasn't going to finish that sentence.

"Okay, listen to me, and believe it. I'm sure there are plenty of things you could do that would make things worse, that would encourage her away from you. I know for a fact, though, this isn't one of them. Nowhere near. You would have to do something seriously bad for that girl to give up on you now, so you have nothing to worry about. She'll give you all the time you need, I promise you. Speaking from experience? Darcy is patient. Not with the little things. She expects taxis to be waiting for her and the Wi-Fi to be at maximum speed and she hates baking because she doesn't like that you have to wait so long for the cake to be finished. But when it comes to the big things? She will wait forever. She will do whatever she can. And she never gives up on people."

I wrapped one arm around myself, not sure if I was cold or just needed the feeling of comfort.

"You think so?" I asked quietly, not caring how childish I sounded.

"I know so." Came the response. "Now, how's your brother doing? Darcy didn't tell me the details, of course, but I gather things are pretty rough?"

"George Wickham is involved," I said hollowly, "so of course things are pretty rough. They're... they're on the way up, though. Jordan spoke to him, to Sander, and I don't know what he said exactly but it helped him to see that he's the victim in all of this. I just... I just hope that we can get everything sorted before long, I can't stay here for much longer. But yes, things are definitely on the way up."

"I'm glad." There was another few seconds of silence. "I don't know George Wickham well. I only met him a couple of times. But... but I wish I'd never met him at all. The things he said..." I heard him take in a deep, shuddering breath. "It was like being at home again. I never told Darcy the things he said, she felt bad enough about his involvement with Jordan. She didn't need to know that he'd hurt me too."

My lungs felt like ice. "Will, did he... what happened? Did he... did he hit you? I need to know, Will, because he hit Sander and I'm going to stop him if it's the last thing I do, I swear it."

There was deathly silence from the other end of the phone.

"He never... physically hurt me," Will said eventually, his voice so small I could barely make it out. "He just said some things. I don't want to talk about it."

I sensed that there was more to the story than this, but didn't push. If Will wanted or needed to tell me, I knew that he would.

"I promise you, Will," I said, my voice trembling. "I'll stop him."

"I know you will," he said, weakly, and I could hear that he was trying not to let his voice betray his tears.

"Don't worry about me; I'll be okay. You do what you need to do."

I nodded. "I will. Are you okay, by yourself?"

There was another moment's silence, and I guessed that he was probably nodding. "I'll be fine. I'll... I'll watch a musical. Eat pizza. I'll be fine." He forced a laugh, trying to lighten the mood. "I'll be better knowing that you're there, helping your brother. You go kick some ass, Lizzy Bennet."

"You got it!" I smiled sadly. "I think – I hope – that this will all be over soon. I'll be back before you know it. Darcy, too."

"I'm glad." He cleared his throat. "I'll speak to you soon, then."

"Yes, I'll speak to you soon!"

We said goodbye, the tone sounding in my ear telling me he'd hung up. It hadn't occurred to me that Will would know George or have ever spoken to him, but now that he mentioned it, it seemed obvious.

Realising that once again I was at a loose end, I looked around for a distraction. I needed something to do while Sander was at the police station, something that would take my mind off things and stop me worrying.

It didn't take me long to realise that nothing would be able to achieve that, but that I could at least keep myself busy. So I cleaned. I did all the washing up, wiped all the kitchen surfaces, vacuumed every room, polished every shelf, baked a cake, mowed the lawn and got the Christmas decorations down from the attic, even though it was still too early to put them up.

I constantly had one ear out for the front door, and when I finally heard it open and close again I dropped the can of bathroom cleaner in my hand and ran towards the hallway.

Sander was leaning against the front door, breathing deeply with his swollen, red-rimmed eyes closed.

"Sander?" I asked cautiously. "Are you okay?"

"I did it," he said, and he almost sounded ashamed. "I handed in the stuff George had asked me to look after. There was... there was a very friendly police woman. She talked to me; explained that she'd have to make a record of it but that there were no charges or anything right now because I was handing stuff in, and she... she wanted me to tell her who gave it to me. Especially... especially because she saw, she saw that I was hurt, and she knew, she guessed how they got there, how the, the bruises were there, but I couldn't tell her. I couldn't tell her, Lizzy, because he's still my friend." He looked up to meet my eyes, and his face was filled with sadness and hurt. "Even with everything he's done, Lizzy, I couldn't betray him. Why couldn't I, Lizzy? I know he's been awful and manipulative and not just to me, but I just... I still couldn't do it. And," he rubbed his nose, sniffing, "It's not like it would have made much difference. The only charge they can press is physical assault, he hasn't done anything else wrong, not in the eyes of the law. I just... I couldn't."

"That's okay," I delicately placed my hand on his shoulder. "I'm so proud of you, Sander, for getting this far, for doing what you've already done. It hasn't been easy, but you did it anyway. I... It took guts, going to the police by yourself like that, and I'm so, so proud of you. And you should be proud of yourself."

"I am," he said, smiling weakly. "I just... what next, Lizzy? George will find out, and he'll be angry, so angry, and I..." he started shaking, tears once again rolling down his cheeks. "What will he do? I'm scared, Lizzy. I'm scared."

I pulled him into a hug as he cried. There wasn't much I could do or much that I could help with, but I could make him feel safe and cared for and loved.

"I'll be here," I vowed. "I'll make sure that he doesn't hurt you. I'll protect you, because I'm your big sister and that's what I do."

I hadn't even realised I was crying too until I choked up at the end.

"It will be okay, Sander, I promise. I swear. I will be here for you, no matter what. Me, Jane, Mark, Mum and Dad, we're all here for you. And we won't let anything or anyone hurt you because we're family."

He pulled away, wiping his eyes, before turning to go upstairs. "I have to go and talk to Mark," he said, a sense of urgency in his tone. "I have to go and fix things. He's my brother, and I screwed up." He paused at the bottom of the stairs. "Do you... do you think he'll... do you think he'll be angry? That he won't listen? What if I can't fix things, what if it's too late?"

"He's your brother," I said, placating. "I'm not going to lie to you, he may well be angry. You two said a lot of things to each other that it won't be easy to forgive. But it's not too late. You've got a long way to go until too late. I know that you two can patch things up. You're not as different as you think you are."

He laughed despite himself. "I guess there is something to all this identical twin stuff then, huh?"

"I guess so," I smiled back, happy as he went upstairs that everything was finally starting to fall into place.

There was one factor, however, that I hadn't considered; one person who we hadn't heard from, who had remained silent since I'd come back to Longbourn. With an involuntary shudder, I realised that I would, inevitably, have to confront George Wickham sooner or later. I couldn't leave without knowing that he was well out of the picture.

For now, though, I would be more than content with the knowledge that my brothers were safe, happy and, with any luck, getting along. I was hopeful. I hadn't heard too much shouting from Mark's room, and I pretended not to notice Sander trawling through sites and forums on asexuality over dinner.

It was fairly late in the evening when I received a message from Darcy. Honestly, I hadn't been expecting anything as I was still half-convinced that I'd managed to put her off for good with my actions that morning. I opened it with trepidation, expecting the worst, but I needn't have worried.

> *Darcy Williams: Hi Lizzy, I hope you and Sander are okay. I just wanted to double-check that it was alright if we came over tomorrow, and if so what time is most convenient?*

It was friendly enough. More than I deserved, really, but it didn't give much away. I guess that was Darcy, though: matter-of-fact and to-the-point. I wrote and re-wrote my message several times before finally sending it. First it was too friendly, then too cold, then too happy, then too sad. Eventually, though, I managed to get something typed out.

> *Lizzy Bennet: Of course it's alright for you to come round! You're welcome to pop by whenever you wish, we're in all day and I'll let you know if plans change. Things with Sander have got a lot better, so please pass on my thanks to Jordan for everything he said! Also, thank you, for coming over. I really appreciated it.*

I closed my eyes as I pressed the send button. Mercifully, I didn't have to wait long for a reply.

> *Darcy Williams: You know I will always be there for you, whenever you need me. And I want to apologise again for what happened earlier on today.*

I couldn't believe her! I royally screw up, and she keeps apologising for it?!

> *Lizzy Bennet: Again, I'm the one who should apologise. I put you in an awkward position, and I shouldn't have done that. I'm so, so sorry. I don't know what I can do to make things okay, but just tell me and I'll do it.*

I watched as those three dots moved up and down for what felt like an age before a reply finally came through.

Darcy Williams: You don't need to do anything. And I wanted to. I wanted to so badly, and the more I think about it the more I regret doing what I did.

My thumbs were flying across the keyboard before I'd even finished reading her message.

Lizzy Bennet: You did the right thing. I know it sucks, but it's the truth. You were right, I was doing it for the wrong reasons, and that was not fair on you. But I promise that, once this is over, I will think about my feelings for you properly, and tell you how I honestly feel. It's the least you deserve.

The reply came quickly.

Darcy Williams: Why is communicating like this so much easier? I miss being able to see you, but apart from that there are no disadvantages to this.

I don't know what possessed me, but I sent her a selfie.

Lizzy Bennet: Problem solved! And let's face it, we were never going to do things conventionally ;)

Oh God.

Oh crap.

I had typed that out and pressed send without thinking about it or checking it first. I read the message again and realised that... that was flirting. Right there.

I was flirting with Darcy Williams.

And I was completely okay with that.

Darcy Williams: Yes, problem solved! I'll send you one in return. And please don't do the semi-colon-closed-bracket thing, it's very irritating and manages to make everything sound dirty.

My phone buzzed again with a selfie, but she hadn't quite got the hang of it. It occurred to me that taking selfies was probably not something Darcy did often. She was looking puzzled at a spot just to the right of the camera and the photo was slightly blurry where the phone had slipped as she took it.

It was perfect.

Lizzy Bennet: I'm not even surprised that you don't like it! Okay, last one, I promise… ;)

Darcy Williams: See, I can't trust anything you say when you do that! Okay, shall I try? ;)

Darcy Williams: No, I don't like it. Never doing it again.

Darcy Williams: I'm sorry, but I have to go now. It's time for dinner.

Lizzy Bennet: Okay, enjoy! See you tomorrow.

Darcy Williams: I look forward to it x

I sat back in my chair. This… this was flirting, right? Surely? It had to be, although the idea of Darcy flirting didn't really fit in my mind. I read back through the messages, and realised that coming from anyone else, I wouldn't think anything of them. But Darcy? This was some seriously unusual behaviour.

But I'd… I'd been flirting. With Darcy Williams. And I was okay with that. In fact, more than okay.

Ecstatically happy.

Chapter 33: Wickham vs. Williams

There was a strange tension in the house the next day. Nobody knew what to say or do. There wasn't anything to be angry or sad about so we all sort of drifted around each other, making   small talk. Sander talked to Dad, explaining more of what had gone on, and told Mum enough to keep her happy. The last thing we needed right now was for Mum to have another panic.

I could tell that Dad was trying to hide his own panic and worry, though. It was unlike him to get worked up about something, so we all knew that if he did, it meant trouble. For Sander's sake, we were all downplaying what had happened. It was clear that he just wanted to get on with things, focus on the present and the future rather than the past, and to be honest I didn't blame him.

I was on edge all morning. I had no idea when Darcy was coming round, so I made sure I was ready first thing. I spent hours trying to distract myself but I was constantly checking my phone, hoping for a message. My phone buzzed once and I grabbed it eagerly, but it was Charlotte asking how things were going. I filled her in before throwing my phone down, annoyed at myself more than anything else.

It was midday before the doorbell finally rang, and I unashamedly dashed down the stairs, pushing a confused Jane out the way to get to the door. I tugged the door open, ignoring the blast of cold air that came in.

"Darcy, you're--"
But it wasn't Darcy.

It was George Wickham.

We stared at each for a second in shock.

"Lizzy!" he said after a few beats. "Wow, I didn't know you were here! How's London going? Man, it's been so long since I've seen you!"

The worst part of it all was... this was the friend I remembered. He hadn't transformed into a cackling villain or cold criminal. He was exactly as I remembered him.

"London's good," I said shortly, still frozen in place. "What are... what are you doing here?"

"I'm here to see Sander," he said cheerfully, not missing a beat. "It was great of you to introduce us back in summer, he's such a cool kid! Is he in?"

I cleared my throat, ignoring the burn I felt from his comment about me introducing them. "I think it's probably best if you don't speak to him right now."

"What?" Even he wasn't good enough of an actor to not look worried; he knew something was up now. "What do you mean, I can't speak to him? Lizzy, what's going on?"

"You know exactly what's going on, George. Why do you want to see him?" I said icily.

"He's my friend! Do I need a reason to see my friend?"

"In this case, yes!" I snapped. "If you have something to say to Sander, you say it to me first."

He shook his head in disbelief. "Why are you being like this, Lizzy? At least let me come in, it's freezing out here."

As much as I hated to admit it, he was right. Although he maybe deserved it, I certainly wasn't getting any warmer standing in the doorway.

"Fine. We can continue this conversation in the sitting room."

I don't know why, but I'd optimistically assumed that he would just follow me straight to the sitting room. I can't say that I was surprised, however, when he called out as soon as I'd shut the front door.

"Sander! Sander, are you in?"

I shouldn't have even been surprised. It was hardly the worst thing he'd done in his life.

"Get in here," I growled, and for a second he actually looked scared before following me into the sitting room.

"Look, Lizzy," he said. "What's going on? We're friends, right? Why are you acting all weird?"

I crossed my arms and looked him straight in the eye. "What do you want from Sander?"

He shrugged. "I haven't seen him in a while, thought I'd pop in and say hi."

"You're lying. You saw him evening before last. Try again."

He ran his hands through his hair, and I could tell he was getting annoyed that his usual charms weren't working.

"Well, I leant him some stuff and figured I'd come and get it back now, you know? Didn't want to put Sander to the hassle. It's no biggy."

"I don't have your *stuff* anymore."

We both whipped our heads round to see Sander standing in the doorway. His arms were wrapped around himself, and you could tell that he was trying to be as small as possible whilst maintaining an impression of bravado. He was – intentionally, I think – only wearing a vest top and pyjama trousers, both of the bruises that George had left on display.

"The police have your stuff. I don't want to hide it for you anymore."

"*What*?!" George twitched towards Sander, but remembered that I was standing there and thought better of it. "What do you... what did you do?"

"I didn't want it anymore," Sander said, his voice small and reedy, "and you wouldn't take it back. So I gave it in. Don't worry, I didn't tell them whose it was. I just... I couldn't have it anymore."

George took a few deep breaths, and you could almost see the steam coming out of his ears.

"What about the cash, huh? What did you do with that?"

"I gave it back to who it belonged to," Sander said, slightly more confidently. "You're my friend, George, but I'm not going to lie and steal for you. Not anymore."

George tried a different tact.

"Sander, that's what friends do, they look out for each other, help each other out. If you were this worried, you could have just given it back to me, you know that, right?"

I had a feeling that this was more to prove a point to me than anything else.

"I tried that." Sander unfolded his arms and raised his chest slightly, displaying the bruise on his collarbone even more. "Maybe I don't want to be your friend anymore." His whole body was shaking as he said it.

"This is *her* fault, isn't it?" George said, pointing towards me but not turning to look at me. Sander shook his head instantly.

"No, George. This isn't Lizzy's fault, it's yours. Friends don't do what you did, and you know it."

George threw his hands up in despair. "I thought you guys were supposed to be my friends, and here you are, ganging up on me! What's it all about, huh? What do you want?" He looked at me dangerously, his eyes burning. "I know what this is about. You thought I was Darcy fucking Williams when you opened the door, didn't you? You've been talking to her! She's somehow persuaded you that I'm this big scary monster who's only out to get what he wants! I thought you were smarter than to listen to that bitch, Lizzy."

I took one step closer to him, even angrier than I had been before. "Don't you dare talk about her like that!" I pointed my finger in his face. "She's a better person than you'll ever be, and you know it. You're consumed with your own bitterness and self-loathing, and you take it out on everyone else. Grow up, George. You can't act like this forever!"

He grabbed my extended arm and I flinched with the tightness of his grip. I heard multiple gasps from the doorway. My shouting had attracted Jane and Mark's attention. I cursed that Mum and Dad were both out, as neither of the Bennet parents were someone you wanted to mess with.

George took a few deep, fuming breaths.

"You're lucky I don't hit girls," he grumbled, letting go of my arm. I was about to retort back, doing everything I could to stop myself from doing something I'd regret, when the doorbell rang.

None of us moved.

"Jane," I asked, my voice a trembling calm, not taking my eyes off George, "Could you see who that is?"

Mark went with her. I could tell that they both wanted to be out of the room as quickly as possible.

The deathly silence in the sitting room made it easy to hear what was going on by the front door.

"Darcy, Jordan!" I heard Jane say, knowing that she'd plastered on her best smile so no one would ever dare to feel unwelcome.

"Hello Jane," came Darcy's voice, stiffly. I realised that this was the first time they'd spoken since before Charlie had left for New York. "Is it alright if we come in?"

Jane must have nodded, because I heard the sounds of them kicking their shoes off and the front door closing.

"Is everything okay?" Jordan asked.

I called out, "We're in the sitting room."

Darcy and Jordan both froze in their tracks when they saw who was with us.

George turned slowly to look at them. "Darcy," he said, curtly. Then he smiled, ever so slightly. "Jordan."

"I suggest you leave," Darcy said coolly, but I could see that her fingers were twitching, betraying her emotion.

"And why should I do that?"

He knew, now; he knew that we all knew exactly what was going on, and saw that his only way out was to play us off each other.

"It's been so long since I've seen you both," he said, cockily. "Especially you, Jordan. I've missed you, mate."

"I can't say the feeling's mutual," Jordan snapped back.

"Leave," Darcy said again, more forcefully. "Leave now, and don't contact anyone in this room again. Understand me?"

George looked around, and something akin to realisation dawned on his face.

"I get it now," he said, nodding smugly. "Defending the girlfriend, are we? Never expected you two to be getting it on. I suppose you're crazy enough for each other, though."

It wasn't clear exactly which one of us he was talking to, but it didn't matter.

"She's not my girlfriend!" we both exclaimed at the same time.

"I see I touched a nerve," he said, still surrounded. "I thought you were cool, Lizzy, really I did, but turns out you're sleeping with the enemy. Never thought you'd stoop that low."

I didn't rise to it, there was no point. There was only one person in this room who deserved to know that much about my personal life, and she was the one person who could confirm that he was lying.

"She's not the enemy," I said coldly. "The world isn't split into heroes and villains. There's people I want in my life, and people I don't. Guess which category you fall into."

I glanced over George's shoulder to see that Sander was standing slightly behind Jordan, clearly trying to stay hidden. I honestly didn't blame him.

Darcy strode over to where we were standing, grabbing George's shoulder and pulling him round to face her.

"Get. *Out*." She said through gritted teeth.

George raised an eyebrow, but I could see that he was starting to get scared.

"Or what?"

"Or I'll call the police."

George shrugged. "I haven't done enough wrong to make that worth your while."

Darcy leant closer to his face, his shirt gripped in her hands. "I'm sure I could find something."

There was a long silence.

"Are you threatening me?" George whispered.

"Glad to see you've caught up," Darcy said, letting him go and brushing her hands together as if to try and clean them. "Now, I suggest you leave. Leave town. Start again. You have one more chance. I guarantee you, we *will* be keeping a better eye on you this time, and should you slip up again? We will do something about it."

He turned round to look at me, only to see Darcy's expression reflected in my own face.

"I promise," I said.

There was a deafening silence as George processed our words. He believed us, that much was obvious, but I couldn't work out what was going on in his head. A hundred emotions flitted across his face as his eyes flicked between me and Darcy. Eventually he seemed to reach some sort of conclusion, nobody breathing as he prepared his response.

He nodded once, slowly. "Understood." He turned to look at where Jordan and Sander were hidden by the shadow of the doorway. "Your brothers are good guys," he said, and it was the first time since he'd turned up that morning that he sounded sincere. "I sometimes wished I wasn't the ass I am. Only sometimes, though."

He made his way to the doorway before turning back, looking from my face to Darcy's and back again.

"Promise me something in return," he said. "When you have kids? Don't use that face. It's terrifying. And let's face it, none of them are going to be as screwed up as me. They won't deserve it." There was a weight behind his words, and for the first time I almost pitied him. A hard life did not excuse all the things he'd done, but that didn't stop it from being so damn *sad*.

I wasn't sure what to make of what he said, and couldn't find a response. I didn't have to, though. Darcy spoke on behalf of both of us.

"We promise," she said confidently, before her gaze faltered. "I mean, um, should the situation arise, of course."

In any other situation I would have laughed and told her that it was okay, but now wasn't the time. I simply nodded my agreement and breathed out a sigh of relief when the door finally shut behind him.

As soon as we heard his car pull out of the drive, the four of us (Jane and Mark having long ago slipped into another room, keeping half an ear open) collapsed onto the sofa, too exhausted to think of anything to say, piled on top of each other.

"I'm sorry," Darcy said eventually.

"What on earth for?!" I sat up to look at her incredulously.

She turned her head to look at me. "I just... I wish I could have done more. Yes, he's gone, but... not properly. There's nothing to stop him coming back, or just going and doing the same thing elsewhere. I should have done something else."

"You did all you could," I said, reaching to hold her hand. "All any of us could have done. And I think – or hope – that he got the message."

She nodded, but I could tell that she wasn't completely convinced.

Sander piped up from where he was pressed up against the arm of the sofa, "Thank you for everything you've done. Both of you. All of you. I... I hate to think what would have happened otherwise. So thank you."

I had almost forgotten that Sander and Jordan were in the room, and quickly pulled away from Darcy. I wasn't sure exactly why, but it didn't feel right being that close to her when there were other people there.

After a few seconds, Darcy cleared her throat. "I think we should, um, probably leave. Is there... is there anything else? Anything at all?" She looked at me with complete sincerity.

I let out a long sigh. "I... I don't think there is. I think... as long as George Wickham stays away for good, that's all that matters."

"You know where we are if you need us," Jordan said, more to Sander than to me. "And... it's been nice. Getting to know you both a bit more. I hope we'll keep getting to know each other."

He gave me another knowing look, and I had a feeling that he was talking about slightly more than just family friends.

"I'm sure we will," Sander said, smiling, and for the first time since I'd come home he looked truly relaxed.

As we walked to the front door, Jordan once again went ahead to give Darcy and I a moment.

"He's not very subtle, is he?" I noted as he busied himself in his phone a few yards away.

"No," Darcy said, the corners of her mouth twitching slightly in a smile. "I'm afraid I'm going to have to go back to London tonight. When do you think you'll be coming back?"

I shrugged. "I'll probably travel tomorrow morning. I wasn't expecting things to be sorted so quickly – and I know they're not sorted, not really, but there's nothing else I can do here. I do think I should at least finish the weekend here. Besides, everyone else will be busy again tomorrow. There's not much use of me being here if everyone else is out."

She nodded in understanding. "Okay, then. I'll see you on Tuesday?"

"Tuesday," I agreed, and we went to hug each other but each leant the same way, awkwardly colliding halfway. We paused for a moment, awkwardly working it out.

"Tuesday," I said again, smiling and waving as they went to Darcy's car.

I went inside once they'd driven off and, after checking Sander was okay, went to go and start packing my things up again. I was busy sorting through the books in my bag when an envelope fell out and onto the floor.

I picked it up, curious, and opened it to find two concert tickets for a concert in two weeks' time at the Southbank Centre. It took me a few seconds to work out what on earth they were doing there when I remembered. They were a gift from Darcy. Two tickets to go and see a concert that Charlie was in.

"Jane?" I called from my room.

There were a few seconds of her scuffling before she stuck her head round me door.

"Lizzy, is everything okay?" she asked, concerned – understandable, given the day's events.

"Yep," I said, looking down at the tickets in my hand. The events involving George were by no means solved but were well on their way to it, and with it came the repair of Sander and Mark's relationship. Now, it was time to think about the happiness of my sister. "How do you fancy coming to visit me in London?"

Chapter 34: All That I Am

With Jane's visit in a fortnight's time organised, I left for London once more on Monday morning. Leaving was hard. I never thought I'd be quite so worried about my brothers. Despite knowing that me being at home would have no difference whatsoever right now, it still didn't feel quite right leaving.

By lunchtime on Monday I was back in London, but I didn't quite have the energy to do anything more than just go home. The euphoria of the previous day's success had long faded, leaving me feeling flat and empty. I drifted around the flat for the afternoon, doing odd bits of housework, but mostly staring into space.

Tomorrow I'd be back at work, and that meant Darcy. It's not that I didn't want to see her, exactly, it's more... well, it's more that I didn't want to have to go through everything that came with seeing her. The worries, the uncertainty, the constant awareness of everything either of us did. Everything just seemed like a huge effort. I hadn't felt this... bland before. Not in years.

Eventually, of course, Charlotte came home from work. It was only when she was surprised to see me that I remembered that I had forgotten to let her know that I was coming back.

"How are you doing?" she asked, gently sitting next to me on my bed where I'd been sat for the last hour, contemplating the pattern that the light made on the door.

I shrugged, apathetic. "I'm okay. I think. Things at home getting better. Sander and Mark are talking to each other again, George Wickham is gone for good. I suppose that's all there is to it."

Charlotte sighed heavily. "What's really bothering you?"

I laughed humourlessly. "How is it that you're so psychic? And before you say anything, I know, you're my best friend. You always know when something's up." I took a deep breath. "Okay, don't you dare say 'I told you so' or anything like that, and I already know about the bet you and Will have going on."

"What bet?" she asked, taken aback.

I smiled wryly. "As your best friend, I can read you. You know exactly what bet I'm talking about."

She rolled her eyes in defeat. "Okay, yeah, that bet. But what does that have to do with anything?"

I looked down at where my fingers were picking at a stray thread on my duvet.

"Charlotte... how is it possible to like someone who... who's been so awful? Even if they're... even if they're better now, even if it turns out that they're actually nice and kind, and they... they actually care about you? How can you like someone who's said and done some... really bad things?"

"Because that's not who they are," Charlotte said knowingly, not missing a beat. I couldn't help but feel that she'd prepared for this conversation. "Some people really are horrible and mean. Most people aren't. And some people... some people pretend to be rude and conceited because it's easier, because it's safer, but that's not who they are. It's only once you really get to know them that you see them for who they really are."

There was a long silence before either of us spoke again.

Eventually, I said in a hollow voice, "Why would Darcy pretend? Why would she... why would she say things that she didn't mean?"

"You'll have to ask her that."

I looked up in alarm. Charlotte was looking far too knowing, and wise as always.

"You'll see her tomorrow, at work. Instead of running everything around in your head, instead of obsessing over it, just ask her."

I nodded nervously. "So, I just... what? Hey, Darcy, here's the photocopying you asked for, fancy telling me why you were a bitch when we first met?"

Charlotte chuckled slightly. "Maybe not in those words. But bring it up at some point. If you don't then everything else, no matter what happens, will just be a series of what-ifs."

"You're right, dammit." I ran my hands through my hair. "I'll talk to her. It's the only way I'll figure out what the hell's going on in my own head."

I jumped slightly as I was pulled into a one-armed hug. "You two will work it out. I know you will."

I kept Charlotte's advice in my head as I steeled myself for arriving into work the following morning. I'd barely slept and so was in the office far too early, telling myself that it was the least I could do since I'd been away for the last week.

By the time half past eight came around I'd gone through both my emails and my physical inbox, getting rid of anything that was no longer relevant and sorting out anything that I could. As the clock ticked closer to nine o'clock, however, I found myself more and more on the edge of my seat, torn between anxiously waiting for Darcy to arrive and hoping that she'd be late.

She arrived, as usual, at quarter to nine, with coffee in hand (reusable cup, of course), greeting everyone as she came up to her office.

"Hi Lizzy," she said almost shyly, pausing as she saw me.

"Oh, um… hi," I eventually stammered out, feeling my face going red. Why wasn't I able to talk to her normally?!

"Are you alright?" There was more to the question than the usual mundanity it held. I could tell that she was genuinely concerned, and given the circumstances in which we'd last seen each other I couldn't blame her.

"Yeah," I replied, feigning confidence.

She nodded, but didn't look convinced.

"Actually," I said, "I, er, was wondering if maybe you wanted to go for lunch today?"

"That would be nice," she said, smiling slightly, and I felt myself relax almost instantaneously. Whatever I'd been worrying about wasn't worrying me anymore.

"Okay," I nodded. "I'll… see you at lunch then."

It was only as we went our separate ways that I saw the people in the surrounding offices quickly turn back to what they were doing, pretending that they hadn't been watching us through their windows and over the cubicles.

Lunch time came around and I met Darcy outside her office with my coat and bag on, ready to go.

"Where shall we go for lunch?" she asked. "We could go back to that restaurant that we went to before? You know, when... when, um, you had to leave early."

"I had a different idea," I said teasingly, glancing sideways to judge her reaction. "This time, I'm paying. But that means we have to go somewhere a bit more affordable. If that's okay with you, of course."

"That's fine," she said, and I could tell that she was trying really, really hard to be relaxed and cool about it so as not to offend me. "Wherever you want to go, that's fine."

"There's a sandwich shop a few streets away that I've been to a few times. It's small and cheap and kind of gross, but there are tables and they do amazing cookies. What do you say?"

She turned to look at me, her gaze filled with trepidation. "It sounds... it sounds like it will be an experience, certainly."

"Think of it as a class in how us lowly interns live," I joked, and she smiled weakly. "Next time we can go somewhere a bit more upmarket. It will be fun."

There was a quiet pause.

"There'll be a next time?"

I looked up, surprised.

"Of course there will. Why, did you think there wouldn't be?"

She shrugged. "I just thought... never mind."

"What?" I put my arm out to stop her walking, turning around so that we were facing each other.

She sighed heavily. "I just... Honestly, I'm surprised that there's a this-time. I thought... I guess I assumed that we wouldn't be doing this anymore. That you… that you wouldn't want to."

"Darcy…" I took a deep breath. "Darcy, I like to think that we're two very intelligent women. But… well, we each have our moments of being completely and utterly stupid. I've had many of them so far, and I could probably list them if you want. This is one of yours."

She nodded, not looking completely reassured, but happy nonetheless that I genuinely did want to be there.

"How's, um, how's work going?" I asked tentatively as we started walking again, desperately looking for some small talk.

"It's going well," Darcy said, and I saw her eyes light up slightly as she started thinking about it. "We're desperately searching for some new offices – as you know, the current ones are quite cramped! We're having a lot more authors and agents come directly to us, though. For a while it was mostly people that my Aunt Catherine had rejected. She has a slightly more… conservative view on what it's acceptable to publish."

"Here we are," I said, indicating to the open door into the sandwich shop. "What exactly do you mean by that?"

"I don't know if you've noticed," Darcy said as we joined the queue. "You probably haven't. The most popular books that Rosings publishes tend not to have much romance at all, being fantasy or crime thrillers, and the romance department is fairly new. It's only been going a few years and hasn't really spread its wings yet. Catherine refuses to publish anything with LGBTQ themes. She reluctantly allowed them to add *The Picture of Dorian*

Gray to their series of classics, but that's about it. It's not widely publicised, of course, and as I said it's not really the kind of thing that they publish anyway, so most people don't pick up on it. It's not something that comes across as glaringly obvious, especially when there's so little LGBTQ fiction out there that isn't considered specialist."

"So, you publish things that she doesn't think are 'acceptable'?"

Darcy nodded. "Yes. If they're good, of course. But now all the literary agents know that, so they come straight to us. It's going pretty well."

We had got to the front of the queue, so I ordered myself a sandwich and specified which toppings I wanted.

"What would you like?" I asked, turning to Darcy, who was looking at the menu boards, bewildered.

She waved vaguely at the board. "The one... the one with the salami."

I translated her order to the bored-looking man behind the counter. "What salad and stuff do you want on it?"

She shook out her hair, raising her posture just slightly. "I'm capable of ordering for myself, thank you."

I held back a snort as mean-and-scary-Darcy came out, somehow refraining from pointing out that the evidence so far was that she was not great at ordering fast food. The server was looking nervous now, unsure whether or not to tell Darcy what dressings they had. She was looking at him expectantly, as if he should know what to do. I almost felt bad. Darcy was obviously struggling with the situation, but surely by the time you're in your mid-twenties you should be able to order fast food?

Taking pity on the people in the queue behind us I pointed to the sticker on the glass that showed the different toppings they had. She nodded quickly as if to let me know that there was no need to show her what to do before ordering.

"Why do you do that?" I asked as we sat at one of the wobbly metal tables.

"Do what?" She was examining her sandwich suspiciously, evidently concerned that it didn't come on a plate.

"You know, that thing you do. Where you're all... Okay, I don't know how to say this and not have it come off the wrong way, but when you're acting all superior, high and mighty, when you're... well, when you're rude. Why do that?"

She looked down, suddenly fascinated by a bit of limp lettuce sticking out of her sandwich. "I... I guess I do it when I'm scared. I, um, have a lot of defences. As you've probably noticed. And this way I can take control of the situation, I can control what people think about me."

"So, you'd rather know that they think that you're up your own arse than be wondering if they actually like you?"

She shrugged. "When you put it like that it sounds stupid, but yeah, kind of. I guess." She took a bite of her sandwich. "This is kind of... disgusting and wonderful at the same time."

"I know, right!" I said through a mouthful of my own. "It's terrible but just... so, *so* good."

She laughed slightly. "I haven't eaten this sort of food since I was a student, wandering home drunk at two in the morning."

"You? Drunk?" I said, pretending to be scandalised, feeling slightly proud when she smiled. "But... I'm sorry to go back to this. Let's face it, we did not get off to the best start. At all. And if there's anything I've learned from the last week, it's that I'm not as good at judging someone's personality as I thought I was, and I obviously misjudged you for a long time. But..." I took a deep breath. "You said that you act all... you know, when you're scared. So why... why so much, and for so long, with me? Even Charlie seemed shocked some of the time, and I guess I was just wondering why, exactly? What is it about me that scared you so much?"

There was a long silence as Darcy planned what to say.

"I... I've never met anyone like you, Lizzy," she said eventually. "You're... you're special. There's something about you... I don't let people get close to me. I think you know all the exceptions. Making friends has never been an easy thing for me to do, and I was an easy target in school. Mixed-race, awkward and stammering, and then openly bisexual. I responded by putting my walls further up, creating this persona of a person who could deal with all of that. Then when my parents died... I guess I kind of forgot who that other person was. The person who wasn't cold and haughty and superior. Until I met you. I couldn't put my finger on it at first, so I lashed out, thinking that maybe if I pushed you away and ignored you then I could convince myself that I you didn't bother me, that you weren't on my radar. But you… you reminded me of who I used to be. Who I really am. You made me want to be that person again. And eventually… eventually I realised that the only way you would feel anything but hatred towards me would be if you saw the real me. If I showed you who I could really be, who I really was. You saw straight through me, Lizzy, you saw me for who I am."

She looked around nervously as she finished, as if suddenly realising exactly what she'd just said, before busying herself in her sandwich. I leant forwards suddenly, placing my hand on her arm. She looked up, alarmed.

"Thank you," I said, slightly overwhelmed, my heartbeat quickening. "Thank you for telling me all that. And I know you think it's stupid, but… but it isn't. It actually all makes perfect sense."

She gave me a watery smile and put her sandwich down so she could put her other hand on top of mine.

We finished our sandwiches in silence and bought a couple of cookies to go before heading back outside, ready to slowly walk to the office. We kept a small distance between us. Crossing it now felt like a big, permanent thing to do.

I thought about everything she'd said about how she'd built up so many defences around herself, and about how I saw her for who she is. I couldn't help but ask myself the question: who is she? For so long I had thought about her one way, and then another, and then another, but I hadn't really sat down and *thought* about who she is, in and of herself.

I could tell that she was watching me out the corner of her eye, so didn't turn to look at her, but one glance was all I needed. Rather than just seeing her, I *looked*; looked for who she was, for everything that made up Darcy Williams. The little things, like the way she always wore a suit jacket no matter the weather, or the way she held a book open so that she didn't break the spine, or the way she pushed at her cuticles when she thought no one was looking. The bigger things, like her passion, her care, her loyalty. Her love.

Her love for her brother, for her friends, for her work.

Her love for me.

It hit me like a freight train, the true importance behind that one simple fact. Of everyone in the world, she had chosen me, and I had taken that for granted all along.

Chapter 35: Hopeless Romantic

Try as we might, Darcy and I didn't get to see much of each other over my remaining days at Pemberley. As we got closer to Christmas the workload for both of us increased, and it was rare that we were both in the office at the same time, let alone with enough time to take a full lunch break. Any time we did find to spend together was usually hurried. Time spent with Darcy seemed to pass incredibly slowly and yet be gone in an instance. A half-hour lunch felt like hours spent together, but at the same time felt like no time had passed at all.

We were still balancing on the edge of friendship and something more. It honestly felt like one thing could tip me over the edge. We would hold hands and hug but never for longer than acceptable for two very close friends. It was sometimes so hard not to lean forwards to kiss her on the cheek or brush her hair out of her eyes, but something stopped me. I'm not sure what it was, or where the uncertainty or fear was coming from. I was sure, however, that now was not the right time. I would know when it was. There was something wonderfully refreshing about our friendship, and the last thing I wanted to do was do anything more that might jeopardise it.

We only managed to really spend time together three more times before, inevitably, it was time for me to return to Rosings. I couldn't say that I was really looking forward to it. Working at Pemberley was much more pleasant, for several reasons. I did miss Will, though, and it would be nice to go back to a more normal routine.

"Well," said Darcy, as I packed up my things at five o'clock on that last Friday. "This is it." I could tell that she was trying, unsuccessfully, not to sound sad about me leaving.

"Back to Rosings I go," I replied, also attempting to sound cheerful. "I'll still see you, though. We can still go for lunch, it's not like I'm very far away. And besides, I'll see you tomorrow. It's Charlie's concert, isn't it?"

She nodded with perhaps a bit too much certainty. "Yes, Charlie's concert tomorrow – are you still coming?"

"Of course!" I said. "And Jane's coming too."

She didn't say anything but nodded in a way that told me that she was glad, even if she didn't feel able to vocalise it.

"I'll see you tomorrow, then," she said almost wistfully.

"Yes, you will!" I was determined that this was not going to be a goodbye. "You'll see me tomorrow. And probably sometime next week, either for lunch or because Will and I are having another movie marathon and pizza. You won't be able to get rid of me!" My attempt at humour was forced and fell flat.

She nodded again, but didn't quite look like she believed me.

I packed up the last of my things, attempting to ram my pencil case into my bag. I stopped still as soon as I'd finished, not really wanting to go.

"Thank you," I said eventually. "For everything. And... for what it's worth, I love it here. Much more than at Rosings."

She smiled. "I'm glad. And for what it's worth from me, I'm sure recruitment would like to see an application from you come summer. If you want to, of course."

She saw me pull a bit of a face at that. "What's wrong? Do... do you not want to? I understand, I'm sorry, I shouldn't have assumed-"

"It's fine," I butted in, feeling bad that I'd caused her to panic. "I would love to work here, I really would. I just... I'm not sure I could be your employee. Not because of you as a person, not at all, because you're a brilliant boss and I would love to work for someone like you, I just..." I took a deep breath, trying to organise my thoughts. "I don't want to have an employer-employee relationship with you. It would just be strange."

"I understand." She was smiling, and looking far too happy for someone who had basically just been rejected. "I'll see you tomorrow, then."

"Tomorrow," I breathed, and I somehow ended up reaching forwards to give her a hug. We met halfway, quickly putting our arms around each other, but lingered for longer than was usual. It was like we'd pressed 'pause' on a fleeting moment as we stood there, embracing, wrapped in each other's warmth. I felt her lips fleetingly brush against my hair as we parted, so faint that I could almost have imagined it, and I felt myself go bright red from my toes right up to my forehead.

She looked slightly bashful as she made her excuses and hurried down the stairs and outside, but I was frozen in place. I just wanted to savour that moment for a few seconds longer; I wasn't ready to let go of it just yet.

Eventually, of course, I had to leave. Apart from anything else I got a text from Jane letting me know that she'd got into London, so she would probably get to my flat before me.

I sat on the Tube on the way home in a daze. It would be so nice to get back to a normal routine with normal people, but I would miss seeing Darcy every day.

As suspected, Jane was already at my flat but was waiting outside because Charlotte was out with Colin.

"Lizzy!" she called as I came up the road, running forwards slightly to meet me. "Oh, it's so good to see you! I know it hasn't been long since I saw you last, but it feels like ages! How are you doing?"

"I'm doing pretty well," I said as I opened the front door. "How about you? And how's everyone at home?"

She talked as we trekked up the stairs to my flat, lugging her overnight bag behind her. "I'm okay – did I tell you that I'm going to spend three months in the new year working at monkey rehabilitation project in South America? It's going to be so exciting, and all those poor monkeys – they're mostly endangered species, so it's really important that we give them every chance we can to get back on their feet."

"Sounds exciting!" I replied, rolling my eyes when she wasn't looking. It sounded like Jane was back to her old self if she was busy picking out gap year projects again. "Make sure to send me lots of photos!"

"I definitely will! As to everyone else at home..." she paused, and her face fell slightly. "Things are getting better. Sander and Mark finally seem to be getting along, they've been spending a lot more time together recently.

Sander's doing pretty well, all things considered. He's still a bit shaken and he's quite jumpy sometimes, but on the whole he seems much happier. You spoke to him the other day, didn't you?"

"Yeah, we skyped for a bit – I wanted to see how he was getting on. He seems to be doing okay. I just wish I could do more, you know?"

"Don't we all," Jane agreed as I let us into the flat. "I'll put the kettle on!"

She was in the kitchen before I could stop her. Only Jane would make other people tea in their own home.

"How are you feeling about tomorrow?" I asked tentatively, following her into the kitchen.

"What do you mean?" she asked, busying herself with the teabags, but I could see from the way her ears turned pink that she knew exactly what I meant.

I sighed in exasperation. "You'll be seeing Charlie for the first time in months, for the first time since he went to New York. Are you... are you feeling okay about it?"

She turned around to face me, a fierceness in her kind eyes. "Actually, I am. I mean, it's not like things can get any worse. It's been long enough now that I'm just getting on with things, and if this gives me some more closure – well, maybe it's for the best. Besides, I might not even get to speak to him. It's just a concert."

I wasn't sure whether she was reassuring herself or trying not to get her hopes up.

"Anyway," she cleared her throat, "What about you and Darcy? You two seemed pretty close when you were at home."

I blushed, and she got a knowing twinkle in her eyes. Luckily for me, though, I was saved by Charlotte arriving home, providing a welcome distraction for Jane.

***

Lunchtime the following day saw Jane and I on the Tube, ready to go to the Southbank Centre for the two o'clock matinee concert. Jane seemed to be purposefully distracting herself, pointing out any and all landmarks that we saw between the Tube station and the concert hall.

"Here we are," I said as we reached the front of the centre, tickets in hand. "We're in the... Queen Elizabeth Hall. I think... yes, that way."

We joined the queue of people at the door, picking up a programme each as we went in.

I was not surprised at all when I found that our tickets were right next to Darcy, Jordan and Will, and even less so when Darcy stood up to give me a hug as we arrived at our seats. I pretended not to see Jordan and Will fist-bump each other behind us.

"How are you doing today?" she asked as we sat down, oblivious to the three pairs of eyes watching our every move.

"I'm pretty good," I smiled, suddenly strangely nervous. Not feeling comfortable settling into a conversation while the others were all around, I said a quick 'Hi' to Jordan and Will before settling into my seat, busying myself with the programme.

I flicked through the first few pages without paying much attention. They were talking about the work that the college did, and seemed to be more of an advertisement than a programme. About halfway through was a section on the people performing in the concert, with a short biography for each of them. Charlie's was first; they'd been organised alphabetically. There was the headshot that I'd seen on his twitter profile, above the words 'Charles Bingley: BMus Piano Performance'. Glancing to where Jane was studiously reading the pages on the history of the college, I read on through his biography.

> *Charles began his formal training in the College's Junior Department in 2002, and went on to study as an undergraduate in 2008 with the Emma Knightley scholarship. Since graduating in 2011 he has performed in some of the world's most prestigious venues, including the Royal Albert Hall, the Beethoven Halle in Bonn, Germany, and Carnegie Hall in New York, working with orchestras such as the Vienna Philharmonic and the London Symphony Orchestra.*
>
> *He would like to dedicate today's performance to JB.*

I carefully nudged Jane, indicating that she should read it. I could tell the moment she'd read that last sentence, the colour immediately rushing to her face.

"Do you think--" she whispered, her voice shaking, "Do you think that means... me?"

"Well, yes!" I said incredulously. "How many other JBs do you think he knows?"

She shrugged. "Well, his surname does begin with a B – it could be a cousin or someone."

Seeing that there was no convincing her, I turned around in my seat. "Darcy – does Charlie have any relatives with a name starting with J? Or any other friends with the initials JB?"

She shook her head knowingly. "No, none at all – just you, Jane."

I knew that she'd been listening to our conversation, although I couldn't really blame her. She had set this whole thing up, and Jane and Charlie's relationship – or lack thereof – was the only big thing left unresolved between us.

If possible Jane went even redder, and carefully brushed her hair down to hide her face as she pretended to read the programme some more.

"I see he's playing some Brahms," Darcy said scornfully, reading the running order. "Of course he's playing Brahms."

I looked up from my lap. "Not a fan?"

"It's just so… overly romantic. Don't get me wrong, I love Romantic music – but I like Wagner and Beethoven and Elgar. Music that has power behind it. This… this is just drivel."

I laughed slightly. "Yeah, because God forbid you ever be overly romantic…"

She turned to look at me in confusion, raising an eyebrow in disbelief. "I have been accused of many things over my life, Lizzy, but never has anyone called me a romantic."

I wouldn't have realised that she'd raised her voice at all if it hadn't been for Will's coughing fit on her other side.

"Maybe not at first," I said playfully, surprising myself by taking her hand, "But honestly? You're the biggest romantic I know."

Jordan joined in Will's coughing: this time, I think, to drown us out rather than to disguise laughter.

I ignored them both.

"You really think so?" Darcy said, disbelievingly.

"I know so," I replied. "I have a whole stack of evidence that, deep down, you're a hopeless romantic. And I lo--"

This time it was my time to start coughing. We were starting to get looks from the people sitting around us.

"I really like that about you," I corrected, once I'd calmed down, stopping Darcy from slapping me on the back.

"You do?" she whispered, but I was saved, thankfully, by the lights dimming and the first performer coming onto the stage.

I don't know much about classical music, but I knew enough to know that all the musicians that we were hearing were very, very good. A glance at the programme told me that the music they were playing spanned over three hundred years of composition. Darcy tried quickly explaining the different hallmarks of each era and composer, but I didn't really understand most of it. I was perfectly content, though, to just sit and enjoy the music. I glanced over at Jane occasionally. She seemed to be enjoying the performance but was also slightly on edge, presumable in anticipation of Charlie coming on stage.

The concert wasn't long enough to justify an interval, and Charlie was the last one to perform. The first piece he played was the Brahms that Darcy had complained about, which I personally rather enjoyed. He played two more pieces after that one; a piece by Mozart and a piece by Chopin. I'd known that Charlie was good, of course I had, but I hadn't understood quite how good. He understood the music, understood how it worked, how it moved. It was almost as if he himself wasn't there. He was just a vessel for the music to appear from, but at the same time he was everywhere. He had a presence while playing that I hadn't seen before, and it filled every corner of the hall. I was completely transfixed all the way through, unable to think of anything except the beautiful music that was ringing around the hall.

There was a long silence after he finished the final chord. Everyone in the hall was still; no one dared make a sound. Charlie hadn't moved his hands off the piano and barely seemed to be breathing as the memory of those last notes rang out. The silence was as much a part of the music as the actual notes were, and no one so much as breathed lest they disturb it.

After what felt like hours, Charlie finally relaxed, putting his hands back by his sides and standing up. The moment he moved the hall erupted into applause; the spell was broken and there was an explosion of sound. People were cheering, some were even on their feet as he turned to the audience, smiled, and bowed. The cheering and clapping kept going as he walked off stage, and it managed to get inexplicably louder as he came back on again. He bowed once more, looking both elated and exhausted at the same time. The moment he moved towards the piano once again for an encore, however, the hall once again fell silent, everyone waiting in anticipation.

He sat there for a few seconds, looking at the piano keys as if contemplating something. He slowly turned his head towards the audience until he was looking right at us. Right at Jane. I felt her tense up beside me as he gave her an imperceptible nod, before he turned back to the piano and began to play.

I recognised the music, although I couldn't tell you what it was. Jane gasped after the first few notes. I looked over, worried, to see her eyes transfixed on the stage.

"He played this for me," she breathed, so quietly that I almost didn't catch it, and I instantly knew exactly why he'd chosen this piece to play. The notes themselves didn't sound that difficult, although I wasn't a very good judge, but the music just... floated around the hall, the patterns echoing around each other.

Darcy leant slightly towards me across our joined hands.

"Bach's first prelude in C," she murmured, still focused on the stage.

The whole hall was completely transfixed, everyone totally absorbed by the performance. As the final few bars were played, that gentle slowing down as the music reached its slow conclusion, it was as if there was a collective sigh from everyone in the building. The last note had barely finished sounding when once again the hall erupted in noise and applause that was somehow even more intense than it had been before.

I looked over at Jane as we stood up to applaud. There were tears streaming down her face.

As the audience eventually filed out of the hall, Jordan led us to the stage door around the back of the building. Jane hadn't said anything at all since the concert, only nodding absently as we talked about how much we enjoyed it. Charlie ran out to meet us, still in his tux, his eyes searching. As soon as he saw us he stopped still, only looking at Jane.

"I'm sorry," he said as we came closer to him, and I could tell that that wasn't what he'd planned to say. "I'm sorry, I'm so, so sorry, I was a stupid big bloody idiot and I know sorry doesn't make it better but…" his voice trailed off as we came within a few metres of him. "Jane? I… I'm--"

"You're sorry. I know," she said in a cool, even tone. Charlie looked like he'd been slapped in the face.

"Jane, I – I don't know what I was thinking, I was just so stupid and scared but I… I love you, Jane. And I know that we weren't together for long, and I know that I screwed up. I royally screwed up. But if there's one thing I'm certain of… it's that I love you."

Jane's hand flew to her mouth as she started crying again. "We… we have to talk about this. We need to talk about this. Things are different now, we can't go back to how we were, things have changed."

Charlie started nodding frantically. "I know, and I'll do anything I can, I promise you that. Jane, I – "

"I love you too, you great idiot!" Jane shouted, then laughed through her tears as she realised what she'd said. "I... I love you. And we can sort everything else out later."

"You – you do?!" Charlie asked incredulously, wiping the tears from his own eyes.

Jane nodded, and it was all they needed. They couldn't hold back any longer, running to close the remaining distance between them as Jane threw herself at Charlie. He picked her up, laughing and spinning her around before they kissed, completely unaware of our presence behind them.

"We should go," I whispered, and the others quickly nodded in agreement, all of us turning around and walking away.

"Surely I can't be the biggest romantic you know after that little display," Darcy asked teasingly as we sat on the bank, overlooking the Thames.

"Yeah, I think you've just been knocked off the top spot," I laughed. "There's still time, though!" I cleared my throat. "Darcy, thank you. For today, I mean."

She shrugged, still looking out over the river. "I had an opportunity to fix one of my mistakes, so I took it. Charlie was never happier than when he was with your sister. It just... it just took me finding some happiness of my own to see that."

I raised an eyebrow. "Okay, you're back in the top spot. Most hopeless romantic award goes to Darcy Williams."

Chapter 36: Iceberg Warnings

Jane Bennet: I'm going to stay at Charlie's tonight – don't wait up for me! See you in the morning.
Jane Bennet: And that's because we need to TALK. Nothing else, Lizzy!!!
Jane Bennet: And thank you. For everything.

***

It was nine o'clock the following morning, just as Charlotte and I were having breakfast, when Jane arrived back.

"Morning Lizzy," she said as I opened the front door, her cheeks flushed pink with either happiness or the cold. Probably the former.

"Morning to you too!" I said, leading the way back to the kitchen. "Someone didn't come home last night, so spill!" I turned and smiled at her expectantly.

"Why are you being so nosy, Lizzy?" she asked, exasperated. "Nothing happened, I told you. We just… we had a lot to talk about. A *lot* to talk about – we parted so suddenly and on such bad terms, we couldn't just pick up again and carry on. He… he needed to know quite how much he hurt me. And I think he already did, really. And we needed to talk about where it went wrong, why things drifted a little bit, all that kind of stuff. So, yeah. That's all. It…" The colour in her cheeks went from a pink dusting to a brilliant red. "The time wasn't right for any other stuff. So, yeah. Shall I make the tea?"

She refilled the kettle, ignoring that we already had tea ready and made, as she determinedly avoided my eyes.

"I'm, er... I'm glad you two are sorting things out, then," I said, trying to put some normality back into the situation.

"Me too," Jane said, turning around to look at me once more, that love-stricken grin back on her face. "What about you, Lizzy? How are things going for you on that front?"

This time it was my turn to blush. "What about me? I don't know what you're talking about."

Charlotte, who had been previously absorbed in her cornflakes, suddenly sat up, grin plastered on her face. "Yeah, Lizzy? What about you?"

I stood for a moment, frozen on the spot, unable to process the words coming at me.

"I don't want to talk about it." I heard the words come out of my mouth without passing through my brain first. I sighed, hanging my head and taking a moment to collect my thoughts before speaking again. "Can't we just go back to talking about Jane? Or you, Charlotte?"

There was a long silence, the other two exchanging a worried glance at my reaction.

Eventually Charlotte spoke, sounding slightly exasperated. "Lizzy, I'm... I'm sorry, I didn't realise."

"That's fine," I said weakly, slowly turning to leave the kitchen. "I'll – I'll be in my room."

I had barely shut the door behind me when there was a delicate knock.

"Lizzy?" Jane's voice floated through. "Lizzy, it's me. Are… are you okay?"

I spun around and opened the door to see Jane standing there, looking sheepish.

"Lizzy, I'm sorry. I didn't realise that… I didn't mean anything by it. I'm sorry."

I sighed heavily. "It's not your fault, and I'm sorry I overreacted. It's just… people have been asking that a lot lately. And I just wish people would stop asking the question for long enough for me to figure the answer out."

We sat down together on the edge of my bed.

"You'll figure it out, Lizzy, I know you will. And there's no hurry. You need to work things out at your own speed, when you're ready. Do it for you. Not for anyone else."

I smiled weakly. "Thank you."

Jane squeezed my shoulders lightly. "It's what big sisters are for. Now, how about some tea?"

"Sounds good," I replied. "Just… give me a minute?"

She nodded before standing up and going back into the kitchen, shutting the door behind her. I could hear her and Charlotte talking in hushed tones, but I didn't make any attempt to make out what they were saying; I didn't think it would take much imagine to recreate the conversation in my head anyway.

Jane was right. There was no point in worrying about working things out, because things would fall into place when the time was right, and not before. But it was funny; everything just seemed… so close. Like it would just take one thing, one tiny push, and I would fall and fall and fall.

I just hoped I liked where I landed.

***

It was very odd on Monday morning, going back into Rosings instead of Pemberley. I smiled greetings to people I hadn't seen in a month, cringing slightly as I saw that Will had taken over the whole of our tiny desk, even having peeled off the tape that I'd laid down to split it in two.

"Good morning, Lizzy!" Colin said as he saw me. "I trust you enjoyed your time at Pemberley, although I doubt it could live up to the splendour of Rosings!"

I decided that smiling and nodding was probably the best policy, making vague gesturing motions towards my seat.

"Here is a list of all the meetings today that you are expected to attend," he said, bustling as usual, but finding the relevant sheet of paper much faster than he used to. Obviously, Charlotte had sorted him out.

I was slowly getting used to the idea of them being together, a process helped by not having to see him at the office for a few weeks. We were very good at pretending that we barely knew each other whenever I saw him outside the office – an occasion which was becoming more and more frequent – and pretending that we never saw each other outside the office when we were actually in it. It was an odd dynamic, but it worked for us. I didn't know if Charlotte had had an effect on him or if I was just getting used to it, but he'd been a lot more tolerable lately.

"Morning, stranger!" Will said jovially, coming down the corridor as I started up my computer. I hadn't really noticed it at the weekend, my attention had been elsewhere, but he'd begun growing a proper beard over the last few weeks and it suited him.

"I saw you two days ago," I deadpanned.

"Bah humbug to you too," he replied, sitting opposite me.

I raised an eyebrow. "It's the first week of December. Too early for Christmas references. I haven't even bought my advent calendar yet."

He gestured to the walls which were decorated with tinsel, a fact that I had resolutely ignored as I had walked in. "Christmas is already here, Scrooge. It's the office Christmas party on Saturday – that's what's taking most of our spare time at the moment. On today's agenda, we still need to finish sorting out the decorations. I have a feeling we'll be putting up paper chains ourselves at this rate, I haven't managed to pin anyone down."

"I didn't realise that it was the Christmas party this weekend," I said, tucking my hair behind my ears. "What's the plan?"

"I've managed to book a function room at a hotel on the Millbank," Will said, starting up his own computer. "I thought I'd have to basically sell my soul for it, but most of London seems to owe iceberg a favour."

"Don't call her that," I chided under my breath, but my heart wasn't really in it, and he carried on regardless.

"Catering's all sorted, DJ's booked, so I think it's pretty much just the decorations left to go." He paused. "Are you... taking anyone? Or planning on it?"

"Are you?" I shot back, not in the mood to go through all of this again.

"Touché."

I stood up, gathering a pile of papers that needed to be delivered to a meeting. "I need to get on, I'm afraid. I should be back in an hour, and I'll help you find decorations then."

He nodded, concentrating too much on his emails to give me a reply.

"Nice beard, by the way," I commented as I finished packing my things up.

He blushed slightly, rubbing his chin self-consciously. "You... you think so?"

"It suits you," I said, smiling.

"Darcy said the same, but... but I think she just said it because, you know. She thought it would make me feel better or something."

"Does it? Make you feel better?"

He leant back in his chair, contemplating. It was odd, talking about his transition like this. It wasn't a topic we particularly avoided, it just never really came up.

"I guess it does," he said eventually, and I saw a small smile appear on his lips. "When I look in the mirror and see facial hair... I like that. It makes it easier to convince myself. That's..." he bit his lip nervously. "That's something I still struggle with. But I'm getting there."

"I'm glad," I said, smiling and putting a hand on his shoulder. "I missed you, you know."

"What can I say, I have that effect on people." He sat up again, his face cocky.

"Don't flatter yourself," I laughed, as I headed back down the corridor to the main offices. "I'll see you later!"

The morning passed as any morning at Rosings did: meetings, fetching coffee, photocopying. The biggest change was spending all our free time trying to book someone to do the decorations for the Christmas party with little success. You'd think that this early on in December someone would be free, but no. We couldn't find anyone to spare an hour on Saturday to stick up some tinsel.

Lunchtime came and I pulled a sandwich out of my bag with every intention of working through the hour. Will did the same. Our to-do lists were too long to justify taking an hour off.

It wasn't uncommon for Colin to come running at us, panicked about something or other, but something about this time felt different. There was a new level of panic, a whole different breed of worry.

"Miss de Bourgh is coming! She's coming here, down here! I don't know why but she will be here in less than a minute and you must be ready! You must be! She never comes down from her floor, not unless there's something so, so urgent that it can't be sent up to her – you must get ready! Quickly! Come on, you two!" We were so bewildered by Colin's flustered manner that it took us a few seconds to register what he was saying. "This is highly important! Miss de Bourgh will be here any second, and you two are cramming food into your mouths! You two need to show some respect--"

"I'm here now, Collins, it's a bit late for that."

Will and I hastily stood up as Catherine de Bourgh approached, attempting to subtly straighten up the papers strewn all over the desk.

"Miss de Bourgh, I can only apologise--"

"Shut up, Collins." She surveyed the scene derisively, looking down her nose at us – an impressive feat as she was easily the shortest of us all. "I am not here to discuss business matters."

She looked straight at me with her hawk-like gaze. I felt as though she was looking right through me. I held her stare, though. I had no reason to be nervous.

"Collins, leave us. You too." She gestured vaguely Will, who looked almost relieved that she didn't know his name, as he scarpered off after Colin. After going a few paces he turned around to retrieve his sandwich, but thought better of it and kept going.

"Miss Bennet," she said coolly, "I trust that you did well at Pemberley. I have had good reports about you."

"Yes, thank you, Miss de Bourgh," I replied, feeling myself shrinking ever so slightly under her gaze.

"Please sit." She gestured to the chair behind me, and I suddenly felt like I was about to be told off in the head teacher's office.

"You may be wondering what it is I wish to speak to you about," she said curtly, her voice giving no hint as to what she was feeling. "I admit, it is certainly unusual for me to meet one of my employees in such a manner, especially one as low down as you. However, this is not a business-related visit. In fact, the matter in hand is rather... delicate, and I wanted to make it very clear that no matter the outcome of this little chat, your employment here and your career will remain unaffected. I have no intention of holding anything against you in a professional context. You are a very good worker, and I do not wish for you to leave my employment until your internship is completed. I hope I am clear in that."

I didn't like where this was going. I did not like where it was going at all.

Catherine de Bourgh cleared her throat in a manner that was clearly meant to look delicate while silencing a stadium. "It has come to my attention, Miss Bennet, that you are of... a certain persuasion. It is not for me to judge you and your ways, and as long as your lifestyle does not interfere with my life at all then I do not wish to criticise or interfere. However, whether intentionally or not, certain matters have come into the light and I cannot allow them to continue.

"As I'm sure you're aware, Miss Williams – who is the manager and owner of Pemberley Publishing House – is my niece. This means that her personal life is my concern, whether she likes it or not. I am sure that you understand that it would not be appropriate for someone of her status and standing to be in a relationship with... to be in an unconventional relationship. With someone like you."

My brain had ground to a halt. Was this really happening? "You mean with a woman?"

"You know what I mean," she said, her voice dangerously clipped. "I don't like the influence you've had on my niece, Miss Bennet, and I suggest that you remove yourself from her life immediately. I want you to promise me that you will put a stop to this at once. That you will not see her, and certainly not in a... romantic context." She spat the last two words out, as though even the thought repulsed her.

I felt my blood boil, the walls closing in on me. I would take Charlotte and Jane and Will and Jordan's pestering a thousand times over if it meant that I didn't have to be here, right here, right now.

But then I remembered all those times I'd got angry. All the times that Darcy and I had got angry at each other, and how little it had accomplished. Anger was human, anger was necessary, but it could be used as a tool rather than wielded as a bloody weapon. In Catherine de Bourgh right now I saw everyone who had ever tried to squash me, to silence me, to silence us all. I could not take this, I could not let it slide. I could not simply ignore it.

And that could only start when I stood up.

"With all due respect," I said, my voice trembling from the sheer amount of pressure it was under, "This is none of your business. Maybe I'm not good enough for Darcy, but if that's the case then it's because she deserves someone caring and loving and intelligent and strong, and I don't think I have enough of any those things to be deserving of her. But it has nothing to do with my gender." I took a step towards her as I felt my whole body tense up, fire lighting in my eyes. "I have fought and fought all my life for the right to love whomever I want to, and Darcy has done the same. It's not up to you to dictate my life, or Darcy's life, or anyone else's. If you're going to prevent your niece from having happiness because of your own petty opinions, then you need to take a good, long look at yourself and decide what's really important. Because the world has enough judgement and hate without you or anyone else adding to it. So, in answer to your question, no, I will not stay away from Darcy. Finding the strength to have pride in myself is one of the hardest things I've ever done, but I won't let your prejudice stop me."

I finished speaking and realised how close I was to Miss de Bourgh – to Catherine – and how much I was towering over her. Her eyes were flitting across my face, and she looked almost scared beneath the fuming anger that surrounded her like a storm.

"I see," she said, her voice dangerously low. "So, you will not adhere to my request?"

"No," I said, a touch triumphantly, "I will not. And you can't do anything to change that, not really. You have no control of my personal life. You may want me to think you do, but we both know that the last thing you want is to be accused of discrimination against your employees. I work here because I respect this business, and I respect you as a businesswoman. That does not mean that I respect or even care about your views on my personal life. And one quick word of advice. You'll find life a lot more enjoyable if you learn to move with the times."

Miss de Bourgh fixed me with an icy stare. "Very well. You've made your opinions quite clear. But it is in your interests to keep me happy, it is in my interests to keep my niece happy, and that cannot be accomplished with such an unsuitable match." She paused, as if for dramatic effect. "I suggest that you don't cross me again."

Holding my glare for a second longer, she turned on her heel and stalked back down the corridor.

"Miss de Bourgh!" I called after her, surprised when she stopped, but not when she didn't turn around. "Just for the record, I didn't make Darcy how she is. I didn't encourage her down a certain path. She's been living openly and proudly for years. I..." I faltered slightly. "I just thought you should know that. You should be proud of your niece. For everything she's been through and everything she's fought for."

Catherine de Bourgh showed no sign of having heard me, but kept walking away from me as she had been before. I couldn't tell if my words had any effect, or if they had changed anything at all, but I felt better just for saying them.

It was as she left my line of sight, and Will and Colin reappeared, desperately asking what was going on, that I realised that I was falling. I had been pushed harder than I ever thought possible, but I was falling, falling, falling, deeper than was possible, but I could see the end, I could see the ground, I could see my destination, I could finally see where I was going, where I had been going all this time. It was so close that all I had to do was reach out and I'd be there, I was just one step away from landing. Only the ground wasn't a place, or an object, or even a state of mind.

It was Darcy Williams.

Chapter 37: Universally Acknowledged

After what felt like the longest week of my life the weekend finally arrived, and with it the office Christmas party. Will and I had agreed that it would be a miracle if the whole thing went according to plan, and between us we had a contingency plan for everything.

Almost everything.

All things considered, everything went off without a hitch. Will and I got to the venue a couple of hours early, already dressed up, and apart from the DJ briefly going to the wrong place, everything and everyone was in the right place at the right time. The first arrival at seven o'clock on the dot was, to neither Will's nor my surprise, Colin, closely followed by Charlotte.

"This truly is marvellous!" he exclaimed as he looked around the hall, Charlotte rolling her eyes jokingly. "I have to say, the two of you have done a magnificent job! Although I'm very disappointed that nobody else is here yet. It's the same every year…"

We luckily only had to wait a few more minutes before other people started arriving, saving us from Colin's lamentations. Before long the hall was nearly full, people who I vaguely recognised getting steadily tipsier before the meal had even been served.

"Iceberg is fashionably late. Shouldn't have expected anything else," Will commented as we watched the hubbub, sipping our drinks. "Surprised Darcy isn't here yet, though, she's always unnervingly punctual."

I spit my drink out, gasping for air as some nearby colleagues looked unimpressed at having been showered in second-hand lemonade. "Darcy? Darcy's coming?"

"Of course she is," Will said, attempting nonchalance. "Jordan, too. Iceberg invites them every year. Although she was very particular, told me where to seat them and everything."

"Yeah, well, God forbid Darcy spends any more time near me and my corrupting influence," I said dryly. "I don't know what Ms de Bourgh expects from me, but I have better things to do than cause a scene."

A wry smile graced Will's face. "Forgive me if I'm wrong, but I thought that making a scene was what us queers did best?"

Before I could formulate a response, he was gone. Darcy had appeared across the hall with Jordan, and he'd gone to greet her. Darcy caught my eye and waved awkwardly, Jordan and Will looking between us expectantly as I waved back. She had a way of demanding attention in a room, a self-assuredness fuelled by self-consciousness.

I moved to go and greet them, but I'd barely taken two steps when Catherine de Bourgh appeared behind them, shaking Will's hand and guiding Darcy and Jordan to their seats. Darcy smiled sadly across at me, and I got the message: *not now*. Obviously Will had filled her in on what had happened. Jordan seemed to show no such discretion, however, making more than a bit of a show of waving at me. His aunt chided him but he pulled a face at her as soon as her back was turned, catching my eye to make sure I'd seen. I couldn't help but laugh, especially as he shrugged innocently when Darcy turned to see what was going on.

At the appearance of our empress of a boss, the crowd of people quickly found their seats, and to Will's credit only a few people subtly changed the name cards. As much stick as I'd given him for hanging around and chatting to people when we should have been working, it had clearly paid off.

Miraculously, the speeches were kept short, the wine was good, and the food was fantastic. Will and I sat through the whole thing with baited breath, waiting for something to go wrong, but nothing happened. Before long, the dance floor was opened up, and our now somewhat tipsy co-workers were attempting to dance.

Will stood up and bowed ridiculously before holding his hand out, pulling his face in something that I assume was an attempt at chivalry. "Milady?"

"Bloody hell, if you insist," I joked, rolling my eyes as he dragged me up to join the throng. Some awful but catchy Christmas song was playing, everyone loudly singing along with the chorus but failing to remember any of the lines to the verses.

Before long Jordan had come up to join us, putting us both to shame with his basic coordination skills. He tried to twirl me and I tripped spectacularly, causing us all to burst out laughing, and Will had a bit more luck in trying to dip Jordan.

The whole time, though, I couldn't take my eyes away from Darcy for more than a few seconds at a time. She was still sitting next to her aunt, clearly caught in a heated debate. A few times I caught her glancing back at me and I quickly looked away, focussing on Will and Jordan for a few seconds before looking back.

As the song changed to something slower and people started to slowly couple off, Will's words from earlier in the night rang more loudly around my head. I looked over to Darcy once more to find that she was no longer pretending not to watch me. She was staring at me outright, and as our eyes met we reached some kind of understanding.

I crossed the room in a few quick strides, coming to a halt in front of Darcy as her aunt watched on incredulously.

"Darcy," I said, surprising myself with my confidence. "Would you like to dance?"

I would endure all the hardships in the world if it meant that I would be able to see her smile like that every day.

"I'd love to," she replied, taking my hand and leading me to the dance floor, neither of us looking back.

"That was very brave of you," Darcy commented once we'd started slowly rotating around each other, my right arm around her waist, our hands clasped just above our shoulders. "You know, with – with my aunt just there. I mean, she is your boss."

"And this whole situation is a lawsuit waiting to happen," I said, and she snorted. "I didn't ask you to dance to prove a point, you know. I asked you because I wanted to dance with you."

"I know," Darcy said, but she looked slightly more at ease from that point on. The whole room could have been watching us, but I wouldn't have noticed it; we were completely wrapped up in ourselves, not saying anything, just holding each other.

Far, far sooner than I'd have liked, the song ended, and once again some terrible pop hit was blasting through the speakers. I wasn't ready to go back to fun and laughter and merriment, not yet.

"I need some air," I announced shortly, a surprised Darcy stepping out of my hold.

"Are you okay?" she asked, searching my face as if to work out what was wrong.

"I'm fine," I added quickly. "I just... I just need a minute. I'll – I'll be on Lambeth Bridge."

I gave her a look, trying to convey why I wanted her to know that, and she nodded in understanding.

"Lambeth Bridge."

I nodded before grabbing my coat and dashing out, not stopping to put it on until I was already out in the cold winter air. Cursing myself for wearing heels, I strode across the uneven pavement, ignoring passers-by as I made my way down the street. It was a clear night, the slightest hint of snow in the air. Darting up the stone steps I stepped out onto Lambeth Bridge, walking along the pavement until I was halfway across before stopping.

I looked out over the Thames, pulling my coat tight around me against the cold December air. London was a city that never slept but Lambeth Bridge was oddly peaceful. A few taxis and buses rambled past behind me, but I didn't take any notice. I had a few precious seconds to clear my head, assemble my raucous thoughts into something coherent. I shivered as my heart jumped into my mouth with every beat, as if my entire body somehow knew that the next few minutes could determine everything.

As if from a dream, I heard the soft, slow click of heels against the pavement, and without turning I knew who it was from the way my heartbeat calmed, and I forgot the cold wind whipping around my face.

"Lizzy?"

I turned to look at her and my breath caught in my throat. She looked beautiful – she always looked beautiful – but it was something else. It was the way that she stood as if she was completely isolated, the loneliest person in the world, her eyes pleading with me and begging me to say *something*.

"Lizzy, is everything okay?"

She'd mistaken my silence for sadness, for a sign that something was wrong.

"Yes," I said quickly, breathing a sigh of relief as she did. "There was – there was something I, something I wanted to talk to you about, that's all."

For a few moments, she stood in silence as we faced each other, but her patience couldn't last forever.

"Before you – can – could I say something first?" Her words stumbled over themselves. She waited for me to nod before continuing. "Lizzy, I will always be there for you, I want you to know that. But my…" she trailed off, looking out over the Thames as if it was easier to say what she wanted to without looking at me, but she forced herself to meet my eyes once more. "My feelings. For you. They haven't changed, if – if anything they've grown stronger, and I – I *have* to know, Lizzy, because I can't live with this for much longer, not without knowing. And if – if you feel the same way that you did three months ago that's fine, I understand, I'll just need some time and then – and then we can be friends, because I can't bear the thought of not being your friend. But unless you tell me I can't help but constantly think about it, and I just…" she furiously wiped a tear from her cheek. "I need to know, Lizzy. That's all."

I looked into her deep, brown eyes, seeing only the woman that I loved, and the universe slowed down for us.

Taking two slow, deliberate steps forward, I took her hand in mine, gently running my thumb over her knuckles and bringing a hand up to cup her cheek.

"Every time I so much as think about you," I whispered, "I fall a little bit more in love."

Our lips met.

For a second we were both frozen, neither of us sure what had just happened, but then Darcy wrapped her free arm around my waist and my hand on her cheek went to cup her neck and our entwined fingers were brought up and held between us. I could feel Darcy's heart beating in her chest, and I knew she could feel mine, and nothing existed except *us*.

Our lips parted but we stayed standing close together, our foreheads touching.

"I love you, Darcy Williams," I breathed, laughing giddily at the grin that spread across Darcy's face as I said those words.

"I love you, Lizzy Bennet," she replied and we kissed again, this time with the promise of each other, of us, of many more kisses to come.

Kissing Darcy was a thousand times better than I could have ever imagined. Neither of us were particularly skilled kissers, but the nearness of her, the intimacy of it? It could have been the worst kiss in the world and I would have loved it. We held each other tightly, determined to never let go, revelling in this wonderful new novelty that already felt like home.

We parted once more and I tucked a strand of Darcy's hair behind her ear, still grinning stupidly up at her.

"I love you," Darcy said again, pure joy written on her face. "It feels wonderful to finally say it!"

"In case I haven't mentioned it, I love you too," I smiled.

She kissed me soundly. "I also love being able to do that!" She put her hand under my chin, her thumb lightly brushing over the dimple in my chin as we kissed softly. "Are you – are you cold? You're shaking, we should go inside."

It was true; I was shaking, although I don't think it was just from the cold.

"Let's not go back to the party," I said, pulling slightly away so I could take both of Darcy's hands in mine. "We could go back to your flat? We could order takeaway, cuddle, and just... be."

"That sounds like the most wonderful thing in the world."

We slowly kissed her once more before we turned to walk back, my heart leaping as our arms went around each other's waists as if it were the most natural thing in the world – and it was. We were completely wrapped in our own world, ignoring the few people that were out on the streets, saying whatever was on our minds, stopping every few yards to say 'I love you' or to kiss or both.

Never have I felt so at home as when we curled up together on the sofa under one blanket, Darcy's arms around me as I rested my head on her shoulder, drifting off to sleep as she watched me, slowly carding her hands through my hair.

I slept more deeply than I had in months. When I woke up, it was initially to confusion; I was impossibly warm and comfortable, and it took a second to remember that the heavy weight over my waist was Darcy's arm. I breathed out an ecstatic laugh as the previous night's events came flooding back, biting my lip so I didn't wake Darcy up.

She looked so peaceful in her sleep, propped up on a pillow that hadn't been there the previous evening. Her brow furrowed slightly as I moved so I stayed exactly as I was, enjoying the timelessness of the moment.

A second blanket had been carefully tucked around us, and I guessed that Will or Jordan must have put it there when they came back, both of us sleeping. I briefly wondered what their reaction was, but I quickly found that I didn't care.

Darcy stirred slightly, making a few muffled sounds as her eyes fluttered open, the corners of her lips curling upwards as she saw me.

"Good morning, darling," she greeted me groggily, her smile widening as I kissed her on the cheek.

"And a very good morning it is," I said, pulling her into my arms as she sat up.

"This might just be the very best morning that there has ever been."

"Well, I agree with you there," I said as we slowly leaned in for another kiss. "I love you, Darcy, so much that I can't even begin to fathom it. And this is by far the happiest that I've ever been."

"Me too," Darcy smiled. "Me too."

Acknowledgements

First of all, I have to thank Jane Austen; this is, after all, her story. Thank you to Rosie, Megan and Narissa, who cheered me on all the way, and to Emily and Holly, for putting up with me while I wrote this. Thank you to Philippa, the only person I know with any knowledge of the publishing industry; your advice has been invaluable! Thank you to Jess, Troy, Sarah and Taryn, for being so supportive through the publishing process and for telling anyone who would listen that I was writing a book. To everyone whose name I just mentioned: thank you for being my friend! I don't know how I got so lucky.

Thank you to anyone who has ever pretended to be interested while I told them what I was writing. Thank you to all of the readers of the original *TSOLAD*; you were what made this experience such a joy and have shaped my life so much.

Last but by no means least, I have to thank Lizzy and Darcy. Without these two ruling my life for so long, I'm not sure I would have had the strength to write so much, or the strength to be honest with the world about who I was. Here's to you two lovely ladies.

Author's Note

I hope you enjoyed this book! Please consider leaving a review or telling a friend; it would really help me out!

You can sign up to my mailing list at my website, www.gracewatsonauthor.wix.com/home

About the Author

Grace Watson is a music student and future cat lady with too many books and not enough bookshelves. She currently lives in Wales. *The Story of Lizzy and Darcy* is her debut novel.

Made in the USA
Monee, IL
08 December 2020